SILENT
SCREAM

SILENT SCREAM

Angela MARSONS

bookouture

Published by Bookouture

An imprint of StoryFire Ltd.
23 Sussex Road, Ickenham, UB10 8PN
United Kingdom

www.bookouture.com

ISBN: 978-1-909490-92-5
eBook ISBN: 978-1-909490-91-8

ACKNOWLEDGEMENTS

Silent Scream has been many books in the making. The character of Kim Stone came to me and refused to go away. In my mind and on the page she has grown into a strong, intelligent female who is not always perfect but is passionate and tenacious and someone you would want on your side.

I would like to thank the team at Bookouture for sharing my passion for Kim Stone and her stories. Their encouragement, enthusiasm and belief has been both heartening and overwhelming. My gratitude to Oliver, Claire and Kim is unending and I feel both proud and honoured to be called a Bookouture author.

In particular I have to thank my wonderful editor and Fairy Godmother, Keshini Naidoo, who has accompanied me on a very long journey with encouragement, belief and advice from our very first conversation and who, along with the team at Bookouture, has turned my dreams into a reality.

I would like to thank all of the Bookouture authors for their warm welcome to the Bookouture family. The support has been truly amazing. And, along with Caroline Mitchell the #bookouturecrimesquad is now well and truly formed.

Finally, I would like to thank my family and friends for their belief and faith in my writing and my dream. A special shout out to Amanda Nicol and Andrew Hyde for their continued support.

My heartfelt thanks to you all.

This book is dedicated to my partner, Julie Forrest, who never stopped believing and never allowed me to forget my dream.

PROLOGUE

Rowley Regis, Black Country
2004

Five figures formed a pentagram around a freshly dug mound. Only they knew it was a grave.

Digging the frozen earth beneath the layers of ice and snow had been like trying to carve stone but they'd taken turns. All of them.

An adult-sized hole would have taken longer.

The shovel had passed from grip to grip. Some were hesitant, tentative. Others more assured. No one resisted and no one spoke.

The innocence of the life taken was known to them all but the pact had been made. Their secrets would be buried.

Five heads bowed towards the dirt, visualising the body beneath soil that already glistened with fresh ice.

As the first flakes dusted the top of the grave, a shudder threaded through the group.

The five figures dispersed, their footprints treading the trail of a star into the fresh, crisp snow.

It was done.

CHAPTER 1

Black Country
Present Day

Teresa Wyatt had the inexplicable feeling that this night would be her last.

She switched off the television and the house fell quiet. It wasn't the normal silence that descended each evening as she and her home gently closed down and unwound towards bedtime.

She wasn't sure what she'd been expecting on the late night news. The announcement had already been made on the local evening news programme. Perhaps she was hoping for a miracle, some last-minute reprieve.

Ever since the first application two years ago she had felt like a prisoner on death row. Intermittently the guards had come, taken her to the chair and then fate had returned her to the safety of the cell. But this time was final. Teresa knew there would be no further objections, no more delays.

She wondered if the others had seen the news. Did they feel the same way she did? Would they admit to themselves that their primary feelings were not remorse but self-preservation?

Had she been a nicer person there might have been a smattering of conscience buried beneath her concern for herself; but there was not.

Had she not gone along with the plan, she would have been ruined, she told herself. The name Teresa Wyatt would have been mentioned with distaste, instead of the respect she now enjoyed.

Teresa had no doubt that the complaint would have been taken seriously. The source had been devious, but believable. But it had been silenced forever – and that was something she would never regret.

But now and again in the years since Crestwood her stomach had lurched at the sight of a similar gait or a hair colour or a tilt of the head.

Teresa stood and tried to throw off the melancholy that shadowed her. She strode to the kitchen and put the single plate and wine glass into the dishwasher.

There was no dog to let out or cat to let in. Just the final night time security check of the deadbolts.

Again, she was struck by a feeling that the safety check was pointless; that nothing could hold back the past. She pushed the thought away. There was nothing to fear. They had all made a pact and it had held strong for ten years. Only the five of them knew the truth.

She knew she was too tense to drift off to sleep immediately but she had called a seven a.m. staff meeting for which she could not be late.

She stepped into the bathroom and began to run the water, adding a generous measure of lavender-infused bubble bath. The scent instantly filled the room. A long soak on top of the earlier glass of wine should induce sleep.

The dressing gown and satin pyjamas were folded neatly on top of the laundry basket as she stepped into the tub.

She closed her eyes and surrendered to the water as it enveloped her. She smiled to herself as the anxiety began to recede. She was just being hypersensitive.

Teresa felt that her life had been divided into two segments. There were thirty-seven years B.C., as she called her life Before Crestwood. Those years had been charmed. Single and ambitious, every decision had been her own. She had answered to no one.

But the years since had been different. A shadow of fear had followed her every move; dictated her actions, influenced her decisions.

She remembered reading somewhere that conscience was no more than the fear of being caught. Teresa was honest enough to admit that, for her, the statement was true.

But their secret was safe. It had to be.

Suddenly, she heard the sound of a glass panel shattering. But the sound was not in the distance. It was at her kitchen door.

Teresa lay perfectly still, her ears straining for further sounds. The noise would not have alerted anyone else. The next detached home sat two hundred feet away, on the other side of a leylandi hedge that rose twenty feet high.

The silence of her house thickened around her. The quiet that followed the loud noise was fraught with menace.

Perhaps it was nothing more than a mindless act of vandalism. Maybe a couple of the students from Saint Joseph's had learned her address. By God, she hoped so.

The blood thundered along her veins, vibrating into her temples. She swallowed, in an attempt to clear her eardrums.

Her body began to react to the sensation that she was no longer alone. She brought herself to a sitting position. The sound of the water rearranging itself was loud as it sloshed against the tub. Her hand slipped on the porcelain and her right side fell back into the water.

A sound at the bottom of the stairs destroyed any vague hope of mindless vandalism.

Teresa knew that she was out of time. In a parallel universe, the muscles in her body reacted to the impending threat, but in this one both her body and her mind were stilled by the inevitable. She knew that there was nowhere left to hide.

As she heard the creak of the stairs she briefly closed her eyes and willed her body to stay calm. There was an element of freedom when finally confronted by the fears that haunted her.

As she felt the cool air enter the room from the doorway, she opened her eyes.

The figure that entered was as black and featureless as a shadow. Utility trousers met a thick black fleece which was covered by a long overcoat. A woollen balaclava covered the face. But why me? Teresa's mind raged. She was not the weakest link.

She shook her head. 'I haven't spoken,' she said. The words were barely audible. Every one of her senses was beginning to close down as her body prepared for death.

The black figure took two steps towards her. Teresa searched for a clue but found none. It could only be one of four.

Teresa felt the betrayal of her body as urine slipped from between her legs into the scented water.

'I promise ... I haven't ...'

Teresa's words trailed away as she tried to lift herself to a sitting position. The bath bubbles had turned the tub slippery.

Her breath came in short, sharp rasps as she considered how best to beg for her life. No, she didn't want to die. It wasn't time. She wasn't ready. There were things that she wanted to do.

She had the sudden image of water flooding her lungs; inflating them like party balloons.

She held out her hand imploringly, finally finding her voice. 'Please ... please ... no ... I don't want to die ...'

The figure leaned over the bath and placed a gloved hand above each breast. Teresa felt the pressure being applied to force her under the water and struggled to sit up. She had to try and explain but the force of the hands increased. Again she tried to rear up from her inert position but it was hopeless. Gravity and brute strength made it impossible for her to fight back.

As the water framed her face she opened her mouth. A small sob escaped from between her lips as she tried one last time. 'I swear ...'

The words were cut short and Teresa watched as the air bubbles escaped from her nose and reached the surface. Her hair swam around her face.

The figure shimmered on the other side of the water barrier.

Teresa's body began to react to the oxygen deprivation and she tried to quell the panic rising inside her. Her arms flailed and the gloved hand was briefly dislodged from her breast bone. She managed to raise her head above the water and got a closer look into the cold, piercing eyes. Recognition sapped the last of her breath.

The brief second of confusion was enough for her attacker to reposition. Two hands forced her body underwater and held her fast.

Her mind was full of disbelief, even as her consciousness began to wane.

Teresa realised that her co-conspirators could not even imagine who it was they had to fear.

CHAPTER 2

Kim Stone stepped around the Kawasaki Ninja to adjust the volume on her iPod. The speakers danced with the silvery notes of Vivaldi's Summer Concerto as they headed towards her favourite part; the finale called 'Storm'.

She placed the socket wrench on the work bench and wiped her hands with a stray rag. She stared at the Triumph Thunderbird she'd been restoring for the past seven months and wondered why it had not captured her tonight.

She glanced at her watch. Almost eleven p.m. The rest of her team would be staggering out of The Dog right about now. And although she didn't touch alcohol, she accompanied her team when she felt she'd earned it.

She retrieved the socket wrench and lowered herself to the knee pad beside the Triumph.

It wasn't a celebration for her.

The terrified face of Laura Yates swam before her eyes as she reached inside the guts of the bike and found the rear end of the crankshaft. She placed the socket head over the nut and turned the wrench in a back and forth motion.

Three guilty verdicts of rape were going to send Terence Hunt away for a very long time.

'But not long enough,' Kim said to herself.

Because there had been a fourth victim.

She turned the wrench again but the nut refused to tighten. She'd already assembled the bearing, sprocket, clamping washer and rotor. The nut was the final puzzle piece and the damn thing refused to tighten against the locking washer.

Kim stared at the nut and silently willed it to move for its own sake. Still nothing. She focused her anger on the arm of the socket wrench and gave it one almighty push. The thread broke and the nut turned freely.

'Damn it,' she shouted, throwing the wrench across the garage.

Laura Yates had trembled in the witness box as she'd recounted the ordeal of being dragged behind a church and repeatedly brutally sexually assaulted for two and a half hours. They had seen with their own eyes how hard it had been for her to sit down. Three months after the attack.

The nineteen-year-old had sat in the gallery as each guilty verdict was read out. Then it came to her case and two words were stated that would change her life forever.

Not Guilty.

And why? Because the girl had consumed a couple of drinks. Forget the eleven stitches that stretched from back to front, the broken rib and the black eye. She must have asked for it, all because she'd had a couple of bloody drinks.

Kim was aware that her hands had started to tremble with rage.

Her team felt that three out of four wasn't bad. And it wasn't. But it wasn't good enough. Not for Kim.

She leaned down to inspect the damage to the bike. It had taken almost six weeks to track down those bloody screws.

She eased the socket into position and turned the wrench again between her thumb and forefinger as her mobile phone began to ring. She dropped the nut and jumped to her feet. A call so close to midnight was never going to be good news.

'D.I. Stone.'

'We have a body, Marm.'

Of course. What else could it have been?

'Where?'

'Hagley Road, Stourbridge.'

Kim knew the area. It was just on the border with their neighbours West Mercia.

'Should we put a call in to D.S. Bryant, Marm?'

Kim cringed. She hated the term Marm. At thirty-four, she wasn't ready to be called Marm.

A picture of her colleague stumbling into a taxi outside The Dog came into her mind.

'No, I think I'll take this on my own,' she said, ending the call.

Kim paused for two seconds as she silenced the iPod. She knew she had to let go of the accusation in the eyes of Laura Yates; real or imagined, she had seen it. And she couldn't get it out of her mind.

She would always know that the justice in which she believed had failed someone it was designed to protect. She had persuaded Laura Yates to trust in both her and the system she represented and Kim couldn't rid herself of the feeling that Laura had been let down. By both of them.

CHAPTER 3

Four minutes after receiving the phone call, Kim was pulling off the drive in the ten-year-old Golf GTI that she used only when the roads were icy or when the firing of the Ninja would be an anti-social act.

The torn jeans stained with oil, grease and dust had been replaced by black canvas trousers and a plain white T-shirt. Her feet were now encased in black patent boots with a quarter-inch heel. Her short black hair required little maintenance. A quick comb from her fingers and she was ready to go.

Her customer would not be concerned.

She weaved the car to the end of the road. The machine felt alien within her control. Although it was only small, Kim had to concentrate on passing distances of parked cars. So much metal around her felt cumbersome.

A mile away from the target property, the smell of burning found its way in through the vents. As she travelled, the smell became stronger. Half a mile out, she could see a column of smoke leaning and reaching above the Clent hills. A quarter mile, and Kim knew she was heading right for it.

Second only in size to The Met, the West Midlands Police covered almost 2.6 million inhabitants.

The Black Country was situated to the north and west of Birmingham and had become one of the most intensely industrialised regions in the country by Victorian times. Its name came from the outcropping coal that made the soil black over large areas. The thirty foot seam of ore and coal was the thickest in Great Britain.

Now, unemployment levels in the area were the third highest in the country. Petty crime was on the increase, along with anti-social behaviour.

The crime scene sat just off the main road that linked Stourbridge to Hagley, an area that did not normally attract high levels of law-breaking. The houses closest to the road were new double-fronted properties with sparkling white roman columns and black leaded windows. Further along the road the houses were spread further apart and were considerably older.

Kim pulled up at the cordon and parked between two fire tenders. Without speaking, she flashed her ID to the officer guarding the perimeter tape. He nodded and lifted it for her to duck underneath.

'What happened?' she asked the first fire officer she found.

He pointed to the remains of the first conifer tree at the edge of the property. 'Fire was started there and spread through most of the trees before we got here.'

Kim noted that of the thirteen trees that formed the property line, only the two closest to the house were untouched.

'You discovered the body?'

He pointed to a fire officer sitting on the ground, talking to a constable. 'Just about everyone else was out watching the commotion but this house stayed dark. Neighbours assured us that the black Range Rover was hers and that she lived alone.'

Kim nodded and approached the fire officer on the ground. He looked pale and she noted a slight tremble to his right hand. Finding a dead body was never pleasant, no matter what training you'd had.

'Did you touch anything?' she asked.

He thought for a second and then shook his head. 'The bathroom door was open but I didn't step inside.'

Kim paused at the front door, reached into the cardboard box to the left and took out blue plastic coverings for her feet.

Kim took the stairs two at a time and entered the bathroom. She immediately located Keats, the pathologist. He was a diminutive figure with a completely bald head, set off by a moustache and a beard that fell into a point below his chin. He'd had the honour of guiding her through her first post mortem eight years earlier.

'Hey, Detective,' he said, looking around her. 'Where's Bryant?'

'Jesus, we're not joined at the hip.'

'Yeah but you're like a Chinese dish. Sweet and sour pork ... but without Bryant you're just sour ... '

'Keats, how amused do you think I am at this time of night?'

'Your sense of humour isn't really evident any time to be fair.'

Oh, how she wanted to retaliate. If she wished to, she could comment on the fact that the creases in his black trousers were not quite straight. Or she could point out that the collar of his shirt was slightly frayed. She could even mention the small bloodstain on the back of his coat.

But right now a naked body lay between them, demanding her full attention.

Kim moved closer to the bath slowly, careful not to slip on the water that was being sloshed around by two white suits.

The body of the female lay partly submerged. Her eyes were open and her dyed blonde hair was fanned out in the water, framing her face.

Her body floated, so that the tip of her breasts broke the surface of the water.

Kim guessed the female to be mid- to-late-forties but well kept. Her upper arms appeared toned but limp flesh hung in the water. Her toenails were painted a soft pink and no stubble showed on her legs.

The volume of water on the floor indicated that a struggle had taken place and that the woman had fought for her life.

Kim heard footsteps thundering up the stairs.

'Detective Inspector Stone, a pleasant surprise.'

Kim groaned, recognising the voice and the sarcasm dripping from the words.

'Detective Inspector Wharton, the pleasure is all mine.'

The two of them had worked together a few times and her disdain had never been hidden. He was a career officer who wanted to climb the ladder as quickly as possible. He had no interest in solving cases, only adding to his tally.

His final humiliation had been when she'd made D.I. before he had. Her early promotion had prompted him to move house and transfer to West Mercia; a smaller force with less competition.

'What are you doing here? I think you'll find this is a West Mercia case.'

'And I think you'll find it's right on the border and I got first dibs.'

Unconsciously, she'd stepped in front of the bath. The victim didn't need any more curious eyes roving over her naked body.

'It's my case, Stone.'

Kim shook her head and folded her arms. 'I ain't budging, Tom.' She tipped her head. 'We could always make this a joint investigation. I was here first, so I'll lead.'

His thin mean face filled with colour. Reporting to her would be done only after gouging out his own eyeballs with a rusty spoon.

She assessed him from head to toe. 'And my first instruction would be to enter the crime scene with appropriate protection.'

He looked down at her feet and then at his own unprotected footwear. More haste, less speed, she thought to herself.

She lowered her voice. 'Don't make this a pissing contest, Tom.'

He gave her a look filled with contempt before turning and storming out of the bathroom.

Kim turned her attention back to the body.

'You'd have won,' Keats said quietly.

'Huh?'

His eyes danced with amusement. 'The pissing contest.'

Kim nodded. She knew.

'Can we get her out of here yet?'

'Just a couple more close ups of her breastbone.'

As he spoke, one of the forensic officers pointed a camera with a lens the length of an exhaust pipe at the woman's breasts.

Kim leaned in closer and saw two marks above each breast. 'Pushed down?'

'I'm thinking so. Preliminary exam shows no other injuries. I'll tell you more after the post mortem.'

'Any guesses on how long?'

Kim could see no evidence of the liver probe, so she was guessing he'd used the rectal thermometer before she'd arrived.

She knew that a body dropped temperature by 1.5 degrees centigrade in the first hour. Normally it was between 1.5 and 1.0 degree centigrade every hour thereafter. She also knew that figure to be affected by many other factors. Not least that the victim was naked and submerged in now-cold water.

He shrugged. 'I'll do further calculations later but I'd say no more than about two hours.'

'When can you ... '

'I've got a ninety-six-year-old lady who expired after falling asleep in her armchair and a twenty-six-year-old male with the needle still in his arm.'

'Nothing urgent then?'

He checked his watch. 'Midday?'

'Eight,' she countered.

'Ten and no earlier,' he grumbled. 'I'm human and need occasional rest.'

'Perfect,' she said. It was the exact time she had in mind. It would give her chance to brief her team and task someone to attend.

Kim heard more footsteps on the stairs. The sound of laboured breathing came closer.

'Sergeant Travis,' she said, without turning. 'What have we got?'

'Officers are canvassing the area. The FOA rounded up a couple of neighbours but the first thing they knew was the fire service rolling up. Alert call was from a passing motorist.'

Kim turned and nodded. The First Officer Attending had done a good job of securing the scene for the forensics team and corralling any potential witnesses but the houses were set back from the road and separated by a quarter acre. Not exactly a mecca for the nosey neighbour.

'Go on,' she said.

'Point of entry was a smashed glass panel in the back door and the fire officer states that the front door was unlocked.'

'Hmmm ... interesting.'

She nodded her thanks and headed down the stairs.

One technician was inspecting the hallway and another was dusting the back door for fingerprints. A designer handbag sat on the breakfast bar. Kim had no idea what the gold monogram fastener meant. She never used handbags but it looked expensive.

A third tech entered from the dining room next door. He nodded towards the handbag. 'Nothing taken. Credit cards and cash still intact.'

Kim nodded and headed out of the house. At the doorway she removed the shoe coverings and placed them into a second box. All protective clothing would be removed from the scene and examined for trace evidence later.

She stepped under the cordon. One fire tender remained on watch to ensure the blaze was totally extinguished. Fire was clever and just one ember that went unnoticed could set the place ablaze within minutes.

She stood at the car, surveying the bigger picture of the scene before her.

Teresa Wyatt lived alone. Nothing appeared to have been taken or even disturbed.

The killer could have left safe in the knowledge that the body would not be discovered until the following morning at the earliest and yet they had started a fire to expedite police attention.

Now all Kim had to do was work out why.

CHAPTER 4

At seven thirty a.m. Kim parked the Ninja at Halesowen police station, just off the ring road that circled a town with a small shopping precinct and a college. The station was located within spitting distance of the magistrates court; convenient, but a bitch for claiming expenses.

The three-storey building was as drab and unwelcoming as any other government building that apologised to taxpaying citizens.

She navigated her way to the detectives' office without offering any morning greetings and none were offered to her. Kim knew she had a reputation for being cold, socially inept and emotionless. This perception deflected banal small talk and that was fine by her.

As usual, she was first into the detectives' office and so fired up the coffee machine. The room held four desks in two sets of two facing each other. Each desk mirrored its partner, with a computer screen and mismatched file trays.

Three of the desks accommodated permanent occupants but the fourth sat empty since they had been downsized a few months earlier. It was where she normally perched herself rather than in her office.

The space with Kim's name on the door was commonly referred to as The Bowl. It was nothing more than an area in the top right hand corner of the room that was partitioned off by plasterboard and glass.

It was a space she used for the occasional 'individual performance directive', otherwise known as a good old-fashioned bollocking.

'Morning, Guv,' Detective Constable Wood called as she slid into her chair. Although her family background was half English and half Nigerian, Stacey had never set foot outside the United Kingdom. Her tight black hair was cut short and close to her head following the removal of her last weave. The smooth caramel skin suited the haircut well.

Stacey's work area was organised and clear. Anything not in the labelled trays was stacked in meticulous piles along the top edge of her desk.

Not far behind was Detective Sergeant Bryant who mumbled a 'Morning, Guv,' as he glanced into The Bowl. His six foot frame looked immaculate, as though he had been dressed for Sunday school by his mother.

Immediately the suit jacket landed on the back of his chair. By the end of the day his tie would have dropped a couple of floors, the top button of his shirt would be open and his shirt sleeves would be rolled up just below his elbows.

She saw him glance at her desk, seeking evidence of a coffee mug. When he saw that she already had coffee he filled the mug labelled 'World's Best Taxi Driver', a present from his nineteen-year-old daughter.

His filing was not a system that anyone else understood but Kim had yet to request any piece of paper that was not in her hands within a few seconds. At the top of his desk was a framed picture of himself and his wife taken at their twenty-fifth wedding anniversary. A picture of his daughter snuggled in his wallet.

DS Kevin Dawson, the third member of her team, didn't keep a photo of anyone special on his desk. Had he wanted to display a picture of the person for whom he felt most affection he would have been greeted by his own likeness throughout his working day.

'Sorry I'm late, Guv,' Dawson called as he slid into his seat opposite Wood and completed her team.

He wasn't officially late. The shift didn't start until eight a.m. but she liked them all in early for a briefing, especially at the beginning of a new case. Kim didn't like to stick to a roster and people who did lasted a very short time on her team.

'Hey, Stacey, you gonna get me a coffee or what?' Dawson asked, checking his mobile phone.

'Of course, Kev, how'd yer like it: milk, two sugars and in yer lap?' she asked sweetly, in her strong Black Country accent.

'Stace, would you like a coffee?' he asked, rising, knowing full well that she didn't touch the stuff. 'You must be tired after fighting warlocks all night,' he quipped, referring to Stacey's addiction to the online game World of Warcraft.

'Actually, Kev, I received a powerful spell from a high priestess that can turn a grown man into a raging dickhead – but looks like someone else got to yer first.'

Dawson held his stomach and offered mock-laughter.

'Guv,' Bryant called over his shoulder. 'The kids are playing up again.' He turned back to the two of them and wagged a finger. 'You two just wait until your mother gets home.'

Kim rolled her eyes and sat at the spare desk, eager to begin. 'Okay, Bryant, hand out the statements. Kev, get the board.'

Dawson took the marker pen and stood next to the whiteboard that occupied the entire back wall.

While Bryant divided up the paperwork she talked through the events of earlier that morning.

'Our victim is Teresa Wyatt, forty-seven years old, highly respected principal of a private boys' school in Stourbridge. No marriage or children. Lived comfortably but not lavishly and had no enemies that we're aware of.'

Kev noted the information as bullet points beneath the heading of 'Victim'.

Bryant's phone rang. He said little before replacing the receiver and nodding in Kim's direction. 'Woody wants you.'

She ignored him. 'Kev, make a second heading, "Crime". No murder weapon, no robbery, so far no forensics and no clues.

'Next heading, "Motive". People are normally murdered because of something they have done, something they are doing or something they are going to do. As far as we know, our victim was not engaged in any kind of dangerous activity.'

'Err ... Guv, the DCI wants you.'

Kim took another gulp of the fresh cuppa. 'Trust me, Bryant, he likes me better when I've had coffee. Kev, the post mortem is at ten. Stace, find out everything you can about our victim. Bryant, contact the school and let them know we're coming.'

'Guv ... '

Kim finished her drink. 'Calm down, Mum, I'm going.'

She took the stairs to the third floor two at a time and knocked lightly before entering.

DCI Woodward was a heavyset man in his mid-fifties. His mixed race origins gifted him smooth brown skin that travelled up and over his hairless head. His black trousers and white shirt were crisp and creased in all the right places. The reading glasses on the tip of his nose did little to disguise the tired eyes behind them.

He waved her in and pointed to a chair, giving her a full view of the glass cabinet holding his model car collection.

The lower shelf housed a selection of classic British models but the upper shelf displayed a history of police vehicles used through the ages. There was an MG TC from the Forties, a Ford Anglia, a Black Maria and a Jaguar XJ40 that took pride of place at the centre.

To the right of the cabinet, fixed firmly to the wall, was a photograph of Woody shaking hands with Tony Blair. To the right of that was a photograph of his eldest son, Patrick, in full dress uniform, right before he was deployed to Afghanistan. He had been clothed in that exact same uniform for his burial fifteen months later.

Woody ended the phone conversation and immediately picked up the stress ball from the edge of his desk. His right hand clenched and relaxed around the clump of putty. Kim realised he reached for it a lot when she was around.

'What do we have so far?'

'Very little, Sir. We were just outlining the investigation when you summoned me.'

His knuckles whitened around the ball but he ignored the dig.

Her eyes wandered to the right of his ear, to his current project on the window sill. It was a Rolls Royce Phantom and construction had not progressed in days.

'You had a run-in with Detective Inspector Wharton, I hear?'

So, the jungle drums had already been busy. 'We exchanged pleasantries over the body.'

There was something about the model that didn't look quite right. To her eye the wheel base looked much too long.

He squeezed the ball harder. 'His DCI has been in touch. A formal complaint against you has been lodged and they want the case.'

Kim rolled her eyes. Couldn't the weasel fight his own battles?

She fought the urge to reach across and pick up the Rolls Royce to rectify the mistake but she contained herself.

She slid her eyes along and met the gaze of her commanding officer. 'But they're not going to get it, are they, Sir?'

He held her gaze for a long minute. 'No, Stone, they are not, however a formal complaint does not look good on your file and quite frankly I'm getting a little bit tired of receiving them.' He swapped the ball to his left hand. 'So, I'm curious to see who you're buddying up with on this one.'

Kim felt like a child being asked to choose a new best friend. Her last performance review had highlighted only one area of improvement; playing nice with others.

'Do I get a choice?'

'Who would you choose?'

'Bryant.'

The ghost of a smile hovered around his lips. 'Then yes, you get to choose.'

So, there was no choice at all, she thought. Bryant provided damage limitation and with the neighbouring force sniffing at her backside Woody wasn't taking any chances; he wanted her in the care of a responsible adult.

She had been on the cusp of offering her boss a little advice that would save him hours of dismantling the rear axle of the Rolls but quickly changed her mind.

'Anything else, Sir?'

Woody put the stress ball back and took off his glasses. 'Keep me updated.'

'Of course.'

'Oh, and Stone ...'

She turned at the door. 'Let your team have some sleep now and again. They're not all charged via a USB port like you.'

Kim left his office, wondering how long it had taken Woody to come up with that little gem.

CHAPTER 5

Kim followed Courtney, the school receptionist, through the hallways of Saint Joseph's on their way to the office of the Acting Principal. From behind, Kim marvelled at the woman's ability to move so swiftly in four-inch heels.

Bryant sighed as they passed classroom after classroom. 'Weren't these just the best days of your life?'

'No.'

They turned into a long corridor on the second floor and were led into an office with a discoloured oblong on the door where the name plate had already been taken off.

The male behind the desk stood. His suit was expensive and his tie was a sky blue silky number. The flat black colour of his hair indicated it had been recently dyed.

He offered his hand across the desk. Kim turned away, examining the contents of the walls. Any certificates or memorabilia containing the name of Teresa Wyatt had already been removed.

Bryant accepted the extended hand.

'Thank you for accommodating our request, Mr Whitehouse.'

'You're the *Deputy* Principal, I understand,' Kim noted.

He nodded and sat. 'I will be stepping in as Acting Principal and if I can be of any assistance in the investigation ...'

'Oh, I'm sure you will be,' Kim interrupted. There was something disingenuous about his manner. Too well rehearsed. The fact he had already moved into Teresa Wyatt's office and removed all traces of her existence was distasteful to say the least. The woman had been dead for less than twelve hours. She guessed that his curriculum vitae had already been updated.

'We'd like a list of all staff members. Please arrange for them to be available to speak with us in alphabetical order.'

The set of his jaw indicated that he didn't respond all that well to instruction. Kim briefly wondered if that was the case with all women or just her.

He lowered his eyes. 'Of course. I'll have Courtney arrange that for you immediately. I've made available a room down the hall that will more than meet your needs to conduct the interviews.'

Kim looked around and shook her head. 'No, I think we'll be just fine right here.'

His mouth opened to respond but good manners prevented him laying total claim to the workspace so soon.

Whitehouse gathered some belongings from the top of the desk and headed towards the door. 'Courtney will be with you shortly.'

As the door closed behind the Acting Principal, Bryant chuckled.

'What?' she asked, taking the chair behind the desk.

'Nothing, Guv.'

He moved one of the chairs to the side of the desk and sat down.

Kim assessed the placement of the remaining chair for the interviewees.

'Move that one back a little.'

Bryant moved the chair so that it was closer to the door. Adrift. There was nothing to lean on or sit against. Now she could observe the body language.

A light knock sounded on the door. They both shouted 'come in' at the same time.

Courtney entered with a piece of paper and a smile that was trying to climb out of her mouth. So, Mr Whitehouse was not all that popular.

'Mr Addlington is outside when you're ready.'

Kim nodded. 'Please show him in.'

'Can I get you anything else? Coffee, tea?'

'You most certainly can. Coffee for both of us.'

Courtney headed to the door and reached it before Kim remembered. 'Thanks, Courtney.'

Courtney nodded and held the door open for the first interviewee.

CHAPTER 6

By four fifteen p.m., after twelve identical conversations, Kim's head hit the desk. There was something satisfying about the thunk of her skull on wood.

'I know what you mean, Guv,' Bryant offered. 'Looks like we've got ourselves a real life saint in the morgue.'

He took a pack of mentholyptus cough sweets from his pocket. By her count that was his fifth.

Two years ago a chest infection had prompted an instruction from the doctor to give up his habit of thirty cigarettes a day. In an effort to get rid of the ripping cough Bryant had popped the sweets non-stop. The smoking had gone but an addiction to the cough sweets had remained.

'You really need to cut down on those, you know.'

'It's that kind of day, Guv.'

And like a seasoned smoker, he indulged more when stressed or bored.

'Who's next?'

Bryant consulted the list. 'Joanna Wade, English Language.'

Kim rolled her eyes as the door opened. In stepped a woman wearing tailored black trousers and a lilac silk shirt. Her long blonde hair was tied back in a ponytail revealing a strong square jaw and little make up.

She sat without offering her hand and crossed her right ankle over her left. Her hands landed neatly in her lap.

'We won't take up too much of your time, Mrs Wade. We just need to ask you a few questions.'

'Ms.'

'Excuse me.'

'It's Ms, Detective, not Mrs, but please call me Joanna.'

The voice was low and controlled with a hint of a northern accent.

'Thank you, Ms Wade. How long have you known Principal Wyatt?'

The teacher smiled. 'I was employed by Principal Wyatt almost three years ago.'

'How was the working relationship between the two of you?'

Ms Wade fixed her gaze on Kim and cocked her head slightly. 'Really, Detective, no foreplay?'

Kim ignored the innuendo and returned the gaze.

'Please answer the question?'

'Of course. We had a reasonable working relationship. Not without its ups and downs, which happens between most females, I find. Teresa was a very focused Principal, rigid in her beliefs and convictions.'

'In what way?'

'Methods of teaching have evolved since Teresa's time in the classroom. Creativity is often needed to instil knowledge into young, fertile minds. We have all tried to adapt to a changing culture but Teresa believed that quiet, disciplined, book learning was the only way to teach and anyone who tried anything different was suitably advised.'

As Joanna Wade talked, Kim assessed her body language to be open and honest. She also noted that the woman had not glanced at Bryant once.

'Can you give me an example?'

'A couple of months ago one of my students turned in a paper whereby half of the prose had been written in abbreviations more commonly used to communicate by text message or on Facebook. I sent all twenty-three students to their lockers to retrieve their mobile phones. I then insisted that they spend the next ten minutes texting each other in correct, grammatical English including appropriate punctuation. This process felt completely alien to them and they all got the point.'

'Which was?'

'That the methods of communication don't translate. It hasn't happened since.'

'And Teresa wasn't happy with this?'

Ms Wade shook her head. 'Not at all. She felt that the boy concerned should have been given detention and that would have sent a clearer message. I dared to disagree and Teresa made a note of insubordination on my file.'

'This isn't the picture we've been getting from other members of staff here, Ms Wade.'

The woman shrugged. 'I can't speak for anyone else, however I would say that there are teachers here who have given up. Their methods of reaching young minds no longer work and they are treading water until retirement. They are content to remain uninspired and uninspiring. I, however, am not.' Again her head cocked to the side and a small smile tugged at her mouth. 'Teaching today's teenagers to appreciate the beauty and finesse of the English language is truly challenging. But, I firmly believe that one should never shy away from a challenge. Don't you agree, Detective?'

Bryant coughed.

Kim offered a small smile in return. The woman's confidence and open dialogue was a breath of fresh air after twelve identical responses. The blatant flirting was amusing.

Kim sat back. 'What can you tell me about Teresa, the woman?'

'Would you like me to toe the line and offer the politically correct epitaph reserved for the recently deceased – or should I be candid?'

'Your honesty would be appreciated.'

Ms Wade re-crossed her legs. 'As a school Principal, Teresa was driven and focused. As a woman, I feel that she was quite a selfish person. As you will see from her desk there are no pictures of anything or anyone important to her. She thought nothing of keeping staff members here until eight or nine o'clock.

'A great deal of her time was spent at spas, shopping for designer clothes and booking expensive holidays.'

Bryant made a couple of notes.

'Is there anything else you feel might be of help to the investigation?'

The woman shook her head.

'Thank you for your time, Ms Wade.'

The woman sat forward. 'If you'd like an alibi, Detective, I was at Liberty Gym practicing my yoga moves. Excellent for muscle flexibility. And if you're interested, I'm there every Thursday night.'

Kim met her gaze. The clear blue eyes sparkled with challenge. She sauntered towards the desk and held out a business card.

Kim had no choice but to hold out her hand. The woman placed the card in Kim's palm and turned the contact into a handshake. Her touch was cool and firm. Her fingers lingered over Kim's palm as the hand withdrew.

'Here's my number. Please feel free to call if I can be of any further assistance.'

'Thank you, Ms Wade, you've been most helpful.'

'Jesus, Guv,' Bryant said as the door closed. 'You didn't need a book to read those signals.'

Kim shrugged. 'You've either got it or you haven't.'

She placed the card into her jacket pocket. 'Any more?'

'No, she was the last.'

They both stood. 'That's it for today. Go home and get some rest,' Kim said.

She had a feeling they were going to need it.

CHAPTER 7

'Okay folks, hope you all got some rest and kissed your loved ones goodbye.'

'Yeah, no social life for the foreseeable future,' Dawson groaned. 'So, no change for Stacey but the rest of us have real lives.'

Kim ignored him. For now. 'The TUBs want this one solved by the end of the week.'

They all knew her acronym stood for Totally Unreasonable Brass. Substitution of the last word was optional, dependent on her mood.

Dawson sighed. 'What if our murderer didn't get the memo, Guv?' he asked, checking his mobile phone.

'Then come next Friday I'll be arresting you and trust me, I can make it stick.'

Dawson laughed.

She remained serious. 'Keep pissing me off, Kev, and it won't be a joke. Now, what did we get from the post mortem?'

He took out his notebook. 'Lungs full of water, definitely drowned. Two bruises just above her breasts. No sign of sexual assault, but difficult to tell.'

'Anything else?'

'Yep, she had chicken korma for dinner.'

'Great, that'll break the case wide open.'

Dawson shrugged. 'Not really much to come out of it, Guv.'

'Bryant?'

He moved a few pieces of paper but Kim knew that any information was already in his head.

'The area was canvassed again yesterday but none of the neighbours saw or heard a thing. A couple of them knew her in passing but it would appear she wasn't a coffee morning kind of person. Not the most sociable of sorts.'

'Oh well, there's a motive. Killed for her lack of community spirit.'

'Folks been killed for less, Guv,' Bryant responded and she had to concede the point. Three months earlier they had investigated the murder of a male nurse who had been killed for two cans of beer and the loose change in his pocket.

'Anything else?'

Bryant picked up another piece of paper. 'Nothing from forensics yet. Obviously no footprint evidence and the fibre analysis has just started.'

Kim thought about Locard's exchange principle. It held the theory that the perpetrator of a crime will bring something to the scene and leave with something from it. It could be anything from a hair to a simple fibre. The art was in finding it. And with a crime scene trampled by eight fire officers and a waterlogged bathroom, trace evidence was not going to raise its hand voluntarily.

'Prints?'

Bryant shook his head. 'And we all know the murder weapon was a pair of hands so we're unlikely to find them thrown in a bush somewhere.'

'You know, Guv, it ain't like this on *CSI*,' Stacey offered. 'Nothing on her phone either. All incoming and outgoing calls are either to St Joseph's or local restaurants. Her contact list ain't all that long.'

'No friends or family at all?'

'Certainly none she cared to keep in touch with. I've requested her home phone records and her laptop is on the way. Maybe there'll be something there.'

Kim grunted. 'So, basically, thirty-six hours in and we've got absolutely bugger all. We know nothing about this woman.'

Bryant stood. 'Give me just a minute, Guv,' he said and left the room.

She rolled her eyes. 'Okay, while Bryant powders his nose, let's recap.' She looked to the board which held barely more information than it had the day before.

'We have a woman in her late forties who was ambitious and hard-working. She was not particularly sociable or popular. She lived alone, with no pets and no family connections. She was not involved in any dangerous activity and seems to have had no hobbies or interests whatsoever.'

'That may not be the case,' Bryant said, taking his seat. 'Apparently she was quite interested in an archaeological dig that's just been authorised to take place somewhere in Rowley Regis.'

'And you know this how?'

'Just spoke to Courtney.'

'Courtney who?'

'Courtney who brought us coffee all day yesterday. I asked if our victim had spoken to anyone different during the last few weeks. Courtney had been asked to get a number for a Professor Milton at Worcester College.'

'I saw something on the local news about that,' Stacey offered. 'The Professor's been trying to get permission to work on that site for ages. It's just a field since the old kids' home caught fire but it's rumoured to hold buried coins. He's been fighting objections for about two years but got the final go ahead this week. It made the national news 'cos of the long court battle.'

Finally, Kim felt the stirrings of excitement. Expressing interest in a local activity was hardly a smoking gun but it was more than they had ten minutes ago.

'Okay, you two carry on digging, excuse the pun. Bryant, go fire up the Batmobile.'

Dawson sighed heavily.

Kim grabbed her jacket and paused at Dawson's desk. 'Stace, don't you need the toilet right about now?'

'No, Guv, I'm fine ...'

'Stacey, leave the room.'

Tact and diplomacy had been invented by someone with too much time on their hands.

'Kev, put your phone down a minute and listen. I know you're going through it a bit right now but you really brought it on yourself. If you'd managed to keep your dick in your pants for another couple of weeks you'd be in the loving embrace of your girlfriend and newborn daughter instead of back in your mum's spare room.'

Kim was not in the habit of employing sensitivity with her team members. She had enough trouble conjuring it for the general public.

'It was a stupid, drunken mistake at a stag party ...'

'Kev, no offence, that's your problem not mine. But if you don't stop sulking like a little girl every time you don't get your own way, that desk over there will not be the only one going spare. Do we understand each other?'

She gave him a hard stare. He swallowed and then nodded.

Without another word Kim left the room and headed down the stairs.

Dawson was a gifted detective but the line he was treading was a very thin one indeed.

CHAPTER 8

For the second time in as many days, Kim walked amongst that air of naïve expectation present at every learning facility.

Bryant headed to the reception desk while she stood to the side. A group of males to her right were laughing at something on a mobile phone. One of the males turned to her. His gaze travelled the length of her body, pausing at her breasts. He tipped his head and smiled.

She mirrored his actions and took in the skinny jeans, V-neck T-shirt and Justin Bieber hairstyle.

She met his gaze and smiled in response. 'Never gonna happen, sweetpea.'

He immediately turned back into the group, praying that his friends had not witnessed the exchange.

'There's something not quite right here,' Bryant said. 'Receptionist looked confused when I asked to see the professor. There's someone coming but I don't think it's going to be him.'

Suddenly the groups began parting like the red sea as a woman four foot in heels bustled through. Her form was small but she travelled like a bullet, slowing for nothing. Her keen eyes searched the area and landed on the two of them.

'Shit, hide,' Bryant said, as she headed right for them.

'Detectives?' she said, offering her hand.

Kim's nose was assaulted by the aroma of Apple Blossom. Tight greying curls clung closely to her head and her nose supported a pair of glasses that Dame Edna wanted back.

Bryant shook the hand. Kim did not. 'And you are?'

'Mrs Pearson, Professor Milton's assistant.'

Okay, clearly the professor was too busy to see them. If they learned nothing from his assistant they would be forced to insist.

'May we ask you some questions about a project Professor Milton is working on?' Bryant asked.

'Very quickly,' she answered. There was no offer to go elsewhere to speak more privately. The woman was clearly going to give them only a little time.

'The professor is interested in an archaeological dig?'

Mrs Pearson nodded. 'Yes, permission was granted a few days ago.'

'What exactly is he looking for?' Bryant asked.

'Valuable coins, Detective.'

Kim raised an eyebrow. 'In a field on the outskirts of Rowley Regis?'

Mrs Pearson sighed as though speaking to an errant toddler. 'You are clearly ignorant of the richness of our immediate locale. Have you never heard of the Staffordshire hoard?'

Kim looked at Bryant. They both shook their heads.

Mrs Pearson made no attempt to hide her disdain. Clearly people outside of academia were philistines.

'One of the most substantial finds of our time was discovered in a field in Lichfield a few years ago. More than three and a half thousand pieces of gold valued at just over three million pounds. Just recently a hoard of silver denarius coins dating back to 31 BC were discovered in Stoke on Trent.'

Kim was intrigued. 'Who gets the money?'

'Well, take the recent find in Bredon Hill, Worcestershire. A man with a metal detector found Roman gold, including coins, and both he and the farmer received over a million and a half.'

'What makes the professor think there's something in Rowley?'

Mrs Pearson shrugged. 'Local legend, myth about a battle that took place in that area.'

'Did he recently take a call from a woman named Teresa Wyatt?'

The woman thought for a moment. 'Yes, I think so. She called a few times, insisting on speaking to Professor Milton. I think he called her back late one afternoon.'

Okay, Kim had had enough. There was something here and she was no longer content to speak to the monkey. She needed the organ grinder to recount the content of that conversation.

'Thank you for your help, Mrs Pearson, but I think regardless of how busy the professor might be we need to speak to him immediately.'

Mrs Pearson looked puzzled then angry. 'Now I have a question for you, Detective. Don't you people talk to each other?'

'Excuse me?' Bryant asked.

'Well you're obviously not from the missing persons unit, otherwise you'd know.'

'Know what, Mrs Pearson?'

She harrumphed and crossed her arms across her chest. 'That Professor Milton has not been seen or heard of for more than forty-eight hours.'

CHAPTER 9

Nicola Adamson closed her eyes against the foreboding that washed over her as she put the key into the lock of the penthouse apartment. Despite her gentle touch the sound still seemed to reverberate around the hall; as did most things at two thirty a.m.

Myra Downs in apartment 4C would be out any second to see who was making all the noise. Nicola could swear the retired accountant slept against the front door.

As expected she heard the familiar sound of her neighbour's deadbolt sliding across the bottom of the door, but she managed to curl herself into her own apartment before the one-woman neighbourhood watch committee spotted her.

Even before she hit the light switch Nicola could feel the difference in her home. It had been taken over, invaded. Although the space was still hers, she was having to share it all. Again.

She removed her shoes and padded through the lounge quietly, headed for the kitchen. Despite the visitor in the spare room she tried to maintain her own habits, her own routine, her own life.

She took a lasagne from the fridge and placed it into the microwave. Work always made her hungry and this was her routine; get back from the club, warm up a meal while taking a shower, then a bite to eat with a glass of red wine before going to bed.

Having to share her home was not going to change that. Nevertheless, she tiptoed across to the bathroom. She was tired and in no mood for drama.

Once in the bathroom Nicola breathed a sigh of relief. Each door she closed behind her was a battle fought and won. She pictured herself inside a computer game where the object was to clear each room whilst outrunning the enemy.

That was unfair, she chided herself as she dropped the clothes in a pile beside the walk-in shower. She had to adjust the temperature dial, which irritated her. Until a week ago no adjustment had been necessary. The dial would have been right where she left it.

She closed her eyes and lifted her face to meet the steaming water. The needles felt good on her skin. She turned away from the spray and craned her neck back. Within seconds the power shower had soaked her long blonde hair. She reached behind to the metal rack but found an empty space. Dammit, the bottle had been placed on the floor again.

She reached down and picked it up. The force of the squeeze sent a stream of shampoo onto the shower glass. Again she swallowed down the irritation. Sharing her space shouldn't be so difficult, but it bloody well was. It was what she'd had to do all her life.

She could feel the tension in her shoulders. Tonight had not been a good night for her.

She'd worked at The Roxburgh for the five years since her twentieth birthday and had loved every minute of it. She didn't care if people thought her job was seedy or degrading. She loved to dance, enjoyed showing off her body and men paid a lot of money to watch her. She didn't strip and there was no touching. It wasn't that kind of club.

There were other clubs in the centre of Birmingham and every dancer at every one of them aspired to work at The Roxburgh. For Nicola it would be the only club at which she would ever work. She intended to retire from dancing when she reached thirty and pursue other interests. Her bank balance supported that plan.

During the last five years she had become the most popular dancer at the venue. She received on average three requests for private dances per night and at two hundred pounds a time it was not to be sniffed at.

She knew she was the anti-Christ for some feminists and to that she raised her middle finger. Women's liberation for her was about the right to choose and she chose to dance; not because she was some vacant crackhead needing the money, but because she enjoyed it.

Even as a child she had enjoyed performing. She had strived for that individuality, that uniqueness that would set her apart, that would make people notice her.

But tonight she had felt dissatisfied with her performance. There had been no complaints from her customers; the Cristal had flowed and two bottles of Dom Perignon had been bought by her last client, making her boss a very happy man.

But Nicola knew. She knew that tonight her mind had not been fully on her work. She had not felt that total submission of herself, her mind and body, to the performance. To her it was the difference between Best Actress or Best Support.

She washed the conditioner from her hair and stepped out of the shower. She towelled herself dry and snuggled into the robe, enjoying the sensation of the warm fabric against her skin. She tied the belt around her waist and stepped out of the bathroom.

She stopped dead. For a moment she had forgotten. Just for a moment.

'Beth,' she breathed.

'Who else?'

Nicola headed to the kitchen. 'Sorry if I woke you,' she said, removing the lasagne from the microwave. She took out two plates and halved the meal.

She placed one plate at her own seat and the other opposite.

'I ay hungry,' Beth said.

Nicola tried not to cringe at Beth's broad Black Country dialect. It was a habit she herself had worked hard to overcome. As children they had both spoken that way but Beth had made no effort to change.

'Have you eaten today?' Nicola asked and then silently reprimanded herself. Would she ever grow out of the habit of being the older twin? Even if it was only by a matter of minutes.

'Yer don't want me here, do yer?'

Nicola stared down into the pasta. Suddenly her appetite was gone. The directness of her sister's question did not surprise her and it was futile to lie. Beth knew her almost as well as she knew herself.

'It's not that I don't want you here, it's just that it's been so long.'

'And whose fault's that, dear sister?'

Nicola swallowed and took her plate to the sink. She dared not look. She could not face the accusation and hurt.

'Do you have plans for tomorrow?' she asked, steering their conversation to something less explosive.

'Of course. Will yo be working again tomorrow night?'

Nicola said nothing. It was obvious that Beth disapproved of her lifestyle.   'Why do yer degrade yerself like that?'

'I enjoy what I do,' Nicola defended. She hated that her voice had risen an octave.

'But yer degree in Sociology. It's a bloody waste.'

'At least I have a degree,' Nicola shot back and instantly regretted it. The silence between them was charged.

'Well, yo took that dream away from me, didn't yer?'

Nicola knew that Beth blamed her for their estrangement but she could never bring herself to ask why.

Nicola stared into the sink, clutching the unit. 'Why did you come back?'

Beth sighed heavily. 'Where else would I go?'

Nicola silently nodded and the air between them calmed.

'It's all gonna start back up again, ain't it?' Beth asked quietly.

Nicola heard the vulnerability in her sister's voice and it made her heart ache. Some bonds could not be broken.

The dirty plate blurred before her eyes and the years without her sister bore down on her.

'And how will yer protect me this time, big sis?'

Nicola wiped at her eyes and turned, reaching out to hold her twin but the bedroom door had already closed.

Nicola emptied the contents of the second plate. She spoke quietly towards the spare bedroom. 'Beth, for whatever reason you hate me, I'm sorry. So very, very sorry.'

CHAPTER 10

At seven a.m. Kim stood before the headstone and pulled the leather jacket tightly around herself. On top of the Rowley hill dominated by Powke Lane cemetery the wind howled around her. It was Saturday and she always made time for family on a Saturday, new case or not.

Grave markers still bore the debris of Christmas gifts left by the living guilty; wreaths reduced to skeletal twigs, poinsettias battered into wilted submission by the weather. A layer of frost glistened on top of the Imperial Red stone.

From the moment she'd found the simple wooden cross marking the space she had saved as much as she could from her two jobs and bought the stone. It had been installed two days after her eighteenth birthday.

Kim gazed at the sparse gold lettering, all she'd been able to afford back then; simply a name and two dates. As usual she was struck by the distance between the two years engraved, no more than a blink.

She kissed her fingers and placed them firmly against the cold stone. 'Good night, sweet Mikey, sleep tight.'

The tears stung her eyes but she fought them back. They were the same words she had spoken right before the last breath had left his fragile, defeated body.

Kim put the memory safely back into the box and donned her helmet. She pushed the Kawasaki Ninja to the exit gate.

There was something disrespectful about igniting the roar of the 1400 cc engine within the confines of the cemetery. A metre out and she spurred the machine into action.

At the bottom of the hill she pulled into an industrial estate awash with 'To Let' signs; a stark testament to the area's industrial history and a suitably barren area from which to make the phone call.

Kim took out her phone. This was not a conversation that took place anywhere near Mikey's grave. She would not allow his final resting place to be contaminated by evil. She had to protect him, even now.

The call was answered on the third ring.

'Nurse Taylor, please.'

The line went dead for a few seconds before she heard the familiar voice.

'Hi, Lily, It's Kim Stone.'

The nurse's voice was warm. 'Hi, Kim, it's lovely to hear from you. I thought you might call today.'

The nurse said the same thing every time and yet it had never changed once. She'd made this call on the twelfth of each month for the last sixteen years.

'How is she?'

'She had a quiet Christmas but she seemed to enjoy the choir that visited ...'

'Any violent episodes?'

'No, not for a while now. Her medication is stable.'

'Anything else?'

'She asked about you again yesterday. Although she has no concept of dates, it's almost like she knows when you're about to call.' The nurse paused. 'You know, if you ever wanted to come and ...'

'Thank you for your time, Lily.'

Kim had never visited and never would. Grantley psychiatric clinic had been home to her mother since Kim was six years old and it was where she belonged.

'I'll tell her you called.'

Kim thanked her again and hit the 'end' button. The nurse treated Kim's monthly phone calls as a welfare check to see how her mother was doing and Kim had never informed her otherwise.

Only Kim knew that she made the call to ensure that the murdering, evil bitch was still safely behind bars.

CHAPTER 11

'Righty, update folks. Kev, what do we know from Mispers?'

'Professor Milton has just divorced for the third time. A bit like Simon Cowell, all his exes have nothing but good to say about him. No natural children of his own but step-father to five. No hostility noted.'

'When did he go missing?'

'Wednesday was the last time he was seen. His assistant at the college raised the alarm when he didn't appear on Thursday morning. He hasn't been in touch with any of his family members, which is apparently very strange.'

'Anything to suggest he's done this before?'

Dawson shook his head. 'To hear the exes talk he's a re-incarnation of Gandhi; mild-mannered and gentle.' Kev consulted his notes. 'The latest ex spoke to him on Tuesday afternoon and he was excited that he finally had permission for the dig.'

'I've been looking into that, Guv,' Stacey offered. 'The original application made by Professor Milton was two years ago. There've been more than twenty objections to the project; environmental, political, cultural. I ain't got anything further on that yet.'

'Keep trying, Stace. Bryant, do we know exactly when our victim spoke to the Professor?'

Bryant held out a piece of paper. 'Courtney faxed me the telephone log. They spoke for twelve minutes on Wednesday at around five thirty.'

Kim crossed her arms. 'Okay, so all we have so far is that our victim had a brief conversation with a university professor on Wednesday afternoon and now one of them is dead and the other is missing.'

A knock sounded on the door. A constable stood in the doorway.

'What?' she barked. She hated interruptions during briefing.

'Marm, I have a gentleman at the desk who wants to speak to you.'

Kim looked at him as though he'd lost his mind.

'I know, Marm, but he insists that he will only speak to you. He says he's a professor ...'

Kim was out of her chair. 'Bryant, with me,' she said, stopping at the door. 'Stace, find out whatever you can about this land.'

She headed out and took the stairs. Bryant almost kept pace with her.

In the reception she was greeted by a male with a full grey beard and a shock of wiry hair.

'Professor Milton?'

He stopped wringing his hands long enough to offer a handshake. Kim took his hand briefly and then gave it back to him.

'Please, come this way.'

Kim guided him through the corridor to interview room 1.

'Bryant, place a call to Mispers so they don't waste any more time. Is there anything we can get you?'

'A sweet cup of tea.'

Bryant nodded and closed the door behind them.

'A lot of people have been worried about you, Professor.'

She didn't intend for the words to sound like a rebuke but she hated any waste of police time. Resources were scant enough.

He nodded his understanding. 'I'm sorry, Detective. I didn't know what to do. I only spoke to Mrs Pearson a few hours ago and she told me about your visit. She said I could trust you.'

Kim was surprised that the old harridan had formed that opinion of her.

'Where have you been?' she asked. It wasn't the question that rolled around in her mouth but if Bryant had been beside her he would have urged caution. The male was clearly trembling and his hands had returned, like magnets, to each other.

'Barmouth, at a bed and breakfast. I just had to get away.'

'But on Wednesday you were over the moon. Mrs Pearson told us.'

He nodded as Bryant entered the room. His hands held a triangle of styrofoam. He sat and pushed one of the cups towards the professor.

Kim continued. 'You spoke to a woman by the name of Teresa Wyatt on that day?'

Professor Milton looked confused. 'Yes, Mrs Pearson mentioned that you asked about that but I'm not sure how it relates to what happened to me later.'

Kim had no idea what had happened to him later but she did know that Teresa Wyatt had turned up dead.

'Can you tell us why Teresa Wyatt called you?'

'Of course. She asked if I would be accepting any volunteers onto the project.'

'What did you say?'

He shook his head. 'No, I only accept volunteers who have completed at least one year at university. Ms Wyatt expressed an interest in the subject of archaeology but hadn't completed any study and certainly wouldn't have been able to before the project commenced at the end of February.'

Kim felt herself deflate. This was not a lead that would help them uncover a killer. It was a harmless conversation.

'Was there anything else?' Bryant asked.

The professor paused. 'She did ask where about we would be commencing the dig, which I found a little strange in the context of the conversation.'

Yes, Kim thought. That was a little strange. 'What happened later?' she asked, recalling his previous comment.

Professor Milton swallowed. 'I got home from work and Tess didn't greet me as she usually did.'

Kim looked at Bryant. Dawson had said the professor was single again.

'Ordinarily she sleeps in the kitchen, next to her water bowl but as soon as I put my key into the lock, she's there, wagging her tail.'

Ah, that made more sense, Kim thought.

'But not Wednesday. I called her as I walked to the kitchen but she didn't come. I found her next to her bed.' He swallowed. 'She was convulsing on the floor. Her eyes were glassy and staring and for a few seconds I didn't even see the note.

'I scooped her up and drove to the vets as quickly as possible but it was too late. She'd gone by the time I got there.' He wiped his right eye.

Kim opened her mouth to ask about the note but Bryant cut her off.

'So sorry to hear that, Professor. Had she been unwell?'

Professor Milton shook his head. 'Not at all. She was only four years old. The vet didn't need to examine her. He could smell the antifreeze on her breath. Apparently, dogs love it because it tastes sweet. The chemical had been poured into her water dish and she'd drunk the lot.'

'You said there was a note?' Bryant prompted gently.

His eyes reddened. 'Yes, the bastard stapled it to her ear.'

Kim winced. 'Do you recall what it said?'

He reached into his jacket. 'I have it here. The vet removed it afterwards.'

Kim took the note. Forensically it would be of no use now. The Professor had handled it, and so had the vet.

She unfolded it and laid it out on the table. It was simple black type on white paper and read:

'KILL THE DIG OR WIFE NUMBER 3 WILL BE NEXT'

'I didn't even go back home. I'm ashamed to admit that I was terrified and still am. Who would do this, Detective?' The professor drained the last of his tea. 'I don't even know where I can go.'

'Mrs Pearson,' Kim offered. She'd seen the expression on the woman's face when she'd spoken of the Professor. That little bulldog wouldn't let anyone near him.

Kim stood and took the note while Bryant shook the man's hand and offered to get him a ride to wherever he wanted to go.

Kim clutched the note and headed back to the office. She couldn't help but feel that somewhere out there was one humungous can of worms and that she'd just been handed the can-opener.

'Okay, Kev, I think we're gonna need fresh coffee. Stace, what did you find out about that land?'

'It's about an acre in size and sits right next to the Rowley crematorium. It's at the tip of a council estate built in the mid-Fifties. Before the housing development it was the site of a steelwork factory.'

Bryant entered the room on his mobile phone. 'Thank you, Courtney. You've been a wonderful help.'

'What?' Bryant asked as six curious eyes landed on him.

'Courtney?' Kim asked. 'Is there something I need to drop to your wife?'

Bryant chuckled as he removed his suit jacket. 'I'm a happily married man, Guv. My wife said so. And anyway, Courtney is mending a broken heart courtesy of Joanna, the English teacher that was coming on to you the other day.'

Dawson turned, his eyes wide. 'Really, Guv?'

'Down boy.' She turned to Bryant. 'Why the call?'

Bryant raised an eyebrow. 'Following your logic of past, present and future I asked Courtney if she had access to Teresa Wyatt's employment history. She's faxing it over.'

'Put that girl on the Christmas list. She's saving us a fortune in warrants.'

Kim turned back to Stacey, trying to visualise the piece of land. 'Hang on, are you talking about that field right next to the crematorium? The one where the travelling fair sets up?'

Stacey turned her monitor and pointed. An image from Google Earth filled the screen. 'Look, there's something fenced off at the road edge but otherwise it's just a waste piece of land.'

Kim's gut was now churning out of control. Every sense she possessed was on high alert.

'Stace, look up the name Crestwood and get me everything you can. I have some calls to make.'

Kim took a breath as she sat at her own desk. A few pieces of the puzzle began to slide into place. And for the first time in her life, she hoped she was wrong.

CHAPTER 12

Tom Curtis turned over and faced away from the window. The daylight didn't normally stop him from sleeping after an eight hour shift at the care home.

The work was exhausting; picking up fat, old people, putting them to bed, dabbing their spittle and wiping their arses.

He'd already avoided two internal investigations but he suspected that this third one might be more problematic. Martha Brown's daughter only visited once a week and when she did she was sure to notice the bruise.

The rest of the staff had turned a blind eye. It was impossible not to lose patience now and again. Being the only male on the team meant he would often turn up for the night shift and find that the heavier jobs had not been done. He was powerless to complain. If he'd been honest on his medical form he would not have a job at all.

But it wasn't even his conscience that kept him awake. He felt nothing for the old folks under his care and if their relatives were affronted they could bloody well take them home and wipe the shitty arses themselves.

No, it was the ringing of his mobile phone that was keeping him awake. Even though he'd switched it off he could still hear it in his head.

He turned and lay on his back, glad that his wife and daughter had already left the house. Today was going to be another dark day.

The dark days had punctuated the last two years, seven months and nineteen days. It was on these days that the urge to drink was overpowering. It was on these days that sobriety was not worth his life.

When he'd left culinary school he had never envisaged that his future would consist of changing the nappies of old people. When he'd graduated he had not foreseen old, wobbly flesh around his neck as he lifted geriatrics in and out of bed. He had not dreamt that he would be hand feeding a group of people who were filled with rigor mortis before they'd taken their last breath.

At twenty-three he'd suffered his first heart attack which had rendered him unemployable on the restaurant scene. Long hours and stressful working conditions were not conducive to the long life of a person with congestive heart disease.

One day he'd been serving haute cuisine in a French restaurant at Water's Edge in Birmingham and the next he'd been preparing turkey burgers and frozen chips for a bunch of worthless kids.

For years he hid his addiction from his wife. He became a master of lies and deceit. On the day he collapsed with a second heart attack his lies had been uncovered when the doctor had advised that the next bender would most probably be his last.

He had not taken a drink since that day.

He reached across and switched on his phone. Immediately it began to ring. He hit the end button to cut off the call, taking the tally of missed calls to fifty-seven in three days. He didn't recognise the number and no name displayed on the screen, but Tom knew who was calling.

And the caller would have spent his time better had he tried to reach Teresa. It was obvious that she'd opened her mouth to someone and it had got her killed.

He suspected that the authorisation for the dig had made them all jittery but he didn't need the check calls. He would keep their damn secrets, just as they had kept his. They had made a pact. He knew that the others viewed him as the fragile connection in the chain of deceit but he hadn't weakened yet.

There had been times, especially on the dark days when he'd been tempted to speak out, to rid himself of the poison. Those thoughts had been more easily silenced by drink.

His mind travelled back, as it did every day. Damn it, he should have said no. He should have stood up to the rest of them and said no. His own wrongdoing seemed so trivial compared to the consequences of his acquiescence.

One time he'd found himself on the wall outside Old Hill police station. For three and a half hours he remained there, chasing the tail of his conscience. He stood, he sat down, he paced, he sat down. He cried, he stood up. And then he walked away.

If he'd been strong enough to tell the truth he might have lost his wife. As a woman and as a mother, if she ever learned of his part in the events she would be sickened by his actions. And the worst part was Tom couldn't blame her.

He threw back the covers. There was no point trying to sleep. He was fully awake. He headed downstairs. He needed coffee, the stronger the better.

He headed to the kitchen and stopped dead at the dining table.

Staring at him was a bottle of Johnnie Walker Blue and a note.

The very sight of the golden brown liquid took the saliva from his mouth. The forty per cent proof bottle cost more than one hundred pounds. It was one of the finest old-aged malt and grain whiskies; the Cristal of the blended whisky world. His body responded. It was like staring into Christmas morning. He tore his eyes away and reached for the note.

WE CAN DO THIS YOUR WAY OR MY WAY BUT IT WILL GET DONE. ENJOY.

He slumped into the chair, his eyes fixed on his best friend and his worst enemy.

It was clear what the sender wanted. They wished for him to die. Alongside his fear sat relief. He had always known that the day of reckoning would come, whether it be in this life or the next.

Tom unscrewed the top of the bottle and the smell reached his nose immediately. He knew that to take a drink would kill him. Not the first sip – he was an alcoholic, there was no such thing as a sip. If he took a drink he would finish the whole bottle and that would bring him death.

If he chose this method to die then no one else need suffer. His wife would think he'd simply weakened and she would be safe. With luck she might never learn of what he'd done. His daughter need never know.

He lifted the bottle slowly and took the first gulp. He paused only a second before raising the bottle to his lips again. This time he didn't stop until the scorch in his chest was unbearable.

The effects hit him immediately. After more than two years his body had lost tolerance and the alcohol burned around his veins all the way to his brain.

He took another swig and smiled. There were worse ways to die.

He swigged again and chuckled. No more bathing old folks. No more dirty nappies. No more wiping dribble.

He raised the bottle to his mouth, taking the liquid half-way down. His body was on fire and he felt euphoric. It was like watching your favourite football team slaughter the opposition.

There would be no more hiding what he'd done. No more fear. He was doing the right thing.

The tears dropped onto his cheeks. Inside Tom felt happy, at peace, but his body was betraying him.

The bottle paused at his mouth as his eyes rested on a photo of his daughter feeding the goats at Dudley Zoo on her sixth birthday.

He squinted at the photo. He didn't remember that frown on her face or the questions in her eyes.

'Sweetheart, I'm sorry,' he said to the picture. 'It was only once, I swear.'

Her expression didn't change. *Are you sure?*

He closed his eyes against the accusation but her face still swam before his eyes.

'Okay, maybe it was more than once but it wasn't my fault, sweetheart. She made me do it. She tempted me. She teased me. I couldn't help myself. It wasn't my fault.'

'But you were an adult?'

Tom closed his eyes against the onslaught of his child's disgust. A tear forced its way out and slid down his cheek.

'Please understand, she was much older than fifteen. She was clever and manipulative and I just gave in. It wasn't my fault. She seduced me and I couldn't fight back.'

'She was a child.'

Tom pulled at his own hair to ease the pain. 'I know, I know, but she wasn't a child. She was a conniving girl who knew how to get what she wanted.'

'But what you did next was unforgivable. Daddy, I hate you.'

Now his whole body cried. He would never see his beautiful little girl again. He would not watch Amy grow into a young lady or be around to protect her from boys. He would never kiss those soft cheeks again or feel her tiny little hand in his.

His head dropped forward and tears fell onto his legs. Through the blurred vision his gaze travelled to his feet and rested on the slippers Amy had bought him for Father's Day. They were monogrammed with the face of Homer Simpson, his favourite character.

No, his mind screamed. There had to be another way. He didn't want to die. He didn't want to lose his family. He had to make them understand.

Maybe he could go to the police. Admit to what he'd done. It wasn't as though he'd been alone. He hadn't even been a decision maker. He'd just gone along with it because he was young and scared. He'd been weak and stupid but damn it he was not a murderer.

Of course he would be punished, but it would be worth it to be able to watch his daughter grow.

Tom wiped away the tears and focused his vision on the bottle. It was over half gone. Oh God, he prayed that it was not too late.

As he placed the bottle back on the table he felt his head being yanked back by the hair.

The bottle fell to the floor as Tom tried to understand what was going on. He felt the cold tip of metal beneath his left ear, a forearm against his neck. He tried to turn but the tip of the blade ripped at his skin.

He watched as a gloved hand moved from left to right beneath his chin.

And that was the last thing he saw.

CHAPTER 13

Kim replaced the receiver after the third call. She hoped she was wrong and that she was about to waste the valuable time of some very important people. She would happily accept a bollocking from Woody if she was wrong. She would get no satisfaction from being right on this one.

Someone did not want that ground excavated.

'What've you got, Stace?' Kim asked, perching on the edge of the spare desk.

'Hope yer sitting comfy, Guv. The building that still stands is part of a bigger facility that was built in the 1940s. Back then, it was designed to house the mentally disturbed soldiers returning from the war.

'The physically disabled were sent to various hospitals in the region but the worst of the psychologically affected were sent to Crestwood. Really, it was a secure unit for the soldiers that could never go back into society. We're talking killing machines that ain't got an 'off' button.

'By the late Seventies the population of about thirty-five individuals had either committed suicide or died of natural causes. The place was then used as a borstal.'

Kim cringed. It was an outdated word that brought all kinds of connotations.

'Go on.'

'There's some real horror stories that came out of the Eighties of abuse and molestation. An enquiry was carried out but no charges were brought. By the early nineties the place 'ad been turned into a children's home for girls but still 'ad a reputation for housing troubled teens.

'Due to budget cuts and building repairs the place was being phased out as we entered the millennium and in '04 there was a fire that emptied it completely.'

'Anyone hurt?'

Stacey shook her head. 'There ain't no headlines to suggest it.'

'Okay, Kev, Stace, start compiling a list of staff members. I want to see ...'

The sound of the fax machine kicking into life silenced her.

They all knew what it was and they all knew what it was going to say.

Bryant reached for the document and perused it quickly. He stood beside Stacey's desk and handed her the C.V. of Teresa Wyatt.

'Here you go, guys, I think you have your first.'

Glances were exchanged between them all as the possibilities began to dawn. No one spoke.

And then the phone rang.

CHAPTER 14

'Jesus, Guv, slow down. This is not a Kawasaki Goldwing.'

'Good to know 'cos there's no such thing.'

'You do know that we're too late to save him?'

Kim slowed as she approached an amber light but thought better of it and sped over the lights of the Pedmore Road. She weaved in and out of vehicles on the dual carriageway that ran alongside the Merry Hill shopping centre.

'And that there's no siren on this?'

'Oh Bryant, loosen up. I haven't killed us yet.' She offered him a sidelong glance. 'And you need to be more worried about the gash on your left arm.' She'd spotted the injury through the fabric of his shirt sleeve during the briefing.

'Just a scratch.'

'Rugby practice last night?'

He nodded.

'You really need to give it up. You're either too old or too slow for the game. Either way you're gonna get hurt.'

'Thanks for that, Guv.'

'Each injury is worse than the last so surely it's time to pack it in.'

She was forced to stop the car at the next set of lights. Bryant unwrapped his left hand from the roof handle and flexed it.

'Can't do it, Guv. Rugby is my yang.'

'Your what?'

'My yang, Guv. My balance. The missus has got me taking ballroom dance classes with her every week. I need the rugby to balance me out.'

Kim negotiated the next traffic island from the inner lane and ignored the horn honks that sounded in her wake.

'So, you prance around the dance floor and then hug other hairy men to balance you out?'

'It's called a scrum, Guv.'

'I'm not judging, honest.' She turned and looked at him, fighting back the smile. 'What I really don't understand is why on earth you offered that information to me voluntarily. You have to know that was a mistake?'

He rested his head back against the seat, closed his eyes and groaned. 'Yeah, starting to see that now.' He turned to her. 'You'll keep it between us, Guv, eh?'

She shook her head. 'Not gonna make promises I can't keep,' she answered honestly.

'So, who were you calling earlier?' he asked, changing the subject.

'Professor Milton.'

'For what?'

'Just making sure he'd reached Mrs Pearson safely.'

'Bollocks,' Bryant said, behind a cough.

As the cars began to move away slowly she shadowed the car in front. It braked and so did she as three lanes filtered into two. Bryant grabbed the handle.

'So, what do we know?'

'Male, late thirties, cut throat. Possible suicide, could be accidental.'

Kim rolled her eyes. A dark humour was necessary to maintain sanity but just sometimes ...

'Where now?'

'Take a left just past the school and we should see it from there.'

Kim screeched around the corner sending Bryant crashing against the passenger door. She drove up the hill and threw on the handbrake at the cordon.

A box porch led straight into the front room, where a WPC sat on the sofa comforting a distraught female. Kim walked through directly into an open plan dining room and kitchen.

'Jesus Christ,' she whispered.

'No, that's just a rumour,' said Keats.

The male was still seated in the dining room chair. His limbs were limp like a rag doll. His head was torn back, the crown almost resting between his shoulder blades. Kim was instantly reminded of a cartoon. The angle looked almost impossible.

The laws of physics dictated that he should have fallen to the floor but the angle of the back of his neck over the top of the chair had kept him in place; the back of his head resting like a hook.

The gaping wound displayed yellow, fatty tissue torn apart by a blade. Blood had spurted onto the wall opposite and drained down his chest, forming a macabre bib. His T-shirt and joggers were sodden red and the stench of metal almost overwhelmed her.

'Jesus Christ,' Bryant offered from behind.

Keats shook his head. 'One of you needs to fire their scriptwriter.'

Kim ignored him as she committed the scene to memory. She stood above the body and looked down. The eyes of the male were open and wide. His face bore the expression of the horror below.

She saw the empty bottle of whisky on the floor. 'Alcohol at this time?' she asked.

'I think half of the bottle is inside him and the other half is in the carpet. It's a damn waste. Johnnie Walker Blue sells for over a hundred a bottle.'

'Bryant, go ... '

'On my way.'

Bryant turned and headed back to the lounge. He was much better with distraught females than she was. In her company they often cried more.

She walked around the body, examining the scene from every angle. Nothing in the immediate area was disturbed and no struggle seemed to have taken place.

A white suit hovered around her.

'Detective, Keegan here is too polite to ask you to move but I'm not,' Keats said. 'Stand back so he can do his job.'

Kim shot Keats a look but stepped back into the corner of the room. With satisfaction she noted that the hem on his right trouser leg was down but damn that smidge of decency that kept the observation on the right side of her lips.

Keegan took digital photographs and then took out a disposable camera and repeated the process.

'His wallet is upstairs so it wasn't robbery,' Keats offered, standing beside her.

Kim already knew that for a fact.

'Type of knife?'

'I'd say plastic handle, seven inch kitchen knife normally used for cutting bread.'

'Detailed description for a prelim exam?'

He shrugged. 'Or it could just be the one in the sink covered in blood.'

'He was murdered with his own damn bread knife?'

'Detective, I wouldn't like to commit myself too early but,' he lowered his voice and leaned towards her. 'I'd hazard a guess that foul play was involved.'

Kim rolled her eyes. Great, today everyone was a comedian.

'Method of entry?'

'Patio door left open to let the cat in and out.'

'Good to see the "Secure Home" campaign was successful.'

Kim stepped closer to the patio door. A technician stood outside, dusting the handle. She studied every inch of the area.

Her gaze paused and she crouched down.

She assessed the back garden; a mixture of gravel and slabs. A clean fence lined the perimeter.

'Keats, who from this team was at Teresa Wyatt's house the other night?'

He glanced at the technicians present. 'That would be just myself.'

So, it was just the two of them.

'Are you wearing the same shoes?'

'Detective, my footwear ...'

'Keats, just answer me.'

He paused for a few seconds, now moving towards her. 'No, I am not.'

And neither was she.

'Look,' she said, pointing.

He squinted at the object, which was no more than an inch long.

'Golden Conifer,' he observed.

Their eyes met as they both realised the repercussions of the discovery.

'Whisky's a bit of a puzzle, Guv,' Bryant said, appearing beside her. 'Our guy was a recovering alcoholic. Been on the wagon for about two years. The wife states that the bottle wasn't in the house this morning and he would never have left the house dressed like that. Also, he's got the same money in his wallet as he did when she left the house. She still checks.'

Kim stood and took an evidence marker from the tech bag. 'Why would the killer bring the whisky?'

Bryant shrugged. 'Dunno, but he had congestive heart failure so the whisky would probably have been enough.'

Kim was puzzled. The murderer had brought a bottle of alcohol, somehow aware that it would probably prove fatal to Tom Curtis, but had almost beheaded him anyway. It made no sense.

'Our killer could have just delivered the bottle and left the scene but that wasn't enough. Why?'

'Sicko wanted to send a message?'

'Either the killer knew of his heart condition but wanted to add the personal touch – or it was a tool to subdue him, to make the job easier.'

Bryant shook his head as Kim's mobile phone rang.

'Stone.'

'Guv, what's the full name of your victim?'

'Tom Curtis ... why?' she asked, hearing the breathless-ness in Dawson's tone. Her stomach rolled at what she knew she was about to hear.

'You're not gonna believe this, but there was a head chef at Crestwood children's home ten years ago. His name was Tom Curtis.'

CHAPTER 15

'Thanks for letting me drive back, Guv. My nerves couldn't take another roller coaster.'

'Yeah well, this ain't *Driving Miss Daisy* and I do want to get back to the station before next weekend.'

Bryant headed towards Halesowen and Kim took out her phone. She redialled a number she'd called earlier.

'Professor Milton ... yes ... Hello. About our discussion earlier, is everything in place?'

'I've made some calls, my dear, and I think I can help with your request.'

'I appreciate that but we now appear to have a second body related to this case and urgency is of the utmost importance.'

She heard his sharp intake of breath. 'It will be done, Detective.'

She thanked him and ended the call.

'What was all that about?'

'Never you mind, just keep driving.'

By the time Bryant pulled into the car park she had called ahead to make a request for a brief meeting with Woody so she entered the building and headed straight for the third floor.

Kim knocked on Woody's door and entered just a second before he instructed her to do so.

'Stone, this had better be good. I was in the middle of ...'

'Sir, the Teresa Wyatt case is much more complicated than we first thought.'

'How so?'

Kim took a deep breath. 'On the day she was murdered, our victim made a call to a Professor Milton who had just received authorisation to excavate an area of land in Rowley Regis.

'She initially asked to be included in the project but was turned down. Then she became quite interested in the area concerned.'

'What significance is in the land?'

'It's the site of the old children's home.'

'Next to the crematorium?'

Kim nodded. 'Both Teresa Wyatt and Tom Curtis are ex-staff members. In the few days since he was granted permission to excavate the land the professor's life has been threatened and his dog killed. And two previous employees of Crestwood have been murdered.'

Woody stared at a spot on the wall behind her. He was already reading the headlines.

'Sir, someone does not want that ground disturbed.'

'Stone, don't go at this at warp speed. There are a lot of politics involved.'

'The equipment will be on site tomorrow.'

His jaw tensed. 'Stone, you know that's impossible. There are all sorts of things we need to do.'

'With all due respect, Sir, that's your worry not mine. With the momentum this case is gathering, we really don't have the luxury of waiting that long.'

He considered her words for a moment. 'I want you on site first thing in the morning and nothing gets dug, not one shovel hits that earth until you get confirmation from me.'

Kim said nothing.

'Stone, do we understand each other?'

'Of course, Sir. Whatever you say.'

She stood and left the room.

CHAPTER 16

Bethany Adamson cursed at the sudden noise in the stillness of the hallway. The metal grid between the elevator and the tiled floor clattered beneath her walking stick.

She moved along the corridor, searching for the keys to the flat. With one hand she tried to single out the entrance key. The whole bunch fell to the ground; metal against metal.

She swore as she bent to retrieve them. A pain shot from her knee to her thigh. Her hand closed around them but not before she heard the deadbolt slide across the old cow's door.

As Beth straightened she felt the gush of warm air that came from the open door of their neighbour.

'Is everything okay out here?' she asked.

There was no concern in the question, only the hint of a reprimand.

Myra Downs stood about five feet high in her fur-trimmed slippers. The bare skin of her feet was scaly and dry. Beth thanked God that the woman was dressed in a full-length dressing gown. Her fleshy arms were folded across an ample breast being flattened down like dog ears. Her lined face was creased in displeasure.

Beth faced her squarely. Nicola might be frightened of the old cow but she was not.

'Nah, Mrs Downs, I was just being raped and pillaged by three blokes but thanks for yer concern.'

The woman huffed. 'There are people trying to sleep, you know.'

'You'd have a better chance if yer wore propped up against the door.'

The woman's face distorted like a bulldog chewing a wasp.

'You know, before you came to stay this floor was a perfectly respectable place and now what with the arguing and the noise at all hours ...'

'Mrs Downs. It's half ten and I dropped me keys. Ger a fuckin' grip.'

The woman's face reddened. 'Well ... well ... how long do you intend to stay?'

Yeah, another resident who didn't want her here. Well, tough bloody luck.

'Probably gonna stay a while. Nic's adding me to the lease.'

It was worth the lie to see the horror register on her face. 'Oh, no, no, I'll be speaking to your sister about ...'

This nosey old bag was really starting to get on her nerves.

'What the bloody hell is yer problem?'

'Loud noise late at night is frightening for single residents, young lady.'

'Who do yer think's gonna ger in. There's three locks and a keycode to protect yer.' Beth looked her up and down. 'And I don't think yer got a lot to fear, to be honest.'

Mrs Downs stepped back from the door. 'I can't deal with you. I'll speak to Nicola. She's far more pleasant than you are.'

Tell me something I don't know, Beth thought.

She continued to stare the old woman down until the door finally closed. She allowed herself a small smile. That little exchange had made her night.

She jangled the keys a few more times before finally letting herself into the apartment.

Beth placed the walking stick over the edge of the sofa and sat down. She rubbed at her knee. The cold was giving it murder.

She reached for the slippers parked on the edge of the sofa. The maroon leather uppers were soft and smooth; the fur luxurious and warm.

She took off the flat-heeled boots and eased her feet into the expensive footwear. They weren't hers but Nicola wouldn't mind. They had always shared. That's what twins did.

She stood and shook out the ache from her knee.

She tapped on Nicola's door lightly. No answer. What had she been expecting? Of course her whore of a sister was not at home. She was out dancing and showing off her body for money.

She opened the door and stepped in. As usual, the room took her breath away. It was the room they'd dreamt of as children as they'd laid side by side at Crestwood.

Their room would have matching pink covers and pillows. An awning would circle the beds, held in place by beautiful lace. They dreamed of a wardrobe as magical as Narnia. Shelves would be filled with stuffed toys and snow globes. Fairy lights would be draped around the head of both beds. Their imagined bedroom would be magical and light and filled with things that were theirs and they would drift off to sleep making shadows on the wall.

Beth stepped further into the room. Her hand trailed along the shelf above the fireplace and landed on the single brown teddy bear at the end. She opened the door to the walk-in closet and stepped inside.

Nicola's clothes, underwear and shoes were folded, stacked and organised according to colour. Two drawers were dedicated to jewellery. One drawer held expensive, delicate pieces stored in their original boxes. Beth spotted one from Cartier and two from De Beers.

The second held bolder, heavier pieces that Beth guessed were used for her work. She closed the drawer quickly and moved further along. She didn't like to think of her sister at work.

A dressing table separated the wardrobe from the shoe cupboard. A single strand of clear fairy lights lined the mirror's edge.

Beth returned to the bedroom and sat on the four-poster bed. It was a room fit for a princess, just as they'd planned. It was the place they had vowed to live together for ever and ever and ever.

It was the room of which they'd dreamed; except there was only one bed.

One bed to be enjoyed by the sister who had it all.

What Nicola had didn't anger Beth anywhere near as much as her sister's refusal to admit what she'd done.

Her pathetic denial of their past infuriated Beth more and more with each passing day. No apology could ever take it back.

Nicola's actions had destroyed their chances of any life together and still she maintained her ignorance of the facts.

I don't know why you hate me. I don't know what I've done. I don't know how I hurt you. On and on and on with the denial.

However much Nicola protested otherwise, Beth felt the truth in her heart.

Somewhere deep inside, she knew.

CHAPTER 17

'Jesus, Bryant, will you keep still?'

He moved from foot to foot. The overnight temperature had dropped to minus three and the ground still held an icy core that seeped up through the shoes and into the bones.

He blew warm breath into his cupped hands. 'For those of us not made of titanium, it's cold enough to freeze the balls off a brass monkey.'

'Man up,' Kim said, walking to the edge of the site.

The area itself was the size of a football pitch. It rose gently towards a row of trees that obscured the north tip from the council estate. On the west side was a road separating the site from the Rowley Regis crematorium. The remains of a large building sat at the southern edge nearest the road, behind a bus stop and a street lamp. The upper floor peered over at a row of terraced houses on the other side of the road. A six foot fence formed a snug perimeter around the structure, obscuring the lower level from view.

She glanced to the west and shook her head. How comforting for kids that had been abandoned, abused and neglected to look out of their windows onto a field for the dead.

There were times when the insensitivity of the system appalled her. It was a building that had become vacant and that was all that had mattered.

She sighed and blew a silent kiss to Mikey's grave, which now lay behind a curtain of mist, sealing them off from the rest of the world two hundred feet in each direction.

A Volvo estate pulled onto a dirt patch at the top of the site.

Kim walked over as Professor Milton and two men exited the vehicle.

'Detective, good to see you again.'

Kim saw a remarkable change in the demeanour of the professor since the previous day. His cheeks were rosy and his eyes bright. His gait was sprightly and purposeful. If that was after one night in the care of Mrs Pearson, she might consider booking in herself.

He turned to his companions as Bryant materialised beside her. 'This is Darren Brown and Carl Newton. They're volunteers that were scheduled to assist on my dig. They'll be operating the equipment.'

Kim felt obliged to come clean with the professor after the trouble he had taken.

'You know this is a hunch, Professor? There may be nothing down there.'

His eyes were serious and his voice low. 'But what if there is, Detective? I've been trying to excavate this land for two years and someone has done their level best to stop me. I'd like to know why.'

Kim was satisfied that he understood.

A Vauxhall Astra pulled in beside the professor's car. A portly male in his fifties got out of the car, followed by a tall, red-headed woman Kim guessed to be in her late twenties.

'David, thank you for coming,' Kim said.

'I don't recall there being a great deal of choice, Detective,' he said with a half-smile.

'Professor Milton, please meet Doctor Matthews.'

The two men shook hands.

Kim had met Doctor David Matthews at the University of Glamorgan which, together with Cardiff University and South Wales police, formed a unique organisation in the UK called the Universities Police Science Institute. It was dedicated to research and training in police-related matters.

Doctor Matthews was an advisor for the Glamorgan Centre for Police Sciences and had been instrumental in setting up the Crime Scene Investigation House at the university.

Kim had attended a seminar there two years earlier and had offered a couple of suggestions for improvement to the scenario training based on her own crime scene experience, which had resulted in her staying on for the weekend.

'May I introduce Cerys Hughes. She is a fully qualified archaeologist and has just completed a degree in forensic science.'

Kim nodded in her direction.

'Okay, it's important you both understand that we have no authority here as yet. My boss is working on the red tape so nothing can be disturbed until the paperwork is in order. If you suspect the presence of anything at all, let me know.'

David Matthews stepped forward. 'You have three hours of our time for these shenanigans and if nothing is detected by then we will be on our way.'

Kim nodded. Three hours of his time for two days of hers. Yep, that seemed fair.

He continued. 'Cerys and I will cut a small feature at the top of the land to begin analysing the soil.'

Kim nodded towards Cerys. The fiery red hair was cut in a sleek bob that rested just below a square jaw line. Her pale blue eyes were piercing. Not naturally beautiful, she had a face that was intriguing, that drew attention.

The woman acknowledged her without smiling and followed David as he walked towards the top edge of the site.

A white Escort van took the last space on the dirt patch.

A woman opened the rear doors. A steaming urn and foil wrapped packages were inside.

Bryant chuckled. 'Did my imagination just conjure her up?'

'No, she's real. Make sure everyone gets a hot drink and a bacon sandwich before they start.'

Bryant smiled. 'You know, Guv, at times ...'

Kim didn't hear the rest of his words as she was already heading down the hill towards the derelict building.

She walked the perimeter of the fence but there was no access point. The front of the building faced onto the road and the houses opposite. Too many prying eyes. She returned to the rear and started looking for an area of vulnerability.

The fencing was not a traditional design of slatted pieces overlaying each other. Each panel was made of strong, thick wood normally used for pallets and lay flush with the one above and below. A tiny sliver of daylight escaped between each nine-inch piece.

She pushed at one of the tall wooden fence posts. It moved back and forth, the bottom of the post rotted in the ground.

'Don't even think about it, Guv,' Bryant said, offering her a hot drink. She took it in her left hand and continued to work her way along the posts. The next two were steady but the fourth rocked to and fro.

'How'd you get Doctor Matthews here? Did you bully him?'

'Define bullying,' she said, pushing at the next post.

'Probably best I don't know. Plausible deniability and all that.'

'It doesn't hurt to have the presence of a forensic archae-ologist on site.'

'Course not, except that at this point we have no authori-sation to instruct anyone to do anything.'

Kim shrugged.

'What if there's nothing down there?'

'Then we all get to go home for tea. But if there is, we have a head start. Doctor Matthews is fully qualified to ...'

'Oh, I know. He's just given me his entire education his-tory but Woody said nothing is to be touched until the pa-perwork is in order.'

'See, now you're just being pedantic.'

'Just trying to protect your ass, Guv.'

'My ass is fine. You should worry more about your own if you're planning to eat that second bacon bap in your pocket.'

'How did you know?'

Kim shook her head. Because he would have brought one down for her, even though he knew she probably wouldn't touch it.

She stood away from the fence and drained her coffee cup. 'Now, more importantly, should I go over or through?'

Bryant groaned. 'How about away from it?'

'Not one of the options I gave.'

'We have no authority to enter.'

'Either help me or leave me to it. Your choice.'

She set the empty cup on the ground as Bryant sighed heavily.

'If you try to go through you'll be leaving the area vulner-able for kids.'

'Over it is then,' Kim said, heading for the middle section of slats between the two stable fence posts. She aimed a kick at one of the panels level with her thigh. It splintered. She kicked it again and the panel cracked in half. She pushed the broken slats inwards so that the stable piece below could be used as a step.

In one fluid movement she put the toe of her left boot on top of the slat and used Bryant's shoulder to push herself up. She grabbed the stable post to her left, threw her right leg over the top of the fence and into the gap on the other side. As she straddled the top of the fence she took a second to steady her balance before bringing her left leg over the top and into the gap. She jumped down backwards, bending her knees to absorb the impact.

The grass around the building was tall and full of nettles. Kim navigated her way to the only cracked window she could see on the ground floor. The height of the fencing had protected the lower windows but all the glass on the upper level had been smashed through.

She spied a grey tin rubbish bin. She removed the lid and smashed it against the damaged window pane.

'What the hell are you doing?' Bryant called.

She ignored him and knocked out another couple of pieces of glass, then took the bin, turned it upside down and stood on it. She carefully folded herself in through the broken window onto a formica unit top that ran the entire length of the wall, pausing only for a double sink.

She looked inside and saw the fire-damaged walls of the kitchen. Kim read that the fire had originated in there. The walls were blackest near the door that led into the corridor. Cobweb curtains adorned every corner of the room.

From somewhere in the building she could hear the sound of water dripping. The water supply would have been turned off at the stop tap. She guessed it was residual rainwater from a roof damaged by fire and time now exposed to the elements.

As she stood in the doorway she saw that the corridor ran the length of the building, splitting it in half. When she looked to her right the walls were painted an off-white. A film of dust was visible in places but was untouched by the fire.

To her left, the wooden beams supporting the floor above were exposed and blackened. The door frames were charred and only a few patches of paint remained on the walls at low level. Wires and cables hung exposed from between the beams.

Debris and fallen ceiling tiles littered the corridor floor. The damage appeared to worsen as it travelled further towards the edge of the building.

Kim stepped back into the kitchen and surveyed the damage again. The wall units closest to the door were mottled with the marble effect of scorched wood. The doors of the fridge and freezer had buckled and were hanging off but the area closest to the six ring cooker sat beneath a light covering of soot.

She opened the door of the wall unit closest to the cooker. Rodent droppings fell onto the hob. A piece of A4 paper was tacked on the inside of the door. The print was still visible. It listed the names of girls on the left hand side and a grid indicating the allocated chore for the week.

Kim paused for a moment. Her hand reached up and touched the first few names. She had been one of these girls, not here and not then but subconsciously she knew every single girl on the list. She knew their loneliness, their pain, their anger.

Kim was suddenly struck by a memory from foster family number five. In the small box room at the back of the house she would hear gentle coo-cooing all through the night from the house next door.

Each time the racing pigeons were released she would watch them, willing them to fly away, escape their captivity and be free. But they never did.

Places like Crestwood were the same. Occasionally the birds would be set free but they always seemed to fly back.

Like prison, release from a children's home came with farewells that held hope and good wishes but never finality.

Her thoughts were interrupted by the sound of a siren in the distance. She clambered onto the work surface and bent herself through the window onto the top of the bin and down on to the ground.

She dragged the bin to the fence just as the siren and the car engine died.

'Morning, Kelvin, why the blues?' Bryant shouted.

Kim rolled her eyes and stood against the fence.

'Had a report that someone was seen inside this building.'

Great, the police were here for her.

Bryant chuckled. 'Nah, it's just me snooping around. Caught a shit job today babysitting this bloody digging crew and I was just curious about what was behind here.'

'But you've not been in the building?' the constable asked doubtfully.

'No, mate, how stupid do you think I am?'

'Fair enough, Detective. I'll leave you to it.'

The constable began to walk away but then turned and took a couple of steps back. 'Shit job from your boss, Detective?' he asked.

'Who else?'

'Gotta tell you, Sir, you have the condolences of most of the station having to work with that ballbreaker.'

Bryant chuckled. 'You know, if she could hear you, she'd probably agree.'

'She is a bit cold, though, eh?'

Kim nodded from behind the fence. Yeah, she was happy with that.

'Nah, she's not as bad as you think.'

Kim almost growled. Yes, she really was.

'In fact, she was only saying the other day that it would be nice if you guys struck up conversation with her now and again.'

She'd bloody kill Bryant. Slowly.

'No problem, Sir. I'll bear that in mind.'

As the constable walked away he transmitted back to the control room that the premises were all in order.

'Bastard,' Kim spat through the fence.

'Oops, sorry, Guv. Didn't realise you were there ... listening.'

Kim stood on the bin, and exited the area the same way she'd entered.

She landed on her feet but fell into Bryant and knocked him sideways.

'Oh, sorry,' she said.

'On the scale of genuine apologies, I'd rate that at minus seven.'

'Detectives,' the professor said, appearing beside them. 'We're ready to begin.'

Bryant caught her gaze and held it as the professor turned and walked away.

'So, did you learn anything on your illegal fact-finding mission?'

. 'Contrary to the written report, that fire did not start in the kitchen.'

CHAPTER 18

Kim caught up with the professor as he neared Bill and Ben, as she had nicknamed his volunteers.

'Doctor Matthews has done an initial survey of the soil to find there is a large clay content.'

Not much of a surprise in the Black Country.

'Such conditions affect the performance of ground penetrating radar so we're going to start with a magnetometer.'

'Gesundheit,' Bryant offered.

The professor ignored her colleague and carried on speaking to her as though she had a clue. Kim rarely questioned the expertise of others. She trusted people to do their jobs effectively and she expected the same in return.

'The magnetometer uses sensors to measure the gradient of the magnetic field. Different materials can cause disturbances and this particular tool can detect anomalies caused by disturbed soils or decayed organic materials.'

Bill started walking towards them with Ben behind. To Kim, he looked like something from *The Terminator*. Over his shoulder rested a black strap fixed to a metal rod approximately six feet in length that he held horizontally at waist height. On the front tip of the pole was a second rod fixed so he carried a giant letter T. Attached to each end of the smaller rod were sensors. Black cables travelled to the reader strapped around his waist and a black canvas holdall was fixed to his back.

'We'll start down there at the bottom edge and work in straight lines. A bit like how you'd mow the lawn.'

Kim nodded and the three of them moved away.

Doctor Matthews and his assistant had retreated to the warmth of the car.

'You gonna be okay with this, Guv?' Bryant asked.

'Why wouldn't I be?' she snapped.

'Well, you know ...'

'No, I don't know and if you feel the need to question my capability, take it to my boss.'

'Guv, I would never do that. It was a question asked out of concern.'

'I'm fine, now leave it alone.'

She never talked about her past but Bryant knew she'd spent time in the care system. He didn't know the things that had happened to her there. He knew she had a mother who was a paranoid schizophrenic. But he didn't know the repercussions of that. He knew she'd once had a twin brother but he didn't know how he'd died. Only one person knew all the events of her past and she was damn sure it was going to stay that way.

The phone in her pocket rang. It was Woody.

'Sir?' she answered, expectantly.

'Still waiting, Stone. I'm just checking that you remember what we talked about.'

'Of course, Sir.'

'Because if you act against my instructions ...'

'Sir, please, you can trust me.'

Bryant shook his head.

'If I don't have the authorisation in the next couple of hours stand Professor Milton down and thank him for his time.'

'Yes, Sir,' she said. Thank God he didn't know about Doctor Matthews.

'I know it's frustrating standing around doing nothing but processes have to be followed.'

'I understand, Sir. I have Bryant here who would like to express his concern about something to do with the handling of the case.'

She held out the phone. Bryant shot her daggers before walking away.

'Oh no, I appear to be mistaken.'

Woody tutted and ended the call. She keyed in Dawson's number. He answered on the second ring.

'What've you got?'

'Not much at the moment, Guv.'

'Got the names of other staff members?'

'Not yet. The local authority isn't quite as accommodating as Courtney. We're trawling through any news reports where Crestwood is mentioned to see if we can come up with anything. The best we've got so far is a Pastor Wilks who did a sponsored walk of the Three Peaks to raise money for a day trip for the girls.'

'Okay, Kev, pass me to Stacey.'

'Morning, Guv.'

'Stace, I need you to start putting together a list of the kids that were here when the place burned down.'

Even if there was nothing found, they would still need to speak to ex-residents of the facility to find a link between Teresa Wyatt and Tom Curtis.

Stacey said she would get right on it and ended the call.

Kim glanced towards the boys. They had progressed about forty feet with the magnetometer but were now standing still, checking the equipment.

Her wandering gaze found Bryant at the edge of the site, his back to her. Uncharacteristically, she felt bad for snapping at him. She knew his question was born out of concern for her wellbeing but she didn't react to kindness all that well.

'Hey, you still got that bacon bap?' she asked, nudging him in the arm.

'Yeah, you want it?'

'No, go throw it in that bin. Your cholesterol level can't take it.'

As soon as the words were out of her mouth she realised that it worked both ways.

'You been talking to my missus?'

Kim smiled. She'd received a text message two days earlier.

Kim heard movement and looked behind.

The professor was approaching at speed. His face was reddened, his features animated.

'Detective, the machine is showing readings of interest. I think we might have something.'

Bryant caught her eye. 'Guv, we don't have any authority.'

She looked at him for a long minute. If there was a body buried in this ground it was not going to stay there a minute longer than necessary.

She nodded to the professor. 'Start digging.'

CHAPTER 19

'Guv, with all due respect, are you out of your bloody mind?'

'Something bugging you, Bryant?'

'Just the fact that you could lose your job for this.'

She shrugged. 'It's mine to lose.'

'Yeah, but sometimes you need to just stop and take a minute to think.'

'Tell you what. You stand there and think on my behalf while I get on with doing my job.'

She walked away from him and headed towards the professor. Doctor Matthews came hurtling across the site like he'd been shot from a catapult.

'Detective, I can't allow this. What the devil do you think you're doing?'

'My job.'

'It's not your job until you have authorisation to excavate.'

'Who said anything about excavation? We're just going to dig a bit.'

All parties had converged and seven of them stood staring at the machine.

'You could damage the entire investigation by acting too hastily.'

'Doctor, if a body is discovered I will adopt the correct protocols immediately but at the moment all we have is an anomaly. For all we know it might be nothing more than a dead dog.' She instantly realised what she'd said. 'Sorry, Professor.'

'This is a potential crime scene,' Matthews argued.

'Which could have been dug by any old metal-detecting enthusiast by now, in which case no protocols would have been followed at all.'

That was her logic and she was sticking to it.

Matthews' mouth tensed when he realised that she was not going to be dissuaded.

His eyes travelled the circle of people and then came back to her. 'Your impetuousness is going to jeopardise the careers of all these people.'

Kim nodded her understanding. She turned to Bill and Ben. 'Pass me the shovel.'

'Guv ...'

Bill and Ben looked to the professor, who was looking at her.

'Jesus Christ,' she growled, grabbing a shovel. 'Doctor Matthews, please feel free to return to the car until authorisation comes through. The rest of you, do whatever the hell you like.'

She lifted her arm and dropped the spade to the ground. Her right foot pushed the blade down as far as it would go. She removed the lump of earth and placed it to her left. She wielded the shovel again.

Doctor Matthews humphed and turned away. 'I cannot be a party to this. Come on, Cerys.'

'In a minute, Doctor,' she said, without looking at him. She caught Kim's eye. 'I'd just like to observe for a while.'

The doctor hesitated before shaking his head. He walked back towards the car.

Kim smiled her thanks to the forensic technician. Her presence offered some protection and she knew it.

She threw down the shovel and repeated the process. The ground was hard and this would be a long process but it was better than standing around doing nothing.

'Oh, for God's sake,' Bryant said, reaching for the second shovel.

He stood opposite her, about six feet away and dropped the shovel into the ground.

The professor looked pained. He shook his head. 'No, no, no. Look if you're going to do this, at least do it properly.'

For the next two hours she and Bryant formed a tag team with Bill and Ben taking turns at digging the feature as directed by both Cerys and Professor Milton.

Cerys had continually circled the area, consulting the data from the magnetometer. She had advised where to dig next and how deep they should go.

Cerys leaned down close to where Kim was digging. 'Detectives, I think you should step out now. Professor, can you pass me your bag of hand tools?'

Kim stepped out of the pit that was now six feet wide by eight feet long and a foot and a half deep.

Kim tried to dust herself down but spatters of damp mud and clay had dried into her trousers up to the knee.

Cerys and Professor Milton consulted over the data and pointed to areas in the pit. The boys entered the pit with gardening hand tools and took direction from Cerys.

Bryant stood beside her. 'There's never a dull day with you, is there?'

'At least you've burned off that bacon bap from earlier.'

'And then some.'

Her own stomach was beginning to rumble. The half slice of toast she'd eaten at six thirty was long gone.

'It's almost two. Not much daylight left,' Bryant observed.

Bill or Ben motioned for Cerys to enter the pit. She knelt down and used something which looked like an oversized blusher brush to dust at a particular area. Kim noted that she cared nothing about the dirt and mud that was now caked to her light blue jeans.

She brushed a second time and then stopped. 'Okay, I need anyone who is not forensically trained to step out of the pit, immediately.'

Cerys remained in the pit alone. She turned and met Kim's gaze. 'We have bones, Detective and unless it had five fingers, it isn't a dead dog.'

No one spoke for a few seconds as they all contemplated the discovery.

Then, as though the newly exposed bones had emitted some kind of siren two squad cars screeched onto the gravel and her mobile began to ring.

It was Woody. Thank God.

'Stone, get back here and bring Bryant with you,' he barked.

'Sir, I need to let you know ...'

'Anything you have to say can wait until you get here.'

'But there are bones in this ground.'

'And I've already told you to get back here immediately and if that's longer than fifteen minutes don't bother coming back at all.'

The line went dead. She turned to Bryant. 'I think he knows.'

Bryant rolled his eyes.

'Go on, I'll see you there.'

Bryant nodded and headed back to his car.

'Listen folks, thanks for your help but if anyone asks, Bryant never touched a thing, okay?'

They all nodded.

Kim sprinted to her bike and donned her helmet and gloves. She pulled away from the site and prepared to face the music.

CHAPTER 20

There is something within her that compels me.

She is surrounded by activity; sirens, vehicles, movement, and yet my eyes never leave her. She stands out from the crowd. A three-dimensional image in a two-dimensional film.

There is unruly energy within her. Like a demon driving her on. It is dark and it intrigues me. Even amongst the crowd, she is alone. Even when she's still, she moves. A hand clench or a foot tap keeps in time with a brain that never rests.

Although I've never seen her before, I know her. I know her intelligence, her restlessness and that natural suspicion in her gaze. She has a sense that is hidden from most. It is indefinable and without name but it is attuned to everything around her. And I've seen it before.

Aaah, Caitlin. Dear sweet adorable Caitlin ...

All too soon, she is gone. A film without its star. My interest wanes but I remain where I am, lost momentarily in my thoughts.

What came first, the chicken or the egg? It is a question I have asked myself often. Did I feel nothing when my mother rejected me, or did she reject me because I felt nothing?

It is a question pored over by many a scholar. Is a psychopath born or made? They have no answer and neither do I.

There was a time when I battled against it, fought it, even tried to understand it but that was a long time ago.

My journey began with a fish. Just an ordinary anonymous goldfish won at a travelling fair by my father. I carried it home. It lived in a bowl for two days and then died.

My sister was inconsolable. I was not. She mourned its loss but I felt nothing. I wanted what she had. I wanted her pain, I wanted her grief. I wanted to feel.

Next came the kitten. Its fur was soft and warm. It was supposed to be ours but it loved her more. It didn't really struggle as I covered its mouth. And after its last breath I waited but still nothing came upon me.

The children at school all had puppies and I wanted one too. But this pet would be all mine. I fed it, I walked it and it lived in my room. This time I was hopeful but the snap of its neck did not pain me. It only fuelled my curiosity. My need to know how far I could go.

The death of three animals brought an embargo on pets. This limited my options for further research and then I realised that the ultimate test had been before me all the time.

Everyone said she was cute; adorable, angelic, perfect. So that was my goal. I knew that she would not come to the pond without tempting. There was a look in her eye. She saw things that others did not.

So I told her there were bunnies; a mummy and her babies. I pointed to the bush, right on the edge. She peered inside. Her back was towards me. I pushed her face down and straddled her neck. She coughed and she spluttered and then she lay still.

Oh, Caitlin, Caitlin, Caitlin. You gave me a gift.

As I dismounted her small body, I finally had all the answers. My condition was not a curse, but a blessing. The sacrifice of my sister finally set me free. Since that day I have been liberated to take what I want and destroy what I don't, without the restraints of guilt or remorse.

Like a missing limb, compassion is simply not there. It cannot be replaced or transplanted and nor would I wish it. It is a shackle that binds lesser mortals to morality and an ethical code. But I have no code to follow.

So, what came first, the chicken or the egg? The answer is, I couldn't care less.

As the sound of the motorbike fades, I turn and walk away.

She would be a worthy adversary.

She will make discoveries along the way which will lead her exactly where I want her to go.

She will uncover secrets of Crestwood but she will never uncover mine.

CHAPTER 21

Despite the head start, Kim pulled into the car park a moment before Bryant. He parked beside her.

'Go and get cleaned up. I'll go see Woody.' She started walking towards the entrance.

'I'm more than happy with my own decisions so don't ...'

'I've got seven minutes to get to his office so hurry up.'

They sprinted up the stairs together and entered the office.

Dawson's eyes widened. 'Jeez, looks like you two had some kind of mud fight.' He chuckled. 'I'd like to have seen that. My money would have been on the Guv.'

Bryant sat down. 'Hell, Dawson, any smart money would have been on the Guv.'

'There are bones,' Kim said, removing her jacket. She ran her fingers through her hair. 'Bryant will fill you in.'

She headed to the door.

'Guv,' Bryant said, stopping her. 'Tell him the truth.'

'Of course,' she replied and headed to the stairs.

By her reckoning she had a minute and a half left by the time she knocked on his door. She waited until he called before entering. It wasn't going to help if she infuriated her boss any further.

She took the four steps to the chair and noted that the stress ball remained on the desk. Okay, now she was in trouble.

'What the hell do you think you're doing, Stone?'

'Err ... could you be more specific?' she asked. She would hate to be apologising for the wrong thing.

'Don't play games with me. The antics of you and Bryant could seriously jeopardise ...'

'Not Bryant, Sir. He just watched.'

Woody glared at her. 'I've got someone who saw him in the hole.'

'And I've got the four people closest to the hole who say he wasn't.'

'And what would Bryant say?'

Kim swallowed. They both knew the answer to that.

'Sir, I'm sorry for what I did. I know it was wrong and I would like to sincerely ...'

'Spare me the speech. It is nauseating and won't do you any good.'

He was right. Kim wasn't sorry at all. 'How did you know?'

'Not that it's any of your business but Doctor Matthews—'

'Yeah, I should have known that he ... '

' ... was absolutely right to call me,' Woody said, raising his voice over hers. 'What the hell did you think you were doing?'

'Sir, I had to get started. My gut said there was a body down there and the idea of waiting for the correct paperwork to come through was ridiculous.'

'Ridiculous or not, there are reasons why we have procedures to follow, not least so that in a court of law we can defend our actions at all times. You would be well served to remember that my instructions are not optional.'

'I understand.'

He sighed heavily. 'The only thing saving your skin right now is that your gut was right and the focus will now change to damage limitation.'

Kim nodded.

'However, at this point I am no longer convinced that you are the right person to lead this investigation.'

She sat forward. 'But, Sir, you can't ...'

'Oh yes I can and at the moment I am seriously considering your removal from this case.'

Kim closed her mouth for a second. Her next words would be important. She decided on total honesty.

Her voice was low. 'Sir, you've seen my file. You're aware of my past, so you have to know there is no one better to head this case.'

'That's as maybe but I need to rely on someone who can follow instructions. If the bones found today are those of a child within the care of social services this case will explode in the media. There will be many individuals trying to distance themselves and I will not give anyone a legal loophole caused by a member of my own team.'

Kim knew he was right. But she also knew she was the right person for the job.

'Now, I suggest you and Bryant get off home and clean yourselves up. You'll have my decision in the morning.'

Kim knew when she was being dismissed and she counted her lucky stars that she'd escaped a full disciplinary.

'You know, Kim ...' he said as she reached the door. Damn, she hated it when Woody called her by her first name.

She turned.

He removed his glasses and met her gaze. 'One of these times your gut is going to be wrong and you will have to face the consequences and that is your choice. But you need to consider those around you. Your team has great respect for you and will follow you into any situation to protect you and gain your approval.'

Kim swallowed. She knew he was talking about one team member in particular.

'And when the day comes that your reckless actions endanger the career or even the life of those around you, it won't be me or even the police force to which you will have to answer.'

Kim felt the rising nausea that had nothing to do with an empty stomach; as she closed the door behind her she found herself wishing for the disciplinary.

The one thing about Woody was that he sure knew how to hit her where it hurt.

CHAPTER 22

The doorbell sounded and Kim didn't even ask who was at the door as she undid the chain. It would be Bryant and he would have Chinese.

'The chow mein fairy has entered the building.'

'You can only stay if there are prawn crackers.' It wasn't a joke.

Bryant removed his outer jacket to display a polo shirt and jeans.

'Love what you've done with the place.'

Kim ignored him. He said the same thing every time he came. To others, her house appeared sparse of personality and adornment. She didn't enjoy personal embellishments. If she chose to move tomorrow she'd need a dozen bin liners and a couple of hours and she'd be ready to roll. Her years in the care system had taught her well.

She served up the beef noodles and egg fried rice. Two thirds for Bryant, one third for her. She passed the plate to him. He took one sofa and she took the other.

She put a forkful of food in her mouth and tried to ignore the disappointment. The theory of food was far more exciting than the practice of eating it. In her mouth it turned into a source of fuel; energy. She pushed in a few more forkfuls and put the plate down.

'Jeez, slow down, you nearly filled a hollow tooth there.'

'I've had enough.'

'You make a sparrow look like a greedy bastard. You need to eat more, Guv.'

Kim shot him a look. Here in her home she was not Detective Inspector and he was not her subordinate. He was just Bryant; the closest thing to a friend she had.

He rolled his eyes. 'Yeah, sorry.'

'And stop fussing. I'm a big girl.'

She took her plate to the kitchen and made a fresh pot of coffee.

'So, tell me, I bring you a handsome, affable man and food you don't eat. Remind me again what I'm getting out of this relationship?'

'My dazzling company,' she deadpanned. She was nothing if not self-aware.

Bryant laughed. 'Hmm ... I'll just leave that hanging without comment 'cos you might be Kim now but eventually you'll be Guv again.' He finished eating and brought his empty plate to the kitchen. 'No, I had something else in mind.'

'Like what?'

'A date.'

'With you?'

He guffawed. 'You wish.'

Kim laughed out loud.

'You know, that's a great sound. You should do it more often.'

Kim knew what was coming. 'The answer is no.'

'You don't even know who.'

'Oh yes I do,' she offered, in pantomime fashion. She'd caught a glimpse of Peter Grant as she'd headed out of the station. As a prosecutor with the CPS their paths still crossed but she had avoided a full conversation since the break-up.

Bryant sighed. 'Come on, Kim. Give him a chance. He's miserable without you. And you're even more miserable without him.'

Kim weighed it up and answered honestly. 'No, I'm really not.'

'He loves you.'

Kim shrugged.

'And you were different when the two of you were together. I wouldn't say happy but perhaps more tolerable.'

'I'm happier now.'

'I don't believe you.'

Kim poured coffee for both of them and they returned to the lounge.

'Look, Kim, I'm sure he's sorry for whatever he did wrong.'

Kim doubted that; because the truth was, Pete hadn't done anything wrong. It was her. It was always her.

'Bryant, how long had Peter and I been seeing each other?'

'Almost a year.'

'And how many times do you think he stayed over?'

'Quite a few.'

'Yep, and do you want to know what lead to that final argument?'

'If you wanna share.'

'Only so you'll get off my back. I finished it because one morning he didn't take his toothbrush with him.'

'Are you kidding?'

Kim shook her head, remembering the day when he'd left for work and she'd gone into the bathroom to see it there, brazenly lying next to hers. No crime scene had ever induced that level of horror.

'I realised that if I'm not prepared to share a toothbrush glass, I'm not prepared to share much of anything else.'

'But surely you could have worked it out.'

'Jesus, this is not *Blind Date* and you're not Cilla Black. Some people are meant to find a soul mate and live happily ever after. And some people are not wired that way. That's all.'

'I just want you to have someone in your life that makes you happy.'

'Do you think it'll make me any less difficult to work with?' Kim asked, signalling that the conversation was over.

He got it. 'Bloody hell – if it was that easy, I'd move in here myself.'

'Yeah, well, make sure you don't leave your toothbrush.'

'No, I'll just bring the glass I put my teeth in at night.'

'No, really, stop there.'

Bryant finished his coffee. 'Alright, enough foreplay. We both know why I'm here. Are you gonna show it to me or not?'

'Well ...'

'Come on, enough with the teasing.'

She jumped up and headed out to the garage. Bryant was no more than two steps behind.

She took her treasure from the workbench and turned to face him. She tenderly peeled back the cotton pillowcase protecting it from the temperature.

Bryant stared in wonder at the motorcycle fuel tank. 'Original?'

'Oh yes.'

'It's a beauty. Where did you get it?'

'eBay.'

'May I?'

Kim passed it to him. She'd spent six weeks trawling the internet for the 1951 model. Far easier to find were parts for the 1953 model and upwards. But she'd never done easy.

Bryant caressed the rubber knee pads fitted on each side of the tank and shook his head. 'Beautiful.'

'That's enough, give it back.'

Bryant handed it to her and walked slowly around the motorbike. 'Wasn't this the model Marlon Brando rode in *The Wild One*?'

Kim jumped up and sat on the workbench. She shook her head. 'Nineteen-fifty.'

'Are you ever gonna ride this bike?'

She nodded. The Triumph would be her therapy. The Ninja was a rush, a challenge. Riding it satisfied a need deep within her, but the Thunderbird was a thing of beauty. Just being near it transported her back to the only three years in her life that she'd felt anything even resembling contentment. A mere interlude.

The sound of a phone ringing startled her. She jumped off the work bench and retrieved her mobile from the kitchen.

She saw the number. 'Hell, no,' she whispered. She darted through the house and into the street. Two houses away from her own, she pressed the answer button. Her home would not be contaminated.

'Kim Stone.'

'Umm ... Miss Stone, I'm ringing about an incident with your mother. She ...'

'And you are?'

'Oh, my apologies. I'm Laura Wilson, the night supervisor at Grantley Care Facility. I'm afraid she's had an episode.'

Kim shook her head, confused. 'Why are you ringing me?'

There was a brief silence. 'Umm ... because you are listed as her emergency contact.'

'Does it say that in the file?'

'Yes.'

'Is she dead?'

'Goodness, no. She took a dislike ...'

'Then you should have read the file better, Miss Wilson – because then you'd have known that there is only one situation for which I require an update and you've already confirmed that not to be the case.'

'I'm so sorry. I had no idea. Please accept my apologies for disturbing you.'

Kim could hear the tremor in the woman's voice and instantly felt bad for her reaction.

'Okay, what did she do now?'

'Earlier today she became convinced that a trainee nurse had been brought in to poison her. She's quite sprightly for a woman approaching her sixties and she charged the nurse and brought her to the ground.'

'Is she okay?'

'She's fine. We've altered her medication slightly to ...'

'I meant the nurse.'

'She was a bit scared but she's okay now. It's part and parcel of working in this profession.'

Yep, all in the normal day of living with a paranoid schizophrenic.

Kim was eager to end the phone call. 'Is there anything else?'

'No, that's all.'

'Thank you for the call but I would appreciate it if you made a further note on the file regarding my previous instruction.'

'Of course, Miss Stone and once again, apologies for my error.'

Kim hit the end button and leaned against the lamp post, banishing all thoughts of her mother from her mind.

She only gave thought to that woman on her terms. And that was once a month at a time and place of her choosing. Within her control.

She left all thoughts of her mother in the street and closed the front door firmly behind her. Kim would not allow her mother's influence into her place of safety.

She took fresh mugs from the cupboard and poured more coffee for herself and Bryant. He said nothing as she re-entered the garage, as though it was the most natural thing in the world for her to take flight from her own home to accept a phone call.

She resumed her seat on the workbench and placed the petrol tank on her lap. She reached for a wire brush, similar in size and shape to a toothbrush and gently brushed at a small patch of rust on the right hand side. Flecks of brown landed on her jeans.

'Surely there's a quicker way of doing that?'

'Oh, Bryant, only a man would be concerned with the speed.'

An easy silence settled between them as she worked.

'He'll keep you on the case, you know,' Bryant said, quietly.

Kim shook her head. She was not so sure. 'I don't know, Bryant. Woody's right when he says I can't be trusted. He knows that regardless of any promises I might make there are some times when I just can't help myself.'

'And that's why he'll keep you on it.'

She looked at him.

'He knows how you work and yet you're still around. There is no disciplinary on your file ... which is beyond shocking, if you want the truth. He knows that you get results and that you won't rest until you solve a case, especially this case.'

Kim said nothing. This case was personal to her and Woody might feel that was detrimental.

'And there's one other reason why he won't remove you from the case.'

'What's that?'

'Because he would be a damn fool to do so – and we both know that Woody is no fool.'

Kim sighed heavily as she put the tank aside. She sincerely hoped her colleague and friend was right.

CHAPTER 23

Nicola Adamson rewound the news report and watched it again.

A tall, solid, black male by the name of Woodward confirmed the discovery of a body on the site of the old Crestwood children's home. His brief statement was followed by an aerial view of the place she had once called home.

Nicola felt instant relief. Finally they were going to uncover the secrets of that godforsaken place.

But then came the fear. How would Beth react to the news? Nicola knew her sister would not open up and talk to her. As children, they had been so close; all they'd had was each other. They had shared everything. Nicola struggled to recall when that had changed.

They had grown apart after Crestwood. Beth had returned four years ago when Nicola had been struck down by glandular fever but once she'd been out of intensive care, Beth had disappeared.

A week ago she had returned and although there were minor irritations at sharing her home, Nicola loved having her sister around. A small voice in the back of her mind offered the question, how long?

When Beth was away Nicola always felt that part of her was missing. Yet when she was back Nicola felt more anxious; always worried about Beth's reactions.

Her sister was changed somehow. There was a remoteness to her personality now; a coldness that showed in a mean set to her features, an impatience with the rest of the world. Nicola felt that every ounce of her sister's joy had been lost.

She checked on the contents of the oven. She had decided to cook Beth's favourite meal of breaded chicken nuggets and potato waffles with a dollop of tomato ketchup. Nicola smiled. It was strange how she'd never grown out of that.

Despite their differences, Nicola wanted to forge a stronger relationship with Beth. She wanted to understand what had driven them apart.

She was hoping they could sit together in their pyjamas and watch a film while eating the juvenile meal that might find its way into Beth's memories.

Living together was not ideal but Nicola wouldn't trade the mild irritations for having Beth back in her life.

And she would do whatever she could to make her stay.

CHAPTER 24

Kim headed into the office after a forty-minute meeting with Woody. Three pairs of eyes looked at her expectantly.

'I'm still heading the case.'

A collective sigh went around the room.

Kim continued. 'The forensic osteoarchaeologist has confirmed the bones to be human and modern, so the area is now a crime scene. Cerys has remained on site and will head up the archaeological side and a forensic anthropologist is due to land from Dundee shortly.'

Dundee University was home to the Centre for Anatomy and Human Identification and had been offering degree courses in forensic anthropology for years. CAHID was regularly contacted for advice and input in high-profile identification cases at home or abroad.

Those strings had been pulled by Woody, who wanted to ensure that everyone who might need to take the stand was impeccably qualified.

'Where are we on Crestwood staff members?'

Dawson picked up a piece of paper. 'I've weeded out various short-term and temporary staff and I'm left with a list of four other members of staff that were recorded as working there when the place burned down.

'As we know, Teresa Wyatt was the deputy manager and Tom Curtis was the head chef. General manager was a guy called Richard Croft. There was a housekeeper there for years by the name of Mary Andrews and two night-watch guys who doubled as caretaker, odd job guys.

'So far, I've tracked Mary Andrews to a nursing home in Timbertree ...'

'Richard Croft, isn't that the name of the Conservative MP for Bromsgrove?' Kim interrupted him. She could swear she'd just read an article that Croft had just completed some kind of bike ride for charity.

'Definitely the same name but I haven't yet been able to link him ...'

'Pass it to Stace,' Kim instructed.

She saw the set expression on Dawson's face.

'Stacey, what have you got on the names of the kids?'

'I've got about seven so far and most of them's from Facebook.'

Kim rolled her eyes.

Stacey shrugged. 'There ain't many records of Crestwood and even less people that wanna talk about the place. My understanding is that the younger kids had already been placed in foster homes or other care facilities around the area. Another six or seven had gone back to family members, leaving around ten kids at the time of the fire.'

'Sounds like a bloody nightmare.'

Stacey grinned. 'To lesser mortals, maybe.'

Kim smiled. Stacey loved a challenge and that was about to be a good thing.

'Right, Bryant, go get the car started.'

Bryant grabbed his jacket and left the office. Kim stepped into The Bowl and sat to remove her biking boots. As she did, she overheard the conversation taking place in the outer office.

'Have yer tried flowers?' Stacey asked.

'Check,' Dawson replied.

'Chocolates?'

'Check.'

'Jewellery?'

No response.

'Are yer kidding? You haven't tried jewellery? Oh, Kev, nothing says "sorry for being a totally amoral arsehole" like a sparkly expensive necklace.'

'Piss off, Stace, what would you know?'

'I'd know, lover boy, 'cos I'm all wooooooman.'

Kim smiled as she tied her right lace.

'Yeah but your love life amongst the world of goblins doesn't count. I need advice from a woman who goes out with men. Like, real ones.'

The conversation ended as Kim stepped back into the office. 'Stace, you're now working on the staff members *and* ex-residents.'

Dawson looked confused.

'Get your coat, you're coming with me.'

He took his suit jacket from the back of the chair.

'I'd get your overcoat as well. You're now staying on site with forensics.'

His face lit up. 'Seriously, Guv?'

Kim nodded. 'I need to know what's going on as soon as it happens. I want you to make a total nuisance of yourself. Keep asking questions, follow people around, listen to conversations and the minute you get anything new, let me know.'

'Will do, Guv,' he said, eagerly.

He followed her down to the waiting car.

She got in the front seat and he got in the back.

'Buckle up, kiddies,' Bryant said, pulling out of the car park.

Kim glanced into the rear view mirror at Dawson's eager, excited face, then turned and looked out of the window.

For a person with no people skills whatsoever, the law of averages dictated that now and again she had to get it right.

CHAPTER 25

The site she'd left yesterday now looked like a small walled city. The entire edge of the property was surrounded by interlocking metal fencing. There was an entrance at the top of the site and one at the bottom, each guarded by two constables. Others roamed the fence edge, keeping within the eye line of other officers. Kim was satisfied that the perimeter was secure.

A corral had been set up along the top of the site for press but she could see they were already spilling out along the fence line. Two white tents had been erected; one around the pit and another for the technicians to store equipment.

Kim headed into the first tent but was not prepared for the sight of the skeleton in the pit – or the effect it would have on her. She had attended many crime scenes; had witnessed bodies in every stage of decomposition, but this one was just bone. When tissue was still present it felt as though there was something to return to the family, something of the person left to bury and mourn. But bones felt anonymous, featureless; like the foundations of a building but without the architecture that made it unique. Kim realised she didn't like that thought one little bit.

She was also shocked by the tiny amount of space the skeleton occupied.

'No clothes?' Kim said as the forensic archaeologist came to stand beside her.

'Good morning, Detective,' said Cerys.

Yep, she always forgot that bit.

'To answer your question, it doesn't mean there weren't any clothes. Only that they're not there now. Different materials deteriorate at different rates. Depends how long they're in the ground. Cotton can disappear in ten years or so, whereas wool can remain intact for decades.' Cerys turned towards her. 'I wasn't too sure you'd be back.'

They both stepped away as technicians took photographs from every angle. A yellow marker had been placed alongside the length of the bones.

'We didn't get much time to chat yesterday,' Kim said.

Cerys tucked a stray piece of hair behind her ear. 'Didn't have you down as the chatting type but okay ... I'm twenty-nine years old, single and childless. My favourite colour is yellow. I have a weakness for chicken-flavoured crisps and I am enlisted in the Territorial Army when I'm not busy knitting.' Cerys paused. 'Okay, I lied about the knitting.'

'All good to know but that's not really what I was asking.'

'Then ask the question you want to, Detective.'

'How qualified are you for this job?' Kim said without flinching.

Cerys tried to hide her smile but her eyes lit up. 'I achieved my degree in archaeology at Oxford eight years ago. I then spent four years travelling on archaeological projects, predominantly in West Africa, came home and earned my forensic science degree and have spent the last two years trying to gain respect in a male-dominated arena. Sound familiar, Detective Inspector?'

Kim laughed out loud and offered her hand. 'Glad to have you on board.'

'Thank you. Now, the bones have been exposed and I'm waiting for the anthropologist to discuss removal. I have to be sure we don't under cut or over cut.'

Kim looked at her blankly.

'Sorry, we need to be as careful as possible that we don't either take too much or too little. We can't go back and do it again.'

Kim's expression remained unchanged.

Cerys thought for a moment. 'Okay, imagine the ground as a brick wall. Each course of the wall is a period in time. If we take too much of the soil we risk encroaching on other events that occurred before the murder and which could give us false information.'

Kim nodded her understanding.

'Once the bones are removed we'll begin sifting the soil for clues.'

'Ah, Detective, there's someone I'd like you to meet.'

Kim heard the familiar voice of Keats, her favourite pathologist.

'Detective Inspector Kim Stone, please meet Doctor Daniel Bate. He is the forensic anthropologist from Dundee and will be working both here and at my lab for the duration of this case.'

The male offering his hand was two inches taller than Kim, with the build of an athlete. His jaw was strong and his hair black. Startling green eyes offered an interesting contrast with the darkness of his features.

Introductions ensued between Cerys, Keats and the new boy. The handshake he offered Kim was strong and firm.

Immediately, Doctor Bate started walking around the pit and Kim took a moment to observe him. He didn't look like a scientist. His build appeared more suited to an outdoor profession that called for physical activity. Kim supposed his attire of jeans and a sweatshirt didn't help.

'So,' Keats said. 'We have the three key people to get to the bottom of this crime. The person who will uncover the clues, the person that will explain the clues and the person who will pull it all together and give us a murderer.'

Kim ignored him and stood beside Doctor Bate.

'Is there anything you can tell us on first inspection?'

He rubbed his chin. 'Yes, I can definitely confirm that there are bones in that pit.'

Kim sighed. 'Well, I can see that myself, Doctor Bate.'

'I understand that you want immediate answers but I have yet to touch the bones and will not presume anything until I have.'

'Relative of yours?' she asked Keats.

Keats laughed. 'I knew you two would hit it off.'

She turned back to the doctor. 'Surely you can offer something?'

'Okay, I can tell you that this poor soul has been down here for at least five years. The body of a typical adult will decompose fully in the space of ten to twelve years; non-adults decay in half the time.

'The first stage of decomposition is autolysis, which is the destruction of the body tissues by enzymes released after death. The second stage is putrefaction, where the soft tissues decay because of the presence of micro-organisms. Eventually the soft tissues become liquid and gas.'

'Get invited to many parties, Doc?' Kim asked.

He laughed out loud. 'My apologies, Detective. I recently returned from the Body Farm in Knoxville, Tennessee where bodies are disposed of in different ways to establish ...'

'Sex?' she asked.

'Not before you've bought me dinner, Detective.'

'Not even a bit funny. Any ideas?'

He shook his head.

She rolled her eyes. 'Don't tell me. You haven't had the chance to examine the body at the lab.'

'It might not make any difference, I'm afraid. If we're dealing with a juvenile the changes to the bones that distinguish the sexes won't have taken place.

'If our victim is sixteen to eighteen then we may have a chance, based on the adaptation of the pelvis, but any younger than that and few scientists will attempt to sex a non-adult by bone.'

'That indicates there are other ways?'

'There are techniques for using dental DNA to identify the X and Y chromosome, but it is both expensive and time-consuming. It's much easier to age a non-adult than sex it. For that we have bone growth and development, dental development and the degree of closure of the joints in the skull. You'll have an approximate age later today.'

'Best guess?' she pushed.

Bate turned to look at her. His eyes were intense and challenging. 'Date, time and place you will arrest the murderer?'

Kim was unfazed. 'It will be Professor Plum in the library on Thursday the eighteenth at eleven o'clock. And although you didn't ask, he'll be holding the candlestick.'

'I'm a scientist, I don't guess.'

'But surely you can deduce something from ...'

'Keats,' he called, over her head. 'Please rescue me from this interrogation before I admit to the Lindbergh kidnapping.'

Kim found the rich Scottish tone at odds with the Black Country accents floating around the dig site. If she closed her eyes he almost sounded like Sean Connery. Almost.

'I knew you two would get along famously.' Keats offered with a smirk. 'Daniel, the boxes have just arrived.'

Kim moved to the end of the pit as more technicians approached, carrying clear plastic boxes. She no longer had any idea which people belonged to which team and she was now pleased that Dawson would be remaining at the site and not her.

If she had to deal with the obstructive doctor much longer she might be responsible for a second burial.

'Made a new friend over there?' Bryant asked.

'Oh yeah, a barrel of laughs, that one.'

'Typical scientist type?'

'Yeah, and I told him as much.'

'Oh right, I bet he loved you for that.'

'It was pretty difficult to tell.'

Bryant chuckled. 'Hardly qualified to judge other people's emotional responses are you, Guv?'

'Bryant, go f—'

'No, no, no,' Doctor Bate shouted stepping into the pit. His voice was loud and commanding. Everyone stopped what they were doing.

He knelt down in the pit beside the man who had been working on the skull. Cerys entered the pit and crouched beside the doctor.

No one spoke as the two of them conferred quietly. Eventually the doctor turned and looked directly at her.

'Detective, I have something for you after all.'

Kim moved closer, her breath caught in her chest. She jumped into the pit beside him. 'Go on.'

'See these bones here?'

She nodded.

'The back bone leads into the neck where there are seven bones that form the cervical vertebrae. This top one is C1; the atlas, the next is C2; the axis.'

His finger continued down the length of the neck pointing out the other C bones from three to seven. Kim saw a clean break between three and four. Instinctively her right hand moved to the back of her own neck. She wondered how the hell he had seen that from up there.

'Spell it out for me, Doc.'

'I can tell you that beyond a shadow of a doubt, this poor soul was decapitated.'

CHAPTER 26

Kim exited the pit. 'Come on, Bryant. We need to get started.'

She glanced at the Toyota pickup that by the process of elimination had to belong to Doctor Daniel Bate. It was dented above the rear wheel arch and covered in mud.

'Jesus Christ, what's that?' Kim exclaimed, jumping backwards.

'Erm ... It's called a dog, Guv.'

Kim peered closer at the furry face that had popped up in the rear passenger side window.

Kim frowned. 'Bryant, is it just me or ...'

'No, Guv, it appears to have only one eye.'

'Detective, stop scaring my dog,' Daniel Bate said, closing the gap between them. 'I assure you, she knows nothing.'

Kim turned to her colleague. 'See, Bryant, dogs do take on their owner's characteristics.'

'You know, Detective, after a four o'clock wake-up call and a three and a half hour drive you are definitely not what the doctor ordered.'

'Is she blind?' Kim asked as he opened the car door. The dog jumped out and sat. Doctor Bate attached a lead to her red collar and shook his head.

'The sight in her right eye is perfect.'

Kim guessed the dog to be a white German Shepherd. She stepped forward offering her hand to the dog's nose. 'Does she bite?'

'Only arrogant detectives.'

Kim rolled her eyes and stroked the dog's head. Her coat was soft and warm.

Kim was confused. If he'd driven it would have taken far longer than a few hours to travel the 350 miles from Dundee. 'What's she doing here?'

'We were taking a few days off after my last case. Scouting rock climbing locations in Cheddar when I got a call from my boss. I was the closest.'

There was no irritation in Daniel's voice, just an acceptance that such calls came with the job.

Kim felt the dog's warm nose nudge at her right hand, which had absently stopped stroking her head.

'Hey, look at that, Detective,' Daniel Bate said with a glint in his eye. 'At least someone on site likes you.'

Kim was prevented from offering a four-letter-word response by the sound of her mobile ringing.

She hit the call button as Daniel turned and walked the dog around the top end of the field.

'What's up, Stace?'

'Where are yer?'

'Just about to leave the site. Why?'

'Are yer facing up or down?'

'What?'

'I've found William Payne, one of the night porters.'

'Give me the address.'

'Look down the hill. Yer should see seven houses in a row. It's the one smack bang in the middle. The back and front garden are fully slabbed.'

Kim was already walking down the hill. 'How the hell do you know that?'

'Google Earth, Guv.'

Kim shook her head and ended the call. Sometimes Stacey really scared her.

'Where did you say we were going?'

'To interview our first witness.'

'Here?' Bryant asked as she opened the waist high gate.

Eerily, the front garden was a sea of grey slabs. The path was only distinguished by a ramp that grew from it and ended at the front door.

After two knocks the door was answered by a tall male with a head full of completely white hair.

'William Payne?'

He nodded.

Bryant took out his warrant card. 'May we come in?'

He made no movement to step back and frowned. 'I don't understand. A police officer already came yesterday and took details.'

Kim glanced at Bryant before speaking. 'Mr Payne, we're here in connection with an investigation concerning Crestwood.'

She had sent no other officers to this address.

Understanding registered on his face. 'Oh, of course, please come in.'

He stood back and Kim took a second to assess him. His hair gave the initial impression of someone much older than his face indicated. It was like two totally separate ageing processes were occurring. The wear on his face placed him only in his early to mid-forties.

'Please be quiet, my daughter is asleep.'

His voice was low and pleasant, with no trace of Black Country accent.

'Come through,' he whispered.

He led them into a single room that ran the length of the house. The first section was the lounge area and beyond was a dining table set before a patio window leading onto the small back garden. A perfect grid of slabs left no room for lawn or shrubs.　Kim heard a noise behind.　It was a gentle rhythmic thunk.

The sound came from a device that appeared to monitor breathing. Attached to the machine was a girl Kim guessed to be in her mid-teens. The wheelchair was an oversized contraption with an IV drip attached to the other side.

Wound around the left arm of the chair was an emergency response pendant with a red button that linked directly to the ambulance service, normally used for the severely disabled. Kim realised this would be little use to the girl around her neck but had been placed less than an inch away from her left hand.

The flannel pyjamas dotted with Betty Boop did not hide the atrophy of the body beneath.

'My daughter, Lucy,' William Payne said from beside her. He leaned over and gently pushed a stray lock of blonde hair behind the girl's ear.

'Please, sit down,' he said, guiding them to the small table. The sound of Jeremy Kyle played quietly in the background.

'May I offer you a cup of coffee?'

They both nodded and William Payne entered the kitchen which was no more than a box just off the lounge area.

He placed three metal coasters on the table before bringing out three china mugs. The smell was delicious and Kim took a sip immediately.

'Colombian Gold?' she asked.

He smiled. 'It is my only vice, Detective. I don't drink or smoke. I don't have a fast car or chase fast women. I just like a good cup of coffee.'

Kim nodded as she took another sip. Bryant gulped as though it was Tesco Value Instant.

'Mr Payne, may we ask ...'

Bryant stopped as Kim nudged his leg beneath the table. She would lead this one.

'May we ask what is wrong with Lucy?'

He smiled. 'Of course, I'm always happy to talk about my little girl. Lucy is fifteen and was born with muscular dystrophy.'

He glanced over at his daughter and his gaze never returned. It gave Kim the opportunity to observe him openly.

'It was clear to us early on that something wasn't quite right. She was slow to start walking and she never grew out of that clumsy, gambolling stage.'

Kim looked around. 'Is Lucy's mother here?'

William turned his attention back to her. There was genuine surprise in his look.

'Excuse me. I often genuinely forget that Lucy ever had a mother. It's been just the two of us for so long.'

'I understand,' Kim said, leaning forward. His voice had dropped to barely more than a whisper.

'Lucy's mother was not a bad person but she had certain expectations and a child with disabilities was not in her master plan. Don't misunderstand me. I'm sure every parent wishes for a perfect child.

'The dream does not normally include the full-time care of an adult that will never be able to take care of themselves. Excuse me for a moment.'

He took a tissue and wiped away a trail of spittle that ran down his daughter's chin.

'Sorry about that. Anyway, Alison really tried at first and while there were certain elements of normality to hang on to she could get by but as the disease progressed it became too much of a struggle. By the time she left she could no longer look at Lucy and hadn't touched her in months. We both agreed it was best she leave. That was thirteen years ago and we haven't seen or heard from her since.'

Despite the matter-of-fact delivery Kim could hear the pain in his voice. He was more forgiving of Lucy's mother than she would have been.

'That's why you took the night job at Crestwood?'

Payne nodded. 'Prior to that I was a landscape architect but I couldn't hold a job and care for Lucy.

'Working the night shift at Crestwood meant I could care for Lucy during the day. My neighbour would often come round and sit with Lucy at night.'

'No second Mrs Payne?' Bryant asked.

William shook his head. 'No, my vows were for life. Divorce may satisfy the law, but it doesn't satisfy God.'

Kim guessed it would have been difficult to meet someone, even if he'd wanted to. Few people were prepared to take on the full-time care of a disabled child that was not their own.

A gurgle sounded from the corner and William was instantly on his feet. He stood before his daughter.

'Morning, sweetheart, sleep well? Would you like a drink?'

Although Kim saw no movement there was obviously some communication between father and daughter, because William pulled around a feeding tube and placed it between her lips. The right index finger of Lucy's hand touched a button on the arm of the chair. A measure of liquid was dispensed through the tube and into her mouth.

'Do you want to listen to music?'

'An audio book?'

He smiled. 'Do you want to turn around?'

Aha, Kim realised. It was blink communication.

As William turned the chair, Kim was struck by the paleness of the smooth skin and the directness of the eyes.

Kim considered the irony of a perfectly functioning brain in a useless body. Surely there could be no crueller fate.

'Lucy sits at the window so she can see outside. She was entranced by the activity yesterday.'

'Mr Payne, you were saying ...' she steered him back on course, gently.

'Yes, of course. The job at Crestwood was easy enough. All I had to do was make sure the place was secure so the girls couldn't just leave and that no one could get in, check the smoke detectors and complete any odd jobs left by the day staff. It was very convenient for me and I was disappointed when it came to an end.'

'The fire?'

He nodded. 'Although the place was being closed anyway I was hopeful for another few months of work.'

'Were you working that night?'

'No, it was Arthur's shift but I heard the alarm as soon as it went off. I'm in the front bedroom, you see.'

'What did you do?'

'I checked on Lucy then ran across the road. Arthur had got most of the girls out but he was choking so I ran in and did a final sweep to make sure there was no one left.

'Miss Wyatt and Tom Curtis were the first to arrive and there was a lot of confusion. Everyone was doing lists to make sure all the girls were accounted for. The paramedics were removing girls for small cuts and smoke inhalation but not informing anyone. I was trying to help but just seemed to be making it worse. I left as the other staff members began to arrive.'

'And what time was that?'

'I'd say about one thirty.'

'Did they identify the cause of the fire?'

'I don't know. I'm not sure how hard they looked. No one was seriously injured and the place was being wound down anyway.'

'You know that both Teresa Wyatt and Tom Curtis have been murdered?'

William stood and approached his daughter. 'Sweetheart, I think it's time for a bit of music, eh?'

Kim didn't see the blinked response but William fitted the earphones and switched on the device.

'Her hearing is perfect, Detective. A normal fifteen-year-old would have been asked to leave the room. This is our equivalent.'

Kim could have kicked her own behind. Without realising it, she had treated Lucy as invisible because of her disability.

It was a mistake she would not make again.

'What can you tell us about the victims?'

'Not much. I rarely saw the day staff. Sometimes Mary, the housekeeper, would stay until I arrived to give me the gossip.'

'What type of gossip?'

'Mainly about Miss Wyatt and Mr Croft arguing. It was a power thing, Mary said.'

'Can you think of anyone who would wish to harm any of the girls?'

William visibly paled and then looked to the window. 'You can't possibly think that anyone ... you really think that body in the ground is one of the girls from Crestwood?'

'We haven't yet ruled it out.'

'I'm sorry but I really don't think I can offer anything to help.'

William stood abruptly. His expression had changed. Still softly spoken, he had decided it was time for them to leave.

Bryant persisted. 'What about the girls? Were they much trouble?'

William began to move away from them. 'Not really. There were a few rebellious ones but they were generally good kids.'

'What do you mean by rebellious?' Bryant asked.

'Just normal things.'

It was clear that William Payne wanted them to leave and Kim began to understand why.

'What kind of ...'

'Bryant, we're done,' Kim said, standing.

William looked at her gratefully.

'But if I could just ask ...'

'I said, we're done.' There was a growl in her voice. Bryant closed his notebook and stood.

Kim walked past William. 'Thank you for your time, Mr Payne. We won't keep you any longer.'

Kim passed by Lucy's chair. She touched the girl's left hand lightly. 'Goodbye, Lucy. It was lovely to meet you.'

At the door Kim turned. 'Mr Payne, if I could trouble you for a minute longer. What did you initially think we were here for?'

'We had an attempted robbery the night before last. They didn't get away with anything but I called it in anyway.'

Kim smiled her thanks as he closed the door behind them.

Once outside the gate Bryant turned to her. 'What was all that about? Didn't you notice how he changed when we started to ask him about the girls? He couldn't get us out of there quickly enough.'

'It's not what you think, Bryant.'

Kim walked across the road and turned, surveying the property. Of the seven houses, it was the only one with an alarm attached prominently to the front of the house. A passive infrared light and sensor was aimed directly at the gate. She had seen an identical sensor covering the rear of the property along with a six foot fence topped with cat spikes.

House breakers did not deliberately challenge themselves with the trickiest home available. And Kim did not believe in coincidences.

Bryant huffed. 'You don't know what I think because you didn't give me chance to find out. He was nervous, Guv.'

Kim shook her head as she walked up the hill.

She passed Daniel Bate walking his dog back towards the car.

'Hey, Detective, just can't keep away, eh?'

'Yeah, Doc. I really can,' she said, without breaking her stride.

'Guv, what the hell is going on?' Bryant asked her as they reached the car. 'You don't normally walk away from a challenge. That bloke was as nervous as hell and you just left it.'

'Yes, I did.'

'He all but physically removed us.'

'Yes, Bryant, he did.' She turned and glared at him over the roof of the car. 'Because he needed to change the nappy on his fifteen-year-old daughter.'

CHAPTER 27

The care home was an exercise in symmetry. Inside the foyer was a glass hatch on either side. To Kim's right was a small empty office and to her left was a room holding a couple of desks and a woman wearing a black T-shirt. The gatekeeper.

'Can I help?' Kim was guessing she'd asked through the glass barrier that separated them.

'Could we speak to one of your patients?'

The female shrugged, not understanding. Kim pointed to the sliding doors but the female shook her head and mouthed 'emergency only.'

For a moment Kim felt as though they were trapped in some kind of decontamination chamber. She pointed to the inner set of doors.

The woman nodded and pointed to an open book on a ledge to the right of the window. She made a squiggle motion with her right hand. Kim guessed that was the instruction to sign in.

'Remind me of the progress we've made in communications,' Kim muttered to Bryant.

They signed in and waited for the buzzer.

As they entered Kim could see immediately that there were two communities. To the left were the more able-bodied residents. One or two moved around the area on walkers, other residents leaned across their wing-backed chairs engaging in

conversation. Philip Schofield droned on about money management. Residents had turned and were looking in their
direction; new faces.

To the right, there was very little sound. A nurse wheeled
around a trolley dispensing medication. No one looked in
their direction.

The woman from behind the glass stepped out of the office. She had donned a badge just above her left breast that
read 'Cath'.

'How can I help you?'

'We'd like to talk to one of your residents; Mary Andrews.'

Cath's hand went to her throat. 'Are you family members?'

'Detectives,' Bryant answered. He continued talking but
the woman's reaction brought a sick feeling to Kim's stomach.
They were too late.

'I'm sorry, but Mary Andrews died ten days ago.'

Before any of this started, Kim thought – or perhaps it had
been the start of it all.

'Thank you,' Bryant said. 'We'll contact the medical ex-
aminer.'

'For what?' Cath asked.

'Clues to her death,' Bryant explained but Kim had already turned away. She pushed on the door but it was locked.

'There was no post mortem carried out on Mary Andrews.
She was terminally ill with pancreatic cancer so it was hardly
any great surprise when she died. There was no reason to subject her family to the process so she was released to Hickton's.'

Kim didn't need to ask. Everyone knew the funeral directors
in Cradley Heath. They'd been burying the locals since 1909.

'Did Mary Andrews have any visitors that day?'

'We have fifty-six residents in this facility, you'll pardon
me if I don't recall.'

Kim heard the hostility and ignored it.

'Do you mind if *we* check the visitor's book?'

Cath considered for a second and then nodded. She pressed a green button that released the doors and Kim stepped back into the foyer.

Kim started turning back the pages while Bryant held open the door with his foot.

'Sir, you'll have to let the door close behind you or an alarm will sound.'

Suitably chastised, Bryant stepped back into the foyer.

'What's wrong with you anyway, got something against old folks?' Kim asked, noting the set expression on Bryant's face.

'Nah, it's just depressing.'

'What?' Kim asked, turning back another couple of pages.

'Knowing this is the last stop. When you're out in the big wide world anything is still possible but once you move into a place like this you know there's only one way you're gonna move out.'

'Hmmm ... cheery thought. Here it is,' she said, stabbing the page. 'Twelve fifteen on the tenth. Visitor signed themselves in to see Mary Andrews with a name that is completely illegible.'

Bryant pointed to the top right corner of the foyer.

Kim turned and knocked on the glass window. Cath scowled at her. Kim pointed to the entry doors. The buzzer sounded.

'We need to view your CCTV.'

Cath looked as though she was about to object then just humphed loudly. 'This way.'

They followed her through the general office and into a space behind.

'Here it is,' she said, leaving them to it.

The space hardly qualified to be called a room. There was a small desk with an old television monitor and playback controls. A single VHS machine chuntered to the side.

'I suppose digital was too much to hope for,' Bryant groaned.

'Yep, good old video tape. Please tell me they're labelled.'

Kim took the only chair as Bryant inspected the shelves of video tapes.

'There are only two for that date. One for day and one for night. Tapes are only changed every twelve hours.'

'So, now we're talking time lapse?'

'Afraid so,' he said, grabbing the tape. From an evidence point of view real time video was acceptable, as it captured everything in full. Time lapse recording grabbed an image every few seconds which gave a mechanical motion to the video, almost like a collection of screen shots.

Kim put the video into the machine. The screen came to life. She forwarded the tape to the rough time of day.

Kim stared at the screen. 'Are you seeing what I'm seeing?'

'Tape degradation. Shit, you can't make out a damn thing.'

Kim sat back in the chair. 'How many times have these tapes been used?'

'Looking at that, we're talking hundreds.'

CCTV tapes were normally destroyed after twelve cycles to prevent what was showing on the screen now.

Kim continued to watch the shadows of figures entering and leaving the foyer.

'Jesus, it could even be me.'

Bryant looked at her seriously. 'Is it you, Guv?'

Kim leaned back and opened the door.

'Cath,' she shouted. 'Got a minute?'

Cath appeared at the door. 'Really, Detective, there's no need to ...'

'We're taking this tape.'

Cath shrugged. 'Okay.'

'Do you have a release form for us to sign?'

'A what?'

Kim rolled her eyes. 'Bryant.'

He ripped a page from his pocket notebook and wrote down the tape rotation number, their names and the police station.

Cath took it, although she was clearly unsure why.

'Cath, you do realise that this system is pretty much useless?'

The woman looked at her as though she was stupid. 'It's a care home, Detective, hardly crime central.'

The woman appeared triumphant.

Kim nodded her agreement as Bryant chose to inspect his nails.

'You're right ... but with better tapes we might now be in a position to identify someone responsible for two, perhaps three, murders and we would certainly be closer to ensuring they did not get the opportunity to murder again.'

Kim smiled pleasantly at the woman's horror-stricken face. 'But thank you for your time and helpful co-operation.'

Kim strode past the woman and let herself out of the building.

'You know, Guv, I always knew there was more cause to fear you when you're smiling.'

'Get that tape to Stacey. She may know a miracle worker who can offer us a clue.'

'Will do. Where to now, Guv?'

Kim took the keys from his hand.

'We're gonna take the ride of your worst nightmare, Bryant,' she said, opening her eyes wide. 'We're going from the care home to the funeral home.'

Bryant shuddered. 'Fine. But if you're driving, just make sure it's not my last ride, eh?'

CHAPTER 28

'Seriously, Guv, I've heard of ambulance chasing but speeding after a bloody corpse?'

Kim closed the road distance between themselves and the car in front. 'You heard the undertaker. She only left two hours ago. If we can get there in time we can stop the ceremony and order a post mortem.'

'The family will be thrilled.'

'Stop whining.'

'You realise we're headed back to the crematorium right next to the site? Ever feel like you're getting nowhere?'

'You have no idea,' she said, sounding the horn at the car in front that was hesitating at a small traffic island. The car turned right.

Kim motored up the Garrett Lane hill and over the canal bridge. Bryant bounced in his seat. She took the fourth exit off the island straight into the crematorium grounds and stopped outside the entrance.

'Damn, no cars or mourners,' she observed.

'Maybe we're early. Perhaps the funeral party is still at the house.'

Kim said nothing as she got out of the car and headed into the building. A young girl sat on the wall, her head bowed.

Kim continued forward. There was a funeral to crash.

Kim shuddered as she entered the building. Wooden benches lined the space on each side of the walkway. The centre aisle led to a curtained area. Red velvet drapes were pulled back to their resting positions.

To the right was an elevated pulpit. A board behind held three hymn numbers.

Kim felt the soullessness of the place. She didn't care much for churches but at least they provided balance. There were weddings, christenings; celebrations of a beginning, to equal out loss. This place existed for death alone.

'May I help you?' asked a voice without a body.

She and Bryant looked at each other.

'Jesus Christ,' Bryant whispered.

'Not quite,' said a figure appearing from behind the pulpit.

Although not fat, the black ministerial robe was not flattering to the man that wore it. His face was not as round as his body shape indicated. His salt and pepper hair was heavy at the sides but thinned in a wide arc over the top of his head like a well-trodden path over a field. Kim guessed he was mid- to late-fifties.

'But may I help in His absence?'

The voice was low and even with a gentle rhythm. Kim's foster mother number five had possessed a telephone voice which bore no resemblance to how she spoke normally. Kim wondered if the minister had a special voice for services.

'We're looking for the funeral party of Mary Andrews,' Bryant said.

'Are you family members?'

Bryant produced his warrant card.

'In that case, you're too late.'

'Damn. Is there any way the process can be stopped?'

The minister looked at his watch. 'She's been in there at eleven hundred degrees for about an hour. I suspect there won't be a lot left.'

'Bugger ... Sorry, Father.'

'I'm a minister, not a priest, dear, but I'll pass your apology on.'

'Thank you for your help,' Bryant said, nudging Kim towards the door.

'Dammit, dammit, dammit,' Kim said, heading back to the car.

Her peripheral vision registered the young girl still sitting on the wall, alone. She reached the car and glanced back. It was obvious that the girl was shivering but it wasn't her problem.

She opened the car door and paused. It really was not her problem.

'Back in a minute,' she said, slamming the door shut.

Kim trotted over to the girl and stood to her side. 'Hey, you okay?'

The young girl looked surprised. She tried to manage a polite smile while nodding. Her eyes were raw recesses in a pale face.

Her feet were encased in flat, patent shoes with black and white bows. She wore thick black tights and a knee-length skirt. A grey shirt was smothered by a double-breasted suit jacket that was both outdated by two decades and oversized. An outfit cobbled together for a funeral but offering no protection against the temperature that had not crept above two degrees.

Kim shrugged and turned away. She'd asked the question. The girl was in no distress other than grieving. She could walk away with a clear conscience. It was not her bloody problem.

'Someone close?' she asked, sitting on the wall.

The girl nodded again. 'My nan.'

'I'm sorry,' Kim offered. 'But sitting here is not going to do you any good.'

'I know but she was more like my mum.'

'But why are you still here?' Kim asked, gently.

The girl looked up at the chimney of the crematorium. Thick smoke funnelled out and dispersed. 'I don't want to leave her until ... I don't want her to be alone.'

The girl's voice broke and the tears rolled over her cheeks. Kim swallowed as she realised who she was talking to.

'Your nan was Mary Andrews?'

The girl's tears stopped as she nodded. 'I'm Paula ... but how did you know that?'

Kim didn't feel the need to give the grieving child any details.

'I'm a detective. Her name has come up in connection with that over there.'

'Oh yes, she used to work at Crestwood. She was the housekeeper for about twenty years.' The girl suddenly smiled. 'She used to take me with her sometimes if she worked at weekends. I'd help with changing the beds or some washing. I'm not sure how much help I was.

'All the girls loved her even though she took no nonsense from them. They seemed to respect her. They didn't cheek her and she got lots of hugs.'

'I bet the rest of the staff loved her as well.'

Paula shrugged and then smiled. 'Uncle Billy did.' She nodded to the bottom of the hill. 'He used to live down there.'

Kim was intrigued. 'How did you know Billy?'

'Sometimes my nan would watch his daughter for a bit so he could go shopping.' The girl smiled and looked up at the chimney. 'She was only supposed to sit and watch Lucy but my nan couldn't do that. She'd always find a couple of jobs to do before he got back, just a bit of ironing or vacuuming. And I'd play with Lucy. When he came back she wouldn't mention anything she'd done. She didn't want thanks, she just wanted to help.'

'It sounds like your nan was a very special lady,' Kim said and meant it.

'We never went back after the fire and my nan said they'd moved away.' Paula thought for a moment. 'You know, a lot changed for my nan after that fire. She'd never been an old nan, if you know what I mean, but after the fire it's like something went out of her.'

Kim found herself wondering why Mary Andrews had lied about William Payne having moved away.

'Did you ever ask her about it?' Kim pushed gently.

She knew she was taking advantage of the girl's need to talk about her grandmother. Talking about a person so recently lost kept them alive in your heart and your mind. It preserved the link, the bond. Kim hoped they were helping each other.

Paula nodded. 'One time and she got very angry with me. I remember it well, because my nan never got angry with me. She told me never to mention that place or those people ever again. So I didn't.'

Kim noted that the girl's body was shivering. Her whole body rocked but smoke continued to billow out of the chimney.

'You know, someone said something to me once and I always remembered it.' Kim recalled it clearly. It had been at the funeral of foster parents number four and she'd been thirteen years old.

The innocent, unlined face turned towards her eagerly, desperate for some comfort, as Kim had been, although she had shown no one.

'I was told that the body is no more than a jacket which gets cast off when it's no longer needed. Your nan isn't there any more, Paula. The jacket she wore caused her pain but she's free of that now.'

Kim looked up at the smoke, thinner now. 'And I think the jacket is gone now, and so should you be.'

The girl stood. 'Thank you. Thank you very much.'

Kim nodded as the girl turned. Any words would cushion the grief for a matter of moments. Intrinsically selfish in nature, grief was for the living. It was a measure of how keenly one felt their own personal loss, and in some cases, as Kim knew, their regret.

Kim watched as Paula trotted down the hill. She had considered telling the girl that Lucy still lived in that same house, but her grandmother had lied to the child for a reason and Kim had to respect that.

The ringing of her phone brought her back to the present. It was Dawson.

'Guv, where are you?'

'So close I can almost smell your aftershave.'

The day was developing into a bad episode of the *Twilight Zone*.

'Good, Guv, 'cos we need you back here right away.'

'What's wrong?' she asked, sprinting towards Bryant.

'That magnet machine has just gone mental. It looks like we have another body.'

CHAPTER 29

Kim travelled the distance faster on foot than Bryant in the car. She passed Doctor Bate and Keats loading boxes into a van.

The doctor turned to face her. 'You know, Detective Inspector, at this rate I may have to consider a restraining order.'

'How's piss off grab ya?' she asked, without stopping.

'Yeah, you were right,' he said to Keats.

She had no idea what Keats had been right about and at this precise moment she couldn't be less interested.

She aimed for the group of people forty feet west of the first tent. The location behind the equipment storage tent meant their activity was obstructed from the view of the press. She thanked the lord for small mercies.

'What's going on?'

Cerys drew her to one side. 'Gareth was checking the rest of the area just to be sure. He got to this point and the magnetometer detected a second anomaly.'

'Jesus Christ,' Kim said, running her hand through her hair. 'Is there something else it could be?'

Cerys shrugged. 'There's always that chance but we won't know until we start digging. In the meantime there's something else I'd like you to see.'

Kim followed Cerys into the utility tent. Fold-out tables had been erected and held small Tupperware boxes. A couple were empty but most were filled with varying amounts of soil.

'We have some small metal fragments that I need to explore further but I thought this might interest you.'

Cerys reached for one of the smaller Tupperware boxes that held fine dirt and what looked like Maltesers.

'What are they?'

Cerys took one out and held it at Kim's eye line.

It was a perfect pink circle with yellow dots.

Kim tipped her head. 'A bead?'

Cerys nodded.

'How many?'

'Seven, so far.'

'Bracelet?'

Cerys shrugged and smiled. 'That's your job, Detective. Of course, there's always the possibility that they are totally separate contexts.'

'Separate what?'

Cerys closed her eyes for a second. 'Remember what I told you about the wall?'

Yes, Kim recalled something about events happening in layers. 'So, you're saying the beads could be completely unrelated to the body?'

'Perhaps.'

'When can I have photographs?'

'Everything taken today will be with you first thing in the morning.'

Kim nodded and headed out of the tent. Yellow paint had been sprayed around the area the machine had indicated.

She turned as Cerys came to stand beside her. 'Why is no one digging yet?'

'It's almost three. We have half an hour of daylight left. Not enough time.'

'Are you kidding? You're just going to leave her down there?'

Cerys turned to her, surprised. 'Firstly, we're not yet sure it isn't a dead dog,' Cerys said using Kim's own example of the previous day. 'And secondly, if there is another body down there it would be foolhardy to assign a sex when the first one ...'

'What is it with you scientists? Is there a special class at university called the extraction of free thinking?'

'If we start disturbing the soil now, knowing we're not able to complete it, we run the risk of exposing the site to the elements. Valuable evidence may be lost.'

Kim shook her head. 'You're all the same, like little android clones who rely on ...'

'I can assure you that we are not all the same. Yesterday, we did it your way but today, we do it mine.'

Kim glowered at her.

Cerys folded her arms. 'I understand your impatience, Detective. In fact I've seen it first-hand, but I will not be bullied into making mistakes. In addition, my team left their homes at four this morning to be here. A team needs rest.'

Cerys began to walk away, but returned. 'I promise, she's safe for one more night.'

'Thank you ... Cerys.'

'You're welcome ... Kim.'

She headed over to Bryant and Dawson and pulled them to one side. 'Okay, guys, they're winding down here for the day. This is gonna break wide open tomorrow if we find another body down there.

'Go home and get some rest while you can. From tomorrow this is going to be non-stop so be sure to let family members know that your shift rota is a distant memory.'

'No problem, Guv,' Dawson offered brightly. His eyes were dark and a little bloodshot but he was learning his lesson.

'Okay, Bryant?'

'As ever, Guv.'

'Right, briefing at seven. Someone let Stacey know.'

As Kim walked away from them both she quietly seethed inside. Waiting was not an activity she did well.

CHAPTER 30

It was almost midnight when Kim entered the garage. The quiet family street beyond had settled into cosy silence. She switched on her iPod and chose Chopin's 'Nocturnes'. The solo piano pieces would ease her through the early morning hours until her body demanded sleep.

After leaving the crime scene she had returned to the station unable to do nothing while there was the potential of another body lying in the ground.

Eventually she had returned home and vacuumed the house throughout. She had mopped the kitchen and used half a bottle of Cillit Bang on the work surfaces. Two washing cycles had ended and the clothes had been dried, ironed and hung in her wardrobe.

The nervous energy had still raged around her body, prompting her to fix a broken shelf in the bathroom, rearrange the furniture in the lounge and tidy out the airing cupboard at the top of the stairs.

Probably just need to cleanse, she thought, stepping into her favourite room of the entire house.

To her left was the Ninja, reversed into the space, poised for their next adventure.

For a moment Kim visualised herself lying into the body of the bike, her breasts and stomach against the petrol tank, her thighs clutched around the leather seat, bending the bike into a series of tight turns; her knees an inch from the ground. The co-ordination of her hands and feet working together to control the beast took every ounce of concentration and erased everything else from her mind.

Riding the Ninja was like breaking in a spirited horse. It was a question of control, of taming a rebel.

Bryant had once told her that she liked to argue with fate. He said fate had dictated that she was beautiful and yet she fought against it by doing nothing to enhance her looks. He said fate had decided that she couldn't cook and yet she tried complex dishes every week. But only she knew that fate had decreed that she would die young and so far she had fought against it. And won.

There were times when the fates chased her to make her what she should have been when she was six years old; a statistic. So, every now and again she tempted them, goaded them into catching her as they had tried to back then.

The restoration of the Triumph Thunderbird was a labour of love, a testament to two people who had tried to make her feel safe, who had tried to love her. The Thunderbird was an emotional journey that bathed her spirit.

In this one room of her house, the stresses and challenges of the working day eased out of her muscles, leaving her relaxed and content. Here she did not have to be the analytical detective dissecting every clue, or the leader of her team guiding and prodding to get the best results. Here, she did not have to justify her ability to do a job she truly loved or battle to mask the social skills she so sorely lacked. Here, she was happy.

She crossed her legs and began to assess the pieces that had taken five months to gather. The '93 genuine Triumph parts would all fit together to form a crankshaft casing. Now all she had to do was figure out how.

Within the overall challenge of restoring a classic motorbike came smaller tasks along the way. The crankshaft casing was the heart of the machine so she began as she always did with a puzzle within a puzzle, she grouped similar type parts together.

Twenty minutes later the washers, gaskets, springs, valves, tubes and pistons were all separated. She opened the diagram that would help guide her through the challenge.

Normally, the process jumped off the page like a three-dimensional hologram. Her mind was able to assess the most logical starting point and she would build from there. Tonight, the instructions remained a muddle of numbers, arrows and shapes.

After ten minutes of scowling at it the page still resembled the writings of the Rosetta Stone.

Dammit, no matter how hard Kim fought she knew this case was having an unsettling effect on her.

She uncrossed her legs and leaned back against the wall. Perhaps it was the amount of time spent in such close proximity to Mikey's grave. Although she took fresh flowers every week she had locked away those memories when she was six years old.

Like a bomb linked to a motion sensor, there would never be a good time to open that package. Every psychologist she'd been sent to had tried to break open that box and had failed. Despite their assurances that she needed to talk about the trauma in order to heal, she had resisted. Because they had all been wrong.

For a few years following Mikey's death Kim had been passed around the mental health profession like a puzzle that could not be fathomed. Looking back, she often wondered if a set of steak knives had been on offer for the professional who could break open the surviving twin of the worst case of neglect the Black Country had ever seen.

She suspected there was no such prize for putting the child back together again.

Silence and aggression had been her best friends. Kim had turned into a difficult child and that had been her intention. She hadn't wanted to be coddled and loved and understood. She hadn't wanted to form bonds with foster parents, mock siblings or paid carers. She'd wanted to be left alone.

Until foster family number four.

Keith and Erica Spencer were a middle-aged couple when they started fostering. Kim had been their first foster child, and as it would turn out, their last.

They were both teachers who had consciously chosen to have no children. Instead they had spent every spare moment travelling the world on motorcycles. After the death of one of their friends they had decided it was time to curtail the constant travel but their passion for bikes had remained.

When she was placed with them at ten years of age Kim had donned her spikes, ready for the usual onslaught of long, probing chats and measured understanding.

She spent the first three months in her room, honing her rejection skills, waiting for their intervention. When it didn't come, Kim found herself venturing downstairs for short periods of time, almost like an animal checking to see if it was safe to come out of hibernation. If either of them were surprised, they didn't show it.

On one such foray she was mildly interested to find Keith restoring an old motorbike in the garage. Initially she sat at the furthest point, just watching. Without turning, Keith explained what he was doing. She never answered, but he carried on anyway.

Each day she moved closer towards his work area until eventually she was sitting right beside him, cross-legged. If Keith was in the garage, so was she.

Gradually Kim started asking questions about the mechanics of the machine, eager to understand how it all came together. Keith showed her diagrams and then demonstrated the practice.

Erica would often have to drag them from the garage to eat her latest gastronomic delight from the countless cookbooks that lined the kitchen shelves. She would roll her eyes fondly while Kim continued to ask questions as they ate to the gentle sound of Erica's classical music collection.

Kim had been with the couple for about eighteen months when Keith turned to her and said, 'Okay, you've watched me do it plenty of times, do you think you could fit that nut and washer into the exhaust housing?'

He moved out of her way and went to get drinks from the kitchen. With that first turn of the nut her passion was born.

Lost in the process, she continued to sort through the parts strewn across the garage floor, eventually fitting another couple of bits to the bike.

A soft chuckle caused her to turn. Both of them stood in the doorway watching her. Erica was teary.

Keith came and took his place beside her. 'Yeah, I think you got the clever genes from me, sweetie,' he said, nudging Kim sideways.

And although she knew it to be impossible, the words had brought an ache to her throat as she had thought of how happy she and Mikey could have been had the fates been kinder.

Two weeks before her thirteenth birthday, her foster mother had brought a hot chocolate to her bedroom and simply placed it on her bedside cabinet. On her way out, Erica had paused at the door. Without turning, her hand had clutched the door handle.

'Kim, you do know how much we love you, don't you?'

Kim had said nothing but had stared hard at Erica's back.

'We could not care more deeply if you were our biological child and we will never try and change you. We love you just the way you are, okay?'

Kim nodded as the words brought tears to her eyes. Without her knowledge this middle-aged couple had touched her heart and offered the first foundations of stability she had ever known.

Two days later, Keith and Erica were killed in a motorway pile-up.

Later she found out that they'd been on their way home from an appointment with a solicitor who specialised in adoption law.

Within an hour of the accident Kim was packed up and returned to the social care system like an unwanted package. There was no celebration, no fanfare upon her return. No acknowledgement of her three-year hiatus. A nod here and there and the latest spare bed.

Kim wiped away a tear that had escaped and travelled down her cheek. This was the problem with journeys to her past. Any happy memory led to tragedy and loss. The reason she didn't visit all that often.

The aroma of the coffee pot called from the kitchen. She pushed herself to her feet and took her mug for a refill.

As she poured the liquid into the mug her eyes moved across the vast collection of cookery books that lined her kitchen shelves.

Suddenly the words that were twenty-one years too late escaped from between her lips.

'Erica, I loved you too.'

CHAPTER 31

Nicola Adamson took a sip of Southern Comfort. Normally, she didn't touch alcohol while she was working but tonight she could not shake the stiffness in her bones. Her joints had been fused together and her muscles injected with cement.

The atmosphere in the club had been electric. A group of Swiss bankers had landed, flush with excitement and cash. The music was thumping and the laughter was infectious. The rest of the girls were busy mingling with the patrons, their smiles genuine and open. All the signs dictated it would be an enjoyable night for all. It was the kind of atmosphere whereby her work required no effort at all. Usually.

Nicola knew she was struggling to throw off the argument with her sister. It had started over something so inconsequential she couldn't even recall but had developed into a massive row that had stopped short of physical blows.

Beth had predictably used the guilt card, quoting what Nicola had and what Beth had not. Eventually Beth had left the flat in a fit of rage and had not returned before Nicola left for work.

Although Beth was an adult and perfectly able to take care of herself Nicola knew she was still the big sister; the protector. Despite the animosity between them she was worried and she couldn't help it.

'Hey, Nic, you okay?'

She jumped slightly. 'I'm fine, Lou.'

The club owner was an ex-wrestler, which was not disguised by the shirt and suit he wore every night to work.

It was his venue and one he'd started from scratch. Lou had had a vision of an upmarket club where attractive ladies danced for the enjoyment of customers. He'd had three principles from day one and they applied to the employees as stringently as the patrons: no nudity, no touching and no disrespect.

For his employees there was a fourth rule; no drugs. He himself chose to oversee the implementation of the first three and a monthly drugs test took care of the fourth.

His principles formed his business plan and his mission statement and he always led by example. No girl that Nicola knew of had ever been made to feel uncomfortable in Lou's presence.

'You're not yourself tonight, girl?'

She considered lying but her boss knew her too well.

'Just a bit distracted, Lou.'

'Do you want to work the bar?'

Nicola shook her head, nodded and then sighed. Honestly, she didn't know what she wanted to do.

He indicated for her to follow him through the door behind the bar. Once in the relative peace of the corridor he stopped walking.

Mary Ellen, an ex-model from San Diego, squeezed between them. Lou waited until she was out of earshot.

'This got anything to do with your sister?'

Nicola felt her jaw drop. 'How do you know about Beth?'

He looked up and down the corridor. 'Look, I wasn't going to say anything but she was here earlier today.'

Nicola felt her mouth dry up. 'She was here?'

Lou nodded. 'Demanded I let you go so you could do something more meaningful with your life.'

'Oh, God, no,' Nicola breathed. She could feel the heat climbing up her face. She'd never felt so humiliated in her life.

'What did you say to her?'

'I told her you were a big girl and perfectly capable of making your own decisions.'

'Thanks, Lou. I'm so sorry. Did she say anything else?'

'Yeah, she called me a few names and accused me of exploiting you. Nothing I haven't heard before.' He rolled his eyes.

Nicola smiled. 'And you said?'

'I thanked her for her comments and asked if there was anything else I could help her with.'

Nicola laughed out loud. It was a welcome release and an antidote to the tension that had built in her body.

Despite his good humour she was mortified that Beth had brought their family issues to her place of work.

'Look, Lou. My heart's not in it tonight so it's probably best if I get home.'

He nodded his understanding. 'I tell you what, out of the two of you I'm glad I got you 'cos your sister is one pissed-off lady.'

'I know,' Nicola said quietly, while thinking to herself, *you have no idea.*

She began walking towards the changing room at the end of the hall.

'Oh, and Nic ...'

She turned.

'Watch yourself. I get the feeling that she's really pissed off at you.'

Nicola sighed heavily and repeated her earlier thought.

You *really* have no idea.

CHAPTER 32

'Okay, Kev, you first,' Kim instructed.

She had already briefed them about the crime scene of the previous day and the discovery of the conifer that linked both crimes.

Cerys had been true to her word and the photographs had been received just after six thirty. An aerial view of the site had been taped to the white board.

Dawson stood and traced the line from the location of the first grave to the edge of the map. 'This is victim number one. Although there's been no formal identification of sex, we believe from the clothing and the recovery of beads that the body is more likely to be female and that she's been down there for approximately ten years.

'The body has now been removed from the site and is at the lab with Keats and Doctor Bate. So far we know for certain she was decapitated.'

'Gruesome,' Stacey said.

Dawson made notes on the white board as he talked.

It bothered Kim that the heading was still 'victim one'. The bones had once formed a person. There had been muscles and skin, perhaps a birthmark. There had been a face with expressions. It was not just bones. This girl had spent enough of her life anonymous and it angered Kim that she still had no name.

Kim recalled clearly her own realisation of just how invisible care kids were. When she was eight years old she had ventured into the linen room for a fresh pillowcase. Her gaze had caught a sheet of paper attached to a clipboard. The front page and the sheets behind were diagrams of each of the seven bedrooms. Each bed was drawn on and numbered; bed one, bed two, bed three with tick boxes below. She had wondered why her name was not listed instead of Bed 19.

Kim quickly realised that it was too much bother to label them according to the girl's name. The occupant changed, but the location of the bed did not.

Kim had perched herself on a wooden stool and leaned on the ironing board to write in every girls' name next to the bed they occupied.

Two days later a cursory check in the linen room had revealed fresh, clean pages; bed one, bed two, bed three.

Her space, her identity, her one little area of safety so easily erased. It was a lesson that she'd never forgotten.

She refocused her attention on Dawson as he pointed at the board. 'This is where the second mass has been detected; approximately fifty feet from the first.'

He drew a line to the edge of the map but marked it only with an asterisk. Her whole body reacted to his use of the word *mass* but she fought it down. As yet, there was no body.

'Thanks, Kev. Today the archaeological team will conduct a full survey of the site to make sure there are no more.'

'Do you expect more bodies, Guv?'

Kim shrugged. She really had no idea.

'Stace, did you manage to look at the tape?'

Stacey rolled her eyes. 'Yeah, it mighta been used for the original recording of *Ben Hur*. It's been taped over hundreds of times. I've gor a friend who might be able to clean it up a bit but he's not on our register of approved ...'

'Send it anyway. From an evidentiary point of view it's worse than useless, because we can never prove foul play in the death of Mary Andrews, but it might just give us something.'

Stacey nodded and made a note. 'Nothin' more on Teresa Wyatt. I've gor her phone records and there's no calls in or out that can't be accounted for. Forensically they found nothing at the scene except for a couple of shoe prints, double trodden.'

Their killer had taken the time to retread his initial footsteps to further confuse any identification. As if the damage done by the fire service wasn't bad enough.

'Both clever and impatient,' Kim observed.

'Why impatient?' Bryant asked.

'The discovery of Teresa Wyatt's body was expedited by arson so that she was found within an hour of her death. Tom Curtis would have most likely died had he continued to drink the whisky but that wasn't good enough for our guy.'

'He wants us to know he's angry,' Bryant mused.

'He certainly has something to say.'

'Well, let's stop him before he says it to anyone else,' Stacey added, hitting a few keys on the computer. 'Okay, following on from Kev's work I can confirm Richard Croft from Crestwood is most definitely the Conservative MP for Bromsgrove.'

'Bloody hell,' Kim said. Woody was going to love this.

'And I've gor an address for both him and the second night watchman.'

The printer kicked into life and Bryant grabbed the single sheet.

'I also have the most up-to-date record of the girls at Crestwood from a local GP but to be honest I'm getting better info from Facebook of who was there at the end.'

'Keep on that, Stace, it may prove useful in helping us identify our first victim. Someone may recognise the beads. For us today the focus is on the staff members. There's nothing to suggest that the ex-occupants are in any danger.

'Bryant and I have already spoken to William Payne. He has a severely disabled daughter. Loved his job but didn't see the other staff members all that often. He's recently been the victim of an attempted break-in which, based on the level of security at his home, makes no sense. Kev, pay him an advisory visit when you get back to site.'

Dawson nodded his understanding.

Kim stood. 'So, we all know what we're doing. Yeah?'

Kim stepped into The Bowl to grab her jacket.

'Come on, Bryant. We're off to the lab to see if Doctor Spock has anything else to tell us.'

Bryant followed her out the door. 'Easy, Guv, it's barely half past seven. Give the guy a chance.'

'He'll be there,' she said, reaching the bottom of the stairs.

She took a deep breath as she opened the passenger side door.

Who the hell knew what they'd turn up today.

CHAPTER 33

As Kim entered the autopsy suite she blinked three times to adjust her vision. The overload of stainless steel was like a dozen flashbulbs all going off at once.

'This place gives me the creeps.'

She turned to Bryant. 'When did you turn into such a little girl?'

'Always been that way, Guv.'

The pathology suite had recently been modernised and now held four separate bays positioned like a small hospital ward.

Each area came complete with a sink, table, wall cabinets and a tray of tools. Many of the instruments looked harmless and not unlike the scissors and scalpels used in routine surgery but others, like the skull chisel, bone saw and rib cutters, looked like they'd been plucked from the imagination of Wes Craven.

Unlike the wards in the main part of the hospital there were no curtains around each bay. These customers cared nothing for false modesty.

The recovered skeleton was laid out in form and looked somehow more forlorn than in the ground. Now the bones were displayed in a sterile environment being scrutinized, analysed and studied. It seemed just another indignity to be suffered.

The table was long and had a lip all the way around that gave the impression of an oversize turkey dish. Kim had the overwhelming urge to cover the bones over.

The ceiling light was pulled down to shoulder height and reminded Kim of the type used at the dentist.

Doctor Bate measured the right femur and noted the measurement on a clipboard.

'Someone's been busy.'

'Early bird catches the worm, as they say. Unless you're an entomologist and then that would be just plain weird.'

Kim clutched her chest. 'Doc, did you just try and make a funny? You did, didn't you?'

The white coat hung open, revealing a pair of faded jeans and a green and blue striped rugby shirt.

'Detective, are you this sarcastic to everyone you meet?'

She thought for two seconds. 'I certainly try to be.'

He turned to face her fully. 'How have you been this successful by being so rude, arrogant, obnoxious ...'

'Hey, easy there, Doc. I have bad points as well. Tell him, Bryant.'

'She does have ...'

'So, what can you tell us about our victim this morning?' Kim interrupted.

The doctor shook his head in despair and turned away. 'Well, for a start, the bones will often reveal more about a victim's life than their death. We can estimate how long they lived, illness, old injuries, height, build, if any deformities were present.

'The age at death inherently affects decay. The younger the person, the faster they will decay. With children, their bones are smaller. They contain less mineral.

'Conversely, an obese person will decay faster because of the large amounts of flesh available to feed micro-organisms and maggots.'

'Fabulous, now is there anything you can tell us that will actually help?'

The Doctor threw his head back and roared with laughter. 'I'll say one thing for you, Detective, you're consistent.'

Kim said nothing and just waited while he put on a pair of simple black-framed glasses.

'We have two fractured metatarsals on the left foot. An injury more consistent with playing football, but this was not an old injury. No fusion of the bones had occurred.'

'Could it be from kicking something?' Bryant asked.

'It could be, but a normal person would kick with their right foot, unless they had been trained to use both feet equally.'

He moved up the table closer to the head.

'I've already shown you the fracture in the cervical verte-brae so we know that the victim was beheaded at some stage. It was a savage attack and the blow that severed the bone was not the first.'

He took a magnifying glass. 'If you look at C1 and C2 you'll see what I mean.'

Kim leaned down beside him. There was a visible ridge in the bone of C1.

'Do you see?'

Kim nodded, noting the smell of mint on his breath.

'Here, hold this,' he said, passing her the magnifier.

He gently turned the body slightly so that the bones of the neck were sideways on. 'Now look at C2.'

He held the body in place while she lowered the glass over the top area of the neck bones closest to the skull. Again she saw a clear ridge.

Kim stepped back as a sick feeling began to build in her stomach. 'But the injury you showed me yesterday was not on the side of the neck.'

The Doctor nodded and for just a second their gaze held in understanding.

'I don't get it,' Bryant said, leaning over the table for a closer look.

'She was alive,' Kim murmured. 'She was moving around when he was trying to take her head off.'

'Sick bastard,' Bryant exhaled, shaking his head.

'Could the injury to the foot have been caused by being stamped on, to render the victim less mobile?'

That would explain why the victim was writhing on the ground but unable to get away.

'That would seem to be a logical conclusion.'

'Be careful you don't commit there, Doc.'

'I can't confirm that theory, Detective, in the absence of any soft tissue but I can state that I have not identified any other obvious cause of death.'

'How long has she been down there?'

'As little as five years, possibly as many as twelve.'

Kim rolled her eyes.

'Look, if I could give you a day, month and year I would but decomposition is affected by many variables; heat, soil content, age, illness, infection. Like yourself I would like to find everybody with a photograph, full medical history, a passport and recent utility bill but unfortunately this is what we've got.'

Kim was unperturbed by his outburst. 'So, what exactly have we got, Doc?'

'My educated estimation is that we have the body of a non-adult, no older than fifteen years of age.'

'Educated estimation? Is that scientific jargon for a guess?'

He shook his head. 'No, I'd testify in a court to that conclusion. My guess is that it is the body of a female.'

Kim was puzzled. 'But yesterday, you said ...'

'There is no scientific rationale.'

'Is this because of the beads?'

He shook his head. 'Cerys brought this over last night.'

He held up a plastic bag containing a piece of cloth. She peered closer. There was a design.

'It's part of a sock. Wool decays much more slowly than other fabrics.'

'But I still don't ...'

'Under the microscope I can just make out the remnants of a pink butterfly.'

'That'll do for me,' Kim said, as she turned and left the lab.

CHAPTER 34

I didn't like the girl from the moment I saw her. There was some-thing pitiable about her: pathetic. And she was ugly.

Everything on her body was a size too small. Her toes wore a tear at the tip of her shoes. Her denim skirt showed a little too much thigh. Even her torso seemed too small for the long limbs that sprung from it.

She was the last girl I expected to cause me a problem. She was so inconsequential that I barely remember her name.

She wasn't the first and she wasn't the last but there was some-thing truly satisfying about ending her misery. She was a girl that no one was ever going to love and no one ever had.

Born to a fifteen-year-old mother on the Hollytree estate the fates had been rather unkind. After giving birth to a second child five years later the mother had fled.

Paternal rejection came six years later when her father dumped her at Crestwood with one bin bag of accrued worldly goods. He made it clear that there would be no weekend visits or hope of return.

The girl stood at the reception desk as her father gave her away; old enough to understand.

He walked away with no hug, touch or farewell but at the very last minute he turned and stared at her. Hard.

Did she, for one brief minute, hope for regret, for some kind of explanation; a justification she could understand. Did she hope for the promise of her father's return, even if it was false?

He walked back and pulled her aside.

'Listen, kid, the onny thing I can say to steer yer right is try 'ard with the books 'cos yo ay never gonner ger a man.'

And then he was gone.

She stole around her peers like a shadow; eager to ingratiate herself, desperate for love or anything that looked remotely like it.

Her limited knowledge of affection dictated that the attention she received from other girls elicited a pathetic gratitude and an undying loyalty that brought forth gifts of food, allowance; anything her two cronies asked for. She trailed after them like a puppy Lurcher and they let her.

It is amusing that the most inconsequential girl ever to walk the earth is now of some importance. Everyone is looking to her for answers and I am happy to have given her that gift.

She said to me one night, 'I have a secret about Tracy.'

I said, 'I have one too.'

I asked her to meet me once the others were asleep. I told her it was our secret and that I had a surprise for her. Bunnies at the lake. The technique never failed.

At one thirty a.m. I watched as the back door opened. A shaft of light lit the gangly body from behind making her silhouette look like a cartoon character.

She tiptoed towards me. I smiled to myself.

This girl was no challenge. Her desperation for attention was sickening.

'I've got something to tell you,' she whispered.

'Go on,' I said eagerly, entering into her game.

'I don't think Tracy ran away.'

'Really?' I asked, feigning surprise. This was not news. The girl had been telling anyone who couldn't escape her quickly enough that she didn't think Tracy had run away.

Her stupid, awkward face was a mask of studiousness.

'See, she ay that kind of person and she left behind her iPod. I found it at the bottom of her bed.'

This was not what I expected her to say but damn it. How had I missed that? The stupid cow had always had it hanging from her ear. Undoubtedly stolen, it had been her prized possession.

'What did you do with it?' I asked.

'It's in my cupboard so nobody nicks it.'

'Have you mentioned this to anyone else?'

She shook her head. 'No one cares. It's like she never existed.'

Of course it was – and that was just how I wanted it.

But now there was the damn iPod.

I smiled widely at her. 'You're a very clever girl.'

The darkness surrounding us did not hide the redness that infused her cheeks.

She smiled, eager to please, to be of some use; to matter.

'And there's something else. She wouldna run off 'cos she was ...'

'Sshh,' I said, placing my finger to my lips. I leaned in closer to her, a co-conspirator, a friend. 'You're right. Tracy didn't run away and I know where she is.' I held out my hand. 'Do you want to go and see her?'

She took my hand and nodded.

I walked her along the patch of grass towards the far corner; the dark part furthest from the building and sheltered by trees. She walked on my right.

She stumbled into the hole and fell backwards. I let her hand go.

Confusion pulled at her face for a moment then she held up her hand in defence as I stepped into the hole.

I searched at the edge for my shovel but the stumble had moved it away.

The delay gave her time to stand up but I needed her lying on the ground. I pulled her head back by a handful of hair. Her face was inches away from mine.

Her breathing was laboured and frantic. I raised the shovel in the air and threw it down on top of her foot. She screamed only once before falling to the ground to clutch at her foot. The agony caused her eyes to roll back in her head as she briefly lost consciousness. I grabbed the sock from the other foot and stuffed it deep into her mouth.

I pulled at her body until she lay lengthways in her grave. I stood to the side and threw the shovel down. It caught her on the side of the neck. The pain brought her back to life. She tried to scream but no sound made it past the sock.

Her eyes darted all around, frantic with fear. I raised the shovel even higher and thrust it down as she writhed around the hole. This one worked better. The sound of the blade ripping through flesh met my ears.

The girl was a fighter. She wriggled again. I kicked her hard in the stomach. She began to choke on her own blood. I kicked her again, turning her onto her back.

I concentrated hard. It was a matter of aim. I raised the shovel once more and swung at her throat. The light left her eyes but her lower half twitched.

It reminded me of felling a tree. The cut was made and one more blow would sever it completely.

I launched the shovel from above. There was a sound of metal on bone.

Then the twitching stopped. Suddenly there was silence.

I placed my right foot onto the shovel and then my left, using it like a pogo stick. I jiggled the blade down until I felt it bed into the soft earth underneath her.

Her eyes never left me as I covered her up. In death she was almost pretty.

I stood back from the grave that would go unnoticed amongst the damage from the travelling fair.

The girl had always been eager to help, to be of use to someone, to have a purpose. And now she had.

I stamped down the grass and stood back.

Then I thanked her for keeping my secret.

Finally, she had done something good.

CHAPTER 35

'What do you think, then?' Bryant asked as she got into the passenger seat.

'About what?'

'The doctor and the archaeologist?'

'Sounds like the start of a bad joke.'

'Come on. You know what I mean. Do you think they're—'

'What the hell is wrong with you?' she snapped. 'Half an hour ago you were acting like a little girl and now you're a gossipy old woman.'

'Hey, the "old" hurts, Guv.'

'I'd rather you were applying your limited brain power to the case and not the sex lives of our colleagues.'

Bryant shrugged and pointed the car in the direction of Bromsgrove. Their next stop was to visit with Richard Croft at his office in the high street.

As they headed through Lye, Kim glanced out of the window, unable to rid herself of the image of a fifteen-year-old girl writhing around on the ground, clutching her broken foot, trying to escape the death blow of a blade. That the first two attempts may have cut through flesh, cartilage and muscle to reach the bone without being fatal sickened her.

She closed her eyes, trying to imagine the fear that had coursed through the body of the child.

Kim remained lost in her thoughts until they reached the outskirts of Bromsgrove and the site that had previously housed the Barnsley Hall asylum.

The mental hospital had opened in 1907 with a capacity of 1200 at its busiest and had been home to her mother for most of the Seventies, when she was released into the community aged twenty-three.

Yeah, good call, Kim thought as they passed the residential estate that had been built after its closure and demolition in the late nineties.

There was great local sadness when the ornate water tower was finally demolished in 2000. The Gothic structure fashioned in red brick with sandstone and terracotta dressing had towered over the facility. Personally, Kim had been thrilled to see its destruction. It was the last reminder of a facility that had severely contributed to the death of her brother.

Bryant pulled into a small car park behind a pet superstore and she focused on pulling herself together.

They took a short cut through a gulley between two shops and were greeted by the smell of the first bake of the day from Gregg's the bakers.

Bryant groaned.

'Don't even think about it,' Kim said.

She looked up and down the properties. 'That's the one,' she said, pointing to a red door that stood between a card shop and a discount clothing store.

An intercom was fixed just below the name plate. Kim pressed it. A female voice answered.

'We'd like to see Mr Croft.'

'I'm sorry, he's not available at the moment. We have a walk-in ...'

'We're investigating a murder, now please open the door.'

Kim was not prepared to conduct police business through an electronic device.

There was a gentle beeping sound and Kim pushed the door. Before her was a narrow staircase leading to the upper floor.

At the top she found a door on either side. The door to her left was solid wood and the door to her right held four glass panels.

She pushed open the door to the right.

Inside was a small, windowless room occupied by a woman Kim guessed to be mid-twenties, with hair pulled back so tightly Kim could see puckering at the temples.

Bryant took out his warrant card and introduced them.

Although small, the space looked tidy and functional. The filing cabinets filled the wall. A year planner and couple of certificates decorated the opposite wall. The sound of Radio 2 played from the computer speakers.

'May we speak with Mr Croft?'

'No, I'm afraid not.'

Kim looked behind her at the door onto the other side of the landing. 'He's not there. He's out making house calls.'

'What is he, a G.P.?' Kim asked, irritated.

What was with these assistants that felt the need to offer protection for middle-aged men? Was there a special college course for it?

'Councillor Croft spends many hours visiting housebound constituents.'

The words 'captive audience' came to Kim's mind, as did visions of him refusing to leave until their vote had been pledged.

'We are trying to conduct a murder investigation so ...'

'I'm sure I can find a suitable appointment time,' she said, reaching for an A4 diary.

'How about you just give him a call and let him know we're here. We'll wait.'

The woman played with the pearl necklace at her throat. 'He cannot be disturbed while making house calls so if you'd like to make an—'

'No, I would not like to make a bloody ...'

'We understand that the councillor is a busy man,' Bryant said, gently nudging Kim to the side. His voice was low and warm, tinged with understanding. 'But we have a murder investigation to conduct. Are you sure he has no available time today?'

Croft's assistant flicked back to the current day but shook her head. Bryant followed her eyes down to the diary.

'I honestly can't fit you in until Thursday morning at ...'

'Are you joking?' Kim barked.

'We'll take whatever you have.'

'Nine fifteen, Detective.'

Bryant nodded and smiled. 'Thank you for your help.'

Bryant turned and guided her out of the door. Once outside, Kim turned to him, fuming.

'Thursday morning, Bryant?'

He shook his head. 'Of course not. His diary said he's working from home all afternoon and we know where he lives.'

'Fine,' she said, satisfied.

'You know, Guv, you can't always bully people into giving you what you want.'

Kim disagreed. It had worked for her so far.

'Have you ever heard of the book *How to Win Friends and Influence People*?'

'Have you ever watched *One Flew over the Cuckoo's Nest*? Because she was Nurse Ratched in the making.'

Bryant laughed out loud. 'I'm just saying there's more than one way to skin a cat.'

'And that's why I have you,' she said, stopping outside a coffee shop. 'Double shot latte for me,' she said, pushing open the door.

Bryant rolled his eyes as she sat at the window.

Despite Bryant's warning, she had never possessed the ability to adapt her behaviour to accommodate other people. Even as a child Kim had been unable to assimilate herself into any kind of collective. She possessed no ability to hide her feelings, her innate reactions having a habit of claiming her face before she had a chance to control it.

'You know, sometimes all you want is a cup of coffee,' Bryant groaned, placing two cups on the table. 'They have more choices than a Chinese takeaway. Apparently this is an Americano.'

Kim shook her head. Sometimes it was like Bryant had stepped out of a time capsule delivered from the late eighties.

'So, why were you getting all tetchy with Nurse Ratched back there?'

'We're getting nowhere, Bryant.'

'Yeah, we're stalling around the onion rings.'

'The what?'

'A case for me is like a three-course meal. The first part is like a starter. You dive right in 'cos you're hungry. There are witnesses, a crime scene, so you gorge on information. And then the main course comes and let's say it's a mixed grill. You gotta work out what's important. There's too much food, too much information. So, should you just go for all the meat and leave the garnishes or forego a sausage so that there's still enough room for dessert?

'Now, most people will agree that pudding is the best bit because when it comes the whole meal comes together and the appetite is satisfied.'

'That's the biggest load of boll—'

'Ah, but look at where we are. We've eaten the starter and we now have two lines of enquiry. We're trying to work out which direction we should take to get to the dessert.'

Kim took a sip of her coffee. Bryant loved to analogise and now and again she chose to indulge him.

'Now, the main course often makes more sense if interrupted for a gut chat.'

Kim smiled. They really had worked together for too long.

'So, come on, hit me with it. What's the gut saying?'

'What was our initial theory?'

'That Teresa Wyatt was murdered because of a personal grudge.'

'And then?'

'After the murder of Tom Curtis we surmised that it is someone connected to Crestwood.'

'The death of Mary Andrews?'

'Didn't really alter our thinking.'

'The discovery of a body in the ground?'

'Leads us to believe that someone is trying to eliminate people involved in crimes that happened ten years ago.'

'So, to summarise, it is our theory that the person who killed our young girl is the person who is murdering the staff so they don't get caught for their original crime?'

'Of course,' Bryant said, emphatically.

And therein lay the disparity in her gut. 'I think it was Einstein who said, if the facts don't fit the theory, change the facts.'

'Huh?'

'The person who murdered our buried victim was measured and methodical. They managed to kill and dispose of at least one body without being caught. They left no clues and would have remained undetected, if not for the tenacity of Professor Milton.

'Fast forward to Tom Curtis. The job was done with the alcohol but that wasn't enough. There was a message loud and clear that this man deserved to die.'

Bryant swallowed. 'Guv, don't tell me your gut is saying what I think it's saying?'

'And what is that?'

'That we're looking for more than one killer?'

Kim took a sip of her latte. 'What I think, Bryant, is that we're going to need a bigger plate.'

CHAPTER 36

'Are you sure this is where she said?' Kim asked.

'Yep, this is the place; The Bull and Bladder. Famous for being the second pub along the Delph Run.'

The Delph Run was a collection of six pubs that were scattered the length of the Delph Road. The Corn Exchange kicked off the stretch at Quarry Bank and it ended with The Bell in Amblecote. It had become a rite of passage for groups of males and more recently, females, to work their way from one end to the other, consuming as much alcohol as their young bodies could contain.

No self-respecting man over the age of eighteen within a two-mile radius would admit to not having conquered the Delph Run.

Bryant had knocked on the door at the home of Arthur Connop to be informed by his indifferent wife where her husband could be found.

The Bull and Bladder was a triple-windowed building furnished with mahogany wood and a mustard-coloured exterior.

'At eleven thirty?' Kim asked. To her it looked like a place where you wiped your feet on the way out.

The outer door led into a small, dark corridor with choices. To the immediate left was the snug. Along the same wall were doorways to the toilets. The doors matched the dark wood on the windows outside and made the small space claustrophobic.

The stench of ale was worse than most crime scenes Kim had ever attended.

Bryant opened the door to the bar on the right. The room was not much lighter than the corridor.

A fixed booth ran the entire circumference of the wall. The upholstery was stained and dirty. Wooden tables sat in front of the banquette encircled by a couple of stools.

In the right hand corner was a newspaper and a half pint of beer.

Bryant approached the bar and spoke to a woman in her early fifties drying glasses with a dubious-looking tea towel.

'Arthur Connop?' he asked.

She nodded towards the door. 'Just in the pisser.'

At that second the door opened and a male no taller than five feet entered, adjusting the belt to his trousers.

'Cheese cob, Maureen,' he said, walking right through them.

Maureen reached under a scratched plastic hood, examined a package and then placed it on the bar.

'Two quid.'

'And a pint of bitter,' he glanced in their direction. 'The coppers can get their own.'

Maureen pulled the pint and placed it on the bar. Arthur counted out the change and placed the money on a grungy beer mat.

'Nothing for us, thanks,' Bryant said, and for that Kim was truly grateful.

Arthur squeezed himself between the table and the banquette and sat down.

'What d'ya want?' he asked as they both took stools on the other side of the table.

'Been expecting us, Mr Connop?'

He rolled his eyes impatiently. 'I day come over on the banana boat. Yo bin digging up where I used to work. Folks I worked with am being knocked off so it weren't gonna be long til yer come looking for me.'

He unwrapped the cling film from the cob that appeared to be the only culinary fare on offer. The stench of onion reached Kim immediately. A small piece of grated cheese fell onto the table. Arthur licked his index finger, touched the table to retrieve the cheese, then ate it off his finger.

Kim was guessing those hands hadn't been washed after his recent trip and suddenly she was fighting down nausea.

Bryant knocked her knee beneath the table. He obviously wished to lead this one and she was more than happy to let him.

'Mr Connop, we're after some background at the moment. Do you think you could help with that?'

'If yer want. Just be quick and leave me in peace.'

Kim was tempted to show him the photos on her phone but just in time remembered a valuable piece of advice offered to her by Woody. If you can't play nice ... let Bryant do it.

Connop's skin was a roadmap of burst capillaries and bore the pallor of lifelong drinking. The whites of his eyes had submitted to the colour of jaundice. His facial hair was white and days old. The wrinkles in his forehead did not revert to a resting position and judging by their depth she guessed this guy had been born pissed off.

He used both hands to hold the cob together as he raised it to his mouth, chewing noisily.

Clearly one to multitask, he spoke at the same time. 'Go on, ask yer questions and fuck off.'

Kim chose to look away as his mouth macerated the food into a mixture of mashed-up cheese and bread.

'What can you tell us about Teresa Wyatt?'

He took a gulp of beer to wash down the sandwich.

He wrinkled his nose. 'A bit up herself and hoity-toity but she day really interfere. She never spoke to the likes of me. Any jobs was writ on the board and I just gor on with 'em.'

'What was her relationship like with the girls?'

'She didn't really 'ave a lot to with 'em. Day to day she wasn't too involved. To be honest, I think it woulda been the same to her if the place was filled with a load of farm animals. Had a bit of a temper from what I heard but other than that there ain't nothing I can tell yer.'

'How about Richard Croft?'

'Fucking wanker,' he said, taking another bite.

'Care to elaborate?'

'Not really. If he's still alive when yer get to him, you'll see what I mean.'

'Did he have much involvement with the girls?'

'You're kiddin ain't yer? He didn't come out of his office long enough to spake to any of 'em. And they all knew better than to bother him. His job was budgets and stuff. Talked a lot about marking benches and performance intimators or some other shit.'

Kim guessed he meant benchmarking and performance indicators, both of which would have meant nothing to the handy man.

Arthur tapped his nose. 'Always dressed above his station, that one.'

'You mean he wore nice clothes?'

'I mean he wore nice everything. Suits, shirts, shoes, ties. He weren't buying that on the salary of a civil servant.'

'Is that why you didn't like him?' Kim asked.

Arthur grunted. 'I didn't like him for a million reasons but that weren't one of 'em.' His face creased in distaste. 'Slimy, nasty bastard. Superior and secretive and ...'

'About what?' Bryant asked.

Arthur shrugged. 'I don't know. But why a man would need two computers on his desk is beyond me. And he'd always pull down the lid of the small one when I went in. Dunno why. It ain't like I could've understood it.'

'Did you know Tom Curtis?'

Arthur nodded as the last of the cob was ground up in his mouth. 'He weren't a bad lad. Young and good looking. He had more to do with them girls than anybody. Do 'em a sarnie if they'd missed tea, that kinda thing. He put a brave face on it.'

'A brave face on what?' Kim asked.

'Bein' at Crestwood, of course. That's the thing, see. Everybody was there for their own reasons. It was a good stepping stone to wherever folks wanted to get. Except Mary. Salt of the earth, that one.'

Kim turned away for a second, thinking about the charges in the care of this group of people who at best, had offered no warmth, guidance or genuine care – and at worst, had done a whole lot more.

'Did you know William Payne?' Bryant asked.

Arthur guffawed. 'Oh, you mean Golden Bollocks?' he asked and then laughed to himself. It wasn't a pleasant sound.

Kim turned and peered closely at the man before her. The effects of the alcohol were loosening him up. His focus was slightly off as he took another good gulp of beer, finishing off his pint.

Kim stood and went to the bar. 'How many has he had?' she asked Maureen.

'A double whisky and he's on his fourth pint.'

'That his usual?'

Maureen nodded as she filled up a bowl with salted nuts for communal use. Kim wouldn't have eaten one with an AK47 at her head.

Maureen turned and threw the empty bag in the bin. 'Once he's finished that pint, he'll ask for another, I'll refuse him. He'll call me a foul name and then he'll stagger home to sleep it off before coming back again tonight.'

'Same routine every day?'

Maureen nodded.

'Jesus.'

'Don't feel too sorry for him, Detective. If you've got any pity going spare, offer it to his wife.

'Arthur's a miserable old man who's been a victim for as long as I've known him. He's not a cuddly old granddad and he's just as obnoxious, drunk or sober.'

Kim smiled at the woman's honesty. By the time she sat back down the last pint was half gone.

'Yeah, fucking Billy this, Billy that. Everyone bent over backwards for fucking Billy. Just 'cos he had a spastic daughter.'

Kim felt the growl rise in her throat. Bryant shook his head at her and so she unclenched her fists. It wouldn't do any good to floor him. He was never going to change.

'Yeah, let's all take care of Billy. Let's give him all the easy jobs and leave all the shit for Arthur. Let's let Billy work whatever hours he wants and Arthur can have all the rest. We all had fucking problems and if he'd just shoved her in a home we'd have never ...'

Kim leaned forward. Close enough to see the last ounce of clarity dawn in his eyes.

'Never what, Mr Connop?' Bryant prompted.

He shook his head and his eyes rolled but his hand eventually found his glass. He raised it to his mouth and finished it.

He held the glass aloft. 'Another, Maureen?' he shouted.

'You've had enough, Arthur.'

'Fucking slag,' he slurred, banging the glass onto the table. He stood and wobbled.

'Arthur, what were you going to say?'

'Nothing. Piss off and leave me alone. You're too fucking late.'

Kim followed him out of the building and grabbed his forearm. Her tolerance for this embittered old man had run out.

She spoke loudly as a car ignited close by.

'Listen, you know that three former staff members have died in the last two weeks. At least two were murdered and unless you tell us what you know you're probably going to be next.'

He fixed her with a look that belied the level of alcohol raging around his body.

'Let 'em come, for fuck's sake. It'd be a welcome relief.'

He pulled his arm from her grasp and stumbled down the road. He swayed into a parked car and then into a wall, like a pinball.

'It's no good, Guv. He's not gonna tell us anything in this state. Maybe we should visit him later when he's had a chance to sleep it off.'

Kim nodded and turned. They headed back to the car parked just around the corner.

As Kim reached to open the car door the air was filled with a sickening thud, followed by a high-pitched scream.

'What the hell? ...' Bryant shouted.

Unlike Bryant, Kim didn't need to ask as she turned and started running back down towards the pub.

In her gut, she already knew.

CHAPTER 37

Kim was beside the prostate form of Arthur Connop within seconds.

'Move away,' she barked.

Three people stepped to the side and Bryant stood between them and the figure on the ground.

Before she turned her attention to the victim, Kim nodded to a youth across the road pointing a mobile phone in their direction.

Bryant sprinted across and without his protection the crowd began to converge on her again.

'Folks, back off right now,' she shouted, as she assessed the damage.

Connop's left leg was hanging in the gutter at an unnatural angle. Kim leaned down and put two fingers to his neck which told her exactly what she already suspected. He was dead.

A young woman with a pushchair was already requesting an ambulance.

Bryant returned and looked down at her. 'Guv, do you want me to ...'

'Get details,' she said. She would not expect her team to do anything she wasn't prepared to do herself. And she was trained. Damn it.

She knelt on the ground as Bryant turned to the witnesses and tried to corral them away from the area.

She rolled him over onto his back, gingerly. His face was mottled with gravel from the road. His eyes stared, unseeing, up to the sky.

She heard the gasp of one of the witnesses but she had no time to worry about the sensitivities of onlookers. It was human nature to peer at things that would later cause nightmares but her priority was Arthur Connop.

Kim gently tilted back his head using two fingers beneath the chin.

His zip-up cardigan had not been fastened so she ripped open his shirt

She placed the heel of her right hand at the centre of his chest and placed her left hand over the top, interlocking her fingers. She pressed down sharply approximately six centimetres. She counted to thirty and stopped.

She moved to Arthur's head and with her left hand pinched his nose shut. She sealed her lips over his mouth and blew steadily.

She watched as his chest rose; the result of artificial respiration. She repeated the process and then returned to compressions.

She knew that CPR was used primarily to preserve intact brain function until further measures could be taken to restore spontaneous blood circulation and breathing. The irony was not lost on her that she was trying to preserve a brain that the owner had spent years trying to destroy.

The squeal of police sirens stopped somewhere behind her. Their first priority would be to close off the road to preserve evidence. Others would take over questioning the witnesses.

Above and around her she was conscious of the activity but her focus remained on the lifeless figure beneath her hands.

A cacophony of voices surrounded her but one broke through her concentration.

'Guv, shall I take over?'

Kim shook her head without looking up. She paused compressions, sure she'd just seen the chest move of its own volition.

She stared hard. It rose again. The light was returning to his eyes and a low guttural groan escaped his lips.

Kim sat back in the road, her arms dead with fatigue.

Arthur Connop looked right at her. She saw an instant of recognition and the glint of understanding as the pain throughout his body travelled along the nerves to his brain. He groaned again and a grimace contorted his features.

Kim laid a hand on his chest. 'Stay still, the ambulance will be here soon.'

His rolling eyes found her as she heard another siren in the distance.

'Ended,' he gasped.

Kim bent her head. 'What's ended, Arthur?'

He swallowed and shook his head from side to side. The effort brought another groan.

She heard the approaching footsteps of the paramedics.

'What did you say?'

'End it,' he managed.

She looked into his eyes and saw the light once again receding.

Her aching arms instinctively moved towards his chest but she felt herself being moved aside.

Two green uniforms blocked her view. The male felt for a pulse and shook his head. The female began compressions as the male began taking equipment from his bag.

Bryant took her arm and guided her away.

'He's in good hands, Guv.'

She looked back as the male paramedic placed the defibrillator pads on Arthur Connop's chest.

She shook her head. 'No, he's gone.'

'What did he say?'

'He asked me to end it.'

She leaned against the wall, fatigue taking the place of adrenaline. 'Whatever the hell went on at Crestwood tormented these people for the rest of their lives.'

Bryant nodded. 'Witnesses saw a white car speeding away. No one actually saw the impact but one swears it was an Audi, the other says a BMW. Could be unrelated, Guv.'

She turned and looked at him. 'Bryant, he stumbles the hundred yards home every day without incident.'

'So, you're not thinking genuine hit-and-run.'

'No, Bryant, I think our killer was out here waiting and the bastard had the gall to do it right in front of us.'

He touched her arm gently. 'Come on, let's get you cleaned up before we ...'

She pulled her arm free. 'What time is it?'

'Just after twelve.'

'Time to pay our local councillor a friendly visit.'

'But, Guv, a couple of hours ...'

'May well make us too late,' she said, heading back towards the car. 'Other than William Payne, our councillor is the only one left.'

CHAPTER 38

'Got any of those mints, Bryant?' Kim asked. She'd used and balled up three wet wipes to clean her face, neck and hands but, psychological or not, the lingering aroma of beer and onion would not go away.

He reached into the side compartment of the driver's door and offered her a fresh packet. She took one and popped it in her mouth.

The menthol aroma blazed a trail right down to her lungs.

'Jesus, do you need a licence for these?' she asked, once her right eye had finished watering.

'Consider the alternative, Guv.'

She took a good hit of the sweet and looked out of the window as they approached Bromsgrove town centre. Bryant took a right past the old union workhouse which had operated until 1948.

Although only ten miles from Stourbridge, it was like entering another world.

The area was first documented in the early ninth century as Bremesgraf and had grown up around farming and nail making. Staunchly Conservative, the affluent, rural population was primarily white British, with four per cent ethnic minority.

'Are you kidding me?' Kim asked as they turned off Littleheath Lane. Houses along this stretch of Lickey End started at seven-figure prices. Tall hedges and long driveways protected the houses from view. Known as 'the banking belt', the area accommodated the corporate professionals with easy access to the M5 and M40. Not the natural habitat of a local MP.

The car stopped at a walled garden separated by a wrought-iron gate.

Bryant wound down the window and pressed the intercom button. A distorted voice answered and Kim couldn't be sure if it was male or female.

'West Midlands police,' Bryant said.

There was no reply but a low thunk signalled the electronic gate sliding behind the left hand wall.

Bryant drove through as soon as the gap was wide enough.

The gravel drive led them to a redbrick courtyard and a two-storey farm house.

The property was L-shaped and Kim could see a detached garage block behind that would have eaten her house for lunch. Despite the mansion space for the vehicles, two cars were parked on a gravel patch to the right of the property.

An open canopy porch trimmed the building and planters holding bay trees were set at regular intervals.

'You wouldn't want to give all this up without a fight, eh?' Kim asked.

Bryant pulled up outside the front door. 'He's a witness, not a suspect, Guv.'

'Of course,' she said, getting out of the car. 'And I'll be sure to remember that when I question him.'

The door was opened before they reached it. Before them stood a male Kim guessed to be Richard Croft.

He wore cream chinos and a navy blue T-shirt. His greying hair was damp and a towel rested around his shoulders.

'Forgive me, I've just jumped out of the pool.'

Of course. She had that very same inconvenience all the time.

'Nice cars,' Kim observed pleasantly nodding towards an Aston Martin DB9 and a Porsche 911. There was a space in between.

Kim saw two CCTV cameras perched on top of the building.

'Security overload for an MP?' she asked, following Richard Croft into the hallway.

He turned. 'Oh, the security is for my wife.'

He turned left and they followed through double glass doors into what Kim assumed was one of the lounge rooms. The ceiling was low and supported with thick beams that had been expertly restored. Caramel leather sofas and mauve walls lightened the space. French doors led to an orangery that appeared to run the entire length of the house.

'Please, take a seat while I arrange for some tea.'

'Oh, how civilised,' Bryant said as Richard Croft left the room. 'He's going to make us tea.'

'I think he said he would *arrange* for some tea. I'm pretty sure that means he isn't making it.'

'Marta will be along in a moment,' Richard Croft said, re-entering the room. The towel had gone and the hair had been combed revealing more grey hair around his temples.

'Your wife?'

He smiled, revealing teeth that were just a little too white. 'Heavens, no. Marta is our live-in. She helps Nina with the boys and the house.'

'And a very lovely house it is too, Councillor.'

'Richard, please,' he offered, magnanimously. 'The house is the love child of my wife. She works hard and expects to relax in a comfortable home.'

'And she does what exactly?'

'She is a human rights barrister. She defends the rights of people you may not particularly wish to spend time with.'

Kim got it immediately. 'Terrorists.'

'*Individuals accused of terrorist activity* would be a more politically correct term.'

Kim tried not to let her emotions show but the distaste must have been obvious.

'Everyone is entitled to make full use of the law, wouldn't you agree, Detective?'

Kim said nothing. She didn't trust her mouth to open. She firmly believed that the law was applicable to everyone and so she had to concede that the defence of that same law should be made available to everyone. So, she agreed with him. She just hated the fact that she agreed with him.

More intriguing than his wife's profession was the total lack of facial movement when the man spoke. Croft's forehead and upper cheek area had not moved once. For Kim, there was something surreal about the process of injecting a derivative of the most acute known toxin into your own body voluntarily. For a man approaching his fifties, it was positively obscene. She felt she was looking at the waxwork dummy and not the man.

He waved at his surroundings. 'Nina likes to live well and I'm just lucky that I have a wife that loves me very much.'

The comment probably left his mouth as self-deprecating and with intent to charm. It met Kim's ears as smug and self-satisfied.

Probably not as much as you love yourself, Kim was tempted to respond – but was luckily prevented by the arrival of a tray being carried by a young slim blonde who also had damp hair.

Kim exchanged a knowing glance with Bryant. Jesus, he and his wife didn't have a moral fibre between them.

She feared for the two perfectly groomed young boys in the photo on the brick fire surround.

Once Marta had left the room Richard poured the contents of the silver pot into three small cups.

Kim could see no milk and could smell no caffeine. She held up her hand and declined.

'I've been meaning to come and see you to offer any assistance but I've just been so busy with my constituents.'

Yes, Kim was sure they insisted he indulge in a midday romp with the hired help. Even the tone of his voice sounded disingenuous. She wondered if she might have found him more believable at the office. But here, amongst the luxury of his surroundings, knowing what he'd been up to, she couldn't help the wave of revulsion that stole over her.

'Well we're here now, so if we could just ask a few questions we'll be on our way.'

'Of course, please, go ahead.'

He took a seat on the sofa opposite and sat back with his right foot lifted onto his left knee.

Kim decided to start at the beginning. Every cell of her being detested this man but she would try to ensure that her personal opinion did not colour her professional judgement.

'You are aware that Teresa Wyatt was murdered recently?'

'Terrible business,' he said, without changing expression. 'I sent flowers.'

'A lovely thought, I'm sure.'

'The least I could do.'

'And you know about Tom Curtis?'

Croft shook his head and lowered it. 'Horrific.'

Kim would bet her house he sent flowers.

'Were you aware that Mary Andrews also recently passed away?'

'No, I wasn't.' He looked towards his desk. 'I must make a note to send ...'

'Flowers,' Kim finished for him. 'Do you recall a staff member named Arthur Connop?'

Richard appeared to ponder for a moment. 'Yes, yes, he was one of the orderlies.'

Kim wondered just what kind of assistance this man may have offered had he managed to find the time to visit the station, because he wasn't being all that forthcoming now.

'We spoke to him earlier today.'

'I hope he's well.'

'He didn't particularly wish the same for you.'

Richard laughed and reached for his cup of green liquid. 'People rarely remember their superiors with fondness, I find. Especially when those individuals are lazy. I had cause to reprimand Mr Connop on more than one occasion.'

'For what?'

'Sleeping on the job, shoddy work ...'

His words trailed away as though there was more.

'And?'

Richard shook his head. 'Just day to day corrections.'

'What about William Payne?'

Kim saw a slight shift in his eyes. 'What about him?'

'Well, he was the other night porter. Did he receive similar reprimands?'

'Not at all. William was a model employee. You know of his personal circumstances, I assume?'

Kim nodded.

'William would have done nothing to risk losing his job.'

'Would you say he was treated more favourably than Arthur Connop?' Kim pushed. There was something here. She could feel it.

'Honestly, we probably did turn a blind eye to one or two things.'

'Like what?'

'Well, we knew now and again that William would pop home at night if his daughter was having a particularly bad time or if his neighbour was unable to watch her, but he never left the girls unattended, so we let it slide. I mean, we knew about it but ...' He shrugged. 'Would you want to change places with him?'

'Anything more than that? Arthur indicated ...'

'Really, Detective. I think Arthur Connop was born bitter. If you've met him you'll know that he is one of life's victims. Every bad thing in his life has been the fault of someone else and not under his own control.'

'And earlier today he may have had a point when a car drove into the back of him, leaving him for dead.'

Richard Croft swallowed. 'And is he ... dead?'

'We don't know yet but it didn't look hopeful.'

'Oh dear. What a terrible, tragic accident.' He sighed deeply. 'Well, in that case there seems no harm in my being completely candid with you, Detective.'

'Please do,' Kim said, unable to see the wild horses that appeared to be dragging words from his mouth.

'Not long before the fire it was brought to my attention that Arthur had been supplying some of the girls with drugs. Nothing hard, but drugs nonetheless.'

'Why?' Kim asked, pointedly. If discovered, his actions would have cost him his job, a criminal record and potentially a few months in Featherstone.

'William was the night shift caretaker, covered by a relief guy for his two nights off. Occasionally Arthur would step in and earn the overtime. Unknown to the rest of the staff, Arthur was spending the first part of his shift at the pub. A fact easily discovered by a group of occupants, who used the situation to their advantage.'

'They blackmailed him?' Bryant asked.

'That's not really a word I'd like to use, Detective.'

As the person in charge of the facility, Kim felt sure it wasn't.

'Arthur obviously kept quiet through fear of losing his job.'

'As well he should,' Kim exploded. 'He was responsible for the safety of fifteen to twenty girls aged anywhere from six to fifteen. Anything could have happened to those kids while he was gone.'

Richard eyed her quizzically. 'You condone the behaviour of these girls, Detective?'

No she did not, but she was yet to find one single person to whom these girls had been entrusted that actually gave a shit.

She chose her words carefully. 'I do not. However, had Arthur been doing his job correctly he would not have been placed in that position in the first place.'

He smiled his agreement. 'Point taken, Detective. But the girls concerned were not model citizens.'

Kim fought down the sudden rush of anger. The behaviour of the girls automatically made them amoral delinquents with no future or promise. And with role models like Arthur Connop, she was not the least bit surprised.

Kim wondered at Richard's sudden disclosure about Arthur. What did he have to gain?

Richard sat forward. 'More tea?'

'Mr Croft, you don't seem particularly worried that all your old colleagues are dying at an unnatural rate?'

'By my count there are two murders, one natural death and an accident that may or may not be fatal.'

'What went on at Crestwood all those years ago?' she asked, pointedly.

Richard Croft did not miss a beat. 'I wish I knew, but I was only there for the last two years of the facility's operation.'

'And in that time the number of runaways definitely increased, don't you agree?'

He met her gaze squarely but a flicker of irritation was threatening his measured composure. Her technique had escalated from general to probing. He didn't like that she was questioning the management of the facility during his tenure.

'Some youngsters don't like rules, no matter how well intentioned they are.'

From Kim's memories the majority of rules were set down for the convenience of the staff and not the occupants.

'You've spoken about Arthur but how involved were *you* with the occupants of Crestwood?'

'Not very. I was brought in to make organisational decisions, to operate the facility efficiently.'

His constant use of the word 'facility' made Crestwood sound more like a secure unit at Broadmoor than a home for abandoned kids.

'Mr Croft, do you have any reason to believe that any of your colleagues would have wanted to harm any of the girls?'

He stood. 'Of course not. How could you even ask such a question? That is a terrible thing to say. Everyone employed at the facility was there to take care of those children.'

'For a monthly salary,' Kim said before she could stop herself.

'And even people that were not,' he shot back. 'Even the pastor could not get through to some of these girls.'

'What about Arthur?'

'He made a mistake. He would never have harmed anyone.'

'I understand that, Mr Croft, but we have the body of what appears to be a teenage girl buried in the grounds of Crestwood and one thing I can deduce with absolute certainty is that she didn't get there by herself.'

He stood still and ran his fingers through his hair; the only physical reaction to her words. His facial expressions were difficult to read beneath the Botox.

'Mr Croft, did you or anyone you know file objections to Professor Milton's dig on the land?'

'Absolutely not. I would have no reason at all to do that.'

She stood and faced him. 'And finally, the last question I have before I leave you in peace. Where were you on the night of Teresa's murder?'

His face turned crimson and he pointed towards the door. 'I would thank you to leave my property immediately. My offer of assistance is revoked and any further questions should be directed through my solicitor.'

Kim moved towards the door. 'Mr Croft. I am more than ready to leave *your wife's* home and I'd like to thank you for your time.'

Kim exited through the front door as a silver Range Rover pulled onto the gravel patch. The driver did not take the available space between the two others, indicating that something else was normally parked there.

A slim female stepped out of the vehicle and retrieved a briefcase from the back seat. She wore a black business suit with a pencil skirt that fell just below the knee. The calves were lifted by four-inch heels. Her hair was black and glossy but pulled back into a severe ponytail.

As they passed, Kim couldn't help but notice that the woman was absolutely stunning. She was rewarded with a tolerant smile and a curt nod.

'Okay, what the hell does *she* see in him?' Bryant asked.

Kim shook her head as she got into the car. The door closed behind the married couple. There were still mysteries in the world after all.

Bryant started the car and put it into reverse. 'Guv, are you ever gonna find a way to play nice?'

'Of course I am, the very moment I find playmates that I like.'

She sighed as she looked back at the property and for a moment thought about William Payne and his daughter Lucy. Fate most definitely had a flawed perspective.

'What're you thinking?' Bryant asked as the gate slid open to release them.

'I'm thinking about his reaction to the news of the buried girl.'

'What about it?'

'He never even asked if we'd made an identification. He wasn't shocked by anything we told him. The Botox may have numbed his face but it couldn't control his eye movement.'

Kim's gut had reacted unfavourably to Mr Richard Croft. He knew something, of that she was sure. But she was still chasing that elusive thread, that final piece of hanging cotton that once pulled, would unravel the secrets of Crestwood.

CHAPTER 39

'What did *they* want?' Nina Croft asked, placing her briefcase down in the hallway.

'They were asking about Crestwood,' Richard answered, as he followed his wife into the kitchen. After fifteen years together there were two things about her that never failed to amaze him.

The first was that she still looked as fantastic as she had the day they'd met. He had fallen head over heels in love with her and unfortunately for him, that had not changed since.

The second was that the icy remoteness had not left her eyes for seven years.

Nina stopped at the floating island in the middle of the vast kitchen. He stood on the other side. She faced him through the Le Creuset kitchenware that had never been used.

'What did you tell them?' she demanded.

Richard lowered his eyes. Seven years ago, after the birth of his second son, he had been in the throes of euphoria. Watching his beautiful wife give birth had provoked in him such fierce protection and love he had thought the bond with his wife had been unbreakable. He had felt he could trust her with anything.

Two days later, after settling Harrison into his cot, Richard had felt close enough to his wife to reveal the secrets held at Crestwood. They had not shared a bed again.

There had been no anger, no recriminations and no threat of turning him in. A freezing fog had fallen between them and it had not lifted since.

'What did they ask?'

He recounted the conversation word for word. She showed no emotion at all until the final couple of questions. Only then did a muscle jump in her cheek. When he'd finished he felt a bead of sweat forming beneath his hairline as he waited for her response.

'Richard, I told you years ago that I would not tolerate your past mistakes affecting my life or the lives of my children.'

'Was that the night you left my bed forever, sweetheart?'

Every now and again the barely tolerant tone of her voice was like a kick to the stomach and sometimes his backbone put in a surprise appearance.

'Yes, my love, any attraction I felt died after your night-time confession. It would have been scandalous enough that an enquiry into Crestwood would have revealed your inability to keep your hands out of the facility's pockets.' She raised her eyes to the ceiling as though speaking to Harrison. 'To take money that was meant for those girls was reprehensible, my love,' she said icily, 'but what you did to cover it up. Well ... quite honestly, words defy me.'

Once more he damned his total honesty to her that night. Yes, he had taken a little extra salary for himself. He had deserved it and the girls hadn't missed it. Their basic needs had been covered at all times.

The disgust in the face of his wife found its way to a heart that refused to let her go. Croft's immediate reaction was to strike back. To hurt her in a way that would provoke any measure of feeling.

He tipped his head and smiled. 'Well, at least I have someone prepared to offer me love, even if my wife will not.'

Richard held his breath. Any reaction that contained real emotion would be welcome. Anything that would indicate the remnants of what they once had.

She laughed out loud. It was not a sound born of joy or happiness. 'You mean Marta?'

This was not the reaction he'd expected. A sly smile was creeping across her face.

The room started to close in on him. 'You ... you know about Marta?'

'Know about it, my sweet ...? I pay very handsomely for it.'

Richard stepped back as though she had slapped him. She was lying. She had to be.

'Oh Richard, you ridiculous old fool. Marta has a large family back in Bulgaria that she supports with this job. Her annual salary ensures that they eat. Her erm ... *overtime* sends both her brothers to school, so if she seems eager to have sex with you it's because she gets paid by the hour. And I am happy to pay, because she deserves every single penny.'

Richard could feel the colour infusing his face as the ugly truth registered. Earlier today Marta had been quite insistent.

'You cold-hearted bitch.'

Nina ignored the insult and turned to the coffee machine. 'I've told you before that I will not have even the hint of scandal attached to my name. I have worked very hard to achieve the life that I live and because of your public standing in the community I don't mind having you along as a passenger. As long as you travel silently.'

Richard felt the disgust at his life wash over him. His only use to his wife was the vicarious kudos of his standing as a member of parliament; a career which gave her an element of respectability that counter-balanced her unsavoury clientele.

'Don't look so shocked, my dear. It is an arrangement that has worked well and should continue to do so.'

His skin crawled at the thought of sharing a bed with Marta after what he had learned. At times, Richard had felt they had a genuine connection and yet he had been nothing more than a salary enhancement.

'But why Marta?' he asked, still stunned from her admission.

'My image is everything and I will not allow you to tarnish it. You are a man and you have certain needs but I would never tolerate you screwing some diseased whore out on the streets and putting my children in danger.'

He watched as Nina took out her mobile phone. 'Now, run along like a good boy while I continue to clean up your mess.'

Richard stood on the cusp of a decision. His hands were clenched at his sides. He could turn and walk away, out of this house, away from Nina's coldness and control.

He could go straight to the police and release the burden inside him. He could be free of this woman and the life he led.

He considered his meagre MP's salary of £65,000. Even creative accounting with his expenses left daylight between him and a six-figure income. His monthly pay barely covered the house utility bills. The salary of his wife paid for the mortgage, the cars and the £5,000 pocket money that landed in his account on the first of each month.

Richard's clenched hands fell to his sides. He turned and walked into the study, carrying his balls on a nine-carat-gold dinner plate.

Only when the door was closed behind him did he wipe at the bead of sweat behind his ear. His last remaining sliver of pride had prevented him doing so in front of his wife.

Teresa and Tom were dead and Arthur on his way. Richard wanted to believe that the deaths were coincidental. He had to believe it ... because not believing it could only mean one thing; that he was probably next.

CHAPTER 40

Kim dialled Stacey's number as Bryant gave their order at the McDonalds drive-thru. It was answered on the second ring.

'Stace, we're going to need any addresses you've got for the ex-occupants of Crestwood 'cos we are rapidly running out of staff members.'

'Yeah, we heard about that here. Woody's already been down here looking for yer.'

'Woody's after me,' she whispered to Bryant as Stacey tapped her keyboard.

Bryant grimaced.

'Okay, first one on the list is, oh actually, it's two of 'em. Twin sisters named Bethany and Nicola Adamson. This address is for Nicola at Brindleyplace in Birmingham.'

Kim read out the address and Bryant jotted it down.

'Okay, can you work on tracking down that pastor you mentioned before? His name came up again so I think he's worth a visit. The girls may have talked to him.'

'On it, Guv.'

'Thanks, Stace. Anything from Dawson?'

'Not to me.'

Kim ended the call.

'We really should have gone back to the station after what happened earlier,' Bryant said.

Kim knew full well they should have briefed Woody about the hit-and-run and followed the procedure that accompanies the witnessing of any 'traumatic incident' but on her team they'd never get out the station.

'I'll do a report later and go talk to Woody but we're running out of time. So far we've lost four people that worked at Crestwood at the time it closed.'

She took a bite of the chicken burger. It tasted like a wedge of cardboard placed between two slabs of MDF. She put it aside and took out her mobile phone.

Dawson answered immediately.

'How's things?' she asked.

'Moving along. Cerys is in the pit with her hand tools so we're not far away from whatever's down there.'

Kim could hear the fatigue in his voice. 'Did you pay a visit to William Payne?'

'Done, Guv. I placed a check call to ADT to make sure the alarm is working. I cleaned and tested the motion sensors front and back which work on a fifteen foot arc. I got him to move a couple of planters away from the fence and change the battery in Lucy's emergency response pendant, just to be sure.

'Oh, and I've briefed every patrolling officer to include Payne's home in their perimeter checks.'

Kim smiled. And that was why he was on the team. There were times that managing Dawson was like mothering a toddler. Some days he tried her patience to the limit and others where he did his job; brilliantly.

'Just so you know, Guv. It came over the radio. Arthur Connop died.'

Kim said nothing. She had known he wasn't going to make it.

'SOCO still have the road closed. You never know, there might be something.'

Kim ended the call. 'Connop,' she whispered.

'Dead?' Bryant asked.

Kim nodded and then sighed. If she was perfectly honest, she was hard pushed to measure the loss of Arthur Connop. His wife had been emphatically disinterested in his whereabouts. No one they'd spoken to had harboured any affection for the man at all, past or present. Perhaps Maureen might feel his loss from the decrease of beer and cobs sold per week but few would seriously mourn his passing.

Kim would have liked to think that the rude, insufferable man had once been a decent human being who had slowly grown bitter with age but his blatant neglect of his charges ten years ago destroyed the false hope. She suspected that Maureen was right that Arthur had always been selfish and mean – but she now had to wonder if he was more than that. How far would he have gone to cover his tracks?

As Bryant wiped at his mouth with a paper serviette Kim glanced at the dashboard clock. It was just after three and a lot of paperwork lay ahead at the station. It had already been a long and taxing day and she could always start working through the list of occupants tomorrow. Her body demanded a shower and some rest.

'You want me to head towards that address in Birmingham, then, Guv?'

She smiled and nodded her head.

CHAPTER 41

Covering seventeen acres, Brindleyplace was the largest mixed-use redevelopment in the UK. Canal-side factories and a Victorian school had been renovated in a range of architectural styles.

The project was started in 1993 and now offered three distinct areas.

Brindleyplace was an assortment of low-rise buildings offering plush office space, retail units and art galleries while Water's Edge housed the bars, restaurants and cafes. The residential element sprawled out from Symphony Court.

'Guv, what the hell are we doing wrong?' Bryant asked as they stood on the fourth floor of the King Edwards Wharf building.

The door was answered by a slim, athletic woman wearing black leggings and a tight sports top. Her face bore the flush of recent exertion or exercise.

'Nicola Adamson?'

'And you are?'

Bryant offered his warrant card and introduced them both.

She stood aside and welcomed them into an open plan penthouse.

Kim stepped onto beech wooden flooring that stretched all the way to the kitchen area.

White leather sofas were set diagonally before a wall bearing a large, flatscreen television. Beneath it were various electronic devices recessed into the wall. No wires or cables were evident.

Spot lights were flush with the ceiling and a couple of down lighters were fixed above a pebble fireplace.

A glass dining table surrounded by teak chairs signalled the end of the lounge. Just beyond that the laminate ended and stone tiles began.

Kim would guess she was looking at around 1500 square feet of living space.

'Can I offer you a drink, tea, coffee?'

Kim nodded. 'Coffee, as strong as you've got.'

Nicola Adamson smiled openly. 'That kind of day, Detective?'

The woman padded into a kitchen formed of white glossy cabinets with accents of brown wood.

Kim didn't answer but continued to move around the space. The left side wall was formed entirely of glass, punctuated only by a few circular stone pillars. Beyond was a balcony and without stepping out Kim could see the view of the Brindley Loop Canal.

Further along the wall of glass Kim saw a treadmill partly obscured by an oriental screen. Well, she reasoned, if you were going to exercise this was surely the way to do it.

It was an impressive space for a woman in her mid-twenties who was home in the middle of the afternoon.

'What do you do?' Kim asked, bluntly.

'Excuse me?'

'Very nice place you have here. I was just wondering what you did to pay for it.'

Kim's tact and diplomacy were somewhere back around eleven a.m. It was growing into a long day and the woman would either answer or she wouldn't.

'I'm not sure how it's your business as my work is certainly not illegal, but I'm a dancer, an exotic dancer, and I happen to be very good at it.'

Kim guessed that she probably was. Her movements were naturally graceful and lithe.

She carried a tray bearing two steaming mugs and a bottle of water. 'I work at The Roxburgh,' she said, as though that explained everything and for Kim it did. The club was membership only and provided adult entertainment for professional people. The stringent management ensured few visits from the local constabulary, unlike other clubs in Birmingham city centre.

'You understand why we're here?' Bryant asked. Having made the mistake of sitting back on the plush sofa he was now struggling to sit forward before the furniture swallowed him whole.

'Of course. I'm not sure how much I can help but feel free to ask me anything.'

'How old were you when you were at Crestwood?'

'It wasn't one whole stretch, Detective. My sister and I were in and out of care from the age of two.'

'How old were you in that picture?' Kim asked of a photo in a silver frame on the small table beside her.

The features of the two girls were as identical as their clothes. Both wore stiff white school shirts from the free uniform shop. Kim remembered those clothes well and the free taunts that came with them.

Both wore matching pink cardigans with an embroidered flower motif on the left hand side. Everything was identical but their hair. One had loose flowing blonde locks and the other had theirs tied back in a bobble.

Nicola reached for the photo and smiled. 'I remember those cardigans so well. Beth lost hers and would steal mine. It was about the only thing we ever fought over.'

Bryant opened his mouth but Kim's expression silenced him. The woman's face had changed. She was no longer looking into the photo, but past it.

'They may not look much but those cardigans were precious. Mary asked for a couple of volunteers to help wipe down all the paintwork. Beth and I offered because Mary was a good woman who did her best. At the end of the day she gave us a few pounds for our work.' Nicola finally raised her eyes. Her expression was both sad and wistful.

'You can't even begin to imagine how we felt. The very next morning we went up into Blackheath, to the market. We spent all day roaming the stalls deciding what to buy and it wasn't so much the cardigans but that they were ours, from new. Not hand-me-downs from the older girls or used garments from the charity shop. They were new and they were ours.'

A tear had escaped from Nicola's right eye. She placed the picture back and wiped at her cheek.

'It sounds silly and you can't really understand ...'

'Yes, I can,' Kim said.

Nicola smiled indulgently and shook her head. 'No, Detective, you really can't ...'

'Yes, I really can,' Kim repeated.

Nicola met her gaze and held it for just a couple of seconds before nodding her understanding.

'To answer your question, we were fourteen in that photo.'

Bryant looked to Kim and she gestured for him to continue. 'Did you spend all your time in care at Crestwood?' he asked.

Nicola shook her head. 'No, our mother was a heroin addict and I'd like to say she tried her best but she didn't. Until we were twelve it was a mixture of foster homes, children's homes and our mother getting clean and taking us back. I don't really remember it all that well.'

Kim could tell from her eyes that the recollection was no trouble at all.

'But you had each other?' Kim said, looking at the photo. For six years she had also known that feeling.

Nicola nodded. 'Yes, we had each other.'

'Miss Adamson, we have reason to believe that the body we've discovered within the grounds is possibly one of the Crestwood occupants.'

'No,' she said, shaking her head. 'You're not serious.'

'Is there anything you can recall about your time there that would help us?'

Nicola's eyes were busy as though searching her memories. Neither she nor Bryant spoke.

Slowly, Nicola began to shake her head. 'I honestly can't think of anything. Beth and I kept to ourselves. There is nothing I can offer.'

'How about your sister? Do you think she would be able to help?'

Nicola shrugged just as Kim's mobile began to ring. Two seconds later, Bryant's sounded. They both fumbled and cut off the calls.

'Sorry about that,' Bryant offered. 'You were saying?'

'Maybe Beth can recall something. She is staying with me at the moment.' Nicola checked her watch. 'She should be home in about half an hour if you'd like to wait.'

Kim's phone began to vibrate in her pocket. 'No, that will be fine,' she said, standing.

Bryant followed suit and offered his hand. 'If you do think of anything, please give us a call.'

'Of course,' she said, walking them to the door.

Kim turned, willing to take a long shot. 'Do you remember any of the girls having a particular fondness for beads?'

'Beads?'

'Perhaps a bracelet?'

Nicola thought for a moment and then clasped her hand over her mouth.

'Yes, yes, there was a girl called Melanie. She was older than me so I didn't know her very well. She was one of the "cool" girls, one of the troublemakers.'

Kim held her breath.

'Yes, now I remember the beads. She gave some to her best friends. They were like a little club.'

Nicola began to nod her head. 'Yes, of course, there were three of them. They all had the beads.'

Kim felt the sinking in her stomach. She was willing to bet that all three of them ran away.

CHAPTER 42

'Shit,' Bryant said as they got into the car.

Kim felt sick. 'You thinking what I'm thinking?'

'If it's that there's possibly another body to find, then yes.'

'Insert the word *probably* for possibly and we're pretty much bang on.' Kim put the seatbelt on and turned. 'You wrote those names down, right?'

Bryant nodded as she took out her phone. He followed suit.

'Two missed calls and a message from Dawson,' she said.

'Mine are from Woody.'

They both keyed into their mailboxes. Kim listened to Dawson's excitable voice and then deleted the message.

'Dawson wants me back at the site straight away.'

Bryant chuckled. 'Woody wants me to get you back to the station within the same timeframe and last I heard, talented as you are, you've yet to master being in two places at the same time.' He turned to her. 'So, Guv, column A or column B?'

Kim looked at him and raised one eyebrow.

'Yeah, I thought that's what you were gonna say.'

CHAPTER 43

Bryant pulled the car onto the dirt patch. It had taken forty minutes to travel eight miles from the centre of Birmingham.

Kim opened the door. 'Check in with Dawson, make sure he's okay.'

'Will do, Guv.'

She trotted to the third tent. The site was beginning to look more like a festival concessions area than a crime scene. She paused at the entrance. She turned and looked down the hill at the middle house and the prisoner within, and gave a little wave. Just in case.

Cerys turned as she entered.

Kim looked down into the pit. 'Where's she gone?' she asked, sexing the body without thinking. There was no sure way of knowing this second body was that of a female except for her gut and that was normally good enough for her.

'Dan has the body in the other tent. It was removed about half an hour ago. We've had chance to sieve a third of the pit and I thought you might like to know we found more ...'

'Beads,' Kim finished for her.

'How did you know?'

Kim shrugged. 'Anything else?'

Cerys sighed heavily and nodded slowly. 'We've carried out a full sweep of the site and found ...'

'One more mass,' Kim interrupted again.

Cerys placed her right hand on her hip. 'Shall I just go home now?'

Kim smiled. 'Sorry, I'm just tired. One of those days. Will this second area be completed tomorrow?'

'First thing in the morning I'll get started on the excavation of area three. We haven't marked it yet. We don't want to give the vultures a head start,' Cerys said, meaning the press. 'We don't yet know for certain that the third anomaly is another body.'

Kim felt the certainty in the pit of her stomach.

'The press are watching our every move so I had the guys complete the sweep and then pack the machine away and keep clear of the area of interest so they don't get suspicious.'

'How will you know exactly where to dig if you haven't marked it?' Kim asked.

'I've paced it from the edge of the tent. Trust me, I'll know.'

Kim did trust her.

'The good news is that site one can be closed down and filled in tomorrow. I just need to sign it off and the first tent can be removed.'

'Anything else of interest?'

'A few bits of cloth; all labelled, bagged and sent back to the lab. May help with identification.'

After their meeting with Nicola, Kim guessed it was only going to be the choice of three.

'Anything else?'

Cerys shook her head and turned away.

Kim appreciated the woman's tenacity. She accepted that her own drive grew from something more than the need to solve this case. Try as she might to convince herself that it was no different; it was. She knew the pain of these girls' past. Not one of them had woken up one day and chosen the future mapped out for them. Their behaviour could not be traced back to an absolute year, month, day and time. It was a progressive journey of peaks and troughs until circumstances eventually stifled hope.

It was never the big things. Kim remembered only ever being called 'child'. All of them had been called 'child' so the staff didn't have to remember their names.

Kim understood that her own motivation came out of a need to seek justice for these forgotten kids; that her pace would not slow until she had.

And she appreciated anyone that tried to keep up with her.

'Hey,' Kim said, as she reached the exit. 'Thanks.'

Cerys smiled.

Kim headed to the utility tent. Daniel had his back to her but she could see that he and two others were busy labelling plastic bags.

'Hey, Doc, what you got?'

'What – no insults, no abuse?'

'Look, I'm tired but I'm sure I could muster ...'

'No, it's fine. Today I could live without it.'

Kim noted that the doctor was more sullen than usual. His shoulders were slightly hunched as he sealed the plastic bag containing the skull. White strips of tape bearing black marker pen listed the site and the bone within.

His assistant reached for the lid to the storage box but Daniel shook his head. 'Not yet.'

Kim was confused. She'd seen bodies packed before with the heaviest bones at the bottom of the box and ascending so that the lighter, more fragile bones lay at the top.

Normally the skull was the last item to be packed.

She stood beside him as he reached for a container the size of a sandwich box, already lined with tissue paper. A collection of small bones was piled to the far right of the table. His hand trembled slightly.

'Adult or non-adult?' Kim asked.

'Definitely non-adult. I can't give you any idea of how she died at the moment. On first inspection there are no obvious areas of trauma to her body.'

His voice was quiet and controlled.

Kim was momentarily confused. 'Hang on, Doc. Because our first victim was juvenile I couldn't threaten you into sexing it but all of a sudden you're referring to this one as a female before you've even taken the bones back to the lab?'

He removed his glasses and rubbed his eyes. 'That's right. I have no hesitation in sexing victim number two, Detective.' He looked back at the sandwich box.

'Because this young lady was pregnant.'

CHAPTER 44

'What a bloody day,' Bryant said, parking the car at the rear of the station. They were the first words spoken since leaving the site. 'Dawson was pretty quiet up there.'

'Are you surprised?'

Dawson had been unable to take his eyes from the small container until the bones were loaded into the larger box, beside the bones of the mother.

'Get off home, Bryant. I'll go see Woody and then I'll be heading home myself.'

It was just after seven and they were entering the thirteenth hour of the sixth working day. Bryant would keep at it right beside her. But he had a family. She did not.

Her last burst of energy was used as she mounted the steps to the third floor. She knocked and waited.

As Woody called for her to enter she marvelled at the level of controlled rage that could be contained in two syllables.

The stress ball was already in his hand when she took a seat.

'You wanted to see me, Sir?'

'Three hours ago, when I called, would have been more appropriate,' he growled.

Kim looked to his right hand and swore she could hear the stress ball crying out for mercy.

'There were developments at the site that required ...'

'Stone, you were involved in a traumatic incident.'

'Bryant's driving isn't that bad,' she quipped weakly. It had been a long day.

'Shut up. You're fully aware of the procedure and the need for your return to the station for a debrief and a welfare check.'

'I was fine, ask Bryant ...'

'You'll excuse me if I choose not to waste my time with that.' He sat back and switched the stress ball to the left hand. Damn, she wasn't out of the woods yet.

'I have an obligation, a duty of care, which you make damn near impossible for me to exercise. You have to be offered support and counselling.'

Kim rolled her eyes. 'When I need someone to tell me how I should be feeling I'll be sure to let you know.'

'That you don't feel anything may well be the problem, Stone.'

'It's not a problem for me, Sir.'

He leaned forward, his eyes boring into her. 'Not right at this moment but eventually all the negativity will affect you and your ability to function.'

Kim doubted that. It was the way she always handled things. The bad things were packed away in boxes and sealed shut. The key was in never opening the boxes and her only question was why more people didn't do that.

The old adage stated that time healed everything. And she had mastered the art of manipulating time. In real time she had failed to save the life of Arthur Connop only seven hours earlier but the activity crammed into those intervening hours distanced the memory. In her mind, the incident could have happened last week. Therefore, the event was much further back in her past than Woody believed.

'Sir, thank you for your concern but I really am fine. I accept that I can't save everyone and I don't beat myself up when people die.'

Woody held up his hand. 'Stone, enough. My decision is made. Once this case is over you will seek counselling or you will face suspension.'

'But ...'

He shook his head. 'If not, the bad inside will destroy you.'

What she held inside was of no concern to her. It was locked up and contained. Her only fear was in letting it out. To release it would most certainly signal her destruction.

She sighed heavily. That was a fight for another day.

'There will be no further discussion on the matter but before you go, there's something else.'

Fabulous, she thought.

'I've received a call from the superintendent who has received a call from the chief superintendent who both want *you* removed from this case.' He sat back. 'So, tell me who the hell you pissed off today.'

There was no point lying to him. Clearly someone's feathers had been well and truly ruffled.

'Sir, I could give you a list but it wouldn't be exhaustive. However, the only person I'm aware of having angered that badly would be Richard Croft but I can't imagine he has that kind of influence.'

There was a brief pause as their eyes met. 'His wife,' they said, together.

'What did you say to him?'

She shrugged. 'Many things,' she answered, thinking Croft's wife must love him very much after all.

'Witness or suspect?'

She pulled a face. 'Bit of both.'

'Dammit, Stone. When will you learn that there is an element of politics when policing at this level?'

'No, Sir, there is an element of politics in policing at *your* level. Mine is still about uncovering the truth.'

Woody glowered at her. Kim hadn't quite meant it the way it had sounded. She relied on the fact that he would know that and chose not to open her mouth to change feet.

She stuck out her chin. 'So, are you gonna follow instructions and remove me?'

'Stone, I do not need goading from you to make use of a perfectly healthy spine. They have already been advised that you will continue to head the case.'

Kim smiled. She should have known.

'The councillor clearly has something to hide or he wouldn't have set his guard dog loose.'

For the first time in days, he offered her the promise of a smile. 'So, I guess I'd better unchain mine.'

'Yes, Sir,' Kim said, with a smile.

CHAPTER 45

Kim looked from Bryant to Stacey. 'Okay, new day. Dawson will be going straight to the site and he'll call when there's more to report.

'So, to recap. Of the six staff members identified, only two remain; Richard Croft and William Payne. Richard Croft doesn't like me very much so I don't think we'll be getting much more from him. But he's hiding something.'

'Guv, two of the objections to the professor's project were filed by the law firm Travis, Dunne and Cohen.'

'Croft's wife?'

Stacey nodded. 'She works under her maiden name of Cohen.'

'So, whatever he's hiding, she knows about.'

'Worth a visit to her office, Guv?' Bryant asked.

Kim shook her head. 'She's already tried to remove me from the case and I'm not giving her any further ammunition.' She shrugged. 'We're not gonna get any help from her. Whatever Croft's hiding, his wife is party to it and will block us at every turn.'

'How far do yer think she'd go?' Stacey asked.

'Depends on the level of potential damage,' Kim answered, recalling the gated house, the cars, not to mention the career.

Kim stood at the board that had been divided into two. The first half had been further quartered. The details of Teresa

Wyatt and Tom Curtis occupied the top two segments. The bottom quarters were occupied by Mary Andrews and Arthur Connop.

'Anything back from forensics on Arthur?' Kim asked.

'Broken glass from a passenger-side headlight and some particles of white paint embedded in his trouser leg. They're trying to match it now.'

Kim stared hard at the left hand side of the board. Despite her inability to prove the murder of Mary Andrews and Arthur Connop, she knew their deaths were linked to something sinister that occurred ten years earlier.

What did you do? she silently asked all of them.

The opposite side of the board was currently divided into two, representing the buried victims so far removed. Kim knew the board would be divided again before the end of the day.

Three names were printed to the side.

Melanie Harris

Tracy Morgan

Louise Dunston

'How's the identification going?' Stacey asked, following Kim's gaze.

Kim didn't turn. 'Apparently these three were a close little group. I'm hoping Doctor Bate can offer us more clues to identify which girl is which.'

'Do yer think there's more than three, Guv?' Stacey asked.

Kim shook her head. There was a reason why a particular group had been targeted.

'Can you find out more about these three on Facebook without being detected?'

'Oh yeah. When I asked if anyone remembered me, one girl asked if I was that shy little black girl with thick glasses and a stutter. And I said yes.'

Kim rolled her eyes. 'What did you find out about the minister?'

'The only minister I could find with any link to Crestwood was Victor Wilks, the guy who did some charity work. His name's come up in a few posts. The girls all refer to him fondly as "Father". He used to visit the place once a month to give a short service for the girls.'

'Background?'

'Hard to know. So far, I've got him spending a few years in Bristol, a couple in Coventry and a year in Manchester. I've thrown out some emails to see if I can get a bite.'

'Where is he now?'

'Dudley.'

'Since when?'

Stacey tapped the keyboard. 'Two years ago.'

'Got an address?'

Stacey passed Kim a piece of paper as Bryant replaced the receiver.

'Guv, that was the front desk. You have a visitor.'

Kim frowned. She was too busy to drop everything for a walk-in.

'Call them back and ...'

'This one ain't shifting, Guv. Your visitor is Bethany Adamson and she is mighty pissed off.'

CHAPTER 46

'May I help you?' Kim asked, at the front desk.

The woman turned and Kim was immediately taken aback. Not by how much the woman resembled Nicola; they were identical twins. The surprise was in how *little* alike they looked.

The woman didn't offer her hand. 'My name is Bethany Adamson and I wanna talk to you.'

Kim stepped back into the corridor and motioned for Bethany Adamson to follow.

A regular kerthunk sounded behind her as she headed for interview room two. Kim hit the key code and held the door open. The woman stepped right past her, using a walking stick in her right hand.

Kim noted that Bethany's boots were flat and functional and rose up to her knees. Beneath were black jeans that hung loose from the knees to the thighs. A bulky winter jacket swamped the slender frame that appeared more frail than that of her sister.

'I don't have much time, Miss Adamson.'

'What I got to say won't take very long, Detective.'

Kim was surprised by the broadness of the Black Country accent.

Kim nodded for her to continue while she appraised the woman's appearance. Had she not known she would have thought that Bethany was the sister of Nicola, albeit much older.

The blonde hair was tied back tightly in a ponytail, with roots that were unwashed and greasy. The face, although identical in structure, appeared thinner, harsher than that of her sister.

The apportionment of vitality and charisma had definitely not been divided in the favour of this twin.

Kim noted that the woman seemed to be resting her entire weight on the walking aid. Kim motioned towards the chair but Bethany shook her head.

Kim remained standing also. They faced each other across the metal interview table.

'Yer spoke to me sister yesterday.'

Kim was shocked at the harshness she saw in the woman's face. Her lips were thin and a frown brought her eyebrows closer together.

Kim nodded. 'Both of your names came up during a current investigation.'

'There's nothing we got to tell yer.'

Kim was intrigued. 'How would you know that?'

Bethany Adamson sought Kim's gaze and their eyes locked. The portals were cold and emotionless. Not even angry or passionate. Just dead and unyielding. If the sum of the face was formed of its individual features, then this woman had never experienced a moment of joy in her life.

'I just know.'

Kim crossed her arms. 'Your sister was a little more accommodating.'

'Well, she don't understand, does she?'

'Understand what?'

Beth sighed heavily. 'Our early years was hard. We was born to a crack whore who checked us in and out of care like library books. As we gor older our chances for any kind of life disappeared 'cos we weren't wanted. All we 'ad was each other.'

'I understand that, Miss Adamson, but ...'

'Our years at Crestwood weren't the happiest times and yer can't possibly understand how it feels to be born to a mother that wants yer only for the child allowance.'

The woman's gaze had Kim and wouldn't let her go.

'Our childhood didn't 'ave any love or stability and we don't wanna keep remembering it. Neither of us.'

Kim understood more than she would ever care to admit. Despite the woman's demeanour, Kim had the urge to try and reach out. She understood where the defensiveness came from, but she had bodies both old and new piling up around her.

'What went on at that place, Beth?' she asked, quietly.

'It's Miss Adamson if yer don't mind, and that's for you to find out, Detective, but don't involve me or me sister. It won't be good for either of us.'

'Not even if it would help catch a killer?'

No emotion registered on the dead face. 'Not even that. Me sister's too polite to ask but I ain't. So leave us alone.'

'If this investigation dictates that I need to speak with either of you again ...'

'I really wouldn't if I was you. If yer don't leave us be, I promise yer will be sorry.'

With surprising speed Bethany Adamson travelled the distance to the door. She was gone before Kim realised she'd just been threatened.

Rather than warning her off, the woman's words had induced the polar opposite.

Now another question burned within Kim.

Nicola and Beth had experienced the exact same childhood but were like opposing seasons of the year. So, what the hell had happened to make Bethany Adamson such a hostile, hateful individual?

CHAPTER 47

The Hollytree housing estate lay between Brierley Hill and Wordsley. The entire council development, constructed in the early Seventies, covered a two-mile area and was now home to at least three registered sex offenders.

On entering, Kim was always reminded of Dante's circles of hell. The outer layer was formed of grey prefab houses with windows that were either broken, boarded or barred. Fences separating properties were long gone. The gardens of empty houses had been used as opportune rubbish dumps for the good of the local community. Old cars with mismatched panels littered the road.

The inner layer was formed of maisonettes with twelve dwellings per block. Each external wall was a competition in sprayed-on vulgarity and offered more detail on the birds and the bees than the school curriculum. It was a battle the council had fought and lost. Kim didn't need to leave the car to know the putrid smell of the hallways that dispensed more drugs than Boots.

At the centre of the estate three high-rise buildings towered over the rest of the estate, keeping watch. Although refuted by the council, these were the homes of families evicted from other council estates in the area. A trail of years served at Her Majesty's Pleasure would have led back to the Ice Age.

'You know, Guv, if it's true that Tolkien named the dark lands of Mordor after the Black Country, he was surely looking this way.'

Kim didn't disagree. It was the land that hope forgot. She knew – because Hollytree had been home for the first six years of her life.

Bryant parked in front of a row of buildings that had once been shops serving the community. The last one to close had been the newsagents at the end after being robbed at knife-point by two twelve-year-old boys.

The centre building, which previously operated as a chip shop, was opened one morning each week as a drop-in centre.

A group of seven girls in their mid-teens hung around the entrance. They filled the doorway with both their bodies and their attitude. Bryant looked at her and Kim smiled in response.

'Don't hurt 'em too hard, eh, Guv?'

'Course not.'

Bryant held back as Kim stood before the ringleader. Her hair was three different hues of purple and the fresh unlined skin of her face was mottled by metal.

She held out her right hand. 'Entrance fee.'

Kim met her gaze, fighting to contain the smile. 'How much?'

'Hundred?'

Kim shook her head. 'Nah, too much. There's a recession you know.'

The girl smirked and crossed her arms. 'That's why I gorra keep me prices high,'

The cronies sniggered and nudged each other.

'Okay, answer a simple question and you got a deal.'

'I ain't gorra answer no questions 'cos you ain't gerrin in, bitch.'

Kim shrugged and began to turn. 'Fine, I'll just walk away but at least my way you had a chance.'

The hesitation lasted a second. 'Goo on then?'

Kim turned back and looked into a face eager for money.

'Tell me how much I'd have to pay if I asked for a fifteen per cent discount?'

Confusion creased the girl's features. 'I don't fuckin' know the ...'

'See, if you went to school, look how much more you'd be able to extort.' Kim leaned in closer so that their faces were an inch apart. 'Now get out of the way before I drag you by your nose ring.'

Kim kept her voice low and allowed her eyes to do the work.

The girl stared back for a full minute. Kim didn't blink.

'Come on, girls, this bitch ain't worth it,' she said, moving to the left. The posse followed.

Once the doorway was clear, Kim turned. 'Hey, lady; a tenner to watch the car.'

The girl hesitated but a second girl nudged her from behind. 'Deal,' she growled.

Bryant followed her into the shell of a building. Anything of value had been removed, including the ceiling tiles. A seven foot crack travelled from the right hand corner towards the middle of the back wall.

Three men stood in the opposite corner. They all turned. Two looked instantly panicked and headed past them to the door. Career criminals were like bloodhounds and could smell police from the neighbouring county.

'Something we said, boys?' Bryant asked.

One of the boys sucked air through his teeth as a sign of disrespect and Kim shook her head. The feeling was mutual.

The remaining man Kim recognised from the crematorium on the day they chased the body of Mary Andrews.

'Pastor Wilks, I didn't recognise you with your clothes on,' Bryant quipped.

Victor Wilks smiled with barely concealed tolerance to a comment he must have heard many times. Although Bryant was not far wrong.

Dressed in robes, Wilks had been an instant figure of reverence, respect, familiarity. Here, in normal surroundings, he looked ordinary, just an average man. Her initial assessment at the crematorium had put him in his late fifties but without the uniform he dropped ten years. The casual clothing of light jeans and blue sweatshirt accentuated a build that was more muscle than fat.

'May I offer you a drink?' he asked, pointing to a silver urn.

Kim noted the last two fingers on his right hand. They curled underneath like a hook. It was an injury she'd seen before in bare knuckle fighters. Together with his above average height she was guessing he'd boxed at some point in his life.

Kim looked at the urn and nudged Bryant, who responded. 'No thank you, Pastor ... Minister ...'

'Victor, please.'

'What the hell do you do here?' Kim asked. No sane person would enter this place by choice.

He smiled. 'Try to offer hope, Detective. This area is one of the most deprived in the country. I try to show them there is another way. It's easy to be judgmental but there is good in everyone, you just have to look.'

Aha, there it is, she thought as his voice changed to sermon mode.

'What's your success rate?' Kim asked, irritated. 'How many of these souls have you saved?'

'I don't deal in numbers, my dear.'

'Luckily,' she said, wandering around the room.

Bryant began to speak about the investigation. 'We understand that you would visit Crestwood regularly; speak to the girls, conduct short services?'

'That's correct.'

'We also understand that now and again you would cover for William Payne?'

'That is also correct. All of us offered cover for him now and again. His situation is unenviable, I'm sure you'll agree. His commitment to his daughter is admirable. He is eternally grateful for the life of Lucy. He cares for her tirelessly. All the staff did their best to support him.' He thought for a moment then added, 'well, most of the staff.'

Kim completed her circuit of the room and stood beside Bryant. 'Talking of the staff, can you tell us who was there during the time you were involved with Crestwood?'

Victor walked to the urn and Kim couldn't help her surprise that the metal instrument had not yet been robbed for scrap.

He dropped a tea bag into a plastic cup. 'Richard Croft had just been installed in the position of manager. His role seemed to be primarily administrative. I think his brief was to tighten budgets and improve efficiency. He had very little contact with the girls and that was how he liked it. I always felt that he never quite moved in, that he was in a rush to get the job done, meet his targets and move on.'

'What about Teresa Wyatt?'

'Well of course, there was friction between the two of them. Teresa was passed over for the manager's job and so was resentful of Richard's position.'

Wilks tried to stir flavour out of the tea bag. 'Teresa was not a particularly warm woman and she and Richard clashed immediately. They hated each other and everyone knew it.'

All very interesting, Kim thought, but not explanatory of there being two or possibly three dead girls in the ground.

'We believe Teresa had a bit of a temper.'

Victor shrugged but said nothing.

'Did you see any evidence of it?'

'Not personally, no.'

'But someone else did?' Kim pushed.

He hesitated and then opened his hands. 'I don't see what harm it can do now. Teresa spoke to me about an impending complaint against her. I'd heard whispers that there'd been the occasional slap or push when Teresa's frustration got the better of her but this one was different. She'd actually punched the girl so hard in the stomach she coughed up blood.'

Kim felt her foot begin to tap. She placed her hand on her knee to keep it still.

'And that was the complaint?'

He shook his head. 'No, Teresa wasn't as concerned about the assault as she was about what the complainant was going to infer.'

'Which was?'

'That Teresa Wyatt had beaten the girl up for refusing to have sex.'

'And did she?'

Victor looked unsure. 'I don't think so. Teresa was honest with me about the assault. She admitted exactly what she'd done but swore it was not about sex. She knew that such an allegation would destroy her. Such a slur would have stuck to her name like a leech for the rest of her life.'

Kim closed her eyes and shook her head. The secrets just kept on coming.

'Who was the complainant?' Kim asked. She would bet her bike, house, and job that it was one of the three.

'She didn't say, Detective. The conversation we had was for her benefit only. She wanted to talk it out to straighten things in her own mind.'

Of course she did, Kim thought. God forbid Teresa Wyatt would have given any thought to telling the truth.

'What about Tom Curtis?' Bryant asked.

Victor had to think for a moment. 'Oh, you mean the kitchen cook? He was a bit of a quiet one. He didn't really clash with anyone. A bit of a sheep, I suppose you'd call him. Got himself told off a couple of times for being a bit too familiar with the girls.'

'Really?' Kim asked.

'He was mid-twenties, the youngest member of staff, so he could relate to them better. Some thought perhaps too well – but it was only rumour, so I'd rather not comment further.'

'But surely you had an opinion.'

Victor's face hardened as he held up his right hand. 'I will not sully the name of a dead man when I myself saw no evidence of impropriety.'

'Inferring that others did?' Kim pushed.

'Not for me to say and I will not speculate.'

'Understood, Victor,' Bryant soothed. 'Please continue.'

'Mary Andrews was a no-nonsense type of woman who probably gave the girls the majority of attention. She was firm but loving and available too. It wasn't just a job to Mary.'

'And Arthur?'

Victor laughed. 'Oh, Arthur Connop; I'd almost forgotten about him. A rather unfortunate individual, I always felt. I often wondered what must have happened in his life to make him so bitter and hostile. Strange little man, didn't like anyone.'

'Particularly William Payne?' Bryant asked.

Victor scrunched up his nose. 'Oh, I don't think it was anything personal. William is a difficult person to dislike. I think Arthur resented the fact that the rest of the staff did things to help William out now and again. He didn't like anyone getting anything he wasn't.'

'How did he interact with the girls?'

'Who, Arthur? Not at all. He hated every single one of them. Because of his nature he was an easy target. They would play tricks on him, hide his tools, that kind of thing.'

'Did they play tricks on William?'

Victor thought for a moment. Something crossed his face but he shook his head.

'Not really, because William worked the night shift so his contact with the girls was minimal.'

Kim sat forward. There was something he was not telling them.

'What can you tell us about the girls there?'

He sat back. 'They weren't a bad bunch. Some of them were there only temporarily due to some kind of family situation. Some were placed in care following accusations of child abuse. Others stayed until another family member claimed them and a few had no family members at all.'

'Do you remember twin girls; Nicola and Bethany?'

A smile came to his eyes. 'Oh yes. They were beautiful little girls. If I remember correctly, Nicola was the more outgoing of the two. Bethany often hid behind her sister and let her do the talking.

'They didn't mix much with the other girls. I suppose because they had each other.'

'So, there were no problem girls?' Kim asked. It didn't sound like any of the children's homes she'd been in.

'Of course there were tougher girls. Young ladies that could not be reached. There were three girls in particular ... I'm sorry, I don't remember their names. They were bad enough separately but once they came together they became a tight little group. They fed off each other and caused all kinds of trouble; stealing, smoking, boys. He looked away. 'And other things.'

'What other things?' Bryant asked.

'It's not really for me to say.'

'Did they hurt someone?' Kim interjected.

Victor got up and stood at the window. 'Not so much physically, Detective.'

'How then?' she asked, looking towards Bryant.

Victor sighed heavily. 'They were crueller than most, especially together.'

'What did they do?' Kim pushed.

Victor remained at the window. 'One of the girls lived locally and knew of Lucy. One day the three of them offered to play with the child while William ran some errands.

'Being a completely trusting person, William took the opportunity to go to the supermarket. When he returned barely an hour later the girls were nowhere to be found and neither was Lucy.

'He searched the house from top to bottom.'

Victor turned and walked back towards them. 'Do you know where he found her?'

Kim felt her jaw begin to tighten.

'They had stripped her naked and forced her small body into the rubbish bin. She didn't have the muscle strength to get out.' He swallowed. 'She was stuck in there for over an hour, covered in rubbish and food and her own dirty nappies. The poor little girl was only three years old.'

Kim felt the nausea rise within her. However far they tried to stretch the fabric of this case it sprang right back to the doorstep of William and Lucy Payne.

It was time for another chat.

CHAPTER 48

'What the hell is going on here?' Kim cried as the car pulled up outside the Payne house. Both a responder and an ambulance were parked outside. The rear doors to the ambulance were wide open.

As she ran around the vehicles two paramedics exited the property with a stretcher.

The small, fragile figure of Lucy hardly filled the narrow makeshift bed. They carried her as though she were a baby. The atrophy of her limbs was clearer out of the chair. An oxygen mask covered her small face but Kim could see her eyes and the fear that radiated out.

Kim touched her arm lightly but the paramedics were moving with a sense of urgency to place her in the back of the ambulance.

William Payne rushed out of the house. His face had been stripped of colour. His eyes were wide and frightened.

'What happened?' Kim asked.

'She was breathless in the night but she seemed better this morning. I was upstairs changing the beds and she must have had difficulty again but she couldn't make a sound. She couldn't alert me.'

They both stood at the rear of the ambulance as the paramedics fixed the stretcher into position.

William's eyes reddened as he fought back the tears. 'She managed to press the button on the pendant and I heard the sirens in the distance. When I came back down she was turning blue.' He shook his head as the tears began to fall. His voice was hoarse and terrified. 'She might die because I couldn't hear her cry for help.'

Kim opened her mouth to offer him reassurance but one of the paramedics jumped out of the vehicle.

'Sir, we need to ...'

'I have to go. Please excuse ...'

Kim nudged him towards the back of the waiting ambulance.

The doors closed behind him and the ambulance sped away with sirens and lights.

Kim felt an ache in her throat as she watched the vehicle disappear from view.

'Didn't look good, eh, Guv?'

Kim shook her head and crossed the road to the dig site.

She entered the tent of victim number two. Cerys was on her knees in the pit. She turned and smiled.

Kim offered her hand. Cerys removed a latex glove and held onto Kim as she stepped out of the pit.

The hand was warm and soft and coated with the talcum powder from inside the glove.

Cerys stepped to the head of the pit. 'I heard sirens. Everything okay?'

Kim shrugged. There was little point explaining about Lucy. Cerys had no part in that area of the investigation and her own emotional reaction to the young girl did not make sense to Kim herself, never mind trying to explain it to someone else.

'Site one's done, then?' Kim asked. The first grave had been refilled and pieces of grass placed on top. It looked like a bad hair transplant. That tent had been removed but another had been erected.

'Anything up there?'

'Getting close. Readings indicate that the mass is less than two feet down.'

Unlike Cerys who, as a scientist, would not assume it to be a body until she saw bone, Kim already knew in her gut that it was the third girl. Now it was just a case of which one was which.

'This one will be signed off later and filled in this afternoon.'

'Anything further?'

'We have the beads,' she said, moving towards a fold-up trestle table. 'Eleven of them. And this.' Cerys held up a plastic bag.

Kim took it from her and felt the thickness of the fabric.

'I'm guessing flannel,' Cerys offered.

'Pyjamas?'

'Possibly, but only the top.'

'No bottoms?'

Cerys shook her head.

Kim said nothing. The absence of a lower garment put a picture in her head that made her teeth grind together.

'Could have been a different fabric, mismatched nightwear, the material may already have decomposed.'

Kim nodded. She could hope.

'Nothing else?'

Cerys handed her a Tupperware dish full of mud-encrusted fragments.

'Small pieces of metal but nothing that I think is linked to her murder.'

'What next?'

Cerys wiped her hands on her jeans. 'Up to site three, coming?'

Kim followed to the latest tent.

'Just in time, Guv,' Dawson said as she entered.

She looked down at the unmistakeable shape of a foot protruding from the dark earth.

Seven people within the tent stared down into the shallow grave. It didn't matter that it was what most of them had expected to find. Each body deserved a moment of respect, a silent declaration of unity when all parties vowed to do their part in bringing the perpetrator to justice.

Cerys turned to face her. Kim met her gaze. It was haunted but firm.

Her voice was low and thick as she said what everyone else around them was thinking.

'Kim, you have got to find the bastard who did this.'

Kim nodded and exited the tent. She had every intention of doing exactly that.

CHAPTER 49

'Guv, I've got a message,' Bryant said as they exited the tent. 'Doctor Dan has something he wants us to see.'

Kim said nothing as she headed back down the hill. Bryant started the car and headed towards Russells Hall hospital. He knew when to leave her alone.

A rage was building inside her. Regardless of what they'd done, these girls had not deserved to die. That someone had felt their lives were disposable sickened her. She had been one of these girls and they had all deserved a fighting chance.

A poor start in life did not dictate the acts of the future. Kim was a testament to that fact. Her early years had promised a life of crime, drugs, suicide attempts and possibly worse. Every road sign had directed her towards destruction of life, either her own or that of others and yet she had shown two fingers to a pre-determined existence. There was nothing to suggest that her three victims would not have achieved the same.

Bryant stopped the car outside the main entrance of the hospital.

She jumped out and started walking. Bryant caught her up as she reached the bank of lifts.

'Jeez, slow down, Guv. The rugby I can manage. Keeping pace with you is another thing entirely.'

She shook her head. 'Come on, Grandpa, quicken up.'

Kim entered the mortuary. She could see that the bones of victim number two had been laid out on a table beside victim number one.

Although dead, Kim couldn't help the feeling of relief that victim number one was no longer alone amongst the stark clinical coldness of the lab. If they'd been friends in life they were now together again.

Any relief she felt was short-lived as she saw a small collection of bones next to the second victim.

'The baby?' she asked.

Daniel nodded.

No pleasantries or greetings were offered by either of them.

Kim looked closer. The bones were so small they bore no correlation to an actual form, which Kim found all the more sad.

And it was Daniel's job to inspect these bones for clues and pretend they were not the building blocks of a baby. A scientific objectivity was required from them all. There was a need to extract the emotion from the process. But he had to dissect clues from a life that never was. It was not something she could do.

There would be no smart mouth today.

'How old?' she asked

'Bones begin developing at thirteen weeks. At birth a newborn has approximately 300 bones. I'd estimate this mite to be somewhere between twenty and twenty-five weeks.'

Most definitely a person, Kim thought. Both ethically and legally. Abortions were not normally carried out after twelve weeks unless a significant risk existed to the mother.

'Be a double murder, then, Guv; both mother and child?'

Kim nodded. Her hand was drawn to the bones. She wanted to cover them. For what reason she had no idea.

Daniel moved around the table and stood between the two girls. 'Don't know if it's going to help but I have extra background on victim number one. She was around five foot four, her diet was poor and I'd say she was undernourished.'

Bryant took out his notebook.

'Her teeth were not cared for and the lower central incisors crossed over. At some stage two fingers on her left hand had been broken and her right tibia had been fractured. These injuries were not sustained close to death.'

'Childhood abuse?'

'More than likely,' he said, turning away, but not before she'd seen a deep swallow in his throat.

He turned to victim number two. 'I don't have the same level of detail yet on our second victim but I thought there was something you needed to know.'

He moved to the top of the table and gently moved the lower jaw of victim number one. 'Take a close look at the inside of the teeth.'

Kim bent in closer. She could see what Daniel had noted about the lower teeth being crooked but other than having no gums or flesh attached the teeth looked relatively normal.

'Now take a look at victim two.'

Kim turned and bent over the skull of the second female. The teeth were reasonably straight and no trauma seemed to be evident but there was something different in the colour of the overall enamel.

'Has victim one been cleaned?' she asked.

Daniel shook his head. 'Neither has been cleaned.'

Kim's tolerance for guessing games was evaporating quickly. 'Spell it out for me, Doc.'

'The dirt present on the teeth of victim number one would have found its way into the mouth cavity over time once the flesh had decomposed, probably five to six years after death. The dirt on the inside of the teeth of our second victim was there from the day she was put in the ground.'

Kim quickly joined the dots scattered by Daniel. There was only one way that the soil could have become fixed to the inside of the teeth so quickly.

This girl had been buried alive.

CHAPTER 50

Tracy was the first to 'run away', and there were times when I wish she hadn't. The pang of regret I felt afterwards was so surprising and unknown that I struggled to name it.

Retrospective thinking does not come naturally to a psychopath unless a plan goes wrong – and then it is only analytical, not emotional.

The world tipped slightly on its axis as I wrestled this intruder to the ground. Upon submission I understood that the regret came not from what I'd done but that I would not see her again; that I would not watch the swing of her hips as she moved around the room.

That the regret was only in correlation to what was lost to me.

The world righted itself.

Despite this, I knew Tracy was different. There are females that even as young girls stand out. They enter a room and heads turn; eyes rove. It is not to do with beauty but an inner core; a spirit that will not be broken. A resolve that ensures that the owner will achieve whatever they set their mind to.

It is attractive and arousing.

I knew that Tracy's nine-year-old body was sold for thirty-five pounds by her mother, Dina. A week later it was sold for considerably more when Dina understood the market value. Two months later, Dina retired from the business completely.

Tracy was removed by social services two days after her fourteenth birthday. She was brought to Crestwood and placed amongst other abused girls who had been beaten, raped, neglected.

She was not thankful.

She was not a victim and she had wanted to stay exactly where she was.

Having learned the hard way that she could trust no one, Tracy had been hiding earnings from Dina for two years. Tracy didn't complain about life's challenges. She simply turned them to her own advantage.

She told me all about her early life. It reminded me of a factual narration being read from a book. Maybe once or twice her voice faltered but she quickly recovered and moved on.

I listened and I nodded and I offered my support.

And then we had sex. Correction ... I had sex and she struggled. Rape is an ugly word and does not define what took place between us.

Afterwards she stood and looked me in the eye. Her gaze was cold, calculating and at odds with such a young face.

'That is gonna cost you big,' she said.

I had no fear about Tracy telling anyone what had occurred between us. She trusted no one, only herself. She would figure a way to use it against me that would have some benefit to herself.

I admired her youthful optimism and was not surprised when she cornered me a few months later.

'I'm pregnant and it's yours,' she said, triumphantly.

I was amused even as I doubted both parts of her statement. One of the things I liked most about Tracy was her ability to manipulate any situation to her own benefit.

'So?' I asked. We both knew that negotiations had been opened.

'I want money,' she said.

I smiled. Of course she did. The real question was, how much. Past transactions posted a figure in my head. It would be the price of an abortion and a little extra. The normal cost of doing business.

I remained silent, using the most powerful negotiation tool available.

She tipped her head and waited. She knew it too.

'How much?' I asked, indulgently. There was something about this girl.

'Enough.'

I nodded. Of course I would give her enough.

'Is five hundred ...'

'Not even close,' she said, narrowing her eyes.

It had been worth a low opening bid. One never knew. It had worked twice before ...

'What did you have in mind?'

'Five grand or I'm opening my mouth.'

I laughed out loud. That was more than a little extra. 'Abortions don't ...'

'I ain't having a fucking abortion. No way. I want money to get away.' She patted her stomach. 'To start again.'

No way in hell was that going to happen. I am a reasonable person. I knew that if she were to make accusations right now she would not be believed; with a walking DNA match I would never be free. The date stamp of its birth would be a constant threat.

That baby could never be born.

I nodded my understanding. I needed time to think; time to prepare.

Later that night I was ready.

'We really should part with a drink,' I said, pouring a generous measure of vodka into a dribble of Coke.

'You got my money?' she asked, raising the glass.

I nodded and patted my top pocket. 'What are you planning to do?'

'I'm gonna go to London, ger a flat and a job and then goo back to school and get some qualifications.'

She continued to talk and I continued to top up her glass. Twenty minutes later her eyes were hooded and her words were slurred.

'Come with me, I want to show you something.' I offered my hand. She ignored it, stood and fell back down. It took a few moments for her to attempt it again. This time she weaved towards the door like a dog on an agility course. I stepped ahead and opened the back door. The sudden gust of fresh air sent her falling into me. I steadied her but her legs buckled forward and she fell to the ground.

She laughed as she tried to push herself up from the floor. I laughed with her as I grabbed her by the upper arms and marched her across the grass.

Twenty-five paces north west and I dropped her. She fell into the hole on her back. She chuckled again. So did I.

I knelt in the pit beside her, my hands at her throat. The feel of her skin against my palms was arousing, even as she tried to swat my hands away. Her eyes were closed and she writhed beneath me in a semi-conscious state. The move of her hips and the swell of her breasts was hypnotic. And could not be ignored. The flimsy shorts were ripped away with one swift movement and immediately I was inside her.

Her body was pliable in my hands as she drifted in and out of consciousness. She moved as though in a dreamlike state. There was no struggle like the first time.

When I stood her eyes had rolled backwards. I crouched beside her in the limited space and reached for the ripped shorts. They were mine to keep forever. They would help me remember.

My hands once more found her throat. My thumbs hovered above her larynx but they just wouldn't press. Her pretty face still smiled from the stupor.

Frustrated, I jumped out of the hole. The first shovel of dirt landed on her torso. She still didn't open her eyes.

I worked frantically, filling the hole within minutes. This method of disposal was new to me.

I stamped the ground down and re-laid the grass.

For half an hour I stayed with her. I didn't want her to be alone.

I sat beside the grave and cursed her for what she had made me do. If only she hadn't been so greedy. If she'd just accepted the money for the abortion everything would have been okay.

But that baby could never have been born.

CHAPTER 51

Bryant sighed heavily as he popped a mint. It was an immediate reaction to leaving a No Smoking environment.

'Can you think of anything worse than being buried alive?' he asked as they reached the car.

'Yeah, being buried alive with you,' she said, trying to lighten her own mood.

'Thanks for that, Guv, but I mean, can you even imagine it?'

She shook her head. It was a manner of death too horrific to comprehend. She guessed most people would wish to go quietly in their sleep. She had always favoured the idea of a gunshot.

Victim number two would have needed to be unconscious or incapacitated in some way when laid in the hole. She would have regained consciousness surrounded by the dense blackness of the ground. She would have been unable to see or hear or move a muscle. She may have tried to scream, a natural reaction to abject terror. Her mouth would have filled with dirt and every breath she struggled to take would have clogged her nose and throat more. The breath would have slowly left her body as her gulping mouth took in nothing but soil.

Kim closed her eyes and tried to imagine the fear; the sheer panic that must have paralysed the half-dressed fifteen-year-old girl. It was a blackness that Kim could not comprehend.

'How does such evil grow in a man; I mean, where does it start?'

Kim shrugged. 'Edmund Burke called it right when he said, *all that is necessary for the triumph of evil is that good men do nothing.*'

'What you saying, Guv?'

'I'm saying these victims could not have been his first. Rarely is cold-blooded murder the first sign of an evil mind. There had to have been earlier signs that were either excused or ignored.'

Bryant nodded and then turned to her. 'How long do you think it took for her to die?'

'Not long,' Kim said, but her mind added that it would have felt like a lifetime.

'Thank God.'

'You know, Bryant. I can't do this anymore,' she said shaking her head.

'What's that, Guv?'

'I can't keep referring to these victims by number; victim one, victim two. They had enough of that when they were alive. We have three bodies and three names and I need to match them up.'

Kim stared out of the window, a sudden memory shouted up. Her fifteenth birthday had fallen between foster family five and six.

Two days before that, a member of staff had approached her.

'It's Kim's birthday tomorrow and we're having a collection for a present. Do you want to give?' he'd asked her.

She had stared at him for a good long minute to see if he would realise that he'd just asked her to contribute to her own collection. His face had remained blank.

'Where to, Guv?' Bryant asked, approaching the exit of the hospital.

With the information they now had from Daniel Bate, Kim knew there was only one person who could help, regardless of the threat she'd received earlier that day.

'Brindleyplace, I think, Bryant. Time to go and see the twins.'

She focused on the road ahead. 'I have to know their names.'

CHAPTER 52

Nicola Adamson opened the door on the second knock, dressed in satin pyjamas. Her hair was mussed and she offered them a wide yawn for a greeting.

'Sorry if we woke you,' Bryant offered.

There was no 'if' about it, even though it was way past lunchtime.

She yawned again and rubbed at her eyes. 'It was a late night at the club. 'Got in about five this morning – last night, whenever.'

Nicola closed the door and headed straight for the kitchen. Although she herself was only thirty-four, Kim wondered if there'd ever been a time when she'd stepped out of bed looking quite so fantastic.

'I'm happy to talk, guys, but let me get some coffee going first.'

Kim moved aside a handbag and sat on the couch. 'Your sister came to see me this morning.'

Nicola's head snapped around. 'She did what?'

'She wasn't very keen on the idea of you helping us.'

Nicola shook her head and looked away. The jar of instant coffee landed back in the cupboard with a thud.

Kim got the impression that this wasn't the first time Beth had interfered.

'What did she say to you?'

'She instructed me to leave you both alone and not to open up old wounds.'

Nicola nodded and the tension seemed to leave her body.

'She's just looking out for me, I suppose. I know she appears to be harsh but she's just being overprotective.' She shrugged as she sat. 'It's just the way twins are.'

Yes, it is, Kim thought.

'But I'm a big girl and I offered to help so if there's anything you'd like to ask me, go ahead.' She smiled. 'Especially now I have coffee.'

'Your sister recently hurt her leg?' Kim asked, wondering if it held any clues to the woman's bitterness.

'No, it's an injury from childhood. She had a bad fall after climbing an apple tree when we were eight years old. The bones of her knee were shattered. Eventually, they mended but in cold weather the injury pains her. Now, what can I help you with?'

Bryant took out his notebook. 'We have more information on our victims and thought maybe you could help us with identification.'

'Of course, if I can.'

'Our first victim was probably the tallest. Most likely thin and her bottom teeth were crooked ...'

'Melanie Harris,' Nicola said with certainty.

'You're sure?'

Nicola nodded. 'Oh yes. She suffered a lot because of those teeth. She took a lot of abuse from girls at school until she joined up with the other two. Nobody bullied her after that. She always looked a little odd beside the other two, being so much taller, like a minder.' Nicola sobered. 'We were told she had run away.'

Kim and Bryant said nothing.

Nicola's head moved from side to side. 'Who would have wanted to hurt Melanie?'

'That's what we're trying to find out.'

'There's a second victim, Nicola,' Kim said, quietly. 'And this one was pregnant.'

Nicola leaned across the table and reached for the handbag Kim had moved. She took out a box of cigarettes and a disposable lighter. Kim had seen no evidence of a smoking habit when they'd visited the previous day.

She placed a cigarette in her mouth but her thumb fumbled with the lighter. She got it on the third attempt.

'Tracy Morgan,' Nicola whispered.

Kim looked at Bryant who raised his eyebrows.

'You're sure?'

'Yes, I'm sure. It's not something I'm particularly proud of but as a youngster I was pretty nosey. My school report always went along the lines of "Nicola would do well if she minded her own business as well as she minds other peoples'".'

Bryant chuckled. 'Yeah, I've got one at home just like that.'

Nicola shrugged. 'Well, I used to sneak around and listen at doorways. I remember hearing Tracy telling the other two she was "up the duff" as she put it.'

'Any idea who she was seeing?' Kim asked. It could be another lead.

'No, I heard her say she was going to speak to the father but I didn't hang around for too long in case they caught me.'

Nicola drew on the cigarette as realisation dawned. 'There's a third, isn't there?'

They said nothing and allowed her a minute to digest the news.

'Is there anything you can tell us about the ...'

'Louise was the other one. I don't recall her last name but she was the ringleader; the toughest. No one messed with Louise. Even after the other two had run away –sorry, after the other two had *gone* – no one dared mess with her.' She paused for a second. 'You know, now I think about it, she was insistent that her mates would not have run away.'

'Is there anything about Louise that would help us confirm an identification?'

Nicola stubbed out the cigarette in a cut glass ashtray. 'Oh yes. Louise had a denture. Three of her teeth were knocked out in a fight with girls from another school. She hated how she looked without it. One of the other girls at Crestwood hid it one night for a laugh. Louise broke her nose.'

'Do you know anything about an incident involving the daughter of William Payne?'

Nicola frowned. 'Oh, you mean the night guy?' She shook her head. 'We never saw him very much. I never heard of anything in particular but I remember them being on lockdown for a month for something. But they were always up to mischief of some kind. Still ... they didn't deserve this.'

Bryant flipped a page in his notebook. 'Do you recall much about Tom Curtis?'

Nicola narrowed her eyes. 'He was younger than the other staff members. He seemed a bit shy and quite a few of the girls had a crush on him.' Nicola's hand flew to her mouth. 'Oh no, you don't think he could have been the father of ...' Her words trailed away as though she couldn't even finish the thought.

The idea had crossed Kim's mind but she chose not to respond.

Kim didn't feel that Nicola could offer anything further at this point.

She stood. 'Thank you for your time, Nicola. Please don't share this information with anyone until the victims have been formally identified.'

'Of course.'

Kim headed to the door and turned. 'Which one went first?'

'Sorry.'

'Who disappeared first, Melanie or Tracy?' Kim asked. Nicola had already told them that Louise was the last.

Nicola scrunched her face in thought. 'Tracy went first because Melanie and Louise thought she'd just disappeared because of the pregnancy.'

Kim nodded and was halfway out the door.

'Detective ...'

Kim turned.

'Regardless of what my sister said to you, I'm more than happy to help in any way I can.'

Kim nodded her thanks and left.

'Where to, Guv?' Bryant asked.

Kim's watch said it was after three o'clock. 'Head back to the station.'

She took out her phone and called Dawson.

'Hey, Guv,' he answered.

'What's the situation on site, Kev?'

'Second grave is being filled in and Cerys has the third body half uncovered. Doctor Bate is on his way. Because she's not as far down they're hoping to have her out by tonight.'

Kim was aware how hard she'd been working her team. 'Once the Doc gets there, stand down for the day. There won't be anything that we can't get first thing in the morning.'

'Guv, I'd rather stay, if that's okay.'

Dawson not taking time off when offered was a first.

'Kev, you okay?'

Attuned to his voice, she caught the sudden thickness.

'Guv, I've watched the bodies of two young girls being removed from this ground so far and if it's okay with you I'd prefer to see it through.'

And sometimes he just shocked her.

'Okay, Kev. I'll give you a call later.'

She hung up and shook her head.

'Are you really that surprised?' Bryan asked.

'No. He's a good kid, if lacking in judgement now and again.'

'And I'd want him on my team any day of the week,' Bryant concluded.

The two of them did not often sing from the same hymn sheet but Bryant could be objective when he needed to be.

Kim got out of the car and Bryant locked it.

'Go check in with Stacey. Put those names on the board.'

She wanted their anonymity erased as soon as possible. 'And then get yourself off home.'

Kim headed towards the bike and paused as she unlocked the helmet.

Something at Nicola's had been wrong. There was something gnawing at her gut, something she should have picked up on.

It was as though her eyes had seen something that her brain hadn't registered.

CHAPTER 53

For the second time in one day Kim saw the main entrance of Russells Hall hospital. She pulled the bike onto the pavement area and took her chances on getting a ticket.

Entering the hospital, she walked through a mixed group of patients and visitors puffing away beneath the 'No Smoking' sign.

She approached the reception desk on her left. A woman, badged as Brenda, smiled up at her.

'Lucy Payne, admitted earlier today?'

'Are you a relative?'

Kim nodded. 'Cousin.'

Brenda hit a few keys on the computer. 'C5, Medical ward.'

Kim headed past the café and checked the directory board. She took a lift to the second floor and headed along the west wing, moving aside for a bed being wheeled back from the operating theatre.

Kim stepped into the ward behind the bed. The area had a gentle buzz of machines and low voices. The prescription trolley crossed from one six bay ward to another.

Kim could see she had just caught the back end of visiting time. Relatives sat in silence having said everything they could think of and now just waited for the clock to hit the hour.

She approached the nurse's station. 'Lucy Payne?'

'Side ward, second door along.'

Kim passed the first door which was a tiny kitchen. She reached the second door and her hand was poised to knock. She caught it just before it made contact with the wood.

Lucy was sleeping peacefully in the huge bed, her head supported by five pillows. A monitor was clipped to her right index finger. A machine beeped rhythmically to her right.

Atop the tall beside cabinet sat a single 'Get Well Soon' card and a stuffed grey teddy bear.

Kim entered the room and stepped past William Payne who snored lightly from the easy chair in the corner.

She stood beside the bed and looked down at the sleeping figure. Lucy looked much younger than her fifteen years.

And yet she had suffered so much. This girl had not asked for this cruel disease that had slowly stolen her strength and mobility and she had not asked for a mother who would abandon her. And she certainly had not asked to be stuffed into a bin by three stupid girls.

Today Lucy had almost died. She had tried to scream and all that had emerged was silence.

Despite the life she led this brave, determined girl had fought back. She had clawed her way up from the brink because, quite simply, she wanted to live. That she had managed to press the emergency button on the pendant was a testament to the fact.

Kim also had not been given high survival odds when she was carried from the high-rise flat on Hollytree. Silent head shakes and deep sighs had accompanied her all the way to the hospital where she was intravenously fed with no real expectation of success. Her six-year-old body weighed a stone and a half. Her hair was falling out in clumps and she was unable to speak. But on day three, she'd sat up.

Kim took a tissue and wiped a thin line of drool from Lucy's chin.

Finally, she understood her affinity with this young girl who she had known only for a few days. Lucy was a fighter. She would not give in to the cards that fate had dealt her. Every day she struggled to live against odds that were not in her favour.

Earlier that day she could have chosen not to press the emergency button. She could have submitted to her illness and chosen the path of eventual peace but she had not and only one thing had stopped her. Hope.

Could this young lady receive a better quality of life than she had now, Kim wondered. Could her existence be made safer and more enjoyable? Kim had no idea, but what she did know was that this tiny slip of a girl had a core of strength and determination that she herself was compelled to admire.

As Kim placed the tissue on the side cupboard she became attuned to a change behind her as the gentle snoring stopped.

She didn't turn. 'You know that we have to talk?' she asked softly.

'Yes, Detective, I know,' William replied, thickly.

Kim nodded and left the room. It was time to go home. She had work to do.

CHAPTER 54

Beth leafed through a magazine. She had no idea what it was but she was making a point.

She could feel Nicola's anxiety. They had not spoken since Beth had returned. She knew her sister. Nicola wanted to ask her what was wrong but was scared of the answer. The truth was, she couldn't cope with the answer.

Nicola had always hated it when people were angry with her. She was a people pleaser. She wanted everyone to be happy. And that trait had cost her. It had cost them both.

And her eagerness to please was going to cost them again.

Beth was so angry she could not raise her head. She stared down at the page. Nicola would not be able to hold her tongue for much longer. Beth turned a page nonchalantly.

'Myra spoke to me yesterday,' Nicola offered. 'She said you were very rude to her.'

'I was,' Beth said. If her sister chose to talk to her about inconsequential matters rather than address the real problems between them, that was fine with her. Nicola would break eventually.

'Why do you have to be so mean? The woman has done nothing to you.'

Beth shrugged. 'She's a nosey old cow who wants to get in everybody's business. Why do yer care what she thinks?'

'Because she's my neighbour and I have to live here.' Nicola paused. 'Did you tell her I was adding you to the lease?'

Beth smiled to herself. That little nugget must have kept the bitch awake for hours.

'Yeah, that was me.'

'Are you trying to make my life difficult while you're here?'

'Yer know, Nic. I asked yer to do something and yer ignored me. Yer asked me to be nice to the old hag and I ignored yer. What's the difference?'

'For goodness sake, Beth, I know you're angry with me. Will you just tell me why?'

Beth smiled inside. She knew her sister so well. She always had.

She turned another page. 'Which reason do yer want?'

'Any reason you'll give me. Anything that will stop this silent treatment. You know I hate it when you're angry with me.'

Oh yes, Beth knew very well.

'I told yer not to talk to her.'

'To who?' Nicola asked. The question in her voice was forced. Nicola knew well and good who she was talking about.

She turned another page, knowing it would frustrate her sister even further. Nicola wanted her full attention. She hated that Beth could still sit and focus on something else instead of being completely consumed by the atmosphere between them. As she was.

'You mean the detective?' Nicola asked.

'Uh-huh.'

'Jesus, Beth, how can you be so cold? They're finding bodies buried where we used to live.'

'And?'

'We knew these girls. We spoke to them, we ate with them. How can you not even care?'

"Cos they ain't nothing to me. I didn't even like 'em, so why should I care now?'

'Because they're dead and whatever they did wrong, they didn't deserve to die. Some monster just put them in the ground and forgot about them. I have to try and help.'

'You're more bothered about them than yer are about me.'

'What are you talking about?'

This time the confusion was real. And there it was. They could never move on until Nicola admitted what she'd done.

'Yer knew what they did to me and yer did fuck all about it.'

'Beth, I don't know who did what to you. Tell me.'

She flicked another page of the magazine and shook her head. 'Ask the detective, maybe she'll tell yer what yer did 'cos you're hell bent on gerring yerself involved.'

'Only because I know it is somehow connected to us.'

Beth's hand stilled in mid-air. The page fell from her grip. That her sister had made that connection was progress in itself. She wanted Nicola to remember. She wanted an apology. She wanted to hear the words she'd waited ten years for.

But not quite yet.

'I'm telling yer, Nic, leave it alone.'

'But I want it all out in the open.' Beth heard the emotion in her sister's voice. She didn't look. She couldn't look.

'Beth, I wish I knew what I'd done to hurt you. How I failed you so terribly. You're my sister. There are too many secrets between us. I love you and I just want to know the truth.'

Beth threw the magazine to the side and stood.

'Nic, be careful what yer wish for ... 'cos yer might just ger it.'

CHAPTER 55

Kim had called a late briefing. The intensity of this case was getting to them all. The least she could do was offer her team an extra hour or two of sleep.

By the time she'd finished updating Woody on current events, Bryant, Stacey and Dawson were at their desks.

'Morning folks, I'm sure you're all aware, but media interest in our case has escalated. The erection of a third tent has provoked a frenzy. It's now front page on every newspaper and there was a talking heads segment on Sky News last night.'

'Yeah, saw it, Guv,' Bryant groaned.

'I'm sure I don't need to remind you that there is no talking to any members of the press, however persuasive. This case is way too volatile to be derailed by a misquoted comment from any of us.'

Kim included herself in that statement. She knew her own limitations when being goaded by the press, which was why she'd wisely been kept away from them.

'And if any of you need a reminder of how shit we're doing, feel free to pop to Woody's office and read any one of the articles.'

Her boss's desk was like a newsagents and during their earlier meeting he'd talked her through every piece.

'Seriously, Guv?' Dawson asked.

Kim nodded. It was best they knew they were under attack. 'Come on, Kev, you know how this works. By day three it's always our fault and we've managed to get to the fifth day since discovering the first set of bones, so I'd say we're doing pretty well.'

Kim felt the wave of negativity breeze through the room.

Kim sighed. 'If media attention is that important to you all you should have chosen a career in showbiz. We're police officers. Nobody likes us.'

'It's a bit soul destroying, though, Guv. Knocks your enthusiasm a bit,' Stacey said.

Kim realised that pep talks were not her forte.

'All of you, look at that wall and I mean look at it hard.'

The whiteboard was much easier on her eye now her girls had names. The board had been divided into three columns:

Victim 1 - Melanie Harris
    Age - 15
    Taller than average, undernourished, tooth defect, butterfly sock
    Decapitated

Victim 2 - Tracy Morgan
    Age - 15
    Pregnant, Pyjama bottoms missing
    Buried alive

Victim 3 - Louise Dunston - ?
    Age - 15
    Denture for top three teeth

'Those three girls lost their lives to a monster. Between them they were raped, beaten, suffocated and buried. This was not a story in a newspaper to them. It was their lives; their reality. We get out of bed every day to find the person who thought they could get away with this crime.

'A few days ago these kids were anonymous, forgotten and silent. But not anymore. Melanie, Tracy and Louise will now have a voice because of us. And make no mistake, we *will* catch the bastard that did this.' Kim paused and looked around the room. 'And if you need any more motivation than that, then you're in the wrong job.'

'Thanks, Guv,' Bryant said, with a nod.

'On board,' Stacey added with a smile.

'Oh yeah,' Dawson chimed.

She took her usual position on the edge of the spare desk. 'Okay, Kev, site progress?'

'Doctor Dan removed the body about two this morning. Cerys did an initial inspection of the grave but they're gonna do the sieving this morning.'

'Did the Doc say anything about a denture?'

'Didn't say much about anything. He's a very strange character, Guv.'

'Mention it to Cerys. Might still be in the grave.'

'Stace, anything?'

'I've now got the mobile phone of Tom Curtis. He 'ad more than fifty missed calls in the two hours before 'is death.'

Kim leaned forward. 'Go on.'

'All came from Croft's mobile.'

'Jesus Christ,' Kim seethed. 'Anything else.'

'The tape from the old folks' home is useless so we ain't got nothing incriminating on the death of Mary Andrews.'

'Anything from SOCO on Arthur Connop?'

'Paint chip analysis says it came from an Audi TT on a five nine plate.'

'Anything else?'

'Yeah, the actual records of Crestwood from the council are shite. I'm still monitoring Facebook unofficially and ringing round ex-residents officially. Some of the registered runaways were actually there that night and some on the list had left weeks before.'

Hmm ... Kim thought. Either gross inefficiency on the side of the council or a deliberate attempt to confuse the final record of occupancy. At this point, either option was a possibility.

Although Kim wasn't totally comfortable with Stacey's presence in the Facebook group it appeared to be bearing more useful information than official records.

'Stace, ask some questions about Tom Curtis. Find out how close he was to the girls. I'd like to know if there were any rumours about inappropriate behaviour.'

'Will do, Guv.'

'Okay, Kev, get back to site and Bryant, I think you and I should pay Councillor Croft another visit.'

'Umm ... Guv, there's one more thing,' Stacey said.

'Go on,' Kim said, reaching for her jacket.

'I got three addresses. Last knowns for each of our girls.'

Kim exchanged a look with Bryant. It was the least favourite job of any detective. Whatever the circumstances of them being placed into care, Kim felt sure there were existing family members who would be deeply affected by the discoveries of their deaths.

Bryant took the list as he walked past Stacey's desk.

First they would check on the living and then do the work of the dead.

CHAPTER 56

Kim nodded towards the squad car parked outside the gate. Although West Midlands Police wouldn't authorise a twenty-four-hour watch of Richard Croft, squad cars had been advised to carry out periodic checks via the intercom when in the area.

Bryant pressed the speaker button and waited for the gate to open. He waited ten seconds and pressed it again.

They looked at each other. On their last visit the response had been immediate.

'Keep pressing,' Kim said, getting out of the car.

She walked back to the squad car. The officer wound down the window.

'How long since you checked?'

'About twenty minutes. Said he was going to work from home this morning and go to the office later. A car came out a few minutes later. The nanny, I think.'

Kim jogged back to Bryant. Richard Croft had been in the house alone for at least twenty minutes. 'Anything?'

He shook his head.

'Okay, we're going in.'

She stood for a second and planned her route over the gate. It was cast of wrought iron forged ornately of flowers, swirls and leaves. Her eyes picked out a trail for her feet close to the wall on the left hand side. She used both hands to rock the gate. It was steady.

Kim remembered Keith telling her that years ago one of the local furnacemen got caught in his wheelbarrow while tipping a load of scrap iron into the furnace and went in with it. The local vicar was called in to say prayers over the molten liquid as it was poured into moulds. She remembered thinking that she hoped he'd been made into something nice.

Sorry, mate, she thought as she began her ascent. She cocked her right leg over spikes one foot high that adorned the top of the gate.

'Not a chance,' Bryant said, from below.

'Come on, you big girl,' Kim said.

'I bloody will be if I try that manoeuvre.'

As Kim descended the eight feet on the other side she thought that with any luck Richard Croft was listening to music too far away from the intercom to hear it. Or that the hi-tech entry system was broken and he was on his way down the drive to let them in. She preferred mildly annoyed to dead.

She ran up the drive, her legs noticing an incline that had not been evident in the car. As she approached the property she saw no signs of activity.

Simultaneously she banged on the door and rang the bell. She stepped back to see where the CCTV cameras were pointed. One was aimed at the front gate and the other at the damn cars. Nothing covered the rear of the house.

'Keep knocking,' she instructed Bryant who had caught up with her and appeared to be intact.

She ran around the side of the house and stumbled over a shovel that had been leaning against the wall.

She felt the crunch underfoot before she saw the broken glass panel.

She screamed Bryant's name at the top of her voice. He appeared from the other side.

The entrance door to the orangery that ran the length of the house had been smashed.

She almost stepped into the house but paused before she put her foot down.

'Follow me,' she said, running back to the front of the property. En route she grabbed the shovel over which she'd stumbled.

She handed it to Bryant. 'Break that window. I don't want that back door contaminated before SOCO gets here.'

Bryant stood as far back as he could and swung the shovel. The panel crashed through on impact.

Kim picked up a brick to smash the jagged edge pieces to make the opening safe to enter.

She stood on the terracotta planter and leaned on Bryant's shoulder for support. Her foot found a solid object beneath the window. She put her weight on it and it held. Only when she was inside did she see that it was an antique writing bureau and that she'd entered through the study.

Once on solid ground, she held out her hand to steady Bryant as he followed her through. The heavy oak door led them into the foyer. She turned left as Bryant headed up the stairs. The next room she entered was the lounge which she recognised from their last visit. She surveyed it quickly.

'Lounge, clear,' she called as she once again entered the foyer. She heard Bryant's call that the master bedroom was clear.

She entered the door to the library and stopped dead.

Lying prostate in the middle of the rug was the figure of Richard Croft, an eight inch kitchen knife stuck in his back.

Kim called Bryant and then knelt down, careful not to touch anything. The pool of blood had soaked into the carpet either side of him.

Bryant appeared beside her. 'Bloody hell.'

Kim put two fingers to his neck. 'He's still alive.'

Bryant took out his mobile phone and called for an ambulance.

Kim went searching for the intercom receiver and found it mounted to the wall beside an oversize Smeg freezer.

She pressed the release button and watched the monitor as the wrought iron gate began to move across.

She noted that the house alarm was not set. Kim marvelled at how people used intruder alarms for the protection of possessions when absent from the home. But not the preservation of life when old colleagues were dying at an unnatural rate.

She shook her head, ran to the front door and threw it open.

The paramedics now had access straight into the building.

She jogged around the side of the house and stopped six feet away from the point of entry. She turned and surveyed the rear garden. On first inspection she could see no obvious points of vulnerability. The back of the property was enclosed not by a wall, but a six-foot-high fence. Decorative trellis increased that height another foot and a half. All of the panels appeared intact.

'Okay, you bastard, if you didn't come over it you must have come through.'

Starting at the top panel, Kim walked the left hand side, pushing on each fence panel in turn. The posts were wooden but sturdy and all the panels down the left were uncluttered with shrubs. A low level herb garden ran alongside it. An intruder attempting entry through any of the side panels would have been immediately exposed to anyone at the rear of the house.

Kim studied the row of fencing that bordered the bottom of the property. Every ten feet was a conifer tree that rose fifteen feet into the air. Most of the trees stood centre panel; except the fourth tree along.

Its three feet width hid a fence panel and post. She strode 100 feet to the bottom of the garden and used her index finger to push the panel lightly. It moved under her touch and Kim saw that the fence panel was no longer attached to the post.

Kim heard footsteps running around the side of the house.

'Marm?' an officer called out.

She stepped out from behind the tree, demonstrating the cleverness of the entry point and possible hiding place.

'What can I do, Marm?'

'Guard that back door. Don't let anyone near it.'

He nodded and stood before the door, facing outwards.

Kim went back behind the conifer and pushed the fence again. It moved easily and offered a gap that was easy enough to slip through.

'Damn it,' she said. This bastard was clever. She stepped away and moved back into the garden to ensure she did nothing further to impede any evidence collection.

She climbed up on the swing set as she heard sirens speed up the drive and stop at the front door.

She looked over the fence to see that the ground on the other side formed a steep bank that led down into the back end of a trading estate. Beyond that was a housing estate that was a warren of streets, gulleys and dead ends.

A bit like this bloody case, Kim thought as she got back down to the ground.

Kim slowly walked the line from the broken fence panel to the rear door looking to the left and the right.

She came to a stop four feet away from the police officer.

'How are you doing, today, Marm?'

Kim opened her mouth to ask him how the hell he thought she was doing when she recognised him as the constable Bryant had spoken to the other day. And he was doing exactly what he'd been told to do, which was engage her in conversation.

Kim rolled her eyes, shook her head and headed to the front of the building. Bryant stood out front watching as the rear doors of the ambulance closed.

'Well?'

'Still breathing, Guv. The knife's still in him. Paramedics don't want to remove it until they get a look at what its holding together. Perversely, it might be the intended murder weapon that's currently keeping him alive.'

'Oh, the irony,' she said, sitting on the stone steps.

'And here comes the help,' Bryant said as a Vauxhall Corsa came to a screeching halt on the gravel. The woman they knew to be Marta got out of the car. Her face was devoid of colour.

'What ... what ...'

Kim remained sitting but Bryant moved towards the young girl.

'Mr Croft has been seriously injured. You need to contact his wife and advise her to get to the hospital as quickly as possible.'

She nodded and stumbled inside.

Two more squad cars squealed into the drive, followed by the SOCO van.

'I dunno,' Bryant said, as Kim got to her feet, 'coppers are like buses. One minute there's none and then ...'

'Sergeant Dodds,' said a burly officer with his hands inside his stab vest. Bryant took him to the side to explain the scene while Kim grabbed the first SOCO officer that got out of the van.

'Follow me,' she said, without introduction. She travelled around the side of the house and took the tall blond male to the bottom of the garden. She pointed behind the tree.

'Broken fence panel is the perimeter breach.' She pointed to the back door. 'That's the point of entry.'

'Got it, Marm.'

She walked back to the front of the house to be greeted by Marta holding out a mobile phone.

'Mrs Croft would like to speak to you.'

Kim took the phone. 'Yes.'

'Detective Inspector, I understand from Marta that there is considerable damage to my home.'

'Not as much as there is to your husband.'

'I'd like a further explanation as to what you are doing at my property. I specifically requested you were to be removed ...'

'Russells Hall, if you're interested,' Kim said and switched off the phone.

She handed it back to Marta as Bryant exited the property.

'Ready?' he asked.

She nodded and they headed back to the car at the end of the drive.

'You building bridges with Mrs Croft, eh, Guv?'

'Oh, we're just growing closer and closer all the time,' Kim said dourly.

'Where to now, Guv?'

'Hollytree Estate,' Kim said quietly. It was a task that could no longer be avoided. 'We're about to ruin one family's day.'

CHAPTER 57

Bryant wound the car through the maze of small streets to the triangle of high-rise buildings at the centre. The estate comprised a total of 540 dwellings with two key gangs responsible for instilling the required level of fear into the residents.

The 'Deltas' were a group of young men who hailed from the Dudley postcode. The 'Bee Boys' were from two streets over, where the Sandwell postcode began.

Bryant parked the car next to the playground. Although the area held a swing set, a see-saw and a few benches, the park had not seen a child in decades. It was known as 'The Pit' and it was where representatives from each group met and settled 'business'. To Kim's knowledge three bodies had been found in The Pit in the last two years and there had been no witness to any one of them.

By Kim's count, almost seventy properties had a direct view of the area and still no one saw a thing.

Their access into Swallow Court was unfettered. Police presence, although unwanted, was not restricted. The community was closed off from the outside world and crimes that took place within the enclave were resolved in the enclave. Gang leaders were safe in the knowledge that any ordinary citizens would never speak openly to police.

'Oh Lordy,' Bryant offered, placing a hand over his nose. Kim had taken a good deep breath before entering the middle block. The foyer was dark and smelled of urine. The area was small and windowless. Two blown bulbs had not been replaced and the only source of illumination was one square ceiling grid shielding a yellowed strip light.

'What floor?' Kim asked.

'Seven. Stairs?'

Kim nodded and headed to the foot of the stairwell. The lifts in these blocks were notoriously faulty and if they got stuck between floors it was unlikely anyone was coming to help.

Knackered or left for dead? It was an easy choice.

By the third floor Bryant had counted seven syringes, three broken beer bottles and two used condoms.

'Now, who said romance is dead?' he asked as they entered the lobby on the seventh floor. 'Right there, Guv,' Bryant said, pointing to flat 28C.

A fist mark was evident in the middle of a door that was opened by a girl Kim guessed to be three or four. She didn't smile or speak and sucked juice from a baby bottle.

'Rhianna, ger away from the fucking door,' called a female voice.

Bryant stepped forward, moving the child out of his way. Kim stepped around her and closed the door.

'Excuse me,' Bryant called as they stood in the dingy corridor. 'Police ... can we ...'

'What the hell ...' they heard amidst a commotion of activity.

'Already smelled it,' Kim called, walking past Bryant into the lounge. The curtains were closed but didn't quite meet in the middle.

A girl with hoop earrings and a pasty expression stood and wafted the air with her hands. The atmosphere was thick with the smell of weed.

'What the fuck yer doin in 'ere? Yo 'ain't got no right ...'

'Rhianna invited us in,' Kim said, almost tripping over a rocker holding a newborn. 'We're here to see Brian Harris.'

'It's me dad. He's abed.'

It was after eleven thirty.

'So, you're Melanie's sister?' Bryant asked.

'Who?' she asked, with a sneer.

Kim heard a door open down the corridor. A half-dressed male headed towards them, raging. 'What the fuckin' hell yo doin?'

'Mr Harris,' Bryant said, affably, standing in front of her. He held up his warrant card and introduced them both. 'We're just here to talk to you about Melanie.'

He stopped short and frowned.

Kim was beginning to think they were at the wrong address. But Melanie had clearly inherited her height from her father. He stood over six feet tall. Every one of his ribs was evident and the waistband of his jeans rested around his skinny hips. His scrawny arms were busy with DIY tattoos.

'What's the little bitch done now?' he said, looking over the back of the sofa. Kim followed his gaze. A dark brown Staffordshire bull terrier lay panting in a cage meant for a large Yorkie. Its teats were distended and red. A cardboard box next to the cage held four puppies snuggled close together. Kim couldn't tell if the eyes on the puppies were yet open but they'd been removed from the bitch for a reason.

A puppy separated from its mother too soon would suffer behavioural problems later on; problems that could be exploited as a status symbol for The Deltas.

Kim looked into the eyes of the older dog who would be bred again at the earliest opportunity.

She looked at Bryant whose gaze also rested on the dogs. They exchanged a glance.

'Whatever that girl's done is fuck all to do with me. I gid 'er away years ago.'

The baby beneath them started to cry.

The female sat down and placed her right foot on the back of the rocker. She took out a iPhone and began texting with one hand.

Brian Harris sat beside his daughter. He nudged her, hard.

'Put kettle on, Tina.'

'Do it yerself, yer lazy bastard.'

'Do it or sling yer hook and tek yer damn kids with yer.'

Tina offered him a filthy look but headed into the kitchen. Rhianna followed closely behind.

Harris leaned forward and lit a cigarette, blowing smoke all over the baby's head.

Bryant forced calm into his voice as he took a seat on the sofa opposite. Kim remained standing.

'Can you tell us the last time you saw your daughter, Mr Harris?'

He shrugged. 'Couldn't say exactly. She was a kid.'

'How old was she when you gave her away?' Kim asked.

Brian Harris showed no emotion at the dig. 'I cor remember, it's been a while.'

'Was she a troubled child?'

'Nah, she just ate a lot. Gutsy little cow,' he said, smiling at his own humour.

Neither Bryant nor she said a word.

'Look, I had two kids to tek care of when their slag of a mother walked out and I did the best I could.'

He shrugged as though his 'Father of the Year' title was just around the corner.

'So, she was just the unlucky one?' Kim asked.

He scrunched up his face showing a row of yellowed teeth. 'She was a funny looking kid. All legs and no meat. She weren't no oil painting.'

Bryant sat forward. 'Did you visit her at all once she'd been placed into care?'

He shook his head. 'Woulda just made it harder for 'er. Had to make a clean break. Don't even know where they shoved her. It mighta bin that place being dug up,' he said, drawing on his cigarette.

'And you didn't think to contact police to see if one of the victims at Crestwood might be your daughter?' Kim asked, exasperated. One shred of emotion would have restored her faith in mankind.

He sat forward. 'Is Melanie one of the dead 'uns?'

Finally, Kim thought, a flicker of interest in the wellbeing of the daughter he abandoned fifteen years ago.

His expression turned to a frown. 'It ain't gonna cost me anything, is it?'

Kim clenched her hands deep into her pockets. There were times she wished she could lock them in there for her own sake.

Tina returned and handed her father a steaming drink. With the look on her face Kim wouldn't trust anything in that mug.

'Mr Harris, we are sorry to inform you that pending a formal identification we do suspect that Melanie is one of the girls recently discovered.'

Brian Harris attempted to look solemn but the selfishness in his eyes won through. 'See, I gid her up years agoo so it ain't really nothing to do with me.'

Kim watched as Rhianna walked around the sofa to the cage. She put her fingers through the bars and began pulling on the jowl of the dog, who had nowhere to go. Kim moved sideways and nudged the child away with her right foot. The child moved towards the puppy box but Kim was saved from acting.

'Tina, get her away from there.'

Tina growled again and stood. She reached for her daughter's hand and led her to the bedroom. With the child out of the room, Kim could bear it no longer. She couldn't use her fists but she had other tools available.

'Mr Harris, I'd like to leave you with a picture in your head. A final memory, if you like. Your fifteen-year-old daughter was murdered horrifically. The bones in her foot were smashed so that she couldn't run away while some sick bastard chopped off her head. She struggled and cried and possibly screamed out for you while the bastard hacked her into bits.' Kim leaned down into the face of the disgusting excuse for a father. 'And that information didn't cost you a damn penny.'

She looked to Bryant. 'We're done.'

She stepped past him and headed to the door. Bryant followed but hesitated before closing the door behind them. 'Wait here, I just wanna ask him one more thing.'

While she waited, Kim realised that hadn't exactly been textbook practice for informing the family of the death of a loved one. But if she had detected just one ounce of love or attachment, even regret, she would have stuck to the rule-book. She decided that the other families would be notified by someone else. She didn't trust herself to remain calm if she were faced with such familial indifference again.

The door to the flat opened again and Kim looked on in shock as her colleague exited the property.

'Bryant, you really have got to be kidding me.'

CHAPTER 58

'Here, you carry the puppies and I'll grab the mother.'

Bryant thrust the box into her arms. The four puppies started moving around and Kim could see that their eyes were open. Just.

'How the hell ...'

'Told him I'd be prepared to overlook the level of criminal activity in his residence on this occasion if he gave me the dogs.' Bryant followed her down the staircase. 'But I never said anything about social services.'

Kim hurried down the rest of the stairs and paused at the car. 'Erm ... what now Doctor Doolittle?'

He placed the bitch onto the back seat of the car and the box right beside her. 'You drive.'

'To where?' she asked, getting in the car.

'Come on, Guv, you know where I live.'

'Jesus,' she exclaimed, putting the car into gear. She negotiated her way out of the estate and then managed to take a quick look behind. The bitch was peering over the top of the box. One of the puppies was straining to reach her nose.

'Don't you ever call me impulsive again, Bryant. What is your missus gonna say about this?'

He shrugged. 'Tell me what choice I had.'

Kim said nothing. Much as they wished to, they knew they were incapable of saving the whole world – but sometimes you just had to deal with what was right in front of you.

Kim paused at a set of lights.

'Guv, look,' Bryant said.

Kim took another look behind. The bitch was licking at the puppy it could reach. The others were trying to claw at the side of the box.

Five minutes later, she pulled up outside his three-bed semi in Romsley.

He stepped out of the car. 'Okay, if you get hold of ...'

'No chance,' Kim said. 'You're on your own with this one.'

'Chicken,' he said.

'Damn right.'

Bryant grabbed the lead of the adult dog. She jumped out of the car of her own accord and stood still. Bryant put the box under his left arm and headed to his front door.

Kim said a silent prayer. Having seen Bryant's missus in a bad mood she feared she might never see her colleague again. She'd give him ten minutes and then she'd be on her way.

She took out her mobile and placed a call to social services. She spoke for a few moments and ended the conversation. An 'at risk' call from a police officer galvanised an immediate response. A case worker would be knocking on the door within the hour. Kim suspected Tina was lost but Rhianna and the baby had a chance.

Bryant's front door opened and he exited. She couldn't be totally sure, but his limbs appeared to be intact.

'Still married?' she asked, moving over to the passenger seat.

'Mum and pups are reunited on a blanket by the kitchen radiator. Chicken and rice is on the stove and the missus is on the internet looking up puppy care.'

'You gonna keep them?'

He nodded. 'For now, until they're old enough.'

'How'd you swing that?'

He shrugged. 'Told her the truth, Guv,' he said, simply.

Kim visualised the dogs in his home being fussed over and spoilt.

She shook her head with despair. 'Okay, now drop me off at the station then get to the hospital. One of us needs to be there to question Croft if the opportunity arises.'

'You not coming?'

Kim shook her head. 'Probably not a good idea. It may be just paranoia on my part, but I don't think Mrs Croft likes me all that much.'

CHAPTER 59

The roar of the Ninja died as Kim pulled onto the dirt track. She removed the helmet and placed it over the right handlebar.

She surveyed the site from the top of the hill. Site one and two had been handed back to the landscape and the utility tent had been removed. The heras fencing no longer lined the property and the press had left the area. The police guard was gone and a few bits of equipment were gathered in the top corner of the site. Once again, it was a piece of spare council land where the travelling fair rested annually to entertain the estate.

Only a few teddy bears and weather-beaten flowers left at the foot of the hill offered any hints to the events of the last few days.

This part of the investigation was over. The clues from the dead had been uncovered and now it was up to her and her team to fit it all together.

One day the names of these three girls would be plastered across a Wikipedia page. It would be a link from the main article depicting Black Country history. The triple murder would forever be a blemish on their heritage.

Readers would skate past the article describing the achievements of the Netherton chain makers who had forged the anchors and chains for the *Titanic* and the twenty Shire horses that had pulled the one hundred tonne load through the town.

The metalworking trade that dated back to the sixteenth century would be forgotten in the face of such a sensational headline.

It would not be a record of the area's finer moments.

'Thought that might be you, Guv,' Dawson said, exiting the tent.

His eyes were being propped up by dark circles. His jeans were dirty and his jumper creased but his hours on site and the commitment to the case had earned him the right to look a little worn.

Kim wanted to compliment him on a job well done but somehow the words stuck in her throat. Normally the day after she gave him a pat on the back he found some new way to piss her off again.

'Dawson, I've gotta say, you frustrate the bloody life out of me. You're a damn good detective but sometimes you act like a three-year-old.' She stopped. This wasn't coming out quite how she'd intended. 'Look, I know this week has been difficult for you but in spite of that you've been a bloody star.'

Dawson threw back his head and laughed. 'Thanks, Guv. Coming from you, that means a lot.'

'I mean it, Kev.'

Their eyes met. He knew it.

'Listen, take tomorrow off. We've all worked eight days straight. Saturday morning we'll spend a few hours over coffee and muffins, Bryant's shout, analysing what we have, and make an action plan for next week.'

'It's been a week, Guv. You still framing me for it?'

She shook her head. 'Nah, I'm thinking Bryant's a better fit.'

She entered the last remaining tent to find Cerys alone at the fold-up table beside the grave.

'Lost all your friends, Cerys?' Kim asked.

Cerys turned and smiled. 'My staff are at the hotel packing up to hit the road. It's been a full-on week.'

Kim nodded her agreement. 'And you?'

Cerys sighed deeply. 'Not quite. This grave will be completed in a couple of hours. I don't think there's anything left to find. Our third victim was not buried as deep as the others but I like to be thorough.'

'So, you'll be leaving later?' Kim asked.

Cerys shook her head. 'No. I'll be here completing the paperwork until quite late.' She reached for a small Tupperware tub. 'Beads again, but of course you already knew that. There were remnants of clothing attached to the body but Daniel has those back at the lab. The garment was too delicate to remove on site.'

'Anything else?'

Cerys pointed to a corner of the grave about one foot square. Her face was drawn and weary. 'Unless there is something of interest just there then I'm afraid not.'

'Did you find a denture?'

Cerys frowned. 'No. Should I have done?'

'It's the final form of identification I was looking for.'

'It certainly hadn't come free from the body, if it was in there at all.'

Damn, without that final piece she couldn't be sure of the accuracy of Nicola's identification.

Kim nodded her understanding and stepped out of the tent. She paused and stepped back in.

'Cerys, are you okay?'

Cerys turned, either surprised by the question or the person asking. She smiled but it was forced and without warmth.

'You know what, Kim, I honestly don't know. My body is filled with a rage that I just can't shake. See, I don't care what these girls did or didn't do. I only know that they were treated as less than human. They were tortured and put into the ground and left to rot and they were only fucking kids. I want to be there when you catch the bastard that did this. I want to do the exact same things to him and what's worrying is that I feel capable of inflicting the same cruelty.'

Kim watched as her body deflated. She sometimes forgot that Cerys had not worked many crime scenes and one as harrowing as this was one hell of an initiation.

The woman looked at her and shook her head. 'How do you do it, Kim? How do you wake up to this every day without going out of your mind?'

Kim considered the question. 'I build stuff. I take a heap of rust and dirt and I build it into something beautiful. I create something that balances the ugliness of what we do. It helps. But do you know what really makes a difference?'

'What?'

'The knowledge that I'll catch him.'

'Do you think so?'

Kim smiled. 'Oh yes, because my passion to do so far exceeds the energy he'll need to avoid me. I won't stop until he's punished for what he did. And, everything you've done here, every clue you've uncovered, every bone you've removed will help me do that. It's bloody hard, Cerys, but it's worth it.'

Cerys nodded and smiled. 'I know and I believe you. You'll get him.'

'Oh, I will. And when I do, I'll give him your regards.'

Silence settled between them. Kim had nothing more to ask of the woman who had worked tirelessly for days at great cost, both physically and emotionally.

Kim moved closer and offered her hand. Although the skin was rough in places the grip was gentle and warm.

'Thank you for everything, Cerys, and have a safe journey home. I hope we meet again.'

Cerys smiled. 'Same here, Detective.'

Kim nodded and left the tent.

She had a denture to find.

CHAPTER 60

Daniel and Keats were gathered around a folder on the table top when she entered.

Daniel moved away as Keats turned. 'Oh, Detective, how lovely to see you.'

Kim glared at him.

'No, seriously, I mean it. For me, absence has most definitely made my heart grow fonder. I find that my sensitive, delicate nature might actually find your acerbic tongue almost tolerable.'

'Yes, you've had quite an easy week of it, haven't you?' she asked, raising her eyebrows.

'I have indeed, Detective.' He began to count on his fingers. 'I've had a double stabbing in Dudley, an elderly male who collapsed into his dinner at his eighty-fifth birthday party and two medical uncertainties. Oh, and the trail of corpses you've left in your wake.'

'Happy to fill the time for you but did you manage to ascertain anything remotely useful?'

He thought for a moment and then shook his head. 'No, I've changed my mind. I now realise that I haven't missed you at all.'

'Keats,' she growled.

'I've sent the post mortem results to your office this morning. Teresa Wyatt was pushed down under the water, as you already know. There was no major struggle due to the victim already being immersed in water. I detected no other marks on the body and no sign of any sexual assault. She was in reasonably good health for her age.

'I don't think the manner of death for Tom Curtis was in any question but what I can tell you is that the bottle of whisky would most probably have killed him. His heart was in such poor condition that it's unlikely he'd have made it to forty-five. Oh, and his last meal was salad and steak. Topside, I think.'

Kim rolled her eyes.

'With Mary Andrews you most certainly did not get to the church on time and to make any reasonable deduction about death I usually need a body.

'Arthur Connop died of massive internal trauma caused by an altercation with a vehicle. His liver was on borrowed time but his other major organs were pretty healthy for a man of his age.'

Keats held up his hands, as if to say, *that's all.*

'No evidence, no trace, nothing?'

'No, Detective, because you're not making a TV show. If we had an hour of titillating entertainment to make I may suddenly find that Teresa Wyatt had swallowed a carpet fibre that can be matched to the home of your suspect. I might even find a stray hair on the body of Tom Curtis that miraculously fell from the killer with the root attached. But I am not a mini-series made for television.'

Kim groaned. She'd had a tooth abscess that had been less painful than a lecture from Keats. His frown told her that he hadn't finished quite yet.

She leaned back against the stainless steel counter and folded her arms.

'How many women did the Yorkshire Ripper murder?' Keats asked.

'Thirteen,' Dan answered.

'And how was he caught?'

'By two police officers who arrested him for driving with false number plates,' she answered.

'So, thirteen bodies later and he still hadn't been caught by stray hairs and carpet fibres. Therefore, I can only pass on what the body tells me. Any kind of forensic evidence will not take the place of good old police work; deduction, gut instinct and intelligent, practical thinking. Which reminds me, where is Bryant?'

Kim offered him a look and he turned back to the workbench. Kim saw the label of the white jacket protruding over the collar. She reached over and popped it back inside with her index finger.

Keats turned. She raised one eyebrow. He smiled and turned back.

Kim turned to Daniel. 'Doc, is there a denture?'

He met her gaze and Kim was struck by the tiredness in his eyes. She knew he had worked at the site until late to remove the body of the third victim. Just as she would have done.

'What, no insults, sarcasm or cutting remarks?'

She sensed that he was like her. Once questions were posed he demanded answers and didn't stop until he got them. On a case like this there was no rota, no clocking on and off time. There was only the need to know. She understood.

She tilted her head and smiled. 'Nah, Doc. Not today.'

He held her gaze and smiled back.

Keats had turned his attention back to the worktop and was flicking through pages in a hardware supplies catalogue.

'There is no denture,' Daniel stated.

'Damn.'

'But there should be. She has three missing front teeth.'

Kim sighed heavily. She now had the names of all three girls. This was incontrovertibly Louise's body.

'Have you checked with Cerys?' He asked.

'It's not there.'

'I've got it,' Keats said, quietly.

Daniel moved along the work area and looked at where Keats had laid his index finger.

Daniel nodded slowly.

'What?' Kim asked.

Keats turned to her, unable to speak. Kim was instantly unnerved. This man had seen bodies in the worst state of decay. He had taken in his stride horrendous crime scenes, decomposition and its subsequent life forms. She had watched him carry out a preliminary examination on a corpse while referring to a community of maggots as 'little fellas'. What the hell could instil such horror in him now?

'Look here,' Daniel instructed, pointing to the pubic bone.

Kim could see there was a crack that ran through the centre of the bone.

She raised her head. 'The pelvis is broken?'

'Look closer.'

Kim leaned down as far as she could and saw the nicks in the edge of the bone. She counted seven in total. The one at the centre was deeper than the others. A zig-zag pattern was evident on both sides of the parted bone. Kim saw that the serration travelled for almost an inch before it met the longer crack in the bone.

Kim stepped back in horror as she looked from Daniel to Keats and back again unable to comprehend what was right in front of her eyes.

'Yes, Detective,' Keats offered hoarsely. 'The bastard tried to saw her in half.'

Silence settled between them as they all stared down at the skeleton that had once been a young girl. Not an angel and not without fault, but a young girl nonetheless.

Kim stepped to the side and almost fell into Daniel.

His arms steadied her. 'You okay?'

She nodded as she moved away from his touch. She didn't trust herself to speak until the nausea had passed.

The sound of her mobile ringing startled them all. It galvanised the room into action as though the pause button had been depressed. It was Bryant and he was calling from somewhere in the building.

Her mouth was dry as she answered the call.

'Guv, I'm wasting my time here.'

'Is he still in surgery?' she asked, looking at her watch. If that was the case it wasn't looking good for Richard Croft.

'No, he was wheeled back to the ward an hour ago. The knife is out and I have that bagged. He's in and out of consciousness but Mrs Croft won't let me anywhere near him.'

'On my way,' she said, ending the call.

'Where are you going now?' Keats asked.

She glanced down at body number three and took a deep breath. 'I'm going to start a fight.'

CHAPTER 61

I sensed that Louise was on to me. She was unlike the other two. Melanie had been shy and needy; desperate for affection and validation. Tracy had been streetwise and sensual but Louise had a mean streak that ran through her like lead.

Louise wasn't like the other two. She hadn't been abused, abandoned or neglected. She just didn't like the new rules that came with a stepfather and a new baby.

Louise liked to be in charge, I saw that from the first day when she decided which bed she would take. The girl who had the bed already dared to say no and got a fractured wrist for her trouble.

It wasn't hard to believe the level of violence she'd inflicted on her seven-month-old brother that had led to her being removed from the home.

Unlike Tracy, Louise had no balance. She was just harsh. There was no sexuality, no humour and I couldn't stand the sight of her.

No one messed with Louise. There was a rage inside her that just ached to be freed. It bubbled amongst the hurt and resentment.

But I knew something about her that no one else did.

Louise was mean, and she was violent. And she also wet the bed.

Assisted by a vibrating wristwatch, at four a.m. Louise would leave her warm bed and head for the toilet. She would not return until her bladder was empty.

'Hello, Louise,' I said, one night as she exited the washroom.

'What do you want?' she asked, covering her mouth.

'I think we should have a little chat. You seem unsettled lately.'

'D'ya think?' she asked, placing her hand on her hip. 'My mates are dropping like flies.'

I shrugged. 'Clearly they don't like you enough to hang around.'

Her face seemed to gather in the middle as her lips pursed and her eyes narrowed. 'Yeah, and maybe they got no say in it.'

Oh, full points for me. It took a psychopath to know one.

There was no reason to play games with Louise. Her fate was assured. But I took the time to have a little fun.

'How so?' I asked.

'I know you've got something to do with it. You pretend to be all nice to us but there's something not right with you.'

I silently congratulated Louise on her perceptiveness.

'You don't really have room to talk. Who would purposely hurt their baby brother? There's a nastiness in you and it drives everyone away. I bet your mates left because they couldn't stand you any longer. Even your own family hate you now.'

She thrust her chin forward. 'I couldn't give a shit.'

'Then why do you still wet the bed?'

She lunged towards me, her closed fist en route to my face, but I was ready. I grabbed her wrist and turned her body so that she fell backwards against me. My forearm was clamped against her throat. She thrashed her head from side to side but I wedged my chin on top of her head. My left hand covered her mouth as she tried to scream.

I walked her forward as she tried to bite at my fingers. Her arms flailed but caused me no harm.

Her efforts to live became weaker as I walked her outside. I placed my right hand on her shoulder and tightened the hold.

I shook the last breath of life out of her like a doll. I felt the end of her existence as her body collapsed against me as though someone had sucked out the bones.

I raised my right hand from her shoulder to her neck just to make sure.

The skin was silent against my fingerprint.

I threw her over my shoulder and carried her outside to the waiting hole.

Unlike the other two, I felt nothing for the flesh that I dropped to the ground. Melanie's neediness had made me feel sick. Her obsequious face had made my skin crawl.

Tracy had inspired desire in me. It was her own greed that had led to her end.

But with Louise there was nothing. She was a means to an end.

She was insurance.

The manner of her death would be misdirection.

So I opened her legs and reached for the saw.

CHAPTER 62

Kim walked the corridors of Russells Hall hospital for the second time in as many days. Because it was outside of visiting hours, she announced herself as a police officer at the intercom.

The first priority of the medical personnel was the care of their patients but they tried to be accommodating to police officers.

Kim walked past the small waiting room at the top of the ward. Bryant stood when he saw her. She motioned for him to sit back down.

She paused at the nurse's station. 'Richard Croft?'

The female in dark blue was short and round. An elasticated belt searched halfway down the uniform for a waist and failed miserably.

'Detective, I don't think he's quite ready for your questions.'

Kim nodded her understanding but wanted some of her own. She leaned forward and spoke quietly. 'Sister, this week I have more than six bodies behind me and they all need answers. Richard Croft was very nearly number seven and may be able to help.'

The frown on the woman deepened.

Kim held up her hand. 'I assure you I will not do anything to upset his condition.'

That was no lie, because Kim had no intention of doing anything at all.

The sister nodded towards the third open doorway off the main ward. 'Just a few minutes, okay?'

Kim nodded her understanding and moved quietly along the corridor,

Kim stood in the doorway and looked not at the inert form in the bed but at the figure of his wife in the easy chair, currently engrossed in the contents of her mobile phone.

As Kim leaned against the doorframe, the head of shiny black hair raised. Nina

Croft's fixed expression was politely tolerant. Clearly the look she reserved for the staff. When her eyes rested on Kim, any remnant of tolerance or politeness fell away.

Kim was momentarily surprised at how such an attractive face could be affected by the venom within. Suddenly, the beauty faded and was replaced by narrowed eyes and a thin, mean mouth.

'What the hell are you doing here?'

'Mrs Croft, your husband needs to be questioned.'

'Not now, Detective Stone, and most definitely not by you.'

Nina Croft stood. Just as Kim had hoped.

Richard Croft moaned from the bed. Kim took a step towards him and Nina instantly blocked her path.

'Get out,' she spat.

Kim tried to walk around her but Nina grabbed her roughly on the arm and pulled her towards the door. Had she not been a serving police officer Kim would have smacked the woman in the mouth. Sometimes the sacrifice was just not worth it.

'Get out of this room and away from my husband right now.'

Nina marched her to the front door of the ward. As they passed the waiting room Kim glanced in and caught Bryant's eye. She nodded backwards to the unguarded room.

Once outside the ward, the woman threw Kim's arm away from her as though it were covered with leprous scabs.

'I don't like your methods, Detective and I don't like you.'

'Trust me when I tell you that will not keep me up at night.'

The woman turned away to re-enter the ward.

'And it's not really my methods you dislike, is it, Mrs Croft?'

Nina turned and stepped back. Good.

'You are not a stupid woman. You would have researched me before you made that call to get me removed from the case. Surely it's my success rate you despise.'

Nina stepped closer. 'No, I despise the fact that you made my husband feel like a suspect, which says to me that you are not equipped to handle this investigation. You are clearly inept ...'

'Why would you want me removed from this case when you know full well that I will solve it, no matter how long it takes?'

Nina Croft continued to glower at her.

'Especially when you know your husband to be at risk. Any normal wife would want the killer caught as quickly as possible to remove their loved one from danger.'

'Be very careful what you say to me, Detective Stone.'

'What are you frightened of, Mrs Croft? Why are you so terrified that I will get the answers? And what the hell did your husband do back then?'

Nina stepped back and crossed her arms. 'You will never prove that he did anything untoward.'

'Interesting that you don't state he did nothing wrong – only that I will be unable to prove it.'

'A play on words, Detective.'

'Your husband knows something about what happened at Crestwood ten years ago and whilst he is managing to hang onto life right now, there are others that have not been so lucky.'

The woman looked unmoved. Kim wasn't sure when she'd met a woman less lacking in empathy than Nina Croft.

Kim shook her head with disbelief. 'You have obstructed this investigation at every turn. You tried, unsuccessfully, to have me removed from the case. You used your legal influence to file objections to the dig ...'

Kim's own words trailed away as the truth dawned. '*You* were the one who killed the professor's dog! When the legal objections failed you decided to try anything to prevent that dig from taking place. Jesus, what the hell is wrong with you?'

Nina shrugged. 'Feel free to arrest me for inappropriate use of staples, Detective.'

A movement beyond Nina Croft's head told her that Bryant had exited the side room.

Kim stepped forward into the woman's face. 'You are a ruthless, cold, miserable excuse for a woman. You care nothing for anyone or anything. I think you know exactly what happened back then and the only person you're interested in protecting is yourself.

'And I promise you this, the day is coming whereby I will visit you again and it will be a very public arrest for obstructing the course of justice.'

Kim paused as Bryant came through the first set of double doors.

'And now you have a reason to make a genuine complaint. So, please, give it your best shot.'

Bryant came to stand beside her.

'Get what you wanted?' she asked.

Bryant nodded and turned to Nina. 'Your husband is asking for you.'

Nina looked from one to the other, realising she'd been tricked. The colour flooded her face. Nina Croft did not like to lose.

'You devious little bitch ...'

Kim turned and walked away.

'Hearts and minds exercise, there, Guv?'

'BFFs now. What did you get?'

'Absolutely bugger all.'

Kim stopped walking. 'Are you joking?'

Bryant shook his head. 'Nope.'

'We have a live victim. Our one survivor of a bastard that's killed at least two people and Croft can give us nothing?'

'Guv, he can barely get two words out but by a yes and no system I managed to work out that he was standing up, and facing away from the door when the knife was plunged into his back. He fell forward and lost consciousness immediately.'

Kim blew air through her lips. 'Minutes, Bryant. We must have missed him by bloody minutes. Whoever it was knew they had a small window of opportunity while Marta was out shopping and knew the only way to get in and out undetected.'

It was dark as they stepped out of the hospital building.

'Look, I've already told Kev. Take the day off tomorrow. On Saturday we'll try and piece everything together. It's been one hell of a week.'

For once Bryant didn't argue.

Kim headed around the side of the hospital to where she'd parked the bike. She turned the corner into the darkness.

As she reached for the helmet which was locked to the wheel her phone began to ring.

CHAPTER 63

She hit the call button. The battery flashed red.

'What's up, Stace?'

'Guv, I've been trawling back through some old posts on Facebook and I've come across something I think yer should know.'

'Go on.'

'About eight months ago one of the girls spotted Tom Curtis at Dudley Zoo with his family. She posted on the board commenting on his weight and wondering what they'd all seen in him back then.

'A few childish jokes followed about him putting his hot dog in someone's bun and crap like that but then they started mentioning our three girls as well.'

Kim closed her eyes against what she knew was coming.

'It's clear he was having sex with one of 'em, Guv.'

Kim thought about the pregnant fifteen-year-old. 'Was Tracy mentioned by name?'

'No, Guv, that's the thing. Tom Curtis was sleeping with *Louise*.'

Kim shook her head as the rage built within her.

'You okay, Guv?'

'I'm fine, Stace. Good work, now get off ...'

Her words trailed away as her phone charge ran out.

She put the phone in her pocket and kicked out at the wall.

'Damn, damn, damn,' Kim growled.

The anger that ripped through her veins had nowhere to go. These bastards had been entrusted with the safety of these girls and they had failed them badly. It seemed that every single one of them had found some way to further abuse these kids.

Child abuse was categorised into four main areas; physical abuse, sexual abuse, emotional maltreatment and neglect. By Kim's count, the staff at Crestwood had pretty much scored a strike on all four. The irony lay in the fact that most of the girls at Crestwood had been placed there to *remove* them from mistreatment.

No girl at Crestwood had been there by choice. She knew from her own experience that homes like this were dumping grounds; a civic amenity, like a landfill site. A place for unwanted and broken individuals where at best, kids were dehumanised and stripped of identity and at worst, they were abused even further.

Kim had seen it herself. Poor treatment became an expectation. And slowly, like a stump being hammered into the soil, your head could only remain above ground for so long.

Kim walked around the bike, trying to expel the heat from her veins. She clenched and unclenched her hands to relieve the building tension.

Each girl had arrived at Crestwood for various reasons, and none of them good.

Melanie had been discarded by her father so easily. Gifted to the state so there was one less mouth at his table. The selection criteria being that she was the less attractive child. How could Melanie not have known that to be the case? How did she reconcile that in her head? Thrown away by the one man who should have cared for her, all because she was ugly.

The child had begged for any scrap of attention, some validation that she was a person worthy of affection. Even trying to buy friendship to find her place. Happy to be the runt of the litter, just as long as the litter accepted her.

That was Melanie's story. But there was not one story. All the children in the system had a story. Kim herself had a story. But hers had not started alone.

A vision of Mikey swam before her eyes. It was not the picture she wanted but it was the one she always got. She stepped back into the darkness of the corner as the emotion thickened her throat.

Three weeks premature, Kim and Mikey had both been born with fragile health. Very soon Kim's health had improved, she had gained weight and her bones had strengthened. Mikey's had not.

Their mother, Patty, had taken them home when they were six weeks old, to a high-rise flat on Hollytree.

Kim's first memory dated back to three days after her fourth birthday and was a vision of her mother holding a pillow tightly over the face of her twin. His short legs had thrashed on the bed as his lungs fought for air. Kim tried to pull her mother away but her grip was firm.

Kim had thrown herself to the floor, opened her mouth wide and sunk her teeth into her mother's calf like a rabid dog. She applied every ounce of pressure she could muster and wouldn't let go. Her mother had spun around and the pillow fell from the bed, but still Kim didn't let go. Her mother had staggered around the room, screaming and trying to kick her free, but only when they were a safe distance from the bed did Kim unlock her jaw.

She remembered running over to the bed and shaking Mikey awake. He spluttered, coughed and gulped at the air. Kim ushered him behind her and stared up at her mother.

The hatred in the eyes of the woman who had birthed them took Kim's breath away. She backed up the bed, keeping Mikey behind.

Her mother moved closer. 'You stupid little bitch. Don't you know he's the fucking devil? He's got to die and then the voices will stop. Don't you fucking get it?'

Kim shook her head. No, she didn't. He wasn't the devil. He was her brother.

'I'll get him, I promise you, I'll get him.'

From that point on, Kim had had to remain one step in front of her mother at all times. There were further attempts during the following year but Kim was never far from Mikey's side.

During the day she kept a badge in her pocket and pricked her lower arm to keep herself alert. At night she took handfuls of coffee from the jar and placed them straight into her mouth, absorbing the bitter granules into her tongue.

Only when she heard the rhythmic sound of her mother's snoring would she allow herself to rest.

There were occasional visits from social services. An overworked individual conducting a ten minute cursory inspection with a mental clipboard; a test she somehow managed to pass.

Kim had wondered many times since just how low the pass grade would have had to have been for them to remain in the care of their mother.

No evidence of crack cocaine – check.

No evidence of parent stumbling and drunk – check.

Children free of obvious scarring – check.

A week after their sixth birthday Kim had exited the lavatory, to find her brother attached to the radiator with handcuffs.

Kim looked at her mother with horror, confused for a few seconds. It was all the time her mother needed. Kim felt her hair being grabbed from behind and bunched in her mother's fist. She was dragged to the radiator and cuffed to her brother.

'If I've gotta get you to get him then that's what I'll have to do.'

Those were the last words she ever heard from her mother.

By the end of that day Kim had managed to squirm her right foot beneath the bed and dislodge a pack of five cream crackers and a half bottle of Coke.

For two days she had been convinced that her mother would return. That one of her rare lucid moments would occur and they would be freed.

On day three she realised that their mother was not coming back and had left them to die. With only two crackers and a few mouthfuls of Coke remaining, Kim stopped eating completely. She divided the last two crackers in half and half again, making eight bites for Mikey.

Every few hours she would try and force her hand through the cuffs, removing slivers of skin each time.

By the end of day five the crackers were gone. A single mouthful of liquid remained in the Coke bottle.

Mikey turned his face towards her; so thin, so pale. 'Kimmy, I peed again,' he whispered.

She looked into his eyes; so distraught at one more puddle amongst the foulness beneath them. His earnest expression made her laugh out loud. And once she started laughing, she couldn't stop. Even though he didn't know why, Mikey joined in until the tears rolled over their cheeks.

And when the tears stopped falling, she held him close. Because she already knew. She whispered into his ear that

Mummy was on her way with a meal and that he just had to hang on. She kissed the side of his head and told him she loved him.

Two hours later he died in her arms.

'Sleep tight, sweet Mikey,' she whispered, as the last breath left his battered, fragile body.

Hours or days later there was a loud noise and then people. Lots of people. Too many. They wanted to take Mikey and she was too weak to fight them off. She had to let him go. Again.

The fourteen day stay in hospital was a blur of tubes, needles and white coats. The days had melded into one.

Day fifteen was much clearer. She was taken from the hospital to the children's home. And she was given bed number nineteen.

'Excuse me, Miss, are you okay?' asked a voice from above.

Kim was startled to realise that she had slid down the wall and was now sitting on the ground.

She wiped away the tears and sprang to a standing position. 'I'm fine, thank you, I'm fine.'

The ambulance driver hesitated for a second but nodded and then wandered away.

Kim stood and breathed deeply to dispel the overwhelming sadness as she placed the memories back in the box. Never would she forgive herself for her failure to protect her brother.

She unlocked the helmet from the wheel. Her body now filled with fight and determination.

No, she would not have it. Kim would not fail these girls because damn it, they mattered to someone. They bloody well mattered to her.

CHAPTER 64

Stacey leaned back in her chair and stretched. A heat burned across the muscles in her neck. She rolled her head to the left and then to the right. Something clicked in her right shoulder blade.

The Guv had said go home and that's what she intended to do.

She closed down the Facebook page and her emails beneath. There were a few at the top still in bold and unread but she would see to them on Saturday morning. All she craved right now was a long hot soak in a bubble bath followed by a takeaway pizza and a dose of *Real Housewives*. She didn't care which one.

The whirring of the computer came to a halt, plunging the room into silence.

Her feet slipped into the shoes beneath the desk. Stacey donned her jacket and walked to the door.

Her left hand hesitated over the light switch but something nagged at the back of her mind. Something she'd seen but couldn't work out the meaning of just yet.

She growled as she stepped back to her desk. The whirring seemed louder, as though it were under duress. Stacey guessed she was projecting.

She keyed in without looking and went straight to her emails. It was the second unread message that quickened her heart. She read from the beginning, her eyes open wide.

By the time she reached the end of the text her mouth had run dry.

With trembling fingers, Stacey reached for the phone.

CHAPTER 65

Kim parked the bike at the side of the fenced-off building. She dismounted and stepped to the side.

It was only eight o'clock but it felt much later. The cold night air had already dropped below freezing, driving families to lock the doors, close the curtains and curl up before a flickering orange flame and a night-time film.

It was a notion that had occurred to Kim when she'd briefly stopped by her home, a place she'd barely seen for the last week, but she knew she couldn't rest. The answers were emerging from the fog but there was one missing piece that still troubled her.

The dig site was now empty. All traces of activity had been removed. To see the site shut down was eerie. The white tents were back in storage awaiting their next victim. The equipment had been removed and would be gone the next day. Along with Cerys.

To the naked eye and in the darkness, the land looked as it had one week earlier. Even the few bunches of flowers and teddy bears had now disappeared.

But Kim knew she could walk to all three graves and identify their exact location. And that fact would remain long after the scars of the landscape had healed.

Kim couldn't help but wonder how long the girls would have remained lost had the professor not been so determined to find buried coins.

But because of his tenacity, three young girls who had lain beneath this unassuming piece of land would now be afforded proper burials. And Kim would attend every one.

She knew the case had touched them all. Cerys had removed the bodies from the ground. Daniel had examined the girls to indicate the manner of death and now it was up to her to pull it all together.

She looked over to the middle house. There was activity inside. Lucy and William were back from the hospital and their life together would continue as normal. For now.

Kim pulled her gaze away from the illuminated window. The time had come for her to have a very difficult conversation with William Payne; but he wasn't going anywhere and there was one missing piece she had to find first.

The denture was here somewhere and somehow, it mattered. That it was not on the body and not in the grave meant that it was still in the building. The location would tell her everything. And this time Kim had come prepared.

She reached into her saddlebag and took out a hammer. She reckoned that by removing two fence panels she'd be able to climb through the gap.

Kim removed the black leather gloves and placed the pencil torch in her mouth. She used the claw of the hammer to remove the nails that held the rough wooden panels against the vertical stumps.

The first two dislodged easily. She tried to prise the panel away from the post but the two fixed to the other side held fast. The top one came loose easily but the bottom one wouldn't budge. She was able to swing the panel down so that it hung vertically, still fixed with one stubborn nail.

It was clear that ten years ago the council budget for decent workmanship far outweighed the budget for quality materials.

Kim repeated the same process with the second panel, providing a space wide enough to climb through. Once on the other side she shook her hands and cupped them to her mouth. The raw wind on her exposed fingers had made the tips numb.

She had deliberately not informed Bryant or the rest of the team of her plans. She had no legal right to enter the building and a warrant would have taken far too long.

Woody's message about the loyalty of her team had been received loud and clear.

Without the aid of daylight, she had to recall from memory the layout of the back of the building. She lit up the ground using her torch. The land was overgrown and littered with bricks and debris.

Kim shone the torch at the open window through which she'd entered the building previously. She tried to traverse a direct path from point A to point B but stumbled over a breeze block. She swore but carried on.

She reached the window and realised she had used the bin to get back over the fence. She travelled back, taking care to avoid the breeze block, then picked up the bin and placed it beneath the broken window.

She shone the torch around the outer edge of the opening to get an idea of where the shards were placed. Kim put the torch in her mouth and used both hands to ease herself through the broken window.

Yes, she was in.

CHAPTER 66

I knew I'd been right when I first saw her. Her diligence and tenacity had served her well. Perhaps too well.

Because it had brought her back to me.

I had initially thought that we would not meet but that was no longer the case.

My insurance, my clever misdirection, had not been enough. For some it would have been. But not for her.

Here she was, alone, late at night, gaining entry to an abandoned building, searching for answers. She would not rest until she had uncovered the secrets.

All of them.

It was only a matter of time before her methodical reasoning brought her to me. I couldn't take that chance.

Had she not been so clever I would have allowed her to live. People have to take responsibility for their own actions.

I remember when I was twelve in the lunch hall. Robbie had a chicken salad sandwich. It looked so much tastier than my ham and cheese. I asked him to trade and he laughed in my face.

A broken rib, a black eye and two fractured fingers later, I had the sandwich and it tasted good.

See, it needn't have happened. If he'd just traded, he would have been fine. I tried to explain this to the teachers but they couldn't understand. They all made excuses for my lack of remorse.

I wasn't troubled. I wasn't seeking attention. I was not acting up because my grandma had died.

I just wanted the sandwich.

It was a shame that the detective had to die. The presence of her keen mind and unerring drive would be missed but she had brought it on herself.

It wasn't my fault.

My only fault lay in the mistake I made some years before, but it was one that I hadn't made since.

But then, even the greatest minds occasionally made errors.

And as I watched her climb in through the fence, I realised that the detective had just made her last.

CHAPTER 67

Kim's feet landed on the Formica worktop and the glass crunched like gravel beneath her boots. In the dark silence, the sound seemed deafening.

She eased herself down onto the ground and cast the torch around the kitchen. Nothing had changed in the few days since her last trespass and this wasn't the area that held her interest.

Still, she paused for a moment, visualising the girls sneaking in when no one was around for a packet of crisps or a drink. How many times had Melanie wandered in and out of this room before she was so brutally beheaded?

Kim headed forward through the room and jumped when something settled on her face. She clawed at her cheeks, dislodging the soft fibres and raised the light to a head-shaped hole in a cobweb at the doorway. She shook her head and rubbed at her face and hair. A single thread tickled at her ear.

As she stepped from the hallway to the corridor a gust of wind howled from above, entering the building through the broken windows. A beam creaked above her head.

For a second, Kim questioned the sensibility of her own choice to enter this building alone and at night, but she would not be frightened off by insects and wind.

She moved along the corridor, taking care to mute the torch as she passed open doorways of rooms that were on the front of the property.

Although the building was surrounded by fencing she couldn't take a chance that the light would be seen from the road or the houses opposite.

On her left she passed a utility room and on her right was the common room. She pictured Louise in that room, holding court, rallying her troops as the group leader – until some bastard tried to saw her in half.

Kim headed for the room at the bottom of the hallway. The room where the fire had been started. The manager's office.

As she entered, she switched off the torch. A streetlight next to the bus stop cast a shadow into the room.

Did you stand in here and ask him for help? Kim silently asked Tracy. Did you come to Richard Croft and seek his advice before you were buried alive? Kim suspected not.

Kim shook away the thought and surveyed the room. Two filing cabinets stood behind the open door. She opened each drawer in turn. The light from the street lamp did not illuminate that far into the room. She searched each one by hand.

Nothing.

She moved to the bookcase on the other side of the doorway. It was a heavy, wooden structure that ended six inches from the ceiling. She ran her hand along each empty shelf, standing on the second shelf up to examine the top. Although her hand was blackened by dark, dusty soot there was nothing to find. She blew away the loose blackened powder and wiped the remainder on her jeans.

She moved to the desk nearest to the window and opened each of the drawers. In the bottom she found a small petty cash tin. She shook it lightly. It was empty.

Kim stood and surveyed the room. The denture was here. She felt it. Where would it be placed to try and ensure its destruction?

Her eyes wandered back to the bookcase nearest the door. The fire had been started in the hallway outside the office door, at the furthest point from the bedrooms of the girls. Somehow the fire had chosen its own direction and headed down the hallway, leaving Croft's office intact.

She put the torch in her pocket and stood before the bookcase. This time she examined every shelf, top and bottom and side panels. She knelt on the floor searching for any gap beneath the lowest shelf.

Nothing.

She sneezed as the dust and soot lifted from the surfaces she had touched.

She stood before the bookcase and opened her arms. She could just about manage to embrace the whole object in a giant hug. She pulled at one side and then the other, budging it forward by an inch at a time. After a few attempts, the bookcase and the wall were separated by about eight inches. Not much, but enough for her to reach behind.

Kim started to move her hand across the plywood backing, sweeping from side to side. Her face was pressed against the side panel as she reached for the furthest point.

The tips of her fingers glided over a smooth surface at odds with the rough plywood. She pushed as far as she could, straining at the shoulder. She touched again. Tape. Her fingers had found the edge of a strip of Sellotape. With one almighty push, she forced herself into the corner.

Instantly, she was reminded of foster family number three, who had used the naughty corner as a form of punishment. She would estimate that approximately one-third of her five-month stay had been spent in that corner. And it hadn't always been her fault. Sometimes it had just been made to look that way.

Kim froze as her hand closed around the unmistakeable shape of a tooth.

The word *punishment* flew around her head and she closed her eyes. She shook her head with disbelief. Why the hell had she not seen it sooner? It had been staring at her from the wipe board. Beheading, Premature Burial and Death by Sawing; all forms of capital punishment.

She retracted her arm from behind the bookcase. The denture could wait. It no longer held the importance that it had earlier.

She had to call for back up. She now had the pieces to finally solve this case. One last visit and her girls could rest peacefully.

Too late, Kim saw a shadow in the hallway cast by the streetlamp.

And then she saw nothing.

CHAPTER 68

Kim opened her eyes to find a strip of fabric jammed into her mouth, tied in a knot at the back of her head.

She had been laid on her side and her hands and feet were bound together in a bunch of limbs, her knees wedged beneath her chin.

The pain throughout her body faded in comparison to the thudding in her head. It originated from the crown and spread like tentacles around to her temples, ears and jawbone.

An icy coldness from the concrete floor was seeping through her clothes and into her bones.

For a moment Kim couldn't recall where she was, or why. Gradually, flashes of the day started to come back to her but it was like a collage. She had a vision of Richard Croft lying face down on the floor in a pool of blood. She vaguely remembered the briefing but couldn't recall if that had happened the previous day. She sensed, more than remembered, that she'd returned to the site and spoken with Cerys.

As the snapshots began to arrange in chronological order Kim recalled that she had returned to Crestwood to find the denture.

Through the haze, she remembered that she'd found it – before the blackness descended.

She had no idea how long she had been unconscious but she knew she was in the manager's office. Dust and soot were caked to her skin.

Her vision started to clear and her eyes adjusted to the light. The room was unchanged and the street lamp outside threw a hazy light into the room.

The silence was broken only by the sound of water dripping somewhere in the distance. The noise offered an eerie presence in its continuous regularity.

Kim pulled at the ties that bound her. They held fast but scored into her flesh. She tried again, ignoring the pain, but the rope burned into her broken skin.

She searched her memory for anything she may have seen in the room that might help her. Nothing came, but she knew she couldn't just lie still and wait.

Something scurried past her head, which galvanised her into action. She tried to inch forward, wriggling like a scorched worm. The effort brought fresh waves of pain emanating through her skull and bile burned the back of her throat. She prayed she would not throw up and choke.

Suddenly she heard a noise and stopped squirming, her senses alert and keen.

She craned her neck towards the doorway. A figure appeared. The form was familiar to her.

Kim blinked through the darkness as her attacker stepped into the shard of light illuminating the room.

Her gaze travelled from the feet, up the legs, torso and shoulders – right into the eyes of William Payne.

CHAPTER 69

William Payne stepped towards her slowly. His eyes held no expression and her head began to move involuntarily from side to side. No, this was not right. Her stomach muscles revolted at the scenario before her. This was not who she'd been expecting.

He leaned down beside her and started trying to undo the knots that bound her like a piece of cattle. His fingers worked quickly but clumsily.

She tried to speak but the fabric in her mouth made her question unintelligible.

He shook his head. 'We don't have much time,' he whispered.

His mouth opened to say more but a low whistling sound came from the top of the corridor.

William put a finger to his lips and stepped back into the shadows of the room. As she couldn't make a sound because of the gag, she guessed he was telling her not to disclose his position.

The humming continued and grew louder. The gait of the visitor was not similar to that of William Payne. These steps were definite, assured, purposeful.

Again, the doorway filled with a shadow, but this time Kim did not have to wait for the owner to step into the beam of light.

This *was* the one she'd been expecting.

CHAPTER 70

'Bryant, you've gotta find the Guv,' Stacey barked into the mouthpiece. 'It's the Pastor. It's Wilks. He killed the girls and I can't get the Guv on the phone.'

'Slow down, Stacc,' Bryant said. The sound of the television in the background was receding. She guessed he was taking the phone to another room. 'What are you talking about?'

'Them emails I sent out just for a punt. There was a hoohar in Bristol twelve years ago when a family got a metal pin in the ashes of their relative. The crematorium was accused of mixing up funerals but after the incident Wilks left in haste.'

'Stace, no offence but that doesn't mean he's guilty of ...'

Stacey held her frustration. She didn't have the time. 'I've checked the archives and two weeks before a kid named Rebecca Shaw ran away from Clifton children's home ...'

'Why would that make the papers?' Bryant asked.

'Because she'd already been in the news when she got run over. Really bad damage to her knees ...'

'That would have required pinning,' Bryant finished.

Stacey could hear the slotting of pieces into place.

'That's how he disposed of 'em before,' Stacey said. 'But he couldn't risk it again.'

She heard Bryant sigh heavily. 'Jesus, Stace, how many are we ...'

'Bryant, you gotta find the Guv. Her phone died when I spoke to her earlier and she didn't sound right.'

'What do you mean?'

'Dunno, she was distracted, agitated. I don't think she was going home. I'm worried that ...'

'Stace, get it circulated that she's missing. It's a bollocking I'm happy to take if she's safe and sound.'

'I will, but Bryant ...'

'Yeah?'

'Just find her.'

The word *alive* went unspoken between them.

'I will, Stace, I promise.'

Stacey replaced the receiver. She believed him. Bryant would find Kim.

She just hoped that he wasn't too late.

CHAPTER 71

He stepped inside the room and placed a shovel against the wall.

Kim watched as his feet moved closer towards her. She could not crane her neck to look up although she desperately wanted to. She wanted to look straight into the eyes of the evil bastard who had tried to saw a girl in half.

His voice was low and jovial, as though discussing where to dine out that evening. 'So kind of your colleagues to dig a few holes for me. That last one was very easy to re-dig. I think you'll be very happy there.'

Kim strained against her ties and tried to spit out the gag.

She felt the tie around her right wrist loosen slightly but not enough.

Victor Wilks laughed out loud. 'This must be a novelty for you, Detective. You're normally the one in control, but not anymore.'

Kim felt the frustration grow inside her. One on one she could take him. She'd beat the living shit out of him. His only method of controlling her was to truss her up like a damn turkey.

He knelt down beside her and finally she could see into his eyes. They were warm with triumph.

'I've done a lot of reading about you, Detective. I understand your passion, I understand your drive. I even understand the affinity you might feel towards your young victims.'

His voice was melodic as though conducting a service for the recently deceased. 'You were one of those girls, weren't you, my dear ... but unlike them, you made yourself into a decent human being.'

Kim strained against the rope. She wanted so badly to wring Wilks' neck and pummel the smug expression from his face.

He stepped back a pace and laughed. 'Oh, Kim. I knew you'd be a fighter. I could sense your spirit the first time I saw you.'

Kim gurgled against the rag.

He tipped his head and read the rage in her eyes. 'You think I won't get away with this?'

Kim nodded and gurgled again.

'Oh, but I will, my dear. You see, this ground will never be touched again. Certainly not in my lifetime.' He chuckled. 'And most definitely not in yours.

'This land is now the original burial site of three murdered teenage girls. No one will be allowed to disturb it again. Now, remind me again who knows you're here?'

Kim squirmed towards him. The shadow of William Payne standing behind the open door was visible to her. She needed the minister to move around so that he would not notice the anomaly in the light.

The movement only prompted Victor to change the leg he was resting his weight on. He was still side on to the doorway.

'And you forget one vital detail, my dear. I have done this before. At least three times – so I think you'll find I'm relatively good at ...'

His words trailed away as the shadow to his left stepped out of the darkness.

Kim groaned as she heard the rush of air. She knew that William had made his move too early. The three steps it had taken him to get to Victor Wilks had offered the minister time to stand and get his footing.

The first strike from William was deflected easily. Although William was younger and taller, Victor Wilks hid pure strength behind his considerable girth.

Victor seized the momentum of William stumbling backwards and was upon him in a second. He raised his fist and struck William to the side of the head. William's head flew to the side.

Victor then gave him a left hook, sending William's head travelling in the other direction. The stance of the minister told Kim that she'd been right about his time in the boxing ring. William didn't stand a chance.

She tried to wriggle further into the middle of the room, hoping to place herself as an obstruction that might cause Victor Wilks to trip and give William the upper hand.

Kim had never felt so damned useless in her life.

'You should be grateful for what I did, you pathetic little shit,' Victor said as William slid down the wall. 'After what those little bitches did to your daughter. You should be bloody thanking me.'

William was halfway down the wall but he lunged forward, aiming for Victor's genitals with his hand.

The motion caused Victor to step backwards out of reach. His right foot kicked her in the head, causing an explosion at the back of her eyes.

It took a few seconds for Kim to blink away the stars but she watched as Victor grabbed William by the throat and lifted him back to a standing position. Victor pinned him against the wall with his left hand at William's neck. She watched in horror as William's eyes rolled in his head.

Victor aimed one last punch at William's head, then released him.

Kim cried out loud as William Payne clutched his chest and fell to the ground.

CHAPTER 72

Having being felled by Wilks' punch, William's face rested inches from her own. Kim quickly looked for signs of life but in the limited light she was unable to tell.

Victor Wilks leaned down between them, then dragged William's inert form away from her as though he was a sack of potatoes.

She watched as he put two fingers to William's neck. 'He's alive. For now.'

Kim breathed a sigh of relief.

Victor came and knelt beside her. He took a knife from his pocket and rested the blade against her throat.

'I'm sure your last wish is to talk to me, Detective – and I'll grant that wish, but if you scream, I'll cut his throat. Are we clear?'

Kim made no movement but continued to stare into the soulless eyes. He was no longer the affable pastor speaking softly to a congregation of mourners, eager for comfort. The smug triumph had disappeared, leaving in its place the blackened heart of a killer.

Wilks pulled the gag from her mouth. It fell and rested around her neck.

'You're gonna pay for what you did, you bastard,' she spat. The words rasped from her throat. The gag had dried the inside of her throat to sandpaper.

She swallowed three times to add moisture to her dry mouth.

He knelt beside the body of William, the blade resting above his carotid artery.

'Oh, I think not, my dear. There is only you that would get close to suspecting me. I saw it in your face the other day. Even if you didn't know it yourself. I knew it wouldn't be long until you put it together.'

'You murdered three innocent girls?'

'I'd hardly call them innocent.'

Kim knew she would have to delay him for as long as possible. No one knew where she was. He was right that no one was coming to help her. Her one chance for escape lay unconscious, six feet away.

But she had to keep him talking. While he was talking, she was breathing.

Kim cursed herself for not putting it together quicker. Something Nicola had said had not rung true. Tracy Morgan would not have said she was going to get money from the father of the child. She would have used the term 'baby's dad' or the man's name. She had meant she was going to get money from The Father.

'Tracy's child was yours?'

'Of course it was mine. The stupid little bitch thought she could blackmail me. She even wanted to keep the child and make a new life for herself.'

'Did you rape her?'

'Let's just say she played hard to get.'

Every cell of her being ached to take that knife and drive it deep between his eyes.

'You evil bastard. How the hell could you do that?'

'Because she was a nothing, Detective. Like many of the others, she had no one. There was no purpose to her life.'

'Why didn't she report you?'

Kim already knew the reason before the sentence was out of her mouth.

'Because it's what she felt she deserved. Deep down inside herself she also knew she was a nothing. Her life – or lack of it – affected no one. Her presence affected nothing. No one cried, no one grieved. She was worthless.'

Kim's own rage began to build. She understood that feeling. Knowing that the only people in your life were being paid to be there ate away at you. The feeling of worthlessness, once absorbed, never went away. Daily, events would occur to reinforce that belief.

'So, Tracy was first?' Kim asked. She had to keep him on track while she worked out how to get herself free.

'Yes, Tracy was first. Her little cronies would have been fine if they hadn't been so persistent. They would keep insisting that Tracy had not run away.'

'But you buried her alive,' Kim said, incredulously.

Wilks shrugged, but Kim saw something pass through his eyes.

'You couldn't kill her yourself?' she asked, with surprise. 'It wasn't intentional to bury her alive. You were going to kill her but you couldn't do it. Oh my God, you actually felt something for that girl.'

'Don't be ridiculous,' he barked. 'I felt nothing for her. I simply gave her vodka so she'd be easier to handle. I had already decided on my course of action.'

Kim felt the bile rise in her throat. A vision swam before her eyes of Tracy Morgan; intoxicated, pliable. It would have proven too tempting for the evil bastard to resist.

'You raped her again, didn't you?'

She saw his smile. 'See, Detective. I knew I was right about you. You certainly know how to use that head of yours.'

'But you're a man of God?'

'And He knows me better than anyone and yet He has afforded me these opportunities. If He felt I was wrong in any way He would have stopped me.

'The other two didn't believe she'd run away. Everyone else did. The rumour was out there that she was pregnant so everyone just felt she'd either run away with the father of the child or gone somewhere to get it taken care of.'

'But not her friends?'

'No, they were persistent little sluts who just wouldn't leave it alone.'

'Did you deliberately frame William Payne?'

'Not with Tracy. I just wanted her gone. But I eventually realised that the same three girls that were a problem for me had done something despicable to his daughter so I decided to take out a little insurance.'

Kim understood. From that point on he had cleverly decided to visit on William's night shifts and offer the caretaker some extra time with his daughter. If the permanent staff knew about it, they turned a blind eye because of Lucy's illness. Victor knew that by doing so the first finger of blame would be pointed at William Payne.

'Who found the denture?' Kim asked.

'Teresa Wyatt. She knew that Louise would not have gone anywhere voluntarily without that denture. She only ever took it out to sleep. So, she put two and two together and got the exact number I'd intended. She checked the night rosters and found that all three girls had gone missing on William's watch. Of course, they all knew about the incident with Lucy. It wasn't much of a leap to believe that he had committed the crimes.'

'So, they covered it up?'

Victor chuckled. 'Oh yes, Detective, they certainly did that.'

'To protect William?'

'Not even for a minute. Oh, on the face of it they all felt for him. His life was unenviable. He watched his child decay more every day and there's nothing he could do about it. Without him, Lucy will have no one. But they did it for themselves.'

Kim didn't like how he was now referring to William in the past tense. She wondered if the grave had been dug wide enough for two.

'I'm sure you already know their secrets. Any kind of official enquiry would have destroyed them all. Richard's embezzling would have been uncovered. Teresa would have faced charges of assault and sexual assault from Melanie. Tom would have been exposed for sleeping with Louise and who would have believed that it was consensual? And Arthur hated all three of them with a passion. They made his life a misery. And the girls were already dead, so there was nothing to gain.'

Kim heard a siren in the distance but knew it could not be for her. Her mind wondered if she could find a way to use it to keep herself alive. She forced herself back on track.

'Who was the ring leader?'

'They jointly made the decision that there was nothing to be gained by going to the police. The remaining girls had to be separated as quickly as possible and incriminating records destroyed.'

'The fire?'

'Yes, the chaos and disbursement of girls would create an administrative nightmare.'

'Did no one speak to William?'

'They didn't need to. A few words from me about his state of mind and rage towards the girls sealed the deal.'

'So, the fire was set?'

'Yes, but the girls were never in danger. The fire was started at the furthest point from the rooms. The alarms kicked in immediately and Arthur Connop was ready and waiting to get the girls out of the building.'

'So, three girls lost their lives. William lost his job and some of the staff members pretty much lost their minds. And you walked away with nothing?'

'Like I said, I have Him on my side.'

'And was He on your side in Manchester, Bristol and wherever the hell else you've been?'

'He is with me always,' Victor said with a smile.

'Are you sure about that?' Kim asked.

She saw doubt cross Victor's face as the siren grew louder. She knew she would not get another opportunity to live. Very shortly he was going to turn that knife on her and bury her in the old grave of one of his victims.

She had to panic him into doing something stupid.

The siren grew louder and Kim had an idea.

'But there is one major thing you forgot, Victor.' She smiled widely. 'And it will be your undoing.'

As Victor leaned in towards her to hear over the siren, William groaned and rolled onto his back.

She saw Lucy's emergency pendant hanging around his neck. It hadn't been his chest he'd been clutching after all.

The siren grew ever louder. Her hands and feet were bound to each other.

'What exactly did I forget, Detective?'

His face was beside her own. He was sure that the siren was not for them and wanted to know what tracks he had left to cover.

Even trussed up, Kim now knew she had the upper hand.

'You already said that I know how to use my head.'

Kim craned her head backwards, then launched it forward, hard. Her forehead met with the bridge of his nose. The fireworks shot through her head and for a second she wasn't sure if the sound of cracked bone was from her or from him.

The wail of pain that came from Wilks' mouth told her it was most definitely him.

His hands reached instinctively for his face, while the knife dropped half a foot from her bound hands. He staggered to his feet and she wriggled her body towards the knife.

'You fucking bitch,' he cried, staggering around the room.

As her bound hands clutched the knife handle, Victor seemed to realise he no longer had possession of it.

Still holding his face, he headed for the shovel in the doorway.

Breaking his nose had bought her a minute but in her bound state one swing of that shovel around her head and she was gone.

The sound of the siren was now deafening.

She turned the knife towards her and hacked at the piece of rope that William had managed to loosen. It cut through but didn't free any of her limbs, although it did offer her another inch or two of movement.

Kim's hand worked quickly. Two more steps and he'd be upon her.

William's right hand shot out and grabbed Victor's ankle. He stumbled and fell but quickly regained his footing.

Kim used her middle finger to pull one of the twines tighter. It tightened around all of her limbs. It was the connecting twine that held her hands to her feet.

She worked harder. Her breath now came in short, sharp bursts as she put every ounce of energy she had into cutting that one connection of rope.

Victor stood above her. Rage burned in his eyes as blood dripped from his nose. In the light of the street lamp the blood had formed a moustache and beard on his face.

He lifted the shovel high into the air, then swung it down. She rolled to the left. The shovel landed on the ground an inch from her head. The sound exploded in her ear.

She could feel the tightness of the rope loosening against the blade. In her mind's eye she could picture the rope fraying under the pressure of the blade.

But it was not fraying quickly enough.

Again, the shovel was raised high above his head. The rage in Wilks' eyes was murderous.

She knew that the next strike would not miss.

The siren had stopped and the sudden silence was ominous.

Victor readjusted the grip of the shovel in his hand, a triumphant gleam in his eyes.

Kim saw the head of the shovel coming down towards her head.

She was out of time. She dropped the knife and put every ounce of strength into pulling her hands apart, praying she'd weakened the correct strand.

Her hands and legs exploded apart and she lunged for his knees, but the downward motion of the shovel could not be stopped. The tool hit the lower part of her back, hard.

She cried out in pain as she swept his legs from beneath him. He toppled backwards to the ground. His right elbow crashed against the wall as he fell.

Kim ignored the pain in her back. She knew she had to make the most of this opportunity. The injuries she'd inflicted would not keep him subdued for long.

She pounced on his legs and climbed up his body. He tried to lift himself up from the waist but Kim was too quick. She pulled herself up and sat astride him. He rolled and writhed beneath her but her knees were locked into his ribs.

Kim heard activity in the kitchen as feet crunched on top of broken glass.

'In here,' she shouted.

Kim looked into eyes that showed only fear for himself. She smiled down at him. 'Looks like He has had enough of your crimes as well.'

Again, Wilks tried to turn his body weight to throw her off.

She balled her fist and punched him square on the nose in the exact spot she'd headbutted him.

He squealed out in pain.

'They were just kids, you bastard.'

She hit him again. 'And that one's from Cerys.'

The glare of a torch landed right on her. A male paramedic shone the light around the room.

'Umm ... Police are en route,' he said, not moving forward, obviously unsure of what had taken place.

'Thank God for that,' she said, reaching for her warrant card.

He glanced at it. 'Okay, what the hell ...'

She pointed to William, who lay groaning beside her. 'See to him first. Head injuries, both sides.'

'Do you need ...'

'I'm fine. See to him.'

Victor wriggled beneath her. 'Oh, keep still,' she said, digging her right knee into his ribs. The second paramedic came storming into the room.

'Police are coming,' he said, looking at her quizzically.

Why were they both so quick to label her the bad guy?

'She *is* the police, Mick,' said the first paramedic, with just a hint of disbelief.

Mick shrugged, then kneeled on the floor on the opposite side of William's head. She recognised the second medic from Lucy's recent episode. She couldn't help but wonder just how many times they'd been called out to the poor child.

'Lucy,' William managed to utter.

'She's fine. She managed to communicate where you were,' Mick said.

What a girl, Kim thought.

'You'll ... never ... prove ...' Victor started to mutter.

'Shut up,' Kim said, using her knee again.

Kim heard more sirens in the distance. They were travelling quickly.

The sirens stopped and within seconds footsteps thundered along the corridor.

Bryant and Dawson burst into the room. And stopped dead.

She smiled. 'Evening, boys. Thanks for coming, but ten minutes sooner would have been good.'

Bryant held out his hand to help her up while Dawson placed Victor's arms above his head.

She ignored the outstretched hand and pushed herself to her feet. She couldn't identify a part of her body that wasn't sending pain messages to her brain but the agony in her back possibly trumped it all. She grimaced as she straightened.

'How did you know?' she asked.

'Stacey got an email from a Minister in Bristol. I'll give you the details later but Guv, there's gonna be more. Burying them wasn't his normal M.O. Before that, he cooked them.'

Kim was not surprised. She closed her eyes and sent a silent prayer for the ones that would never be found.

She took a deep breath. 'Get him up, Kev.'

Dawson and Bryant each grabbed an arm and lifted.

The animosity in Victor's stare burned into her skin. If he thought that would frighten her he needed to think again. He'd clearly never seen Woody in a really bad mood. Now that was something else.

'Victor Wilks, I'm arresting you for the murder of Tracy Morgan and her unborn child, Melanie Harris and Louise Dunston. You do not have to say anything but anything you do say may be given in evidence, you evil murdering bastard.'

She enjoyed how he looked at her, utter hatred in his eyes. 'Get him out of my sight, guys.'

Bryant hesitated. 'Guv ...'

She held up her hand. 'I'm fine. Just get him safely to the station. I won't be far behind.'

She could see the concern in her colleague's eyes. If she let him hang around for too long he'd be frogmarching her to the hospital. And right now she just didn't have the time.

Kim grimaced as she leaned down beside William.

The paramedic closest to her turned his head. 'Miss, you need some attention ...'

Kim ignored him and nodded towards William. 'How is he?'

'Severe concussion. Thinks I'm holding up eight fingers on one hand so he needs to go to hospital.'

'Lucy,' William said again.

Kim touched his hand lightly. 'I'll make sure she's okay.'

She thanked the paramedics and headed out of the building. Every bone in her body screamed at her. She exited just in time to see Victor Wilks being driven away.

Kim wondered how many lives he had claimed. How many other vulnerable, damaged girls had he abused – and how would they ever know.

'But no more, Victor,' she said as the car disappeared. 'You'll get no more.'

CHAPTER 73

Kim darted across the road and tried the door handle. It was open.

She closed the door behind her and entered the lounge.

'Oh, hell no,' Kim exclaimed rushing into the room.

Lucy lay sprawled face-down on the floor in front of her wheelchair.

Kim bent to her and a pain ripped across her lower back.

'Lucy, it's okay,' she said, stroking the girl's hair.

She stood and quickly assessed the fastest method of gathering up the child.

Kim knelt down again and gently turned Lucy so that she was lying on her back. The young eyes were filled with panic.

'It's okay, sweetheart. Can you give me the sign for yes?'

Lucy offered two blinks.

'I'm going to lift you under the arms, is that okay?'

Two blinks.

Kim leaned forward and placed a hand beneath Lucy's neck and raised the top half of her body to a supported sitting position. She knew that Lucy's muscles could not support her own weight so she pulled her closer so that Lucy's body was leaning into her own to prevent her from falling backwards.

She placed a hand under each of Lucy's armpits and hauled her to a standing position. The body was limp and offered no resistance. Although not the weight of a normal fifteen-year-old, the strain on Kim's injured back almost made her cry out loud.

'Tell you what, for this dance, I'll lead,' Kim said, as she turned Lucy around and gently lowered her into the chair.

Kim moved the footstool so that she was sitting in front of Lucy. She took the girl's right hand and held it.

'Are you okay? Are you hurt?'

No blinks. Kim quickly realised she'd asked two questions.

'Sorry, are you okay?'

Two blinks.

'Were you trying to get to your dad?'

Two blinks.

Kim squeezed the hand tighter. Jesus, this girl had some heart.

'He's going to be okay. He got a bang to the head and he's got to go to hospital to be checked over but he's fine.'

Relief filled the teenager's eyes.

Lucy then motioned her head slightly towards Kim.

'Lucy, I'm sorry, I don't understand.'

Kim saw the irritation in her face. She repeated the movement, but more forcefully.

'Oooooooo,' she managed.

Kim felt the frustration of this poor child's torment. Her brain worked perfectly but her ability to communicate those thoughts was a prison worse than she could imagine.

She repeated the motion and the sound together and the intensity in the eyes gave Kim the answer.

The emotion thickened her throat. 'You want to know if I'm okay?'

Two blinks.

Kim looked down at the fragile hand she was holding. Her vision blurred for a second but she coughed it away.

'I'm fine, Lucy, and that is thanks to your dad.' Kim thought of those few seconds he'd bought her by grabbing Victor's ankles. 'He pretty much saved my life.'

Pride shone from the expressive eyes.

'Now, I have to go. Is there anyone I can get to look after you?'

Lucy began to blink as the front door opened. A female voice sounded from the hallway.

'Well, I don't know what kind of circus is going on over there but ...' A rotund woman in her late fifties paused in the doorway and crossed her arms. 'And who might you be?'

'Detective Inspector Stone.'

'Hmmm ... lovely.'

She stood in front of Kim so she could get a good view of Lucy. 'You okay, Luce?'

Lucy must have signalled yes so the woman stood aside, but her eyes were fixed on Kim.

'Where's William?'

'He has to go to the hospital,' Kim answered quickly.

'What the devil have you done to him?' she asked, sternly. 'Is he okay?'

'He's fine but he'll probably be at the hospital for most of the night.'

'Well, it's a good job I came round to check then, isn't it? Right, I'll go and get the kettle on and then we'll have us a nice takeaway, Luce. I'll order pizza, your favourite.'

The woman took off into the kitchen but her presence could still be heard.

'I don't know what on earth you people think you're doing over there; police, ambulances, machines, tents. I thought it was all done with but no, you had to start it all up again tonight ...'

Kim hid her smile until she looked at Lucy, who rolled her eyes. The laughter exploded from her mouth.

'I need to go, Lucy, okay?'

Two blinks.

'Is there anything you need?'

Two blinks.

Kim assessed the situation. The booming voice could still be heard from the kitchen.

Kim got it and placed a hand to her right ear.

Two blinks.

Kim stood and reached for the iPod on the window sill. She placed the earphones into Lucy's ears and the controller on the arm of the chair near to Lucy's right hand.

'Got it?'

Two blinks and a cheeky glint. Kim couldn't help chuckling. She pointed to the door. 'I have to … '

Two blinks.

Kim touched her arm lightly and headed for the door.

The ambulance was just pulling away as a second squad car pulled up.

Kim walked across the road, back to the girls' home. There was a gaping hole, like a missing tooth where the paramedics had crashed through the fence.

'Guys, in the office at the end of the hallway there's a cabinet near to the door. On the back of it is a denture. Get it bagged and logged and up to the lab.'

They nodded and headed into the building.

Suddenly the place was silent again. There was nothing to indicate what had just happened. No marker to display that this was where she had very nearly lost her life.

And the reason she hadn't was because of an emergency aid pendant. A simple tool that helped Lucy get through everyday life had been her saviour.

Kim stopped dead as she realised what she'd been missing. A sickness overwhelmed her as every last piece of the puzzle fell into place.

'Oh, Jesus ...' she whispered into the darkness.

'Got the denture, Marm,' one of the PCs said as they came around the side of the building.

She realised there was more work to do and there was only one person who could help.

'Constable, would you please be good enough to pass me your phone?'

CHAPTER 74

As the bike purred to a stop on the gravel patch, Kim felt more like herself. She'd showered, changed and polished the Triumph. It sat in her garage, gleaming like a museum piece.

There had been no point trying to close her eyes. Every cell of her being had willed the blackness from the sky so she could get back to the site and finish this case.

She spotted Cerys at the bottom of the field just outside the opening that had been smashed through by the paramedics a few hours earlier.

The sun wasn't up yet but it was on its way.

'So, you weren't lying when you called me last night. It really is just the two of us?' Cerys asked.

'Yep,' Kim answered. She was about to take action that could very easily cost her dearly. Woody's words rang in her ears. She would not take her team down with her.

'I saw Dan as I was leaving the hotel. He's sent you a report but he confirmed that the denture you found definitely belonged to Louise Dunston.'

Kim nodded her understanding.

Cerys began pressing buttons on the machine and logging figures into a small notebook.

'Okay, it's ready now. Just how sure are you that we're going to find something?'

Kim took a breath, closed her eyes and analysed her gut. 'More sure than I'd like to be.'

'You realise that anything we find will never stand up in court?'

Kim nodded. If she was right, it would never get to court.

Kim stepped forward and held out her hands. 'Give it to me and tell me what to do. I think I've caused you enough trouble this week.'

'I'm a big girl and I can take care of myself,' Cerys snapped. 'And no offence, but this is an expensive piece of equipment that I will not entrust to you.'

Kim sighed with frustration. 'Cerys, will you just ...'

'Shut up, Kim. Give me the backpack first.'

Kim reached down, lifted the holdall and held it while Cerys put her arms through the straps.

Cerys fixed the monitor around her waist. Kim reached for the strap and hauled the metal rod onto Cerys's shoulder.

She stood back. 'I had you more as a Prada wearer.'

Cerys shook her head. 'Okay, I've had a look around the area and there's a lot of crap on the ground. It all needs moving.'

'I'm assuming that's my job?'

'See anybody else here?'

'Okay, where?'

'I'll survey the rear of the building first. The front of the building looks right onto the road and houses so if we're looking for what you think we are, that area would have been too exposed.'

'Can I help, Detective?'

Kim turned to find that William Payne had walked around the side of the fencing. He looked pale and tired. Kim stepped towards him.

'How are you feeling?'

He smiled. 'Sore, but there's no permanent damage. They sent me home a couple of hours ago.'

'What about Lucy?'

'Take a look.'

Kim walked to the edge of the fencing. The curtain had been pulled back and Lucy peered through the window.

Kim waved and then turned her attention back to William. 'I don't think you're in any fit state ...'

'Detective, I don't know what you're doing here today but I know that Lucy and I have somehow become a part of this. I'd really like to help.'

Kim was torn.

'They were just kids, Detective. Hardened, abandoned, neglected kids. What they did to Lucy was wrong, I know that and so did they. All three of them came back the next day of their own free will and apologised for what they'd done.'

'And you accepted their apology?'

He shrugged. 'Doesn't matter. Lucy did.'

Kim shook her head in wonder. 'You know that your daughter is a true inspiration?'

'Oh yes,' he smiled, proudly. 'She's what gets me out of bed every morning.'

Kim tipped her head. 'And you're not so bad yourself. Last night, if you hadn't managed to loosen that rope or grab Victor ...'

'It wasn't brave at all, Detective. I saw you go into the building and just came to see if you needed any help. Then I saw Victor Wilks digging a hole ...'

His words trailed away as he blushed. Kim understood that he was an accidental hero but he'd saved her life all the same.

'Even so ...'

'Enough,' William said, holding up his hands. 'Now, please tell me what I can do to help.'

Kim smiled to herself. This was a man who wanted no thanks, no praise and no sympathy.

'Okay, see that bin by the window. We need to fill it with anything on the ground that might interfere with the machine.'

William started on the left and Kim on the right. They worked their way from the fence perimeter into the middle, picking up anything that got in the way.

'Folks, the machine works much better if there's less grass,' Cerys called from the perimeter.

Kim looked around. In some places the weeds were knee high.

She bent to start pulling when suddenly the machine made a sound.

Kim straightened and focused on Cerys.

She walked back ten feet and moved forward slowly. Again, the machine cried out.

Cerys looked towards Kim. 'Looks like your gut called it right.'

CHAPTER 75

Cerys looked from her to William and then back again.

Kim covered the ground between them and took the weeds from his hand. 'William, I have to ask you to leave the area now.'

He looked pained as his eyes rested on the area of ground that held Cerys's attention. He nodded.

She took his right hand. 'William, none of this is your fault, you have to know that. No one died because of you. It was just made to look that way by an evil, devious man with no conscience.'

His gaze met hers. It would take time for him to believe it.

'I'll leave you to it, Detective.'

She squeezed his hand. 'My name is Kim and I want to thank you for everything you've done.'

William coloured with embarrassment. She let go of his hand. 'Now get back to your wonderful daughter.'

He smiled widely. 'Thank you, Det— Kim. I will.'

Kim waited until he'd gone and stepped over to where Cerys had laid down the machine.

Cerys turned to her. 'Whatever's down there is not very deep.'

Kim nodded and swallowed.

Cerys passed her the keys to the van. 'There are shovels in the back. Go and fetch them while I mark it out.'

Kim sprinted to the van, grabbed two shovels and ran back down the hill. The painkillers she'd taken earlier were starting to wear off. The pain pounded across her lower back.

Cerys had marked out the area. Kim saw immediately that it was smaller than the rest.

Cerys took one more look at the readings regurgitated from the magnetometer and pointed. 'You work that side but don't go too hard.'

Kim threw the shovel into the ground. A pain speared the width of her back but she ignored it and focused on what she needed to do.

The two of them worked without speaking for the next half an hour.

'Okay, Kim, stop and get out,' Cerys said, suddenly.

The pit was approximately five feet long but three feet wide, with a depth of no more than a foot.

Family pets were buried deeper.

Cerys walked around the perimeter of the pit twice before she got in. She used the hand tools to remove small mounds of dirt and place it to the side of the pit.

Kim didn't speak. Her eyes were on Cerys.

Cerys continued digging. The mounds of earth got smaller. She used the edge of the small trowel to scrape along a section in the middle of the pit.

On the third scrape, sections of white began to appear.

Cerys took a soft brush and dragged it along the surface. More white emerged.

Kim's stomach turned as she knew beyond a shadow of a doubt that she was looking at bone.

'That, Kim, is most definitely an arm.'

Cerys continued to dig and dust until she revealed what looked to be a shoulder joint. Kim stared as more and more bone was revealed.

'Cerys, what's that?' Kim asked, staring at something protruding from the shoulder joint.

Cerys dusted it once and Kim could see that it was fabric.

Kim's heart began to hammer in her chest.

'Cerys, dust it again.'

She did and Kim swore. Cerys turned and their eyes met.

'Is this what you were looking for?'

Kim nodded, her feet already moving slowly towards the bike.

'Cerys ... I have to ...'

'Go,' she said, taking out her phone. 'I'll call it in.'

Kim sprinted up the hill as fast as her legs would move.

CHAPTER 76

Kim knocked on the door and took a deep breath.

The door opened.

'Detective, good morning. Please come in.'

'Good morning, Nicola,' Kim said, entering the flat.

Nicola closed the door and stood in front of it. 'You're alone today?'

Kim nodded. 'I have to give my team some time off.'

'But not yourself?'

'Soon, Nicola. Very soon.'

'Please, sit.'

Kim did so. As she lowered herself down her eyes rested on the edge of the sofa, and her mind now fully registered the significance of what she had glimpsed on her last visit.

'How can I help?' Nicola asked.

Kim took a second to analyse Nicola's expression. It was open and earnest. Kim detected no deceit at all. Dammit.

'We've uncovered another body.'

Nicola's hand flew to her mouth. 'Oh God, no.'

The shock was genuine.

'Nicola, do you have any idea at all who the fourth victim could be?'

Nicola stood and paced back and forth behind the sofa. 'I can't even begin to imagine who ...'

'Nicola, was there a fourth member in that group?'

Nicola frowned. Her eye movement indicated she was searching her memory.

'No, Detective. I'm sure there were only three.'

Kim sighed and stood as though to leave. 'Oh, perhaps Beth might recall another girl?' Kim asked, hopefully.

Nicola shook her head. 'Beth's out shopping at the moment but when she comes back ...'

'Are you sure?' Kim asked.

'Of course I'm sure,' Nicola said, smiling.

Kim nodded towards the edge of the sofa. 'Then why didn't she take her stick?'

Nicola's eyes rested on the walking aid hooked over the back of the sofa. Her expression was one of genuine confusion.

Kim took the momentum and strode across the room. She headed for the first door and just hoped it was the right one.

'Perhaps she hasn't left yet. Perhaps she will ...'

'Detective, don't go in there. Beth doesn't like ...'

Her words trailed away as Kim pushed open the door.

Nicola was beside her and they surveyed the room together. The single bed was a box spring and mattress. There were no sheets or a duvet cover. A two-drawer cabinet sat beside the unused bed.

Kim strode to the wardrobe in the corner and opened it. Seven empty coat hangers stared back at her.

Kim looked back at Nicola who stood, horrified, in the doorway.

Kim waited for a response but Nicola continued to stare into the empty room.

A single tear rolled down her cheek. 'She's gone again – and she never even said goodbye.'

Kim ushered Nicola out of the doorway and closed the door behind her. She guided Nicola to the sofa and sat beside her.

'Has Beth done this before?' she asked, gently.

Nicola nodded. 'She's been doing it ever since we left Crestwood.' A fresh wave of tears rolled over her cheeks. She wiped them away with the sleeve of her jumper 'She's always so angry with me but she won't tell me why. This is what she does. She comes back and then just leaves me again. It's so unfair. She knows I have no one else.'

Kim went to the kitchen and retrieved a few squares of kitchen roll. She sat and handed the tissue to Nicola. The tears were not over yet.

'Can you remember when she last came back?'

Nicola stopped crying and thought. She sniffed and nodded. 'It was two years ago, when I had glandular fever and was taken into hospital. I woke up and there she was, sitting beside the bed.'

'And the time before that?'

'I'd had a minor car accident, just a shunt really. I wasn't badly injured but it frightened me a lot at the time. I hadn't been driving very long.'

'So, she's been in and out of your life since leaving Crestwood. Do you have any idea why she might be angry with you?'

Nicola shook her head vehemently. 'She won't tell me.'

Kim heard the exasperation in Nicola's voice and realised this was going to be even harder than she'd imagined.

Kim reached for Nicola's hand. 'I need you to think back to the day of the fire. I think there's something there that you may have forgotten. Do you think you could do that if I'm right here with you?'

'There's nothing,' she said, confused.

Kim squeezed the hand. 'It's okay, Nicola. I'm right here. Tell me step-by-step what you remember from that day and we'll see what we can piece together.'

Nicola stared forward, her eyes focused on the opposite wall. 'I know it was cold and Beth and I had argued about something. She was giving me the silent treatment so I went to the common room.'

'Who was in the common room?' Kim asked, gently.

Nicola shook her head and then frowned. 'No one. They were all outside, building a snowman.'

'So, what did you do?'

Nicola tipped her head. 'I heard voices, shouting. It was coming from Mr Croft's office.'

'What did you hear, Nicola?'

Kim was holding onto Nicola's hand but her thumb rested on the slim wrist. The pulse had quickened.

'They were talking about William, about covering something up. They were saying he would get into trouble, that he'd go to prison. They were talking about what would happen to Lucy.'

'Do you remember who you heard in there?'

'Mr Croft and Miss Wyatt were arguing. Father Wilks was talking quietly and I heard Tom Curtis and Arthur Connop in the background.'

Five of them, Kim thought. 'What about Mary Andrews?'

Nicola shook her head. 'She'd been off sick with the flu.'

'What happened next, Nicola?'

'Father Wilks opened the door and saw me. He looked angry. I ran away.'

Kim could feel the palm of Nicola's hand turning clammy. 'Where did you go?'

'I went to find Beth. She was in our room. I was sick of people being angry with me.'

Kim's voice was barely a whisper. 'So, what did you do?'

'I told her ... I told her ...'

Kim squeezed the hand but Nicola's head was already shaking from side to side. Her eyes were darting around, searching her own memory, hoping to rearrange the past.

'No. No. No. No. No.'

Kim tried to hang on to the hand but Nicola broke free easily.

She paced around the room like a caged animal looking for somewhere to hide.

The panic was rising in her. Her movements were quick and frantic.

'No, it can't be ... I couldn't have ...'

Nicola's hands thumped down on the breakfast bar. She turned and started banging her fists into the wall units and then punching herself in the head.

Kim ran over and grabbed Nicola from behind, forcing her arms to her sides to prevent her from any further damage to her own body.

'What did you tell Beth?'

Nicola struggled to free herself from Kim's hold but she had interlocked her fingers and she wasn't about to let go.

'Please stop, I can't ...'

Kim's voice grew louder. 'Nicola, you have to remember. What did you tell Beth?'

Nicola's head thrashed from side to side. Kim craned her own neck back to avoid being struck.

Kim was shouting in her ear. 'Tell me, Nicola. What did you tell your sister?'

'I told her she could have the damned cardigan if it would make her happy,' Nicola screamed.

Silence fell between them. Suddenly the fight left Nicola's body and she fell to the ground, taking Kim with her.

Kim refused to let go. She sat on the floor, holding Nicola close. Kim knew the events of ten years ago were finally playing in her mind.

'She took it, didn't she?'

Nicola nodded and Kim could feel the tears dripping onto her hands.

'So, they all thought she was you, didn't they, because of the cardigan?'

Nicola nodded again. 'One minute I looked outside and she was playing with the others and then I couldn't find her. I kept asking people and they all told me she was somewhere else. In the end I went to my room to wait for her but she never came.

'Later, just before the fire, I saw them out of the kitchen window. They were all standing around a hole and I knew. I didn't know what to do. I was scared they were going to come back for me so when the fire started I was just relieved that they couldn't get me anymore.'

Kim knew that Beth wouldn't have been able to run away. Her knee wouldn't have allowed it in that cold weather.

'When did Beth come back, Nicola?'

'About two weeks ago,' she answered hoarsely.

When the announcement was made about the dig and once again Nicola felt frightened.

'You know now that you brought her back, don't you, Nicola?'

'Noooooo ...'

The sound was that of a keening animal. A poor wounded soul that was writhing in pain. Kim held fast while Nicola tried to escape the events in her own head.

The knowledge of what she'd done as Beth was not to be shared now. It was a realisation Nicola would reach eventually in the care of a good psychiatrist.

As she sat rocking the young, broken girl whose guilt had gained control of her, Kim doubted that Nicola would ever be fit to stand trial for the murder of Teresa Wyatt, Tom Curtis and Arthur Connop

After a few minutes, Kim gently eased herself backwards. It was time to make the call.

CHAPTER 77

William added a drop of cold milk to the porridge. He bent his little finger and touched the knuckle to the food. Perfect.

He smiled. Lucy's favourite.

His daughter had been washed and changed and now awaited her breakfast. After that he would clean the bathroom and change the beds. Following lunch the oven was in for a deep clean.

He smiled again. He knew people felt sorry for him and the life he lived but, he reasoned, those people did not know Lucy.

His daughter's spirit inspired him every single day. She was the most courageous and thoughtful person he had ever known.

He understood that her biggest frustration was her inability to speak clearly and some days the effort of communicating all that occurred in her head through eye movement tired her.

But between them they had a pact. On the darker days, he would ask her if she'd had enough. William had told her years ago that he would always respect her wishes and that he would never prolong her life through his own selfish needs.

On those days he would ask her the question and hold his breath while he waited for the answer. The hesitations had grown longer, while the breath in his chest grew fuller, but so far he'd always received one blink.

He dreaded the day it all got too much for her to bear and he received two blinks. He only hoped he had the strength to keep his promise. For her sake.

William pushed the thought away. Yesterday had been a good day. Lucy had had a visitor.

William hadn't recognised her at first. The young girl introduced herself as Paula Andrews and after studying her for a few seconds he had remembered her as the granddaughter of Mary Andrews who had used to visit with her grandmother to play with Lucy. He had been genuinely saddened when Mary had recently passed away. She had been a great friend to him during his years at Crestwood. Her burial had taken place a few days earlier and although he had not attended he had watched the funeral procession from his bedroom window.

Lucy had recognised Paula instantly and had been delighted with the visit. Within minutes they had formed their own method of communication from which William had been excluded. He had never been happier.

To her credit, Paula had shown no reaction to the physical change in her old friend.

He had skulked away to the kitchen for a few moments, nervous for the wellbeing of his daughter. He would never stop anyone visiting with his child but he was powerless to bring about their return. But he accepted that he could not protect her from every disappointment life had to offer.

Somehow the two girls had found a way to play a board game. He had heard Paula exclaim, 'Lucy Payne, you haven't changed a bit. You were always a little cheat.'

William had heard Lucy's gurgle which he knew to be a laugh and his heart had leaped.

He had ventured outside for just half an hour and pulled out a few weeds from between the slabs, safe in the knowledge that his daughter was okay. Just those few minutes in the cold morning air had revitalised him for the rest of the day.

Two hours later, Paula had sought his permission to visit again.

He had given it gladly.

He took the porridge through to the living room and sat on the footstool. Lucy's complexion was rosy and bright, her eyes alert and focused. Today was a good day. Paula's visit had been good for both of them.

'Don't you ever get bored of porridge?'

One blink.

He rolled his eyes. She copied. He laughed out loud.

He brought a spoonful of oats to her mouth. She took it and scrunched her face in appreciation. The second spoonful was on its way when the doorbell sounded.

He placed the dish on the windowsill.

He opened the door and panic rose in him immediately.

Before him stood a male and female both dressed in black trouser suits. He carried a briefcase but she had a shoulder bag.

He immediately thought of social services but they were not due for a visit and they always let him know first. In the early days following the departure of his wife, William had been forced into battle with the authorities to keep his daughter. He had jumped through hoops and performed like a circus animal to show that he was capable. Sensing his determination, social services had started to work with him to keep the two of them together and the job at Crestwood had sealed the deal. But still, the fear lived within him that one day he would lose her.

'Mr Payne, Mr William Payne?'

He nodded.

The female smiled widely and took a business card from her pocket. 'My name is Hannah Evans from Enterprise Electronics. We're here to see Lucy.'

'But ... I don't ... what?'

She rubbed her hands together and blew into them. 'Mr Payne, may we come in?'

William stepped aside.

Hannah Evans stepped into the lounge and stood before his daughter. The man sat and opened his briefcase.

'Good morning, Lucy. My name is Hannah and I am very pleased to meet you.'

Her smile was open and warm, her tone friendly and calm, unlike the condescending tone used by most adults.

'Are you well today?'

Lucy blinked.

'That means yes,' William offered.

Hannah remained where she was and smiled in his direction. 'I know that, Mr Payne. The language of blinking is quite common in people with communication limitations.'

Hannah Evans rolled her eyes at his daughter, who gurgled in response.

'Umm ... excuse me,' William said, bewildered. 'But I don't understand who you are or what you are doing here.'

'It's really quite simple, Mr Payne. We specialise in the most advanced technological systems that can be operated with the least amount of physical activity. We, as a company, exist to make life far more exciting and interesting for people with physical restrictions.'

William's mind was spinning. 'But I don't get it. I haven't spoken to ... I have no money for ...'

'My understanding is that the cost has been taken care of.'
She held up her hands. 'That is not my area of the business
and I have my instructions.'

William felt as though he had been transported to an
alternate universe. His mind scrambled for answers but he
found none.

Hannah turned her attention back to his daughter.

'Lucy, I have only one question. Do you have control of
at least one finger?'

Two blinks.

Hannah smiled widely at William. 'Then I think there is
much we can do here.'

CHAPTER 78

Kim looked at the offering before her and decided that Aunt Bessie was a damn liar.

She placed the ingredients box next to her own attempt just removed from the oven for comparison. Nope, no amount of icing or glittery embellishments would save them.

Kim threw the box in the bin. She felt betrayed.

She raised her eyes to the ceiling. 'I try, Erica. I promise, I try.'

She heard the sound of a knock on the front door.

'It's open,' she called.

Bryant entered wearing jeans and a sweatshirt, carrying a pizza box.

'Missed you at work today,' he said, placing the box on the counter top.

She rolled her eyes. 'Woody's order and I dare not ignore any more 'cos this cat's on its last life.'

'Is that what he said?'

She nodded and counted off her fingers. 'Apparently I notched up two formal complaints about my attitude. I disregarded direct instructions on three occasions and failed to follow correct protocols ...' she counted off the rest of her fingers, '... well, at least that many times.'

Bryant's head fell into his waiting hands. 'Oh Lord, was it brutal?'

Kim thought for a moment and nodded. 'Yeah, pretty much. He had quite a lot to say.'

'And what did you say?'

'I told him that his model was missing the cantilever springs from the rear axle.'

Bryant roared with laughter and she joined in. She supposed it was kind of funny in hindsight.

But it was her way of saying thank you. She was under no illusion that she should have lost her job. And Woody had been clear that it was only the results that had saved her.

Had even one of her hunches been wrong, The Bowl would now belong to someone else.

This case had brought her closer to losing the most important thing in her life and yet it had been worth it.

'How long has he given you for the other thing?'

Kim growled as she took down two mugs from the cupboard. 'A month.'

'Jeez, how you gonna get out of that?'

Kim shrugged. She had four weeks to speak with a psychologist or face suspension.

'You don't think he'd actually go through with it, do you?'

Kim recalled the resolute expression on Woody's face. 'Oh yeah, he'll do it.'

'Well, you'll be pleased to know that Richard Croft was looking much better earlier.'

'He was?'

'Well, he was until I read him his rights.'

Kim would have liked to have been there for that. 'Oh, do tell me that Mrs Croft was present?'

'She most certainly was. For a few seconds she bore a resemblance to a constipated camel but she recovered quickly enough to gather up her laptop and paperwork, stating that her lawyer will be in touch.'

'With us?'

'With Richard. I smell a speedy divorce somewhere in his future.'

'What did he say?'

'Oh, he confirmed that Victor was the one that killed Beth. The rest of them just helped bury the body. He said it was the idea of Teresa Wyatt to start the fire to cause confusion with the records and the runaways and the girls who had already been relocated.'

'Do you believe him?'

'I dunno. Doesn't really matter. He'll get a decent lawyer, but he'll do jail time without a doubt. More importantly, his life as he knew it is over. His wife, house, career and probably his kids are gone.'

Kim didn't speak. There was nothing to say. She felt nothing but revulsion for Richard Croft. He had escaped with his life.

Bryant looked thoughtful. 'Do you reckon Victor Wilks is all bad? I mean, I know what he's done but he worked the estate and stuff so maybe there was some good in him.'

Sometimes Bryant seemed younger than his years. She was just sorry that she was the one who had to tell him that Father Christmas wasn't real.

She shook her head. 'No, Bryant. He was attracted to places devoid of hope and filled with despair, where he could project himself as a beacon of hope amongst the misery. That was his true gratification, his true power trip. Sex with frightened, vulnerable, young girls fulfilled a physical need within him. He placed himself in environments where accusations of rape would be far harder to prove and anyone who became problematic was disposed of.

'He killed them and enjoyed it. He did it because he could and because he felt justified in ending the life of anyone who obstructed him. There will be victims of Wilks' that originated from Hollytree and however hard it is to swallow we may never uncover them all.'

The sprawling estate had notched up eighteen runaways since Victor's return two years earlier. Add in the disappearances of girls unreported by family members who had not noticed or didn't care and that figure probably doubled.

'Bastard,' Bryant muttered.

Kim agreed but she consoled herself with the thought that Victor Wilks would never walk free again.

'Did you find the car?' she asked.

He nodded. 'Garage behind the apartments registered to Nicola Adamson. White Audi with a dented front wing.'

Kim shook her head. Try as she might, she could not muster any sympathy for Teresa Wyatt, Tom Curtis, Richard Croft or Arthur Connop. Together with Victor Wilks, they had hidden the deaths of three young girls and denied them justice for a decade, all to hide their own sordid secrets. Every single one of them had found a way to abuse them some more.

Even worse, they had been instrumental in the death of another innocent whose only crime had been wanting to wear her sister's pink cardigan.

'I'm curious, Kim, what made you first think it was two separate killers?'

'Manner of death,' she answered. 'As we uncovered the girls it was obvious that they had been killed with a great deal of physical force and yet the current murders were not. No effort was required to push Teresa under the water. Tom's throat was cut from behind, Arthur was knocked over with a car and Richard was stabbed in the back. All methods that called for cunning, patience and stealth, not physical strength.'

'What about the fire at Teresa's house? What was the point of that?'

'There was a very thin layer of snow on the ground, Bryant. There would have been a lot of forensic evidence to find with footprints and even the walking stick but eight firefighters, two tenders and a high-powered hose soon destroyed that.'

'Clever.'

'Exactly, so it had to be a woman.'

'Yeah, but she got caught.'

'Yeah, by a woman.'

Bryant rolled his eyes and groaned all at the same time.

He sobered. 'How do you think Nicola will react when she realises the truth?'

Kim shrugged. 'It really wasn't Nicola that did it. It was Beth.'

Bryant looked doubtful. 'You really believe that?'

Bless him, he was a meat and potatoes man.

'Oh yes, Bryant, I do.'

'It's all a bit *X-Files* for me.'

Kim sighed. 'Beth only came back in Nicola's time of need, when she was ill or frightened. Nicola's subconscious used her like a security blanket. Nicola never fully accepted that her sister was dead. Her subconscious mind blocked the memories so that she could live. It protected her from the guilt.

'Now imagine that, as Beth, Nicola's memories were readily available. She had access to the overheard conversation in the office, she had access to the knowledge of what occurred so although Nicola couldn't access the memories, her alter ego could.'

Kim fully believed that Nicola's conscious mind was oblivious to the fact that her subconscious mind had brought back Beth. And after meeting 'Beth', she was in no doubt that it had not been an act.

She turned to Bryant. 'Try and imagine someone's psyche splitting in half. Nicola had control of normal day to day activities. She was able to function adequately but someone else had control of her subconscious mind.'

He shook his head. 'Nah, still not buying it – and I don't think a jury will either.'

Kim suspected Bryant was right but she doubted that Nicola would ever be declared competent to stand trial. For Kim, the internal struggle between Nicola and Beth had been evident at the crime scenes of both Teresa and Tom. The arrival of the police had been expedited on both occasions. Some part of the split psyche had wanted to be stopped.

Nicola was not a bad or evil person and her punishment would come as the memories returned to her.

Kim knew first hand that survivor guilt had the power to shape a mind; and that was why she prayed her own boxes never got opened.

'How do you think Wilks managed to stay alive?'

'More luck than judgement,' Kim said. 'He would have been next and she would have got him.'

Bryant shook his head. 'One thing I don't understand is how the hell did it go unnoticed that there was only one twin?'

'The records were a mess, Bryant. Remember, the place was already being emptied. The records of the runaways were not up-to-date and on the night of the fire just about everyone was producing lists. The ambulance service was removing girls to hospital to be checked. It was chaos and that was the intention. No two lists from that night match up.'

'But why didn't Nicola speak up?'

'The kid was terrified. She was convinced they would realise their mistake with the cardigan and come looking for her.'

'What about Mary Andrews? Do you think that was Nicola or Beth or whoever the hell it was?'

Kim shook her head. 'There was no evidence to suggest that she died of anything other than the disease. Mary was the only one not present or mentioned that day so Nicola had no reason to target her.' Kim sighed heavily. 'I think Mary Andrews was the only person any of them could trust. Except for William, who worked nights, every single one of them found some way to exploit these girls even further. Is it any wonder they weren't girl scouts?'

'That's a charitable way of putting it,' Bryant offered.

She opened her mouth to argue the point but closed it again. Bryant believed that a moral code was ingrained into the conscience at birth. He believed it to be as genetic as eye colour or height. Kim knew it wasn't. Conscience, and use of it, was a learned behaviour. It came from good examples and strong role models. The inherent difference between right and wrong is perfected throughout life and not pre-printed on the brain.

The social background of Tracy, Melanie and Louise dictated that those codes would forever be warped. Just as abused children often go on to abuse.

Bryant would never be convinced but Kim knew – because she had been there. And a three-year interval had saved more than her life.

Bryant took a sip of his coffee. 'So, what was going on between you and the Doc? There was definitely a meeting of the minds.'

'Bryant,' she warned.

'Oh come on, Kim. Given more time there would have been sparks.'

'And what do sparks cause?'

'Fire,' he said, opening his eyes wide.

'And have you ever known a fire without damage?'

Bryant opened his mouth, thought for a second and then closed it again. 'There really is no answer to that.'

'Precisely.'

'Probably a good thing,' Bryant said, thoughtfully. 'The Doc was a bit too much like you.' He smirked. 'Jesus, imagine the kids you would have ...'

'Bryant, I think you should mind your own damn business,' she snapped. Sometimes he knew her a little too well.

And yet, if she met Daniel again, who knew?

'Yeah, I probably should but it's unlikely that I will.'

Kim smiled. 'How's life at Battersea Dog's Home?'

'Pups are doing well. They're all taken. My niece is having Pebbles. Bam Bam is going to the neighbour. Yogi has been reserved by my daughter's best friend and Boo Boo is going to Stacey's sister.'

'You haven't saddled the poor things with those names for life, have you?'

Bryant shook his head. 'Nah, just so we can tell them apart for now.'

'What about the mum?'

'She'll be staying with me. She's only four and the vet estimates she's had three litters already. Her work is done.'

For a second, just a fleeting second, Kim had the urge to hug this bear of a man with the warmest of hearts. He was her colleague and her one true friend.

But she let the moment pass.

He stepped off the bar stool. 'So, I'll cut to the real reason for my visit. It is finished, isn't it?'

'Yes, Bryant, it's finished.'

He rubbed his hands. 'Can I, can I, can I?'

Kim laughed at his childish excitement.

He darted through the adjoining door to the garage.

She took the cakes and emptied them into the bin. She immersed the cake tin into hot soapy water.

Bryant returned to the doorway. 'Umm ... Kim, it's not there.'

'Oh really, how about that?'

He leaned against the door frame with his arms folded. 'You sold it, didn't you?'

Kim said nothing.

Bryant was deflated, confused. 'But you loved that bike like a child. You've been working towards riding the damn thing for months. I just don't get it. It meant the world to you.'

'You know, Bryant, some things just mean more.'

She wiped the cake tin and put it away. Bryant's expression was puzzled. He didn't understand.

But Kim did – and that was all that mattered.

LETTER FROM ANGELA

First of all, I want to say a huge thank you for choosing to read *Silent Scream*. I hope you enjoyed the first installment of Kim's journey and hope you feel the same way I do. Whilst not always perfect she is someone you would want fighting your corner.

If you did enjoy it, I would be forever grateful if you'd write a review. I'd love to hear what you think, and it can also help other readers discover one of my books for the first time. Or maybe you can recommend it to your friends and family ...

A story begins as a seed of an idea that grows from watching and listening to everyone around you. Each individual is unique and we all have a story. I want to capture as many of those tales as I can and I hope you will join both Kim Stone and myself on our travels; wherever they may lead.

If so I'd love to hear from you - get in touch on my Facebook or Goodreads page, twitter or through my website.

Thank you so much for your support, it is hugely appreciated.

Angela Marsons

www.angelamarsons-books.com

www.facebook.com/angelamarsonsauthor

www.twitter.com/WriteAngie